COP THIS!

CHRIS NYST

HarperCollins*Publishers*

HarperCollins*Publishers*

First published in Australia in 1999
Reprinted in 2000
by HarperCollins*Publishers* Pty Limited
ACN 009 913 517
A member of the HarperCollins*Publishers* (Australia) Pty Limited Group
http://www.harpercollins.com.au

Copyright © Chris Nyst

This book is copyright.
Apart from any fair dealing for the purposes of private study, research,
criticism or review, as permitted under the Copyright Act, no part may be
reproduced by any process without written permission.
Inquiries should be addressed to the publishers.

HarperCollins*Publishers*
25 Ryde Road, Pymble, Sydney, NSW 2073, Australia
31 View Road, Glenfield, Auckland 10, New Zealand
77–85 Fulham Palace Road, London, W6 8JB, United Kingdom
Hazelton Lanes, 55 Avenue Road, Suite 2900, Toronto, Ontario M5R 3L2
and 1995 Markham Road, Scarborough, Ontario M1B 5M8, Canada
10 East 53rd Street, New York NY 10022, USA

National Library of Australia Cataloguing-in-Publication data:

Nyst, Chris.
    Cop this.
    ISBN 0 7322 6458 8
    I.Title.
A823.3

Cover image: Black Cherry: KlausLahnstein/The Photo Library
Printed in Australia by Griffin Press Pty Ltd on 50gsm Ensobulky

8 7 6 5 4 3 2
03 02 01 00

1

Merv Harris was a hard bastard. He played A-grade Rugby League when he was just a kid of seventeen, back when the game was more like war than a game. At eighteen he made his name as a pug when he knocked Morrie Bennett arse-up in the front bar of the Stonsey pub. And he'd been a copper now for twenty-three long years, twelve of them in the CI Branch. There wasn't much Merv Harris hadn't seen and done.

But as Detective Sergeant Mervyn Henry Harris surveyed the scene outside Mickey's Poolhouse on that crisp morning in the June of 1969 he could only shake his head. Nothing had prepared him for this.

Dawn was breaking and the forensics and uniforms were crawling all over the charred ruin in the heart of the red-light district of Brisbane's Fortitude Valley. The street was closed off, the barricades lined with police cars. Even at this hour people were drifting to the scene, their uncomprehending faces squinting through the early morning light at the burnt-out remnants of Mickey's Poolhouse. The front wall was completely gone. The roof had fallen in and the first floor was a blackened web of bearers clinging tentatively to the back wall.

The firies were back there now, pulling down loose beams and sheets of iron, making the place as safe as possible for the police to do their job. It had that ugly, jagged look that gave you a sick feeling in your guts and made you know something had gone terribly wrong. Like when you walked into an empty house and instantly knew things weren't right, even before the smell first hit you.

The forensic boys were at the front part of the building, stepping carefully through the debris that had once been the ground floor. They had been pulling pieces of half-burnt human bodies out of the rubble all morning, and Merv knew there were more to come.

It shouldn't have come as such a shock. For too long now the Valley knock shops and the illegal gaming houses had flashed their gaudy lights and thumbed their noses at every poor silly bastard in Brisbane. Mickey's had always been the flashiest of them all, overflowing every night with long-haired poofters, and molls, and half-smart Yanks on R'n'R from Vietnam. You could get a beer and a game of pool with the desperates downstairs if you wanted to but everyone knew the real action was on the first floor where the gaming tables went all night. The coppers and the politicians publicly denied there were casinos in the town but everyone knew different. And now the heavies had moved in. So what did they expect?

That was the way it was in the Valley. If you stuck your head up someone was going to pull your nose. That's the kind of cesspool it was. If you wanted to punt your wages away on the tables, or risk the pox with some sheila, or piss it all up against the wall, fair enough. But the Valley spelt trouble. And no one knew that better than Merv Harris. 'Stay out of the Valley!' his old man used to warn him as he'd jump on the No 17 tram for town on a Saturday arvo. He'd been ignoring that advice ever since.

But it was good advice. Good for schoolboys, good for coppers and good for smart-arse mug lair poofters like Johnny Morris.

'Where's that fucken Morris?' Harris barked at no one in particular.

'Out of town. S'posed to be in Gympie for the night,' said one of the bleary-eyed detectives behind him.

'Gympie? That'd be fucken right! Get on to someone in the Branch in Gympie. I want that bludger back down here today.'

Someone had hidden a home-made bomb inside a rubbish bin on the footpath outside Mickey's some time after one o'clock on Sunday morning. An old drunk had set her off when he was scrounging through the bin, and the whole street had gone up. There were bits and pieces of that old derro everywhere. Merv's stomach turned as he watched the forensic boys scooping something up into a plastic body bag.

He had known there was something brewing in the Valley for a while. Someone had decided to send a message to the boys but things had obviously got a long way out of hand. Merv knew Mickey's flamboyant manager John Morris would undoubtedly know plenty. Morris was too smart by half, and it was altogether too convenient that he just happened to be in Gympie the night half the Valley went up in smoke. If Morris thought he was going to swerve the shit by leaving town he had another think coming.

And Merv Harris knew the shit would come, thick and fast. He also knew that as Chief of Homicide he was going to have to wear most of it. The Commissioner, suck-arse little prick that he was, had already been on the blower. 'I've promised the Premier we'll put every available resource on this thing, Merv — I know you fellows won't let me down.' Dickhead ...

When George Curran's car pulled into the police cordon Harris strode straight to it, swung the rear door open and slid onto the back seat alongside Tommy Wilson.

Tom looked sick, which wasn't surprising. He had no balls for this sort of thing. Barry Reilly was driving. He was young but he was a good copper and he could be depended on. George Curran was in the passenger seat.

'This is a hell of a mess, Merv.'

'Too right it is, George.'

'What's the body count?'

'Eight so far. But I'd say there'll be more.'

'Shit!'

Merv could see the tension in Curran's cold grey eyes. It surprised him to see George so unsettled, even in these circumstances. George Curran was the toughest man he knew and there wasn't a better cop alive. Merv had walked the beat with him in his first week in the job and George had taught him everything there was to know. Everything. He was one tough old bastard.

'Well,' Curran sighed. 'We can't afford an inquest on this thing, Mervyn.'

Curran was right. With at least eight people dead the Coroner would move pretty quickly and the press would be jumping up and down. One way and another there'd be a lot of pressure to convene a coronial inquiry unless there was an early arrest. And an inquest would mean a whole lot of shit they could do without. There would be outrage about the fact that police had been warned this was going to happen. And there would be new questions about the Gaye Welham affair and what was going on between Morris and the boys down at Licensing.

'We know whose name's on this one,' said Curran quietly. 'I think we ought to speak to Mr Arnold straight away.'

George was right. A quick arrest would divert public attention. This one had to be bedded down quick smart or the whole Gaye Welham bun fight was going to blow up in their faces all over again.

Merv Harris, and just about every other copper in town, wished he had never laid eyes on that silly bitch Gaye Welham. The whole episode confirmed what he had known since he was fifteen — that molls were all mad and weren't to be trusted.

That one had nearly got out of control. It could have blown up into another Empire Hotel Inquiry. It was all very well when it was just that silly old fart Nev Waller jumping up in state parliament every six months whinging about police copping a sling out of SP betting and prostitution. People just wrote Waller off as another commie Labor Party ratbag trying to stir the pot. No one really cared. SP bookies were a national institution, and who the hell really wanted to get rid of molls anyway? So what if the coppers got a sling — they were the ones that had to control the whole mess. Even the smarter blokes in the Labor Party knew that. They didn't want to know about that ratbag Waller. They knew how the world turned and they knew they needed the coppers just as much as the other mob did.

No, Nev Waller was no problem. But when that silly bitch Gaye Welham went to the papers, things started to look serious. That photograph of that silly old Arthur Rodgie with his hand on Gaye's tit didn't help too much either. How a bloke with nearly forty years in the Force could trust a slut like Gaye with that photo was beyond Merv Harris.

The photo made the front page of the *Truth* on the Sunday; Arthur made retirement on the Wednesday.

That was where George Curran came into his own. He knew how to hose down a nasty situation like no one else. He convinced Arthur Rodgie to publicly confess on the Wednesday that, yes, he'd had a brief fling with this woman Welham but, no, of course it had nothing to do with his position as Inspector in Charge of Licensing and as for police receiving graft payments, that was ridiculous. George even convinced old Arthur to take the gold watch.

Within three days George got hold of Gaye's psych history and leaked it to the press. When that reporter Gordon Yates from the *Courier* came out on the following Friday claiming to have a twenty-five page sworn affidavit in which Gaye Welham named seventeen serving police officers in connection with prostitution and sly grog down in the Valley and claimed that Johnny Morris was making regular graft payments to the Licensing Branch, the pressure was really on.

The journos were having a field day and things were starting to look shaky. Suddenly the Labor boys could sniff a Royal Commission and they were all trying to jump into the act. There was a lot of pressure mounting on the government to call an inquiry. If it hadn't been for George Curran there's no telling what might have happened.

'Gaye's a very smart girl,' he told the worried assembly in the Day Room that Tuesday morning. 'She just needs a few days to think about where her best interests lie.'

Three days later Gaye had retracted the whole story and left town. Gordon Yates had to acknowledge that he personally witnessed Gaye tearfully admit to a select group of journalists, police and politicians in the Commissioner's office that the whole thing had been an elaborate hoax dreamed up by an unstable girl distraught at having been spurned by Inspector Rodgie after their brief affair. Yates had received, along with all the others, a copy of her new two-page affidavit retracting everything and apologising sincerely.

The Premier had publicly congratulated the Commissioner on having so quickly and successfully investigated the matter. Gordon Yates wore a lot of egg on his face, and the 'serious consideration being given to the laying of false complaint charges against Gaye Welham' was soon forgotten.

It had George Curran stamped all over it. He was a tough old bastard who had dragged himself up to the top of his own personal dungheap and no halfwit sheila like Gaye Welham was ever going to do him down. He'd joined the Merchant Navy at fourteen and he came out a real hard nut. He once told Merv the sea had taught him to survive and the old bastard knew more about survival than anyone Merv knew.

Merv had taken his first sling from George — ten bob as his share to 'look the other way' at the 'Unders and Overs' at the Gympie Show. George taught him that a good copper had to use his scone.

And old George was a good copper. Probably the best Merv had ever known. There was no one better to have by your side in a stink. Merv was there the day George walked straight up and king-hit 'Jingles' Devine after Devine had just wasted young Naughten with a sawn-off .22 right there in front of them. He knew what real police work was all about and he believed in looking after your own. 'Because when all is said and done,' he used to say, 'nobody gives a shit about us coppers, except us coppers.' And he was right.

When George came into the job back in '35 the Masons had the whole show by the balls. A Roman Catholic boy had Buckley's chance of ever making it beyond the rank of Sergeant. But George Curran changed all that.

These days the goat-riders were on the outer and the Paddys called the shots. True, George didn't sit in the Commissioner's office, but he didn't need the title. He had the power. And no one was likely to take that power away from him. Not the Masons, not the journos or the pollies, certainly not some pissant slut like Gaye Welham. Not even the Premier of the whole bloody State was likely to topple George Curran without one almighty shit-fight. And not one of them had the balls for it. And that made Mervyn Henry Harris feel very secure.

Merv sat back in the police car outside Mickey's looking silently at George. The two men understood each other perfectly. With carnage of this magnitude the public would soon look for a head to kick. Unless the police served them up a culprit quickly a lot of very embarrassing questions would resurface.

Yes, George was right, as always. John Arnold was a living certainty for this one and the sooner they brought him in the better.

1969 was shaping up as Gordon Yates's worst year yet. Which was depressing, given that he'd had some very discouraging years of late. Six years ago he'd come from England as a senior journalist with impressive credentials, including a short stint with no less respected a journal than the *Times* and his future in Brisbane seemed assured. He had quickly secured a job with the city's major daily, the *Courier-Mail*, and he was sure he would now be Chief of Staff at least were it not for his taste for the local XXXX Bitter Ale.

Gordon was a drunk. But, for all that, he was a good writer and a hard worker, he told himself, and he did not in the least deserve the absolutely rotten luck that had come his way of late. And that dreadful Gaye Welham business had really topped it off. It was a great story, but Gaye was never going to be strong enough to go the distance. He realised now that he had known it all along but even though it had excited him so much, he just couldn't find the energy to go that extra mile. A little more digging, a little more hard work, might have given him the back-up he needed. But Gordon could not quite find the energy, so he broke the story anyway.

And of course it all collapsed like a house of cards. Just like his career ...

When he had walked out of the Commissioner's office with Gaye's two-page affidavit that day, Inspector George Curran had taken him by the arm and suggested, almost paternally, 'Gordon, you should find yourself a hobby, old son.'

Trying to find a story these days was impossible. The police wouldn't speak to him, the Government had black-banned him and even the Opposition fellows had clammed up for fear of getting the police offside.

By the time he heard the news of the bombing it was seven o'clock. As usual he had been lying awake trying to piece together the events of the previous evening.

He rolled to the edge of the bed, reached out and turned on the morning news. What he heard struck him like a falling brick.

Brisbane was just starting to stir as the four unmarked Falcons rolled into Manning Street. The suburbs had already been stunned by the horror of the news being barked out by every radio station in every corner of that complacent, lazy city.

Suddenly the world was on the doorstep of this oversized country town and its residents were in shock. *Eleven confirmed dead ... Suspected underworld feud ... Illegal casino bombed ... Gangland war ...* Such things happened in Chicago, maybe in Sydney, but surely not in Brisbane.

Merv Harris spun the car radio dial to 'off'. He did not need to be reminded that news was spreading quickly. By midday the stunned public would be asking how such a thing could happen in their fair city, by nightfall they would want to know why, and by morning they would want to know what the boys in blue were doing to provide answers. Merv Harris was going to get them those answers, and he was going to get them from a grub called Johnny Arnold.

George Curran wasn't with them but he had hand-picked the team and every one of them was solid as a rock. All of them were dependable and all of them, except maybe Tom Wilson, could handle themselves in a stink. That was good, because even though Arnold didn't have any form for using weapons, he could go a bit and he was likely to be pretty desperate with this blue hanging over him.

The young blokes would go round the back — Barry Reilly, Mick Staines and Phil Vincent. They'd be fit enough to catch anyone who tried to bolt down the back steps. And Bernie Doyle and Gerry Walsh would be there to make sure they didn't fuck it up. It always paid to have a couple of older heads along — otherwise the young bucks would end up shooting some poor bastard. Bill Potter and Tom Wilson would go in the front way with Harris, and Frank Delaney and Marty Nolan would hang out the front and watch the windows. George had stipulated that Tommy Wilson was to lead the raid and take the running with Arnold. It didn't seem too bright to be trusting an empty hat like Tom with this job but no doubt the old bloke had it all worked out. He was always working the angles, old George.

Harris eyeballed the house as soon as they swung into Manning Street and he kept his eyes fixed on it as they swept along the narrow street. It was a typical little shit-heap 1920s worker's cottage jammed on a twelve perch block between the other fleapit dumps that made up Manning Street. Harris knew the area better than he cared to.

Arnold lived in No 14 with the Douglas brothers. A bunch of hippies on this side. They were just 'longhairs no-cares' — no threat. The Sands, in No 16, were all right, for boories. So the sides weren't too bad, but the house had those bloody central front steps and the verandah was closed in. That meant that if someone inside wanted to have a go, the first bloke up the stairs was duckshit. Maybe that's why George had nominated Tom.

The first car gave a little screech as it lurched to a halt outside No 16. Mug lairs! Why not hire a fucken brass band to announce our arrival, thought Harris, as Bill Potter guided their car swiftly in behind. The young blokes were already over the front fence and sprinting along the side of the house.

'Let's go,' barked Wilson from behind him and he was gone. Harris was still fumbling with the car door when he heard Wilson at the top of the stairs pounding on the door and calling, 'Police! Open up!' Merv was right behind Potter as they came through the front gate and he was starting up the stairs when he heard someone inside call, 'Just a sec!'

A sec was all the time it took to pull a sawn-off out of the bottom of the wardrobe! Harris vaulted up the rickety stairs, his service revolver dancing around in front of his face. He leapt past Wilson and rammed his shoulder into the old verandah door. It crunched and cracked, splinters flying in a dozen directions, and Harris staggered into the darkened hallway.

Potter and Wilson were already on top of him and he could see Reilly and Staines surging up the central hallway from the rear. Then, between the merging forces bounded Les Douglas, a skinny, tattooed weasel in leopard-skin underpants.

'Who else is here?' grunted Harris.

'No one. Just me.'

Harris glanced past him to where Reilly and the others were emerging from various rooms. The dump was empty.

Harris relaxed and started to move down the hallway. Wilson took up the questioning.

'We're looking for John Arnold. Where is he?'

That's when Douglas decided he'd be a bit half-smart. God only knows why. Maybe he was trying to protect Arnold, maybe it was the dopey way Tom had of asking questions or maybe it was just that Les Douglas was a two-bit piece of dog turd. Whatever it was Merv Harris couldn't cop half-smart crims.

'John who?' said Douglas truculently.

Fortunately, the fist Merv threw was his left. It was less powerful than his right, and it didn't have a gun in it at the time. It wasn't particularly well aimed either but when it connected with Douglas above the right eye his head hit the wall with an audible *c-r-a-c-k* as though the wood or his head had split wide open. Douglas grunted then crumpled into a squat against the wall.

The suddenness of it stunned the group and for a long moment they gazed in shock at Harris's contorted face and the twisted heap perched awkwardly in front of him.

Then, to their relief, 'Shit, mate, what are you doing to me?' Douglas whined at last, spitting away blood streaming from his eyebrow down to his mouth and chin.

'John fucking Arnold! That's John who, you arsehole!' Harris bellowed.

Douglas blew a thick red bubble and spat again. 'I dunno where he is. He didn't come home last night.'

'When did you see him last?'

'Yesterday arvo. I was coming out of Billy Peters' tattoo shop. Johnny was just near Manhattan Walk there.'

'Did he say where he was going?'

'No, mate. He just said he was going to see a bloke about a job.'

'Where?'

'I dunno. Dead set, I don't. That's all he said and then he headed up towards the bridge. I haven't seen him since.'

'All his gear's still there,' offered Delaney.

'Looks like he's gone into smoke,' ventured Staines.

'We'll fucken see about that,' Harris grunted. 'Frank, get this grub down to the station and get a statement from him. And get some uniforms over here. I want this place gone over with a fine-tooth comb.'

He paced deliberately back to Douglas and stood over him menacingly, glaring at him as though he wanted to bite his face off and spit it into a bucket.

'I want John Arnold's arse on a plate!'

2

Monday was bitterly cold. At seven-thirty a bleak westerly was howling through the city streets. Brian Leary was grateful for the warmth of his pin-striped double-breaster. It was no longer fashionable but the quality British fabric and Stuart's yeoman tailoring still served him well, particularly on days when the first westerlies warned of worse to come.

The Forbes Henderson Building was a narrow two-storey brick box at the 'top end' of Elizabeth Street. It was called the 'top end' only because it was the end closest to Victoria Bridge, not because it aspired to be anything other than what it was — a grubby, unfashionable back street of the city. Still, it had adequately accommodated the firm of Messrs BM Leary & Doyle, Solicitors & Notaries, these past ten years. Neil Doyle had built up a solid practice in cottage conveyancing and probate work without the cachet of a Queen Street address and for Brian, with his busy criminal practice, the quick dash through Barry & Roberts, up to George Street and down to the police courts couldn't be more convenient.

Brian made his way out of the windy foyer and into the lift. It gave an arthritic shudder, then lumbered to the first floor. He was, as usual, the first to arrive. In the gloom he could just make out the outline of the doorway halfway down the narrow hallway and the brass sign that read 'BM Leary & Doyle — Solicitors'. The rest was darkness, and this morning it was a forbidding darkness that made him eager to enter his office and switch on the lights. As he walked down the hallway his right hand was in his pocket, his fingers on his keys. He stopped, suddenly conscious of a presence up ahead in the darkness.

'Who's there?'

The darkness moved and shuffled. 'Is that you, Mr Leary?' said a gravelly whisper.

'Yes. Who is it? I can't see you there.'

A muscular, tattooed man in a tight black T-shirt and faded blue jeans emerged into the half-light. 'It's me, sir. Johnny Arnold.'

Brian turned and slipped the key into the lock. Anyone wearing a T-shirt on a morning as cold as this had obviously left somewhere in a big hurry.

'You'd better come in.'

John Edward Arnold was born in an East End bomb shelter at the height of the blitz. The precious little his family had scraped together was blown to smithereens that year, and his Mum was never quite the same again. John and his brother Freddy went into the Home in '48. They were never told where the girls had gone. Johnny Arnold missed his sisters terribly and at first he cried into his lumpy pillow every night. But then he learned that crying didn't change a thing. So he stopped crying.

In 1952 they sent young John Arnold to a Home just south of Sydney, Australia. He never saw or heard from Freddy again. Every day, one by one, Johnny's friends at the Home disappeared to farms, or apprenticeships, or other Homes, or who knew where. Friends were temporary. The day he turned fifteen Johnny got himself a job, and he got himself out of that Home.

He was barely sixteen when he was caught coming through the window of the greengrocer's at Glebe, copping six months in the reformatory for his trouble. But nobody could do six months in the reform school easier than Johnny Arnold. Or so it seemed.

At nineteen John Arnold looked like a grown man. He was built like a prizefighter and as hard as steel. He was his own man, and kept himself to himself. Everyone knew you didn't pick Johnny Arnold. He could fight like a threshing machine and the smarter ones knew you'd never beat him while he still drew breath. He walked the city streets like they were his own and sleazy Kings Cross became his home.

Every Easter when the Show came to town Johnny and his mates would be down at the boxing tent trying to earn a few bob seeing out a round or two with one of Jimmy Sharman's boys. By the time Johnny was out of his teens Sharman figured it was cheaper to give the boy a few quid to stay away.

At night Johnny worked on the door at Denny Bourke's pub and, every now and then, if there was something on the go, he would be in it. The odd break-and-enter and the occasional insurance job if someone wanted something disappeared. Not that he went looking but if one of the lads needed a hand and there was a quid in it, Johnny would oblige. Every penny was welcome because sooner or later he was going to be back on that ship. He had to find some people he hadn't seen in a long, long time.

In the Easter of 1964 John Arnold got a job working the ferris wheel at the Royal Sydney Show. The pay was pretty ordinary but the wallopers had closed down Denny's pub and work was hard to find. That August he followed the Show up to Brisbane and worked the dodgems in Sideshow Alley at the Ekka.

That's where he met Wayne Douglas, who worked at the Haunted House, and later Wayne's twin brother Les, who worked on Hunter Brothers' dunny cart. The Douglas boys were ugly little men, missing teeth and covered with home-made tattoos. But they were staunch and they stuck to each other like shit to a blanket. Orphaned at four, these boys had clung together through twelve years at the Nudgee Orphanage and a lot of other hard knocks besides. John Arnold knew better than most what that meant.

When the Show closed down Arnold stayed on in Brisbane and moved in with the Douglas brothers. He and Wayne took a job at the Golden Circle Cannery at Northgate and they were making reasonable money. But travelling costs were killing them so one day Wayne brought home someone else's '59 Zephyr. They got it resprayed down at Monty's Garage and a week later the coppers picked them up. They did six months apiece in Boggo Road.

After that the years had more or less just rolled along for Johnny Arnold. He came close to his fare a few times but never did quite raise it. For the past four years he had been back and forth between Sydney and Brisbane with the occasional forced holiday at Her Majesty's expense. Every day it seemed to get a little harder to remember why those fading memories had once seemed so important.

John Arnold would have been handsome but for a nose bent and flattened, sitting slightly out of position on a face of otherwise noble features. His body was strong and muscular, perfectly proportioned and seemingly as hard and cold as his tough East London accent.

'The Bulls are after me for the Mickey's bombing,' he said.

'Come in,' said Brian, leading the way to his office.

Johnny first bumped Brian Leary back in '66 after he had been pinched on possession of housebreaking implements, resist arrest and assault police. The implements were found by old Mrs King in the front yard of her boarding house at the 'Gabba after she'd surprised an unwelcome visitor who promptly bolted into the night.

When the uniformed boys spotted Johnny outside the South Brisbane Library ten minutes later, they pegged him as being right for it. And he was. He'd have copped it sweet too, if it hadn't been for them young coppers. Just because he wouldn't sign up on a statement the uniforms decided to give him a bit of a touch-up. Not that that worried him too much. He'd copped a belting before, and from better than these blokes. But when they put 'resist arrest' and 'assault police' on him to explain the bruises they left on him, that's when he blued. He wasn't going to cop that so he'd done three weeks on remand waiting for a hearing date and by the time the Douglas boys scrounged enough dosh to get him a solicitor there were only about two hours to spare before Johnny was to front the beak.

He liked the look of this bloke Leary pretty much from the jump. You could tell he was fair dinkum. When Johnny told him he was right for the implements but he wasn't going to cop any of that other shit, the little bloke seemed to understand and when the prosecutor refused to drop the load-up charges, Leary just said, 'Right then, we box on.'

And box on he did. For two whole days he fought like a terrier. He fought the coppers, he fought the prosecutor, and he fought the bloody magistrate. He copped all the shit that magistrate served up to him, and just kept stepping up to them. He went like a champion.

Johnny Arnold had seen more than his fair share of lawyers before — four-eyed little faggots who might go a round or two for show but had no balls and would lie down like dogs the minute their fee was assured. This bloke fought for Johnny Arnold and he did it for real. Johnny Arnold didn't forget that kind of thing.

'This is a shameful business, Mr Arnold,' Brian Leary said, as he sat down and faced his client. 'Did you have some part in it?'

'No, Mr Leary, I never. That's not my caper.'

Brian Leary remembered now that when he last met Arnold, in a curious way he had discerned a kind of basic honesty in the man.

'Then why would the police be looking for you?'

''Cause I knew it was on. And I went gabbing about it round town.'

'How did you know it was on?'

Arnold sighed heavily, then said, 'After I done me bird for that blue up here I went back to Sydney. I had digs down Woolloomooloo and I was working on the door at a strip show in the Cross. Living down the 'Loo you run into just about everyone. Anyhow, there was a lot of talk about that Tipple was looking to take over the games up in Brisbane.'

'Tipple?'

'Harry Tipple. He practically runs Sydney. Got his finger in every game in town. Plenty of pull with the coppers. He gets a tickle off all the Sydney houses and he slings the coppers. If you want to open up down there, you got to square off with Tipple first. Word was he was looking to set up the same deal in Brisbane.'

'How would he do that?'

'Simple, just sell off a bit of insurance. You know, a few quid a week and you don't have no nasty fires or nothing.'

'I see. So what does Tipple have to do with you?' said Brian.

'I know a few blokes who muscle for him, that's all. Fellas I done time with in Long Bay are on his payroll.'

'And?'

'And one of them come in to see me at the club. He knew I'd spent a bit of time up here and I suppose he figured I might know a few of the players like. Anyway, he said Tipple wanted a few blokes to do the rounds of the Brisbane clubs and put the word on them. Wanted to know if I was interested.'

'What did you tell him?'

'I told him Tipple was pulling himself. No one here had hardly heard of him. But this bloke reckoned Tipple had it all worked out. They was going to put the word around and then they'd put a cracker under one or two of the smaller shows. He reckoned that as soon as one went off the rest would be pretty keen to do business. I told him to leave me out of it.'

'Why?'

Arnold shrugged his shoulders. 'Well,' he said, 'that's not my go, is it?'

'No other reason?'

'Because I'm me own man, that's all. And I'm not into cracking heads and standing over blokes. Simple as that. You work for Tipple and you fall in with the likes of that grub Nagel and the rest of them. That's not my go.'

'Who's Nagel?'

'He's just another nancy boy who thinks he's Little Caesar because he carries a shooter. All I'm saying is that Johnny Arnold works for Johnny Arnold, that's who. I don't like Tipple and I don't like his boys. And that's why I told them to leave me out.'

'None of that tells me why the police are looking for you.'

'I come back to Brisbane three weeks ago. Three days before I left Sydney, Washington's went up.'

'You're talking about Washington's Disco in the Valley?'

'Yeah. They used to run a couple of tables out the back. Anyway, someone put the torch to Washington's. So I get a visit from the coppers about a week later and they was trying to put it on me. It was that Harris. Took me three hours to convince them I wasn't even in town. Even after they rung me boss in Sydney and he told them I was working that night they reckoned I was in on it. In the end I shoved me bus ticket in front of Harris's ugly dial and they just had to accept it.

'They weren't happy though. Before Harris left he says to me, "You make sure you keep your two feet in the one shoe, or I'll be back. And next time I'll have your agates on a stick."

'Anyway,' he continued, 'I asked around. Tipple got some young blokes up here on the job. I never heard of them but apparently they've been around a bit. Longhairs they are. Supposed to be on drugs. They reckoned Washington's was just a little taste and unless the clubs come to the party there'd be some real bad luck going around. Next thing Nagel's in town to do the talking for Tipple and they say he's put the word on Johnny Morris, the manager of Mickey's, but the owners won't come into it. And the dogs are barking that Tipple's going to make an example of them and get these longhairs to fix them up.'

'So how did you come into it?'

'I figured that if Mickey's Poolhouse went off Harris and the rest of them'd be up me arse in no time flat. Anyway, about eleven o'clock Saturday morning I run into that reporter bloke — what's his name? — yeah, Gordon Yates, from the *Courier*, down the Shamrock. I had a bit of a whisper in his ear. I never give him no names or nothing. I just told him it was on, that some Sydney interests were trying to take over the Brisbane games and that Mickey's was going to go up.

'I hoped he might do a story in the paper. So it'd be too hot for them to go ahead with it. But he's got as drunk as ten men and then he's gone and fronted a bunch of d's in the back bar of the Trans and told them that Johnny Arnold's told him Mickey's Poolhouse is going to get torched. The bomb went off about five hours later. They reckon four car loads of wallopers hit my place about seven o'clock yesterday morning.'

Arnold stared across the desk at Brian Leary. Both men knew the situation. The police needed a head and right now John Arnold's neck was on the chopping block.

'So what now, Mr Leary?'

'That, Mr Arnold, depends very much on what you want to do. You're obviously quite right — you will be a prime suspect. Perhaps the only suspect. My view is that we should front up to them immediately but if we do there's every chance you'll be arrested and charged.'

Arnold had already arrived at the same conclusion. 'But if I go to ground and they end up pinching me some time when I ain't got you to front for me they'll drop a brick on me for sure.'

The 'brick' John Arnold spoke of was as familiar to Brian Leary as it was to every policeman from probationary constable to Commissioner. It seemed that every day, in every court in the state, in every two-bit town from Cairns to Coolangatta, the 'brick' was alleged by a defendant and denied by a policeman. Sometimes it was called a 'brief', sometimes a 'verbal', but it amounted to the same thing — a fabricated account by a police officer of a conversation said to have been conducted with the defendant in which the defendant confessed to having committed the offence charged.

If the police were to be believed, the brick was a myth, invented by the criminal class to disown the rash confessions they made spontaneously in police stations but were unwilling to commit to writing and quick to deny once they were elsewhere.

If many of Brian's clients were to be believed, the brick was a fundamental tool of trade for the Queensland Police Force, the cornerstone of a system of law enforcement based on the fabrication of evidence and perjury in the courts.

Arnold had summed up the situation perfectly. Brian nodded and added, 'If we front up today I can't guarantee you won't be charged but I can at least do my best to ensure they don't get up to any tricks.'

Arnold's expression hardened, as if to steel himself for the ordeal to come. 'I think that's what we got to do, Mr Leary. We got to go and have ourselves a parley with the wallopers.'

3

As the police Falcon cruised down Melbourne Street towards the city, Merv Harris cast a passing eye over the Greyhound bus depot. He did it out of habit. A lifetime as a copper had taught him it doesn't hurt to know who's leaving town and who's arriving.

There were the usual cow cockies wandering around looking lost and kids heading back to boarding school but nothing interesting. No one caught his eye. No one looked away self-consciously or took a second glance. Outside the pub a line of desperates was squatting in the doorway or limping around waiting for the doors to open. All familiar faces.

Merv Harris was getting very pissed off. Since early Sunday morning every ratbag pollie, journo and do-gooder in town had been on the blower every five minutes wanting to know what the police were doing about the bombing at Mickey's Poolhouse. And so far they had nothing.

He had been sure they'd get something from Arnold's mate Les Douglas, even if Les had to make it up. They'd had him in there for eight hours but he'd shown more courage than anyone thought he had, including Les. He must have been more frightened of Arnold than he was of us, thought Harris. He shouldn't have blown up at him, and he regretted it now in a way, but Douglas had been around long enough to know the drill.

They'd have been happy with anything, even a couple of words of conversation tying Arnold to Johnny Morris or to the Poolhouse or mentioning extortion jobs or even something that might have been an ingredient for a bomb. But the prick wouldn't come into it, and they had nothing. So he copped what he deserved.

But they still had nothing. Johnny Morris had come and gone without Harris even getting the chance to speak to him. That was the way George Curran wanted it. George wanted to take care of Morris personally and Merv knew why. The press were buzzing like flies around shit and Morris had a mouth as big as Hitler's gas-bill. Someone had to shut him down before the journos got to him.

Morris had looked like a man about to give birth to a Besser brick when he arrived at the Valley Station. Harris didn't know what it was that Old George said to him but whatever it was it had obviously scared the living shit right out of that fat prick Morris. When he walked out of Curran's office his dial was as white as a sheet.

It had the desired effect, too — after that day he never opened his fat gob to a living soul about the Mickey's bombing. If Johnny Morris ever knew anything Old George flushed it down the shithouse that day.

So, one way and another, Merv was getting pissed off.

He was coming across the William Jolly Bridge when he picked up the radio message that John Arnold had just fronted up to the Valley CI Branch with a solicitor.

Nine minutes later Harris burst in through the back door of the Valley Station. The first thing he heard was that arsehole Brian Leary mouthing off at the front desk. He knew the voice well enough. Leary acted for every grubby no-hoper in town, and Merv had come up against him a hundred times in Court. He was always whinging about something, and this time was obviously no exception. It sounded as though he was filling someone's ear about being held off his client. Merv could hear the snivelling little rat moaning to the desk sergeant.

'Mr Arnold attended here voluntarily with me this morning. For the past fifteen minutes I have been denied any access to him. This behaviour is quite unlawful and I demand immediate access to my client.'

The next line from Leary was punctuated by a rumbling response. Merv recognised Des Clarke, a good old Sarge who, through a lifetime in the Force, had learned to stonewall better than most. Leary was on his high horse all right, but Merv knew old Des would play him with a straight bat all day if necessary.

Things were on hold down here but what in Christ's name was going on? Harris charged up the stairs. The Day Room was empty except for young Johnston whose two index fingers were stabbing intermittently at the keys of an old typewriter.

'Where's Arnold?' demanded Harris.

Johnston looked up, startled. 'In there,' he said nodding towards an interview room to his left. 'With Sergeant Wilson.'

What sort of a lamebrain stunt was that fuck-knuckle Tom Wilson trying to pull this time? Harris strode to the door of the interview room and threw it open. Arnold was sitting bolt upright with his chest thrust forward and his jaw set like stone, looking like the figurehead of the good ship *Venus* punching through a stormy sea. Tom Wilson, Frank Delaney and young Nolan stood in a semicircle in front of him. In unison their heads swivelled in Merv's direction.

Look at them, he thought. Larry, Curly and Mo! He was tempted to bop their heads together. Instead, he marshalled all his self-restraint and said in a quiet, almost civil tone, 'Tom, could I see you for a minute?'

Wilson, bewildered, glanced either side of him with a 'who me?' expression and muttered, 'Yes. Sure, Merv.'

The two stepped quietly out of the room. Harris closed the door gently behind them and led the way out into the stairwell. Then he turned, hands jammed on his hips, and thrust his jaw to within about two inches of Tom Wilson's face.

'Tom, what the fuck are you doing?'

Tom faltered for a moment then struck back with righteous indignation. 'I'm questioning Arnold about the bloody bombing, Merv!'

'Listen, shit-for-brains,' roared Harris. 'The bloke's come in here with his bloody solicitor and you've got the bastard locked up downstairs so he can't get at him! Where do you think that brilliant fucking stunt is going to get us? You could sign him up for the bloody Jack the Ripper murders and any judge would toss you on your ear in two seconds flat. As soon as he heard you'd held the bloke off his solicitor he'd wipe his arse with any bloody confession we tried to put up.'

The penny dropped. Tom stood there open-mouthed like a pug who'd just been KO'd but had not got around to falling over yet. It wasn't a new experience for him.

'Try and use your fucking scone, eh?' Harris concluded, then stormed off back to the interview room muttering obscenities.

As he barrelled into the room he grunted, 'What are you doing here, Arnold? Your solicitor's looking for you downstairs. Frank, get down there and tell Mr Leary his client's up here. Nolan, go and get them both a cup of tea.'

An unfortunate misunderstanding ... The duty sergeant had thought Mr Leary was to wait downstairs so that the interview could be in the uniform section where there was better access to a telephone in case

Mr Leary needed to call his office, and the detectives assumed the interview would be conducted upstairs and they were waiting for Mr Leary to join them. A breakdown in communications, mainly because the Government refused to install an intercom system in the station and police resources were sorely stretched. Unfortunate but, not to worry, everything was now sorted out and they could get on with the interview.

The excuses fooled nobody. Nobody believed them and nobody believed anybody believed them. Still, they had to be made and, for the record, they were made.

Brian Leary announced that he had received clear and unequivocal instructions from his client that he was not guilty of any involvement in the Mickey's Poolhouse incident and was in a position to provide a detailed account of his movements at all relevant times. His client had become aware that police wanted him for questioning in relation to the matter and he was now willing to provide a signed statement denying any involvement and accounting for his movements.

Tom Wilson and Frank Delaney conducted the formal interview. It took the form of a Record of Interview — questions and answers recorded in typewritten form. Tom Wilson was the fastest two-finger typist in the Branch so he got the nod on the typewriter and Frank did the questioning.

Merv Harris sat outside the Day Room fuming. This was the worst possible development. He knew for certain that John Arnold had a hand in this business. He'd opened his mouth about it on the Saturday morning to that journalist bloke Yates. Yates had already given the police a statement saying how Arnold had told him at the Shamrock that the Poolhouse was all set to go. Arnold knew all about it the day before it happened. Yeah, he was right for this one, no question.

But he was in there now, no doubt sprouting a whole lot of bullshit they wouldn't be able to disprove and getting on record a complete denial, in writing, signed, sealed and delivered. And of course it all just served to confirm what Merv had known all along — that grub Arnold was as round as a bloody hoop for the Mickey's bombing. You don't show up with a solicitor if you've got nothing to hide. Yeah, he was right for it all right and the half-smart little bastard knew the score — front up with a lawyer and deny the whole thing in writing so the coppers can't put a verbal on you.

So Johnny Arnold thought he knew just how to outsmart the coppers, did he? Well he had another think coming. 'You don't know jack shit, arsehole,' Harris growled in the empty room.

John Arnold's statement was confined to a denial of any involvement in the bombing and an account of his movements during all relevant times. He mentioned nothing of the approach made to him or the persons involved. Despite Brian's exhortations, he had stipulated back at the office that while he was willing to tell the police about himself, he wasn't 'in the business of lagging blokes' no matter what the consequences.

'I ain't no give-up, Mr Leary,' he had said almost apologetically. 'People know me for what I am, and that's what I am. I ain't going to start dogging on blokes now.'

So that was it. He told his story.

Saturday afternoon he had spent scratching around the South Brisbane pubs looking for a bit of door work or whatever he could get. He'd had a beer in the Ship Inn and another at the Plough Inn and dropped in at the Manhattan but he 'did no good'. So he decided to hitch down to the Gold Coast because he'd heard that

Johnny Forrest was looking for blokes to work on the door of his turnout at Surfers Paradise.

That was at about five o'clock Saturday afternoon and he ran into Les Douglas outside the Manhattan just as he was heading out to walk across the bridge to North Quay to catch the bus out to Mt Gravatt. From there he would be able to hitch a ride straight through to the Coast. He got to the old Mt Gravatt tram terminus at about a quarter-past-six, he reckoned, and he was lucky enough to be picked up by a truckie going through to Murwillumbah so he was in Surfers not much later than about eight. No, he couldn't remember much about the truckie and he didn't know what his name was.

The first thing he did when he hit Surfers was go and grab a burger from 'that wog bloke in Cavill Avenue underneath the Captain's Table Restaurant'. Then he took a stroll over to the Admiral Bimbo, which was Johnny Forrest's restaurant, arriving there, he reckoned, at about eight-thirty. He ran into a couple of blokes he knew 'just to say hello to like' and had a couple of beers before catching up with Johnny at about nine o'clock when he 'put the bite on him for a start'. Forrest couldn't help him; the job had been filled. So he had a couple more beers at the Admiral and then headed over to the beer garden of the Surfers Paradise Hotel 'just to see what was happening over there'.

He had a few more pots in the beer garden and then he chatted up a couple of 'hippie-looking birds'. One of them was a fat sheila with long, straight, blonde hair. He wasn't sure but he thought her name was Glenda — something like that. The other one was a good-looking sort but 'a bit stuck up'. He remembered her name because it was so unusual. Romy, it was. Romy claimed to be a go-go dancer. They were both up from Sydney and had been staying at Coolangatta.

At closing time he bought three 'tallies' and they all went and sat on the beach. He was starting to think he 'might have been a show with the two of them' but then one of them lit up a reefer and passed it around and after he had a couple of drags he was 'shot to bits'.

Last thing he remembered was the girls talking about trying to hitch back to Sydney that night and heading off down the beach. Next thing it was just breaking day and he woke up, freezing cold, still on the beach. He walked down Cavill Avenue to the highway and it would have been about six o'clock when he scored a lift with a bloke in a 'fairly new Ford Falcon'. The bloke was a salesman, 'real chatty'. Problem was, Arnold fell asleep and couldn't remember much at all about the bloke except that he dropped him off outside the Mater Hospital, about a mile from his house, at about seven-thirty on the Sunday morning.

'What a complete bucket of pig-shit!' Merv Harris was striding around the Day Room waving the Record of Interview and growling at the assembled group of detectives perched on various desks and chairs.

'Fuck!' he roared from time to time, exploding without warning. He fumed for what seemed a long time while the others waited for the rage to work through his system. No use talking to Merv when he was like this. He was just as likely to deck you. He had a short fuse and when he blew up you just kept your head down.

When it was finally safe Delaney was the first to speak. 'We had nothing to hold him on Merv,' he ventured.

Harris shook his head. 'The bloke's just knocked eleven people and him and his lawyer can walk straight out the front door thumbing their noses at us!'

'What do you do, Merv?' Delaney shrugged. 'He's got us by the short and curlies.'

Harris snorted. 'Listen Frank, there's not too many things get on my goat but the one thing that really pisses me off, the thing that gets up my nose like nothing else, is smart-arse two-bit fucking crims who think they can put one over on us coppers.' He glared around at the others. 'And I can tell youse all one thing for certain. That grub might think he's very clever today but this one's not over by a long hop. He's going to wear this one. I'll make sure he does. Mark my words, sure as your arse points to the ground, Johnny Arnold's going to put his hand up for that bloody bomb!'

The first thing was to check out the bullshit alibi. Arnold was smart enough to have made it all pretty vague and no doubt he'd have his tracks covered on the detail he did give but with a half-smart grub like that you never knew. He might just fuck it up. So the first job was to check out his bullshit story.

It didn't take long for it to start coming apart.

Sure, it was true that Arnold did the rounds of the South Brisbane pubs on the Saturday afternoon but two of the publicans said he had done the same thing on the previous Monday, when they'd told him there was nothing going so they were surprised to see him back so soon. As far as Merv was concerned it had all the hallmarks of a half-smart crim trying to work himself up a false alibi.

The next stop was John Francis Archibald Forrest, part-time 'restaurateur' and full-time crook. Johnny ran the Admiral Bimbo, a hole-in-the-wall dive that pretended to be a restaurant. Truth was you were more likely to get a fuck than a feed in the Admiral and everyone knew it.

It was an open secret that Forrest was paying his dues to the boys in Licensing to keep the doors open.

But then, so what? Merv had no problem with coppers getting a bit of a sling out of the sly grog shops. Why shouldn't they? No one really wanted to close them down anyway. The punters wanted to be able to get a beer and a trollop after closing time and they would do it, one way or the other. All the pollies wanted was for the coppers to keep it under the carpet where the mums and dads didn't have to look at it, and everyone was happy. So Licensing kept a lid on it all and maybe the boys copped a little earn on the side. So what? That was just one of the perks of the job.

Forrest was ex-Navy, a big blockhead who had joined up just after the war and fought well enough as a welterweight for the Navy to avoid being court-martialled before finally being discharged under dubious circumstances back in '58. He was known as Long John, a nickname he apparently acquired as a result of an on-stage performance with a stripper in a Hong Kong nightclub, and one which particularly suited him, Merv thought, given that he was the biggest pirate unhung.

After the Navy he had teamed up with a con-man by the name of Billy Wherrit. Billy was as smooth as chewed chook shit and together he and Forrest had pulled off some major scams. Legend had it that they stung the South Africans for nearly a hundred grand and when some hit-man followed them to Sydney they were forced to sling him a poultice to run dead. Or so the story went. You'd never know the truth of it — these blokes were professional bullshit artists. Anyway, whatever did happen over there, it seemed to have put the wind up the boys because after that they went their separate ways, Wherrit heading south and Johnny Forrest carving out a slice for himself in Queensland.

He had been a busy boy, too. He always walked that thin grey line between legal and larcenous and he always had a good excuse as to why he had his mitts in some other bastard's pockets. He'd been pinched more times than a barmaid's bum but they hadn't convicted him once. He even had a few thickhead coppers around the town starting to think he might just be a 'legitimate businessman'. But not Merv. Merv knew him for what he was, a shifty bastard. Johnny Forrest had more moves than a maggot in a shit-tin. But he wasn't about to put one over on Merv Harris.

As soon as Forrest was brought into the interview room Harris dropped it on him. 'I want to know about Saturday night.'

For the first time in his life Long John looked like he was stuck for something to say. He was a big, red, rounded man, with no eyebrows to speak of, short-cropped ginger hair and a florid complexion.

He rubbed his bristly head with his short, fat fingers and genuinely looked like a man about to make a full confession. Which was something Johnny Forrest would never have done unless there was just no other way around it. But what else could he do? There was always a crew in the Admiral on a Saturday night, and how was he to know whether there might have been a copper or two in there when it happened? Obviously the jacks knew all about it. Otherwise they wouldn't have dragged him in here to the Surfers Paradise Station. He may as well be upfront, and try and talk his way out of it.

'Look, Mr Harris, I don't know how many times I've told her she's not to flash the "map of Tasmania" but you know what them mad sheilas are like.'

'The what?'

'The "map of Tassie", the muff. I've told her a thousand times that she's got to keep the G-string on. She can get all the rest of the gear off but she's got to keep the "map of Tasmania" under wraps. That's what you blokes told me and them's the rules. And I've told her a thousand times. But you know these mad bloody dancers. They can't help themselves, it's the artistic urges. As soon as the boys start yelling for more — whooshka — off she comes!'

Harris glanced up at the bemused faces of Potter and Delaney, who were standing behind the seated Forrest. They had all seen the Admiral Bimbo's resident 'exotic dancer' Bernice go through her routine.

Harris rubbed his eyes, and punched out a sigh. 'We could close you down. You know that, don't you, Johnny?'

'Of course I do, Mr Harris. But what could I do? I couldn't stop the show. The place was full of Yankee R'n'R boys, half-mad with the piss. They'd have wrecked the joint.'

Forrest was trying hard to look as sincere as he possibly could and was impressing absolutely no one.

'Do you know John Arnold?'

Forrest was a little surprised, but nonetheless relieved, by the apparent change of subject and answered without hesitation. 'Johnny from down the Cross? Yeah, I know him.'

'Did you see him Saturday night?'

Another easy question. No danger here, thought Forrest. Things were looking up. 'Yeah, I did actually. He was in early on, about nine I think it was.'

Harris studied Forrest, sizing him up. He didn't believe for a second that Johnny Forrest would have had anything to do with the Mickey's job. That was way out of his line. And Forrest wasn't the type to stick his neck out to protect the likes of Arnold. They knew each other because they were both low-life scum but they played different games and it was unlikely that they were mates. Forrest was a good ten years older than Arnold and they moved in different circles. Forrest was more likely to employ John Arnold than to have a beer with him. Maybe that's why Arnold had chosen him to provide his alibi. Get down to the Coast, front Johnny Forrest about a job to put yourself sixty miles away from the scene, and then drive straight back in time to do the job.

'What time did he leave?'

'I don't know, Mr Harris. I was only talking to him for about ten minutes. He was scrounging after door work.'

'Why did he come to you?'

'To be honest with you, Mr Harris, I'm buggered if I know. He's never worked down here before so far as I know. He's always been a city boy. He reckoned someone told him I was looking for a bouncer. But that's bullshit. Young Darryl and I take care of that sort of thing. I don't know where he heard that from.'

Yes, this was one bullshit alibi that was definitely starting to come apart at the seams. Everything Merv had heard so far had only served to confirm what he had known all along — that John Arnold had put that cracker in the rubbish bin out front of Mickey's Poolhouse and killed eleven people in the process.

Arnold's only problem was that he had done it in Merv Harris's backyard, and Merv Harris was going to nail his arse to the wall for it.

Harris did his best to get round Arnold's mates, but it was amazing how few of them were still around. When he and Delaney dropped into Billy Peters' tattoo shop on the Wednesday morning, Billy had his feet up reading a 'Hot Stuff' comic. He glanced at his visitors and jeered, 'Here they are, Bluey and Curl!'

Harris glared back at him. He'd love to kick Billy's guts in for him but there was no point in belting Billy Peters. He was hard as nails — all you'd do is hurt your hands. Anyway, they weren't here for pleasure.

Delaney did the talking because he knew Merv couldn't bring himself to chat up Billy Peters. 'What do you know, Billy?'

'Same as you blokes. Somebody torched the Poolhouse and youse are up everyone's arse about it.'

'We know who done it. We just want to know why. What's on the go, Billy?'

'You blokes know a lot more than me. I heard youse are red hot for Johnny Arnold on it.'

'What's he reckon?'

'Mate, don't come around here asking me those sort of questions. I hardly know the bloke. Listen, what are you trying to do to a bloke? Youse are already sending me broke shaking every bastard down. Dead set, it's crook for business. Every villain in town's gone into smoke.'

Harris could no longer control himself. 'What do you know about Arnold?' he demanded.

Peters stared back truculently. 'I don't know fucken nothing about Arnold. Right?'

Harris glared at Peters for a long moment. Delaney could almost hear the little bulbs fusing in Merv's brain. If he went for Peters they were in for an almighty stink.

'Right?' repeated Peters. Billy was a cranky bastard, almost as cranky as Merv.

'Yeah, right,' said Harris evenly, and Delaney breathed a sigh of relief. Billy went back to his comic.

'So did you hear anything about the Poolhouse, Billy?' resumed Delaney.

'Mate, the dogs in the street were barking that Morris was heading for a fall. He knew it himself. Why do you think Nagel and them was up here last week?'

'Nagel? Was he up here, was he?'

'Yeah. Him and Slippers and Barry Charles. Word is they were in Mickey's on Thursday night having a natter to Morris. He hasn't brought those blokes up unless he was expecting something.'

That was the first time Harris had ever heard Billy Peters say something he didn't already know. And it might even be true. Arthur Nagel, Mick 'Slippers' Donnell and Barry Charles were just the sort of low-life that a half-baked hood like Morris would import if he was feeling a bit vulnerable.

They were all gunnies from Sydney with a reputation for standing over blokes and collecting debts for the bookies. Like most of their type they seemed to find their way to Queensland every now and then for no apparent reason. It wouldn't be the first time Merv had stopped by the Greyhound depot just to welcome one of them to town and search his bag for hardware and remind him that this was Queensland and if he so much as farted in the wrong direction Merv Harris would personally kick his arse around his ears. If he saw them driving into town he'd always pull them over and if there were two of them together Merv would book them for consorting.

He hated those Sydney grubs, half-baked jumped-up Saturday matinee gangsters strutting around the town like they owned the joint. They were the worst kind of arseholes, in their flash cars and fancy suits, pretending they were something they weren't.

Merv could understand blokes brought up hard who did their best the best way that they could but these grubs were nothing more than mug lair crims who watched too many movies. Half of them couldn't knock the skin off a rice pudding if push came to shove. But they all fancied themselves with a pistol in their pocket and they walked around with a big reputation.

Even the Sydney coppers treated them like human beings, and that was one thing Merv couldn't stomach.

A trip to Sydney every now and then to extradite some hero back to Queensland always meant a few nights down the Cross with the Sydney coppers with all the piss and molls laid on. It was always a bit of fun and there were some good blokes among the Sydney d's. But one thing Merv couldn't stomach was the way they'd drink with low-life crims and speak to them as if they had some right to be there. It was a Sydney thing, and Merv couldn't understand it.

In recent years old George had told Merv to ease up on these Sydney blow-ins, not to run them in unless they started to play up. George hated mug lair Sydney spivs as much as anyone but obviously the word was coming through from Sydney. The coppers down there were skimming from the bookies and the dirty girls and no doubt they had business with these blokes from time to time. Merv could understand that fair enough but they ought to be regularly reminded of the fact that they were just grubby crims.

George was becoming much too sensitive about the Sydney coppers. Merv could understand that it was important to keep a good exchange of information going, to encourage cooperation with the New South Wales police but George was always up their arse these days and all that didn't sit too good with Merv. He didn't like the way some of them Sydney coppers seemed to go about things and he particularly didn't like the company they kept. Company the likes of Nagel and his mob.

If what Billy Peters had just said was true, Nagel, Charles and Donnell had slipped into town very quietly and that meant they probably weren't up here on holidays. They were a long way out of their territory and chances were that they'd been especially handpicked to come up here to deal with Arnold.

Word had it there was plenty of bad blood between Nagel and John Arnold. According to the touts, Nagel and his mates had beat the absolute piss'n'pickhandles out of one of Arnold's best chinas from the Balmain footy club over some two-bit gambling debts and it was on for young and old. They reckoned Arnold was getting all around the town threatening to give Arthur Nagel a fair dinkum flogging and Nagel was saying that if Arnold didn't pull his head in, him and the boys would send him off. Arnold did get hold of him though, apparently. Stood him up in the street somewhere down in the Cross and gave him an absolute hiding on all accounts.

For a while there was plenty of talk about Arnold getting knocked for it, but then it seems that popular opinion went against that idea and the word went out on the street that it would be a weak act for Nagel to take Arnold other than by himself and fair and square. So Nagel had dropped off, for the time being anyway. Mind you, Arnold obviously wasn't altogether convinced that Nagel's boys had dropped off him because it was only a couple of days after all that that he headed up to Brisbane.

So truce or no truce, the scores weren't exactly settled between Arthur Nagel and Johnny Arnold and if Morris had John Edward Arnold breathing down his throat for protection payments Nagel was a pretty good choice to bring in as a bit of muscle. Only problem was that these boys didn't know shit from breakfast when it came to keeping peace and it was Harris's guess that maybe that's why things had blown up. Literally.

It all fell into line and for the first time since Sunday morning Harris started to feel like he was getting somewhere. Arnold wants to get a little racket going in Brisbane so he gets around big-noting himself in all the clubs and standing over the likes of Morris. So Morris calls in a couple of Bigs. But he pulls the wrong rein when he calls in Nagel, thinking he'll be keen to deal with Arnold, because suddenly it's personal, with Nagel and Arnold both trying to sort each other out and Johnny Morris the meat in the sandwich. Well, Arnold sorted them out all right and he just happened to blow up half the Valley in the process.

All this meant that Harris had to get to John Morris because he could put the finger right on Arnold. Harris knew old George would want Morris kept out of it if possible. Nobody wanted him getting cross-examined about payments to the boys in Licensing. But now it was clear that Morris had imported Sydney muscle it was a new ball game. Morris had obviously been threatened and therefore he could give the evidence they needed to pin Arnold.

'Forget it, Merv,' was George Curran's response as he stared impassively through the little waft of steam that curled gently over his mid-morning cup of tea.

'George, this has got nothing to do with Licensing.'

'Forget it, Merv,' repeated Curran. 'Morris has been to see a solicitor. Says he doesn't want to say anything to anyone.'

Harris watched in frustration while the older man slurped his hot tea. 'We've got nothing, George. It's four days now, the press is going berserk, the Coroner's already been on the blower. If Arnold's got any brains at all he won't hang around forever. We've got to do something, George. So far we've got nothing.'

'We've got all we need, Merv. We've got the culprit. John Edward Arnold. I've arranged for a couple of fellows to come up from Sydney Homicide tonight. Something tells me there's going to be a major breakthrough in this case sometime early tomorrow morning.'

4

'Michael!'
'Yeah, yeah.'

These days Brian Leary's bark had little bite. Michael rolled over and pulled the pillow over his head waiting for his mother's backup call. It wasn't long coming.

'Michael, get up this minute! If you want a lift with your father you'd better get a move on.'

'Yeah, righto.' Michael dropped his feet to the floor and sat on the side of his bed. Brand new day; same old shit. He snatched the alarm clock from his bedside table, shook it, then stared at it until his eyes came into focus. Ten-past-seven. He hadn't set the alarm on that old clock all year. No need to. No one in this house was about to let him oversleep.

He skipped across the hallway into the bathroom and closed the door behind him. The tiled floor, cold as charity, drained the stiffness from his groin. He reached into the shower recess and spun the hot tap on full blast. As steam billowed up and filled the room he watched his naked image disappearing in the bathroom mirror.

'Michael!'
'Yeah, all right. I'm in the shower!'

Jesus! It seemed like everyone was up him for the rent these days. He was sick of people telling him what to do. He swiped his palm across the mirror and curled his lip. He looked insolent, malevolent, like Eric Burdon on the cover of the 'War' LP. He was one of the revolution generation. *My generation.* Fuck the world. Today he felt rebellious. Maybe today he would tell the old man he wasn't going in to work.

Michael dragged the razor across his chin. On cold mornings like this one he wondered whether he'd made the right decision to take the job working with his father. It was good to have a bit of money but working for a living was a drag.

He'd been a good rather than an outstanding scholar. But he had matriculated to the university and now he sometimes regretted not going there. The oldies could have paid the fees but he didn't want to be a burden on them so he decided to be a hero and do his legal studies through the Solicitors Board and gain exposure to the 'practical face of law', as his father called it.

He had entered into articles with his father's partner, Neil Thomas Doyle, at a weekly wage of slightly less than thirteen dollars, and since then had spent his weekdays licking stamps, folding letters into envelopes, running errands, making cups of tea, filing documents and generally jumping as high and as often as he was told to. The offices were old and dowdy, like the secretaries, and everybody, but everybody, told him what to do. Stories of wild times at the university with girls and grog and grass and all-night parties made the practical face of law seem very drab indeed.

As Michael sat down at the kitchen table his mother slapped a bowl of cornflakes in front of him. Cath was a morning mover and shaker, fussing around as if intent on sweeping them both out the door as quickly as possible.

Opposite him, Brian's head was buried in the paper, frowning. He was wearing his lawyer face, alert and serious. Brian looked different on Saturdays and Sundays. It was as though he kept another Brian in the wardrobe dressed up in a shirt and tie, with a serious, abstracted expression, and every Monday that Brian would emerge, ready for another week. Something about the head behind the paper was particularly irritating this morning and Michael was half-inclined to reach across and ruffle his father's Brylcreamed hair.

'Dad.'

'Mmm ...'

'Dad?'

The lawyer looked up from his newspaper. Michael turned the words over in his head ... *I won't be in today. Decided to stay home and take a sickie. Thought I might ask Suzie Burrows up the road to come over and have sexual intercourse with me. That OK with you?*

His father stared at him a moment and his face softened slightly. Michael looked at him, and wondered did his father ever feel this way? Did he ever wake up on cold mornings with an erection and a head full of lustful dreams? Was he sick to shit of people telling him what to do? He'd love to ask. Just once. But he knew he never would.

His father's eyebrows did a little skip, waiting for the question, so Michael fired out a standard. 'Are we going down to the beach house this weekend?'

'Maybe.'

Michael shovelled up a spoonful of cornflakes. He liked it when his old man talked about the beach house. It seemed to turn him back into a human being.

'I was talking to Kevvy Lonnigan yesterday. He reckons the tailor were running on the weekend.'

Brian Leary the fisherman glanced up from his paper. 'Is that so?'

'So Kevvy says.' Michael pushed the spoon into his mouth and crunched on its contents. He had his father's interest. 'He reckons he and his Dad really got amongst them on Sunday morning.'

Brian scoffed, 'Old man Lonnigan couldn't catch a cold on a winter's night!'

There he is, thought Michael. The human being. Fishing always did it. When the old man got down on the beach with his surf rod and the fishing gear he became a different person. In his daggy old army shorts, T-shirt on its last legs and battered straw hat he was just another bloke.

'We'll have to get down there on the weekend, and show them how it's done then.'

'That'd be good.' Michael pushed the spoon back into his bowl and smiled. This was power of a sort, knowing exactly the right levers to pull.

In the background the news droned from the radio. Michael heard his mother draw in a sharp breath. The radio voice was saying something about a man being arrested for the bombing of that poolhall in the Valley.

The edge of the discarded newspaper dropped into Michael's cornflakes. His father was bounding to the front door.

'You'll have to catch the bus this morning, son!'

Brian Leary arrived at the City Watchhouse just before eight, but it was nearly twenty-past before the Watchhouse keeper was finally willing to reveal that, yes, John Arnold was the person arrested earlier that morning on a murder charge arising out of the Mickey's Poolhouse bombing but he wasn't presently at the Watchhouse.

So far as the sergeant knew, he had been taken back to Police Headquarters in Makerston Street. No, he didn't know for certain why Mr Arnold had been removed from the Watchhouse after being formally charged but he understood from what detectives involved in the matter had mentioned that the gentleman had been very remorseful and quite emotional and quite possibly it was considered appropriate to remove the prisoner to surroundings in which he would be more comfortable in his distressed state.

By the time Brian scurried up North Quay to Police Headquarters eight-thirty had come and gone but it wasn't until after nine and some loud and insistent complaints that Inspector George Curran finally appeared, apologising profusely for the mix-up, and explaining that he had only now learned that Brian had instructions from Mr Arnold and was trying to track him down.

'I'm told he's in a pretty poor mental state, Mr Leary,' Curran said compassionately. 'He's pretty shook up, as you can imagine. I haven't seen him myself but I believe he broke down completely. The fellows were trying to get the Government Medical Officer over to have a look at him, but apparently they couldn't raise anyone over at the GMO's office.'

For a moment Brian thought of heading back to Herschel Street to try to chase down the GMO but that could wait for now.

'I'd like to see Mr Arnold immediately.'

'Of course. I'll just find out where he is and get him straight up here. You can talk to him in my room if you like. Just take a seat and I'll get them to bring him up.'

Brian was pleased that at last he seemed to be making progress and he relaxed a little as Curran disappeared from view.

'Oh, Mr Leary,' said George Curran, reappearing in the doorway. 'You could probably do with a cup of tea. How do you have it?'

The tea came and went without further word from Inspector Curran and by nine-fifteen Brian was again anxious. By the time he managed to convince the duty sergeant to track down Inspector Curran for him and Curran finally reappeared, it was getting on for half-past-nine.

'Sorry about that, Mr Leary,' said Curran with apparent sincerity, shaking his head ruefully. 'I've been all over the shop trying to sort that out for you and in the middle of it all I got sidetracked with an operational matter for the Commissioner. But I've located him now. He's gone back to the Watchhouse so they can print him and process him for court.'

Despite the cold weather Brian raised a sweat almost running back up North Quay to the Watchhouse. Arnold would be led into the No 1 Magistrates Court at ten o'clock and Brian needed to get to him immediately.

When the Watchhouse keeper told him the prisoner had already left for court, it was clear the dirty tricks campaign was under way, which mean that, for some reason, the police wanted to delay his access to Arnold as long as possible. That suggested that the claims Arnold had broken down and in a fit of remorse had presented police with a full confession of complicity in the Mickey's Poolhouse bombing were to be viewed with the utmost circumspection.

His suspicions were confirmed the moment he saw John Arnold.

If he had spotted the cops out front ten seconds earlier, Johnny Arnold would have been home free. He was up early that morning. For some reason he couldn't sleep and by six he had the billy on for a cuppa. He was sitting in the half-light, drinking his tea, when a faint rustle outside stung him like a cattle prod.

He darted through the lounge and into the sleep-out, peering through the window to the yard below. There they were, half-crouched, service revolvers drawn, at the foot of the front steps.

The silence exploded as Arnold bolted frantically towards the back door. A human battering ram charged the front door as the back door crashed open in a hail of splintering wood. The house was suddenly full of men shouting and running from room to room. Arnold darted, jumped, vaulted, pushed, scrambled, and struggled desperately until finally he was pinned under the weight of three men, a revolved jammed against his forehead.

'I want to see my solicitor!' he croaked hoarsely.

The hand with the gun came away for a moment, then slammed back with a sickening thud.

'Shut your fucking mouth, cunt.' The words were spat out by a hard-eyed crew-cut at the end of the revolver. 'You won't be getting no fucking solicitor. All you'll be getting is a bullet in the brain.'

As they dragged him to his feet and propped him against the wall Arnold's legs buckled. The crew-cut, Plain Clothes Constable First Class Darryl Batch, was tramping through the house, checking every room. Wayne Douglas, opting for the better part of valour, had moved out two days previously, leaving Arnold in the house alone.

'I want a solicitor,' Arnold groaned again.

Batch leaned over him, baring his teeth in a snarl. 'Shut the fuck up!' He lifted the revolver again and pressed it hard into Arnold's cheek pushing the flesh upwards until the eye above was almost closed. 'Now listen, killer, we're all going down to the car now. And if you so much as look sideways you're dead.'

The raiding party consisted of six detectives, all of the rank of Constable First Class. George Curran had stipulated to Merv Harris that they had to be young blokes with no prior involvement in the Mickey's Poolhouse investigation, but they had to have 'plenty of balls'. Their job was simply to pinch Arnold and get him to the station. They didn't have to worry about a charge or anything else. George had all that worked out. There would be a suitable holding charge, something to justify holding him in custody long enough to wring a story out of him.

George told Merv to put Batch in charge. He was only young but he was hard, and he'd do what had to be done. And when the pressure was on he'd stick to a story like shit to a blanket, no risk.

Within fifteen minutes Arnold was sitting in an interview room in the Valley Station surrounded by a ring of detectives watching Merv Harris go through his routine.

'I want to know everything you know about that bloody bomb, shithead!' he barked, leaning over his captive.

'I want my solicitor,' repeated Arnold firmly.

With that, Harris swung his full weight behind a backhand swipe with a telephone directory which collected Arnold under his right ear and all but knocked him out of his chair.

'Wrong answer, shithead!'

Arnold straightened himself in the chair, lifted his eyes towards his tormentor, then lowered them again, staring impassively ahead.

'I got a right to have my solicitor here.'

Harris leaned over until his face was close to Arnold's. 'Listen, sport,' he spat. 'You've got no fucking rights around here. Understand? We're the fucking law around here. We do what we like. You understand me? You've been lighting bungers, killer, and you're going to tell me all about it. I don't care if it takes all day and all night. You're going to sing to me like a fucking nightingale even if I've got to pull every fucking tooth out of your ugly fucking head!'

Arnold stared silently back at Harris for a long moment, and then repeated doggedly, 'I want to see my solicitor.'

Harris erupted, flailing wildly at his captive. Pieces of the phone book scattered, fluttered and flew in every direction. Arnold fell backwards, Harris clawing at him violently. They ended up sprawled together on the floor, Harris pinioning Arnold's neck with his left hand while the right hand held a service revolver to the centre of his forehead.

'I've just about had you, you cheeky bastard,' he snarled. 'I'm gonna send you off!'

The younger detectives were chalk-faced, with the exception of Batch, who watched the show with interest, a wry smile on his face. Even the older hands were apprehensive. They had seen Harris go through his routine before and they knew he was just trying to scare the shit out of this bloke but it was never fun to watch. When Merv was in this kind of mood he was right out there on the edge and you never knew for sure he wouldn't topple over.

'Come on, Merv, give him a break,' said Delaney on cue, as he had done so often before. 'He'll cooperate. He just needs a bit of time to think.'

Harris lowered the pistol and eased back slightly — all according to the script. 'You want some time to think? Okay, killer, I'll give you time to think. I'm going out to organise a typewriter and some paper. I'll be back in exactly five minutes. And when I get back we're going to sit down and you're going to tell me all about it. And if you piss me around any more I'm going to get very, very angry.'

Arnold's eyes blazed with defiance. 'Go fuck yourself, copper!'

Harris leapt to his feet and stood over Arnold menacingly. He raised his revolver slowly and took careful aim. Delaney felt the muscles in his chest tighten. His heart was beating so hard it hurt.

'You're a tough man, Johnny.' Harris's voice was so controlled the tension in his colleagues eased a little. 'But you know as well as I do nobody's going to miss you. And if a bloke who's just murdered eleven innocent people was to pull a knife in a police station and we had to blow him away, who's going to give a shit? We'd all be bloody heroes. You think about that for a while, tough guy.'

Harris turned and strode out of the interview room, leaving Delaney to convince their captive he'd better cooperate or there was no telling what 'that mad bastard Harris' might do.

In the excitement Merv did not notice Arthur Wallace, one of the two Sydney detectives George Curran had introduced him to earlier that morning as being up 'to help us with the pinch', slip quietly out of the interview room.

Merv had paid little heed to either Wallace or his partner Barry Dent. He couldn't see why they were there at all — the local boys were quite capable of dealing with grubs like Arnold without their help. It was typical of George these days, always bringing in the Sydney team. No doubt he had his own good reasons

— he always did — but for the life of him Merv couldn't work out what they were.

When Harris stepped into the corridor he saw Curran and Wallace coming towards him, Tom Wilson tagging behind like a drover's dog.

'How's it going in there?' said Curran as they met.

'We're just giving him some thinking time,' replied Harris. 'He'll come round.'

'No time for that, mate,' Curran frowned. 'The press have got onto it. They know we've made an arrest. We've got to have a brief around him for ten o'clock court.'

'Bloody journos! How did they get wind of it?'

'No idea.' Curran sighed heavily. 'But it means we're going to have to wrap it up straight away. His solicitor will be knocking our door down as soon as the news breaks.'

'George, I reckon there's a whole lot more to this than Arnold. If we lean on him a bit we might get the whole story.'

'Turn it up, Mervyn, you know better than that!' said Curran sharply. 'Arnold won't tell us diddleyshit. Now let's wrap a brief around him and get him into court. I've had Tom here write him up for it in a Record of Interview.'

He thrust a copy of a five-page Record of Interview towards Harris, who took it and skimmed the contents.

'Seems Arnold's conscience got the better of him and he had to make a clean breast of it.'

'He won't sign it,' said Harris, still reading.

'Of course not,' replied Curran. 'That's covered at the end.'

Harris flipped over to the last page. His eyes fixed on question and answer 58.

58. Q: Do you wish to sign this Record of Interview? You are not obliged to do so unless you wish.

A: Gentlemen, I want you to understand my position. I've told you my story because I had to. The guilt was too much for me to keep it a secret. But I never sign anything. That's how I was brought up. It has been the code that I have always followed in the past, and that's my desire in this case.

Curran was becoming impatient. 'Can't wait all day, Merv. Gerry Walsh is taking the running on it. You're corroborating, along with Tom and Frank Delaney. Dent is in there as an observer. Keep the young blokes right out of it ... except for young Batch, I want him in as well.'

'Yeah, right.' Merv Harris wasn't happy but nobody had expected the press to get onto it and now they had there'd be lawyers around in no time flat. And that would stuff everything up.

Harris walked back into the room and grunted a few orders which quickly cleared the room except for himself, Wilson, Delaney, Walsh, the young fellow Batch and the Sydney bloke, Dent.

'So you won't talk, eh?' Tom Wilson sounded like an actor in a B-grade movie. 'Fair enough.'

He leaned forward and tucked a folded copy of the Record of Interview into the breast pocket of Arnold's shirt.

'Cop this!'

At last things were looking up for Gordon Yates. Inspector George Curran seemed to have forgotten, or at least forgiven, his role in that embarrassing Gaye Welham affair, and it now looked like he might have some chance of getting on to a few police stories again.

When he was awakened at seven-thirty that morning Gordon had recognised the voice on the phone immediately. No name was given but there was no mistaking George Curran's gravelly drawl. The message was simple — a suspect had been picked up and was being questioned in relation to the Mickey's Poolhouse bombing and an early arrest was expected. The leak was unofficial.

What a scoop! Yates was straight on to his editor, who let it out to the radio stations. It was a Gordon Yates exclusive, and it would establish him once again as a respected journalist with first-class sources. This was just what he needed to get back on track.

Not that day, or any day thereafter, did Gordon Yates stop to wonder why George Curran had decided to leak that story to him. He was simply grateful that he had.

5

The trial of John Edward Arnold started in the Brisbane Supreme Court on Monday the seventeenth of November 1969, before a jury of twelve good men and the Honourable Mr Justice Daniel P Everett, better known in legal circles as 'Fancy Dan'.

His Honour was a plodder about whom, it was generally agreed, there was nothing at all fancy. He had done little to distinguish himself in his long career at Crown Law, but had made few enemies and only small mistakes, so that his appointment to the bench had evoked more genuine surprise than acrimony. The almost universal response among his colleagues at the bar was 'Fancy Dan Everett getting the nod!' Hence the nickname — Fancy Dan.

The Chief Crown Prosecutor, Howard Walker, had over twenty years' experience as a prosecutor and he was certainly no fool. Some said he would have been a first-class success at the private bar, if only he had the courage to leave the security of the Crown. Howard had ability, but not much courage.

Arnold's solicitors Messrs BM Leary & Doyle had briefed Mr Eugene Sullivan, barrister-at-law. Sullivan had been an outstanding law student and a brilliant academic. It was generally agreed that his fine legal mind was wasted in crime. Had he turned to civil or commercial work he might have taken silk by now, or even an appointment to the bench. But for reasons most of his peers found hard to fathom he seemed to favour crime.

For weeks Brian Leary and Eugene Sullivan had been starting over coffee in the quiet, pre-dawn mildness of the mornings, and sitting late into the sweltering nights, poring over the pre-trial transcripts. Public outrage had hung over this trial like a summer storm and both men felt the weight resting heavily on their shoulders.

This was Australia's most horrific tragedy in living memory. And it had happened here in Brisbane, the leafy, sprawling capital of the country's tropical north, the town that Queenslanders had always thought the southerners had forgotten. The underworld had slaughtered eleven innocent victims to increase its power over Brisbane, and her citizens were terrified. Newspapers carried daily stories speculating about the influence of southern crime syndicates in Queensland. The Police Department circulated posters reminding people of the escalating violence in the city and warning them to take precautions.

John Arnold's legal team knew all too well that fear was the dominant emotion in the city. Whoever was on this jury would prefer to be convinced that this accused was guilty of the crime as charged. As soon as that had been established, Brisbane could sleep safely once again.

Howard Walker commenced the prosecution case by telling the jury in summary form that they would later hear evidence that the accused had admitted to police he had set the bomb, thus convincing them from the outset that the man was guilty. Then he opened with non-contentious evidence setting the scene of the tragedy and identifying the victims.

None of this could be challenged by the defence who, for the first three days, were left to sit meekly watching as the jurors' outrage built with each addition to the evidence.

Howard Walker played it perfectly, and by day four he had the jury eating from his hand.

Leary and Sullivan had known all along that once the fight began in earnest, the defence would have to win and keep on winning. Every police witness would be supported by another, and unless the battlefield was strewn with the corpses of their collective credibility, John Arnold would have no hope of survival. This jury would not accord him the benefit of any presumption of innocence or reasonable doubt. They would have to be convinced, and convinced totally. There was no room for a points decision here — this one had to be a knockout.

Michael Leary strode down Elizabeth Street, his mind filled with lascivious thoughts. For two months now he had been doing his best to win onto Denise, a curvaceous blonde who worked behind the Requisitions Counter of the Titles Office. She was no beauty, but her generous cleavage gave fair warning of the yielding softness of ample breasts, and her super-short miniskirts always revealed a tantalising expanse of rounded upper thighs and lacy underwear. One of the few perks of working for his father's firm was the fact that its Titles Office file was stored in the very bottom drawer of the cabinet marked 'A to L', ensuring a tempting glimpse of the attributes of the fair Denise.

Yesterday, she had smiled at him warmly, giggled generously in response to his carefully rehearsed quips, and even offered a seductive 'Oh, Michael, geez you're awful.' He felt sure that he was making progress. As he stepped in through the entrance of the Forbes Henderson building he thought of her generous curves, and as he struggled out of the rickety lift he could almost see those lacy undies peeping out below her miniskirt.

'Well, if it isn't the late Mr Michael Leary,' observed Neil Doyle laconically, without looking up from his desk.

'Sorry, Mr Doyle, I missed the bus.'

'You'd better get in there,' Doyle advised, nodding towards Brian Leary's office. 'Your Dad's on the warpath.'

Michael was surprised to hear his father was in the office. In recent times he went straight to Sullivan's chambers at the crack of dawn and would not be seen in the office until the luncheon adjournment.

'I've got to see the bank manager at ten-thirty,' said Brian Leary, when his initial barrage about his son's tardiness had run its course. 'You'll have to sit in for me and instruct counsel until I get back. Mr Sullivan will be at the Supreme Court. You can meet him there.'

Michael had been sent to 'instruct counsel' once or twice before, on chamber applications and adjournments, but never on a trial. The task appeared to him to involve nothing more complicated than sitting beside the barrister at the bar table, trying to look busy by taking notes, passing requested books and documents, pouring the occasional glass of water, and generally jumping when the barrister clicked his fingers. Still, this was the notorious Arnold trial, and Michael was excited by the prospect of having a role in it.

'You're privileged, greatly privileged, to be instructing a fine advocate in Mr Sullivan.' Michael hated it when his father spoke like this. 'He'll need you to take careful notes of the evidence.'

Brian was at his desk, piling papers into his briefcase. 'Don't disappoint me, now. I should be there by midday.' Brian Leary, the lawyer, at his pompous, sanctimonious, sententious worst!

Brian clipped his briefcase closed, pushed the Arnold file into Michael's arms, and was gone.

Michael was confident he would recognise Mr Eugene Sullivan. One of his friends had once pointed out a tall stick-insect of a man pacing sedately along George Street, and identified him as the great Mr E P Sullivan of counsel. But when Michael arrived at the Supreme Court shortly after nine-thirty, he was confronted by an army of vaguely familiar personages, legal gentlemen of all shapes and sizes, none of whom he could identify as Mr Sullivan. He scanned the various faces, knowing he could never interrupt the undoubtedly important conversations of these undoubtedly important men to inquire.

And then he saw him, at the end of the long corridor, the same odd-looking scarecrow pointed out to him in George Street, awkward in his angular and spindly build, and yet imposing, by virtue of his upright carriage. His sparse hair was shorn in the severest short-back-and-sides Michael had seen in a long time. The face was strong and powerful, with piercing, dark-blue eyes, a sharp nose, and a square, determined jaw. He moved slowly and deliberately, occasionally taking a deep draw on the cigarette held between his long, thin fingers.

'Excuse me. Mr Sullivan?'

Michael's words seemed to jolt the man out of a trance.

'I'm Mr Leary's clerk, Michael. I'll be instructing you this morning.'

'Aaah,' replied Sullivan, as if he'd received tidings of great moment. He paused, then added, 'By all means,' and after a moment's deep thought, 'Good.'

He sucked hard on his cigarette and resumed pacing without another word to his instructing clerk.

Howard Walker commenced the fourth day of the trial by calling Constable First Class Darryl Arthur Batch of the Fortitude Valley Criminal Investigation Branch to the witness stand. As he walked to the stand he looked to Michael like one of those clean-cut Rugby Union types. Tall, upright, muscular and muscle-brained.

The prosecutor introduced him to the court. 'Detective Batch, you're a Constable First Class attached to the Fortitude Valley Criminal Investigation Branch, is that so?'

'Yes sir, that's right.'

Walker led him quickly to the business at hand, and Batch recited the story like a well-drilled soldier. 'I know the accused now before the court. I remember Thursday the nineteenth of June 1969. At that time I was attached to the Fortitude Valley Criminal Investigation Branch.'

The evidence rolled irresistibly forward, crunching its way into the collective consciousness of the packed courtroom. It was evidence everyone had been waiting for three days to hear, and the jury hung on every word.

'At approximately 6 am that morning, as a result of information received, I proceeded in company with Detective Constable Lippett and other police officers to an address situated at No 14 Manning Street South Brisbane. I there had a conversation with the accused. I said, "Good morning, sir. Are you John Edward Arnold?" The accused immediately appeared to become agitated and said in a raised voice, "Piss off coppers. My solicitor has told you I don't want to talk to you. I haven't done anything. Now piss off". I replied, "Now sir, there's no need for that. We are simply making inquiries in relation to certain stolen property. May we come in please?" Mr Arnold replied, "No you can't. I told you, piss off."'

Howard Walker knew the right time to break a monologue. 'At that point did you make any particular observation of the residence?'

'Yes sir, I did. I observed in the lounge room of the premises a television set which matched the description of one of the items of stolen property complained of, and I said to the accused, "I recognise certain property on your premises which I suspect may have been stolen or otherwise unlawfully obtained. I intend therefore to enter the premises for the purpose of conducting a search." At this point the accused ran back into the premises out of my view.

'I then proceeded to enter the premises in company with Constable Lippett. We entered the lounge room of the premises and I satisfied myself that the television set was not the subject of any complaint and we then prepared to leave the premises. At that point the accused reappeared and I observed that he was holding in his hand a large screwdriver which he brandished at Constable Lippett and myself.'

As he spoke the witness looked at the jury, his gaze moving from one to another, occasionally holding the attention of an individual, establishing a trust.

Turning to the judge he said, 'Your Honour, at this point I had a further conversation with the accused. I have an independent recollection of the conversation, but for the purposes of accuracy and to refresh my memory, I seek leave to refer to notes of the conversation which I recorded in my official police notebook shortly after the conversation occurred.'

The request was worded according to the standard formula police officers used every day in the criminal courts but it was delivered with such deference that Fancy Dan was swept up in a wave of mutual courtesy.

'Yes, of course, Officer Batch,' he smiled benignly.

Michael thought he heard a muffled groan from the spindly form beside him.

'Thank you, Your Honour,' said Batch, producing his official police notebook, which he flipped open. 'The accused pushed Constable Lippett in the chest with his left hand and produced the screwdriver in his right hand saying, "I'm getting out of here. Get out of my way copper, or I'll stick you".'

Michael heard murmuring from the dock behind him, which continued to rumble as Batch proceeded with his account.

'I then saw Constable Lippett draw his police service revolver which he pointed at the accused, saying "Drop the screwdriver". The accused dropped the screwdriver and Lippett then touched the accused on his right shoulder and said, "I now arrest you on a charge of assault".'

The murmuring from the dock suddenly exploded. 'This is lies!' shouted Arnold. 'This man is lying!'

Sullivan turned in his seat. 'Sit down, Mr Arnold,' he commanded. 'Sit down and control yourself!' Having despatched the order he turned back to his notes as Arnold resumed his seat. 'Get over there and control your client, lad,' Sullivan murmured, without looking up.

As Michael hurried to the dock and whispered directions to the accused to remain silent, His Honour Fancy Dan was still recovering his composure.

'Thank you for your invaluable assistance, Mr Sullivan,' the judge said icily. 'But in future I'd prefer to control my own court, if you don't mind.'

'Not at all, Your Honour,' replied Sullivan, still immersed in his notes.

'Kindly ensure that we are not interrupted by any further outbursts from the accused.'

'Certainly, Your Honour.'

The judge turned back to the witness with a kindly smile. 'You may proceed now, Officer Batch.'

'Thank you, Your Honour,' said Batch with a courteous nod. 'I then accompanied the accused and Detective Constable Lippett to the Fortitude Valley Police Station. In the police car on the way to the Valley Station Constable Lippett said to the accused, "Why did you try to run from us, John?" The accused then appeared to become quite emotional. He put both hands to his face and said, "Wouldn't you if you'd done what I'd done? Kill me now". I said, "John, are you referring to the Mickey's bombing?" The accused said, "Shoot me. Put me out of my misery. I nearly died when I heard that eleven people had been killed. The bomb was just to frighten them. I didn't mean it to go off!"'

Michael heard more rumblings from the dock, and moved quickly from his seat to avert another outburst.

'Constable Lippett and I then accompanied the accused to an interview room, where he became extremely emotional,' continued Batch. 'He sat down at a desk, put his head in his arms, and sobbed loudly for several minutes. At one point he lifted his head and then brought it very forcefully down onto the desk several times saying, "Kill me. Kill me. Why don't you kill me, you bastards?"

'Lippett then said, "You're obviously upset, John. We'll leave you here for a while to collect yourself". Lippett and myself then left the interview room and took up with Senior Sergeant Wilson and other senior officers. When we returned to the interview room Senior Sergeant Wilson said to the accused, "Are you feeling better now, John?" The accused replied, "Yes thanks. I've been sick ever since it happened". I said, "Are you admitting that you were involved in the deaths of the eleven victims of the Mickey's bombing?" The accused replied, "Yes. It was not intended that way. I just wanted to intimidate the owners of the Poolhouse". Senior Sergeant Wilson then warned the accused that he need not say anything further and that anything he did say would be taken down and would later be used in evidence.'

The jury was spellbound.

'Was there any mention of a solicitor?' Howard Walker asked.

'Yes, sir,' replied Batch. 'Senior Sergeant Wilson said to the accused "John, would you like me to get your solicitor down here before we start?" But the accused replied, "No, he'll just tell me to say nothing. I've got to get this off my conscience. There's eleven people dead".'

'Did the accused participate in a Record of Interview with Senior Sergeant Walsh?'

'He did.'

'And did you perform the typing duties to record that interview?'

'I did, sir.'

Howard Walker held out a document in the direction of the witness and said, 'Would you look at this document please?'

The court bailiff delivered the item to the witness.

'Is that the Record of Interview which you typed that morning?'

'It is.'

'And does it accurately record the conversation which took place between Senior Sergeant Walsh and the accused?'

'It does.'

Walker turned with an air of triumph to the judge. 'Your Honour, I tender that Record of Interview, and I ask that it be read to the gentlemen of the jury.'

The judge's pimply-faced associate, self-important in his black jacket and white bib, read the Record of Interview, his high-pitched, cultivated voice lending a mild element of farce to the text.

As the reading progressed, Michael thought how completely Arnold was trapped by the evidence of his guilt. He was starting to feel an increasing sense of embarrassment for the defence team, of which he was temporarily and publicly a member.

'That is the evidence of this witness, Your Honour,' announced Walker when the public humiliation was complete, and, his gaze sweeping across the faces of the jury, he resumed his seat.

'Cross-examination, Mr Sullivan?' murmured His Honour mechanically, as if he expected Sullivan to have the good grace to forgo that thankless task in the face of the evidence just given.

Sullivan sat silent and motionless for a good three to four seconds, his head propped against his hand. His eyes were half-closed, and for one terrifying moment it occurred to Michael that he was asleep. Just as he was about to stir him, Sullivan placed his hands on the lectern and, looking directly at Batch, rose slowly to his feet, his long body unfolding like an extension ladder. In his close-cropped horsehair wig, black bar jacket and robes Sullivan looked impressive — positively regal, Michael thought. He hoped they had more than just that in their favour.

When Sullivan spoke his rich, clear voice filled the courtroom. 'Witness, it is a fact, is it not, that your evidence here today has been a litany of lies, that every word you have attributed to my client Mr Arnold is a complete fabrication by you in total disregard of the solemn oath you lately took to tell the whole truth in this matter?'

Batch replied unhesitatingly, 'That is incorrect, sir.'

Sullivan hardly paused for the response. 'Put simply, witness, you're trying to verbal Mr Arnold, aren't you?'

'Verbal him, sir? I'm not sure I follow what you mean.'

'Don't you, Constable? Do you not understand the meaning of the term "verbal"?'

Batch answered tentatively, 'I believe I've heard the term, sir.'

'Yes, I'm sure you have. It's a police term, isn't it? It refers to the practice of fabricating a verbal confession.'

'That's an allegation that's sometimes made by lawyers, sir. Yes.'

'Yes, and that's what you're trying to do to Mr Arnold here today, isn't it, Mr Batch?'

'No sir.'

Batch sat upright in the witness box. His face seemed impenetrable, like the stone faces carved into Mt Rushmore, and Michael feared that any attempt to storm this bulwark could be dangerous as well as futile. If Sullivan sensed any danger he didn't show it but rolled on undeterred.

'Incidentally, Mr Batch, there is no signed confession at all, is there?'

'No sir.'

'There is a signed denial by my client.'

'Yes sir, that's true.'

'But no signed confession.'

'That's correct, sir.'

'Yes, that is correct.' Sullivan held that thought for a moment, as if trying to get his brain around it, and then continued quietly, 'Police officers were the only witnesses to this alleged verbal confession, is that right?'

'That's right.'

'No one else to confirm or deny it?'

'That's right.'

'So if this were a police verbal, a fabrication, we'd have absolutely no way of knowing, would we?'

'It's not a fabrication, sir, it's the truth.'

'We do know for certain that three days earlier

Mr Arnold denied any involvement in clear and unequivocal terms.'

'Yes sir.'

Sullivan's voice was silken. 'Of course, on that occasion there was an independent witness present, wasn't there, Mr Batch?'

'Yes sir, I believe his solicitor was with him that day.'

'That's right. And on that occasion Mr Arnold submitted himself to interrogation by police officers for a period of four hours. Isn't that so, Mr Batch?'

'Yes, I believe so.'

'And the result was a twelve-page Record of Interview in which he explained in detail his movements throughout the period leading up to and including the night of the Mickey's Poolhouse bombing?'

'Yes sir.'

'And the last answer he gave in that interview was as follows: "Like I told you, I never had nothing to do with that bomb. I've told you all I know and I don't have nothing more to say to you". Is that right?'

'I believe that's the answer recorded at the time sir, yes.'

Sullivan paused for a moment, then continued with a new sternness in his voice. 'So when there was an independent witness Mr Arnold made a complete, adamant and detailed denial of any involvement in the matter, but when he's alone and behind closed doors with you police, he suddenly sings like a canary. Is that what you say?'

'He confessed his guilt, sir.'

'I put it to you that he made no such confession.'

'He did, sir.'

Sullivan looked around the courtroom as though he assumed the support of his audience, and his melodious voice boomed out to every corner. 'Is it the case, Mr Batch, that on the nineteenth of June 1969 you went to the residence of Mr Arnold knowing full well, as a result of what he had clearly told police officers three days earlier, that he did not wish to have anything more to say to police on this matter?'

'Sir, I knew nothing about the accused's interview with police on the sixteenth until after we got him back to the Valley Station. Otherwise I would have contacted his solicitor before approaching him.'

'Are you trying to tell the gentlemen of the jury that at the time you went to Mr Arnold's house you did not know he was the prime suspect for the Mickey's Poolhouse bombing?'

'I knew nothing about the man, sir. In fact, we didn't even know his name. Our information was simply that some stolen property had been delivered to No 14 Manning Street.'

Sullivan, who had been skimming a statement held in his right hand, tossed it onto the bar table, conveying his disgust.

'Oh please, Mr Batch,' he admonished. 'Do try to get your story straight! You've just told us the first words you said to my client were "Are you John Edward Arnold?" Isn't that so?'

'Well, I, er ...' Batch was suddenly stumbling like a champ who had walked into a lucky punch.

Sullivan kept coming. 'Isn't that what you've just told us, witness?'

'Yes, well, sir, I may have been mistaken there. We may have had a name ...' Batch needed time to think but there was none to spare.

'You must have, mustn't you?'

'Yes sir, I think you're right.' For better or for worse, there was no way out. 'Now that I think about it we had a name and an address, but we had no other knowledge. The name meant nothing to me.'

'I suggest that's nonsense,' Sullivan said, adding emphatically, 'I suggest that you were directed by your superiors, Senior Sergeant Wilson and/or Senior Sergeant Harris, to go to Arnold's residence and pick him up on a holding charge, any charge, so he could be brought back to the Fortitude Valley Police Station, and fitted up for the Mickey's Poolhouse bombing.'

'You're wrong there, sir. I knew of no connection between Arnold and the bombing case.'

'Constable Batch,' Sullivan probed. 'You were working a midnight–to–8 am shift on the nineteenth. Is that right?

'That's right.'

'Normally there are only two detectives rostered on that shift in the Valley Station, isn't that so?'

'Yes sir.'

'How many detectives went with you from the Valley Station to my client's residence that morning?'

'There were six of us, sir.'

'Why is it that there were six detectives rostered on the midnight–to–8 am shift that morning, Constable?'

Batch hesitated for a second. 'You'd have to ask the Duty Sergeant that, sir.'

'You say you wanted to make a routine inquiry about some stolen property?'

'That's correct.'

'Why is it that six detectives were needed to make a routine inquiry of that kind?'

'Well, I, er ...' The champ was back on the ropes, and starting to look at home in that position. 'I-I'm not actually sure now why we felt that.'

'It was because you knew you were going to arrest John Arnold for the Mickey's bombing, wasn't it?'

'No sir.'

'There are only four desks in the detectives area of the Valley Station, aren't there?'

'Yes sir, but you can operate comfortably with up to six officers in that area in my experience.'

'Is that so? Well you had your full complement then.'

'Yes sir.'

'That's right. And in addition to that, you had a further four senior detectives who weren't rostered on for that shift but came in on overtime that morning. Isn't that so, Constable?'

'Well, I, er ... I'm really not sure, Mr Sullivan.'

'Oh come now, Mr Batch, you must have noticed them — Walsh, Harris, Wilson and Delaney. All senior detectives.'

'Er ... well, yes. Now that you mention it, I think they were in early that morning.'

'And there were two others there as well, weren't there? Two Sydney detectives — Dent and Wallace.'

'Yes. Yes, that's right. From memory they were in at the Valley Station that morning.'

'That's twelve. Twelve detectives in an office designed for four. What were all those people doing in there at five in the morning?'

'You'd have to ask them that, sir.'

'No, witness, I'm asking you. You were there. What on earth were all these detectives doing at the Valley CIB that morning?'

'I don't recall, sir.'

'Surely you must, Mr Batch. Surely you must. The place would have been like rush hour in Queen Street that morning.'

'I don't recall, sir.'

'You must have at least run into Wilson or Harris that morning. Did you mention to either of them that you were on your way to see John Arnold?'

'We never discussed Arnold until I got back to the Valley CIB.'

'And coincidentally, of course, all of those officers I've just mentioned were at the Valley Station when you got back there with Arnold.'

'That's correct.'

'I suggest to you again, witness, that on the morning of the nineteenth of June 1969 you attended a meeting of senior detectives at the Fortitude Valley Police Station, at which it was decided that you and others were to go and collect Mr Arnold so that he could be unlawfully detained and fitted up for the bombing of the Mickey's Poolhouse!'

'No sir, I knew nothing about Mr Arnold.'

Sullivan treated the response as an irrelevance and moved on to his next point. 'You say you knew nothing about Mr Arnold. You say you entered Arnold's house because you thought you had identified a stolen television receiver.'

'That's right.'

'Where were you standing at the time?'

'At the front door, sir.'

'And from there you identified this television receiver in the living room. That was your evidence-in-chief, wasn't it?'

'That's right, sir.'

Sullivan drew from a neat pile of papers in front of him a large black-and-white photograph. 'I want you to look at this photograph, witness,' he said, sliding the photograph along the bar table to Walker, who studied it and returned it without comment. Sullivan held the photograph out in front of him until it was whisked away by the court orderly who delivered it to the witness box.

Batch looked at the photograph, his stony face expressionless. But when he looked up his eyes were blinking and uncertain, and Michael imagined tiny pebbles crumbling away from the edges of that hard rock face.

'That photograph shows the view from the front door of No 14 Manning Street, doesn't it?'

'Yes.'

'And it shows, doesn't it, Mr Batch, that the front doorway of that residence leads into a long central hallway? There is no view of the living room from the front door of that residence, is there, Mr Batch?'

'I ... it doesn't seem so from that photograph, sir, no.'

'No, it doesn't, does it?' said Sullivan, in a voice charged with irony. Then, turning to the judge, he announced, 'I tender that photograph, Your Honour, and I ask that it be shown to the members of the jury at this stage.'

The photograph was formally admitted into evidence, and passed from juror to juror in the solemn silence of the courtroom. As each one studied it in turn, Michael could see the resentment creep into their faces, one by one. Nobody likes to be conned, as they had been by Mr Batch.

Now Sullivan forged on confidently. 'Mr Batch, you claim you knew nothing of Arnold's being a suspect in the Mickey's case.'

'That's right.'

'And suddenly all this confession business comes out of the blue while you're on the way back to the station. Lippett asked Mr Arnold the perfectly obvious question, why on earth he had tried to run from you police, and he replied, rather cryptically I suggest "Wouldn't you if you'd done what I had?" That answer might have referred to anything. He gave absolutely no hint as to what he was talking about. Isn't that so?'

'That's correct.'

'That's correct,' repeated Sullivan. Then he leaned forward, studying the witness in silence, drawing out the jury's suspense. 'Tell the gentlemen of the jury,

Mr Batch,' he said in an almost coaxing tone, 'tell them again what you claim were your very next words.'

Batch fumbled with the pages of his notebook. 'Well, I, er ...'

Sullivan pounced on the opportunity to capitalise on Batch's hesitation. 'Come now, don't be shy, Mr Batch. Go ahead. Read out what you claim you replied to that innocuous comment by Mr Arnold.'

'Well, er, I said ...' Batch was suddenly bumbling like a rank amateur, making what should have been a minor cross-examination point into a winner. 'I said, "John, are you referring to the Mickey's bombing?"'

Sullivan punched out the next question accusingly. 'If, as you assure us, witness, not one soul had ever mentioned Arnold's name to you in connection with the Mickey's bombing, what on earth prompted you to make that comment?'

'I, er ... well, I ...' Batch was on the ropes with his guard down, out on his feet. The response, when it finally came, satisfied no one, not even himself. 'I don't know. I really can't recall.'

'Just a lucky guess, I suppose,' quipped Sullivan, wringing the most out of the jury's reaction. 'What is it the policeman on the television says? Call it a hunch, call it a guess.'

The jury grinned and turned to Batch, awaiting his reply.

'I suppose you could call it that, sir.'

One or two of the jurors shook their heads, so slightly that it almost went unnoticed. But not by Sullivan. Now he was certain he had them. Now was the time to give them their first look at Mr Arnold's instructions. They had sat here for three days wondering whether the defence was going to make a fight of it; now was the time to let them know.

For the rest of the morning the jury heard how Arnold had been bashed, bullied, abused, and finally verballed. Sullivan put the facts, Batch denied them, and though the jurors were hearing things they didn't want to believe, they were no longer willing to accept Batch's word that they did not happen.

Sullivan wanted the jury to retire for the luncheon adjournment with the full picture of the contest clearly in their minds, so at about a quarter-to-one he started rounding off his cross-examination.

'You, perhaps predictably, deny most of what I have put to you as being the truth of what really happened. But let's summarise a few matters that aren't in dispute, shall we? First of all, I take it you accept that when Mr Arnold left the Valley Station with his solicitor Mr Leary at shortly after 3 pm on the sixteenth of June, he evinced a clear intention not to enter into any further discussion with police about the matter?'

'Yes.'

'And, indeed, when you first confronted him at his residence on the morning of the fifteenth he confirmed that intention, didn't he?'

'He spoke to us, sir.'

'Indeed he did. According to you he said "Piss off copper. My solicitor told you I don't want to talk to you".'

'That's right.'

'Clearly reaffirming his resolve not to talk to you.'

'I suppose so, yes.'

'And you say that in the same breath he also reaffirmed his innocence, saying "I haven't done —hing!" That's what you say he said, isn't it?'

moment he is alone in the car with you
—denly starts to confess all. Is that what

'That's right.'

'That was an extraordinary reversal, wasn't it?'

'I don't know.'

'Can you suggest anything that might have prompted this change in his attitude?'

'He became very emotional. I believe he wanted to clear his conscience.'

'Of course!' Sullivan sneered. 'An emotional outpouring. You would have the gentlemen of the jury believe that Mr Arnold collapsed under the weight of his mounting guilt.'

'That's what happened. He sort of broke down like.'

'He broke down, you say, and, on your account, he continued to pour out his overburdened soul to you police right up until he was finally lodged in the Watchhouse at about 9.30 am on that morning of the nineteenth of June this year.'

'Yes sir. Even after he had appeared before the magistrate he told me that he was very remorseful for what he'd done.'

'Is that so?'

'Yes sir.'

Sullivan paused, and, without taking his eyes off the witness for a moment, he reached down to the bar table, picked up a springback folder and placed it on the lectern.

'You've never mentioned that before in evidence, either in this court or at the preliminary hearing in the Magistrates Court, have you, Mr Batch?' he said quietly.

'Actually, to tell you the truth I'd forgotten about it until just now, Mr Sullivan.'

Sullivan opened the folder and removed a page from a newspaper and placed it on the lectern. When he spoke again it was in a strong, stern voice that punched out an accelerating rhythm.

'Do you accept, Constable Batch, that the June twentieth edition of the *Courier-Mail* newspaper reported that when the accused was first brought before the magistrate at 10 am on the nineteenth of June this year, and brief particulars of the police case were read out by the prosecutor, Mr Arnold was heard to say in a loud voice, "It's all lies! I'm innocent!"?'

Batch shifted in his seat. 'Ah, well, yes, I believe he did say that, sir. But he was very up and down, very changeable.'

'You say that for about four hours on the sixteenth he continuously and strenuously denied his guilt. When confronted by you three days later he again denied it. Then for no apparent reason he confesses his guilt the moment he is alone in police custody, and continues to do so for three-and-a-half hours until he is brought into public view in the courtroom, whereupon he immediately and emphatically again denies his guilt. But immediately he's back behind closed doors with you police, once again away from the scrutiny of any independent person, he confesses his guilt to you again. Is that what you're asking the gentlemen of the jury to believe, Mr Batch?'

'He was very changeable, sir.'

'Very changeable indeed!'

There were muffled snickers from the jury and Sullivan paused to let them run their course. Then he continued curtly, 'After his appearance in the Magistrates Court Mr Arnold was taken by you and other police officers to Boggo Road Prison, where you checked him in to the Remand Centre at exactly 11. 40 am. Correct?'

'I believe so.'

'Within thirty minutes of being out of police custody and in the hands of prison authorities he handed prison officials a letter addressed to Senior Sergeant Wilson again denying any involvement in the bombing, and alleging assaults by you police and the complete fabrication of the Record of Interview you've tendered here today.'

'That's what he alleged.'

'This is the man who, you would have the jury believe, was so stricken with the need to purge himself of his unbearable guilt, that less than two hours earlier he was weeping and wailing and gnashing his teeth and baring his soul to you and your associates.'

'He was anxious to tell us what had happened, sir.'

'Anxious to tell you what had happened! I see. Freely and voluntarily confessing all. Is that it?'

'That's right.'

'That's virtually from when you arrested him at about 6 am until he appeared in court at 10. For virtually four hours he was falling over himself to assist you police by confessing to an involvement in this crime. Is that what you're saying?'

'He was extremely cooperative virtually right up until he saw his solicitor at 10.'

Sullivan broke the rhythm of the exchange and paused, bending his spindly body over the lectern and leaning over as though engaged in affable conversation with the witness.

'Tell me this, Constable,' he said in an almost-conspiratorial tone. 'You had this extremely cooperative fellow falling over himself to assist you for four long hours' — he gave the words 'extremely cooperative' an emphasis Batch had not — 'I take it you'd have been vitally interested in getting a signed statement of some sort from the man, wouldn't you?'

'We would have liked to, sir, yes.'

'Of course you would,' Sullivan boomed congenially. 'Because you knew that if he gave you a signed statement, he wouldn't be able to come along to a court later and allege that you were trying to verbal him, would he?'

'That's true.'

'Of course not. And for that reason you'd have loved to get a signed statement from him if you could.' He paused again, and the congeniality drained away. 'Mr Batch, you had a total of four pages in your notebook recording an alleged confession, you had a further five pages of typewritten alleged confession in the form of the Record of Interview, all made, you say, by this extremely cooperative and penitent man. So tell His Honour and the good gentlemen of the jury — tell us all if you will — how many pages of these alleged confessions did Mr Arnold sign to confirm their truth and accuracy during this four-hour period when you say he was falling over himself to assist you?'

'None.'

Sullivan eyed him quizzically as though he genuinely thought he might have misheard the response. 'I'm sorry?'

Batch cleared his throat. 'None, sir. The accused was asked to sign the notes but declined. He said his solicitor had advised him never to sign anything.'

'His solicitor?' Sullivan exclaimed. 'Does this come from the same penitent soul you claim declined to have his solicitor present for the interview because, quote/unquote: "He'll just tell me to say nothing. I've got to get this off my conscience"?'

Batch looked utterly miserable.

Sullivan continued relentlessly, 'Do you seriously expect the gentlemen of the jury to accept that, witness? Do you seriously suggest that a man who was so remorseful he felt obliged to reject contact with his solicitor, broke down and made his confession and then refused to sign on the basis of the same solicitor's advice?'

'That's what happened, sir,' Batch said doggedly.

'May the witness see exhibit 27, Your Honour — the Record of Interview,' said Sullivan. As the orderly neared the witness box he continued, 'Look at answer 58, witness, and tell the gentlemen of the jury what you say Arnold replied when asked to put his signature on this confession you claim he made.'

Batch fumbled with the document and eventually responded, 'The accused replied "I'm sorry gentlemen but I must decline. I want to indicate my position. I have related to you my side of the events but as a matter of invariable policy I never sign anything. It has always been the code I've followed in the past and that is my desire in this case".'

'And you say those were the words my client used?'

'They were exactly the words he used.'

'Are you telling us that a twenty-nine-year-old Cockney doorman spontaneously produced an answer displaying that scope of vocabulary and grammatical precision?'

Batch frowned, as if confused. 'Geez, Mr Sullivan, I'm not sure I get your point.'

'The point is, witness,' Sullivan fired back. 'Are you sure the answer wasn't more like "I don't know nuffin about nuffin"?'

Batch felt obliged to pretend he shared the jury's amusement with this sally, and he replied with an attempt at a smile, 'No, sir.'

'It's a verbal, Mr Batch,' Sullivan roared. 'A complete and utter fabrication. Just like virtually everything you have said here today. Isn't it?'

'No, sir,' said Batch, the remnants of the awkward grin fading. 'That's what he said all right.' He shifted uncomfortably in his chair, then added, 'That was evidently the code he followed. He had a personal policy of never signing anything.'

'No, Mr Batch,' said Sullivan quietly in the hush of the courtroom. 'No, that's not true,' he repeated, shaking his head in an exaggerated gesture that threatened to dislodge his wig. Then, taking a firm hold of the lectern, he thundered in the accusing tones of a fire-and-brimstone preacher, 'That is not true, and you know it's not true! There's one piece of evidence that not only proves it's not true, but discredits your whole pathetic account, I suggest. You see, three days earlier, in the presence of his solicitor, Arnold did sign something, and he signed it not once, not twice, not thrice, but thirteen times. What he signed was the Record of Interview, Mr Batch, the one he gave to police at the Valley Station on the sixteenth, the one in which he denied again and again and again that he had any involvement in this heinous crime, the one in which he particularised in minute detail all of the events in which he was involved at all material times so as to demonstrate his innocence clearly. Isn't that so, Mr Batch?'

'He did sign that Record of Interview, sir, yes.'

'And isn't it the case that despite lengthy and probing inquiries, investigating police have been unable to disprove any part of his account given in that signed Record of Interview?'

'We can't actually prove he lied on that occasion sir, no.'

'No,' said Sullivan decisively. 'You can't, can you?'

He turned to the judge and said quietly, 'I have nothing further, Your Honour,' and then sat down, as the courtroom clock ticked over to one o'clock.

6

Tony Artlett had always been a smart-arse, but he was still Michael Leary's best mate. They went back a long way. They'd started in the same class at St Lawrence's in the seventh grade, when Artlett was a pampered doctor's son with a superior attitude and an inferior position in the schoolyard pecking order. Tony was clever, studious and self-opinionated, all of them unfortunate qualities in a schoolboy, particularly at St Lawrence's in those days.

It was an inner-city Catholic boys' school with more than its fair share of street-wise city toughs forced to stay on until they reached the legal age to go to work. Most left after 'scholarship', to sell newspapers on street corners or stack fruit crates at the Markets. Later, others went to take apprenticeships and the like, leaving a smaller group of boys to finish off the Senior years. It was in those last two years that Michael and Tony became friends, and when they both enrolled in law — Artlett at the university and Michael through the Board — the friendship continued.

As the two of them sat on the grassy slope below the university refectory passing the bottle of beer between them, Michael glowed with excitement. When his father had returned to court, he had asked him cautiously if he might stay on for the rest of the day. Brian had shot him one of his searching looks, and it was hard to know whether he was pleased or pissed off with him. But he had said yes, and that's what counted.

So many impressions; so many emotions. That tough guy Batch — mean as shit, even when he was coming apart at the seams. And the old bloke, Sullivan, the stick man. He was kind of neat. And the long, shapely legs of the blonde court reporter who had sat for hours right in front of him.

'I wouldn't mind doing a bit of crime when I get through,' Michael said, passing the bottle to his friend.

'Crime?' Tony said disdainfully, taking a healthy swig. 'Are you out of your tiny mind? Crime's for losers, mate. Crime doesn't pay — didn't anybody ever teach you that? Property and commercial work is where the money is.'

Sometimes Artlett was full of shit, and best ignored. 'Maybe even at the bar. I'd make a good criminal law barrister, I reckon.'

'Barrister?' Artlett scoffed. 'Are you kidding? It's not coincidence that barristers are listed in the dictionary between "bankruptcy" and "bastards". A first year commercial law solicitor with a good Queen Street firm will earn three times what any junior barrister can, particularly one doing crime. Jesus! Leary, forget all that bullshit.'

'Maybe,' said Michael quietly, before he threw his head back and drained the last of the bottle. 'One thing's certain, that's the last of the beer.' He lobbed the empty bottle onto the grass. 'A dead marine, if ever I saw one. How about we check out what's happening in the refec?'

'Good idea!' Artlett scrambled to his feet and they both moved up towards the lights. Upstairs, the band in the refectory was pounding out something by The Doors. The solid beat reverberated in Michael's head as the crowd stomped up and down. As they mounted the steps the band stopped, and laughter spilled into the courtyard to greet them.

Suddenly, an amplified voice rang out:

The National Liberation Front supports the proper exercise by the people of Vietnam of their legitimate right to assert their sovereign independence and self-determination through struggle, and the collusion of the Australian government in the American military opposition to that struggle makes this country an accomplice in the imperialist aggression being practised by the US military in Vietnam today!

The young man standing at the microphone outside the Union Building belted home each point emphatically. The crowd was spilling out of the refec into the courtyard, to be ambushed by the young orator with the wispy beard and long frizzy hair. Around him were posters printed in the colours of the NLF and banners bearing slogans, 'Stop US Imperialism' and 'Support the NLF', and to one side sat his supporters, mainly lissom girls, their flowing hair adorned by leather headbands, and wearing cheesecloth Indian skirts and T-shirts stretched tight over breasts unrestrained by imperialist bras.

Michael moved closer, Tony a pace behind him. The speaker had captured the attention of only a small section of the crowd. Some revellers tried to ignore him, others catcalled, or threw paper cups, or told the speaker to piss off, or made farting noises or obscene gestures. Through it all the young man at the microphone continued undaunted.

'You ignore the lessons of history, my friend!'

Michael was startled to hear Tony's raised voice and embarrassed to find the crowd's attention had turned to them. He wanted to step away, to distance himself from

Tony, but he remained, hoping their moment in the spotlight would pass quickly.

'Australian soldiers in Vietnam are murdering innocent women and children!' the speaker continued.

Tony Artlett leapt onto the wooden seating in the courtyard, as if to claim the moral high-ground. To Michael's horror, he seemed determined to continue the debate, but he was interrupted by an angry third voice that thundered from beside the podium.

'Piss off, ya bloody rad poofter!'

An empty beer can came hurtling from a group of young men striding down the ramp from the Relaxation building. It rolled and banged and rattled to a stop beside the man at the microphone. He kicked the can to one side, but did not miss a beat. One of the converted in the crowd said something to the young men as they advanced, but he was pushed aside and shouted down as a burly Rugby type stepped up to the speaker.

'Go on, I said piss off!'

One shove of the footballer's heavy hand sent the slightly-built speaker staggering, and as the big man kept on coming, pushing with his beefy hands, the young man stumbled backwards, until he lurched off the cement podium, staggered briefly on the steps, then fell heavily onto the grass. The big man took a wild swipe with his gym boot, but missed, and nearly went to ground himself as his victim backed away in the direction of the Great Court.

Suddenly the courtyard erupted into a free-for-all. Cheers and screams intermingled as the crowd converged on the microphone and people pushed and shoved each other wildly. Michael could just see one of the supporters as she screamed and flailed wildly at two men who were carrying the PA gear away. Further back a fist fight had developed and a group of men were trying hard to separate the combatants.

'The Vietnam conflict will be won or lost right here in this country Michael!' Tony Artlett's face was flushed, his hazel eyes bright with the excitement of the moment. 'Each one of us must choose a side!'

Michael's head was still woolly from the beer, and he looked blankly at his friend, wondering what the hell he was on about, as Artlett turned and pushed his way towards the heart of the melee. *Choose a side? What's that supposed to mean?*

Michael stood at the edge of the crowd, his eyes following his friend into the fray, wondering what he had missed, and hoping he might catch another glimpse of one of those big-breasted revolutionary girls.

George Curran sat pensively among the sombre night-time shadows lurking in the corners of the Warders' Office in the old section of the gaol. It was built back in the old days, when a prison was a prison, and it still had that hard, cold, lonely feel about it. Every tiny movement echoed into the faraway ceilings, ringing a hollow emptiness into the soul of a solitary man. As George sat alone in the yellow light of that dingy office, the melancholy of the old prison matched his mood.

Things were going bad. Batch had done well enough for a young bloke with limited court experience, but in the end he'd copped a pizzling from that bastard Sullivan, and from there on it was all downhill. The other young blokes were hopeless, and by the time some of the older heads hit the witness box it was a bigger salvage job than raising the *Titanic*.

Even Merv had come out smelling like a bucket of shit, and there was no harder nut to crack than Merv.

Mind you, it was no bloody wonder the troops were in trouble, given the hopeless bloody brief they'd been served up by that imbecile Wilson. You'd think it would be a simple enough exercise to drop a decent verbal on a grub, but trust Tom to go and fuck it up. And from there on everyone had been sliding backwards at a million miles an hour.

He blamed himself. He should have known better than to leave Tom Wilson to his own resources. He'd given him the outline and explained to him how the story was to go. All Tom had to do was connect the dots. But of course he'd fucked it up. Someone like Merv Harris would have had the grub stitched up like a sack of spuds. It was a shame he couldn't leave this one to Merv. Merv would have just as likely sniffed out the real story, and there's no telling what he might have done.

He was a good bloke was Merv, none better. But he saw the world in black and white, and there was no telling which way he would have jumped. So George had to go with Wilson and, as usual, Tom had fucked it up. And, as usual, it was up to George to mop up the mess. Sullivan and his mob were getting around like it was all over bar the shouting, and the press were running around like a bunch of chooks with their heads cut off, but for George's money this one wasn't over by a long hop.

Okay, the jury might be convinced that the coppers verballed that grub Arnold, and as long as that's all the Crown had they'd give Arnold the nod. But George knew the public was pretty stirred up about this one, and that meant that if he could convince them the grub might — even might — be right for that bomb, they wouldn't give a square shit about what tricks the coppers had been up to; they'd wipe that

Arnold like a dirty bum. If he could convince that jury Arnold was right for this one, they'd hang his balls out to dry.

The clang of heavy metal doors interrupted his thoughts. He could tell from the jingle of keys and the thud of prison boots on the wooden verandah that his old mate was returning from H Wing.

Dougherty puffed and grunted as he lugged his fat rump around the desk and dropped it into the wooden swivel chair on the other side.

'Stone's out there on the verandah now,' he gasped, still catching his breath from the effort.

'What warder's with him?'

'Fraser. He's no worries.'

'What's the story with Stone?'

'He's in year four of a twelve-year stretch for rape and sodomy. He got to some young kid in G Wing last week. Fucked him pretty bad.'

'Can we make it disappear if we have to?'

'Yeah, sure, I think so.'

'I don't want the warder in here with us.'

'That's OK. I'll bring Stone in meself. Fraser can't hear nothing from out on the verandah.'

George and Hughie understood each other well, and George liked that. He'd helped Hughie out along the way, and Hughie was grateful for it. He wouldn't have this job today if it weren't for George, make no mistake about it. Besides, George had helped him make a couple of bob on the side to boot, and it was as well to remember that. He showed a good Irish heart, old George, and Hughie didn't need to be told what was needed. He dragged himself back out of the chair and lumbered out into the darkness, reappearing almost immediately with a shifty-eyed weasel of a man who stood submissively before his captors.

Curran sat slumped against the desk, idly rolling a pencil back and forth on the wooden surface. In the silence of that sullen room you could hear the burbling sound of the hexagonal surface rolling one way, then another.

Eventually he spoke, in the low, gentle tones of a Father Confessor. 'Hello, Lindsay.'

'Hello, Mr Curran.'

Curran looked up at Lindsay Stone. 'What's this I hear about you getting up to your old tricks again, Lindsay?'

'Not me, boss.'

'That's not what I hear, Lindsay. I hear you've been kid-fucking again.'

'No boss, that wouldn't be right.'

'I think it is, Lindsay. And I think it means that unless you get some big help pretty quick your stinking fucking rock-spider carcase is going to rot in this hole.' A humourless smile crept across his lips. 'But you're a very fortunate lad, Lindsay. Your kindly old Uncle George is here to help you.'

Several cars were parked in the street outside the Leary house when Michael nosed his battered VW into the driveway. He groaned and rolled his eyes. He'd have to sneak in, otherwise his father would insist that he pay his respects to the old codgers' club.

Brian was no boozer but every so often on a Friday he'd slip across to the Grosvenor after court for a few drinks with his mates. Often as not they'd all repair back to the house, where the old boys would pay Cath extravagant compliments until she excused herself and retired to bed, leaving them to get right up the turps and tell each other lies or whatever it was they did, until they tottered out the door in the wee small hours of the morning.

As he walked towards the back door he heard his father seeing off a couple of early pikers, then car doors closing and engines starting up. Only the stayers left, he thought.

Inside the house he could hear just one man talking, in a tone that sounded serious and formal. Through the living room window he glimpsed the profile of old Father Tom Moran, slumped low in the best armchair, fast asleep. For once it wasn't Father Tom holding the floor.

As Michael quietly opened the back door, he recognised immediately the voice speaking in the living room. It was the old recording Brian had often played when he and Dan were youngsters, played it so often they half-memorised it. It was years since Michael had heard that crackly old 78. From the safety of the kitchen he cocked an ear to catch the mellow brogue of a once-venerated Irish actor passionately reciting the speech that the Irish patriot Robert Emmet had made at his trial.

Michael was well out of it here, for this recital was guaranteed to move the living room to tears. He knew the story well. Emmet was an Irish patriot tried for high treason for his efforts to free Ireland. He made no defence at his trial and the jury convicted him without even leaving the jury box. When asked whether he had anything to say before the death penalty was imposed upon him, Emmet, a true Irishman, seized the opportunity and delivered a powerful oration which outraged the court and ignited the patriotic fervour of Ireland. Michael had often heard his grandfather tell how 'to this day' Irish patriots would proudly carry a banner inscribed '*Remember Emmet*'. Brian Leary had done his best to make sure his sons did not forget.

... this is my hope: (the melodious voice intoned in competition with the scratches of the old record) *I wish that my memory and name may animate those who survive me, while I look down with complacency on the destruction of that perfidious government which upholds its domination by blasphemy of the Most High ...*

As Michael moved stealthily from the kitchen to the hallway he glanced in at the living room. It was safe: his father's back was towards him so there was no danger of being hauled in there. If any of the others saw him, they were unlikely to dishonour Emmet by interrupting his hallowed words.

The group was sitting pensively. Opposite Father Tom the human stick man, Sullivan, sat straight-backed and crossed-legged in the other armchair, a Jamiesons in one hand and a cigarette in the other. Brian was on a chair pressed into service from the dining table, leaning forward, his elbows on his knees, glass in hand.

On the sofa sat a little old man whose face was familiar. He had a thinning crop of snow white hair and such a mischievous sparkle in his eyes that to Michael he looked like an oversized leprechaun. He looked up, noticed Michael, smiled and nodded his acknowledgment.

Michael remembered him now. His name was Casey. He had been a famous barrister of whom Brian often spoke in reverent terms. On the rare occasions he came to their home, he was treated with a deference usually reserved for clergy.

Michael smiled at old Mr Casey then moved on to his room. He peeled his shirt off, flopped onto his bed, and lay back in the darkness, with only the passion of a long-dead hero to disturb his thoughts. He mouthed the words, a few gaps when memory failed him, in unison with the speaker.

Why did your Lordships insult me? Or rather, why insult justice, in demanding of me why sentence of death should not be pronounced against me? I know, My Lords, that form prescribes that you should ask the question. The form also presents the right of answering. This, no doubt, may be dispensed with, and so might the whole ceremony of the trial, since sentence was already pronounced at Dublin Castle before the jury were empanelled ...

Grandad Leary, born within spitting distance of the Ring of Kerry, used to quote 'the great man' often. When he'd had a few he'd rant about the Easter Uprising, and the black-hearted Black'n'Tans, and the great Wolfe Tone, and Parnell, and all that ancient history of little or no relevance to Michael or Dan, or likely anyone else except the old men sitting in the living room enthralled by the words of the long-dead revolutionary.

Michael lay in the darkness thinking about his grandfather, and how much he missed him. His eyes were heavy, about to close, his brain about to switch off for the night, when a raised voice in the living room roused him.

'We've got them, Dan! They're in serious trouble.' Emmet had retired or had been sacked, and Sullivan had the floor. 'This could be the opportunity to get something really significant done.'

There was a murmured response Michael didn't quite catch, and then he heard his father, 'But Sully's right, Dan. We're travelling well in this thing. And if Arnold gets acquitted in the face of that confessional material, people are going to want to know why. This is our chance to force a Royal Commission on the whole method of proof in criminal trials in this country. The verbal could be gone forever.'

There was a pause, and then another softly spoken response, which Michael didn't pick up at first. He strained his ears. Mr Casey was telling them a story about someone he had known long ago.

'... Goodness knows how long Des'd been practising, but certainly since before the turn of the century. He came from a fine Irish family. His father was a well-known physician in Dublin, and it was only wanderlust that brought Des to this country.

'When I first met him he was probably the busiest solicitor in Brisbane. And for maybe thirty years he'd been fighting hammer and tongs with the local constabulary, and he still wouldn't give an inch. He was renowned for it. Anyway, I did a couple of things with him, and I remember one day being particularly disillusioned about another damn fool decision by a police magistrate, and I was young and foolish enough to let it get to me. So Des offered me some words of encouragement, which was very kind of him. And I said to him, "Des, where in heaven's name do you find the energy to keep going?" And he said, in that lovely brogue he had, "Sure, Daniel, 'tis easy and 'tis simple. I'm a great hater!"'

Michael heard his father chuckle, then Casey went on. 'So I said, naively as I see it now, "But Des, we've got to do something about them". And he said "We *are* doing something, Daniel. I've been doing it every day for the past thirty years. And if you have any worth as a lawyer, you'll do exactly the same thing".'

Casey paused dramatically, and when he recommenced Michael was struck by the power in his voice. 'One client at a time. That was Des's advice. All you can really do is stand up every day for whomever you are representing at the time, and fight the good fight as best you can. Forget about Royal Commissions. As Des said to me all those years ago, if you want to change the world, do it one client at a time.'

After that silence fell, as though Casey had said something profound, and Michael wondered what it might have been.

Eventually Sullivan said, 'Maybe so.' There was another pause before he added, 'Mind you, if the jury acquits this fellow, there'll be some significant changes in our part of the world, you mark my words.'

'I think we should be pressuring the Attorney to do something about these roosters,' added Brian.

With that he and Sullivan launched into an exchange about what should be done, and how, and why, and as the two droned on Michael's heavy eyes lost focus, and rolled back in his head.

He never heard Dan Casey's voice again.

7

On Wednesday the tenth of December 1969 Brian Leary sat in court, conscious of an uneasiness in the pit of his stomach. It was that irrational sense of foreboding that sometimes came when things were going better than expected.

During the preceding seventeen days all the witnesses referred to in Walker's opening address had been called, and Sullivan had systematically dismantled them. On the evidence so far the jury had to have a reasonable doubt. The question was whether that would be enough. This morning the last witness on the Crown's list, a police sergeant called Wallis, would give largely non-contentious evidence concerning signs of powder burning at the scene, and perhaps be briefly cross-examined, before Howard Walker would announce, 'That is the case for the prosecution, Your Honour'.

That meant it was decision time for the defence. Once the Crown closed its case Arnold would be called upon to say whether he intended to give evidence on his own behalf or call witnesses in his defence, or both. Arnold had no witnesses to support him so the big question was, should he take the witness stand? Brian put little stock in the adage that 'The best way to wreck a good defence is to call your client', but in this case there were sound reasons for Arnold not to give or call any evidence at all.

First and most important, it wasn't necessary. He had already given his full account in the signed Record of Interview, which would be with the jury in the jury room. The only thing he could add would be to deny the verbal and tell the true story of what happened at Police Headquarters that day. But Sullivan had so effectively attacked the police evidence of the verbal that it seemed acceptable to rely on the jury's discounting it.

If the defence called no evidence Sullivan had the invaluable right of last address to the jury, which meant he would be able to counter any propositions Walker put forward in his closing statement and have the last say before the judge instructed them as to the law and they retired to consider their verdict. If, on the other hand, the defence went into evidence, Sullivan must address first, with Walker following him.

That was a tactical consideration. More important was the worry that, if Arnold gave evidence, he would have to attack the character of Crown witnesses by alleging police fabrication, and that meant Walker would apply for, and probably get, permission to cross-examine him on his prior convictions. The jury would then learn of his sorry past, which included priors for assault, malicious damage and possession of an offensive weapon. Brian knew that juries found it a lot harder to believe, and a lot easier to convict, a 'known criminal'.

Sullivan was on his feet asking Sergeant Wallis some routine questions in cross-examination when Brian noticed unusual movement at the other end of the bar table. Merv Harris was crouched between the prosecutor and his clerk, whispering. He came and went a couple of times, as did another officer, before Sullivan concluded his brief interrogation of Wallis and resumed his seat. As he did so, Walker pushed a document along the bar table to him, and stood up to address the judge.

'I have no re-examination, Your Honour. Might Sergeant Wallis be excused from further attendance?'

Sullivan and Brian Leary hurriedly studied the document that had been put before them.

'Yes, you may stand down,' said the judge mechanically. Then, with more enthusiasm, he said, 'Mr Walker, I take it that that completes the Crown case.'

'No, Your Honour, I have one further witness whose evidence has only now been brought to my attention. I have provided my learned friend with a copy of his statement, Your Honour, and the Crown is in a position to proceed with the evidence immediately.'

'Very well,' replied His Honour, his voice tinged with resentment of this further extension of what had already been a lengthy trial.

'I object, Your Honour,' said Sullivan, jumping to his feet. 'I have just this moment been handed a copy of this man's statement. I need time to consider it and to obtain instructions on its contents from my client.'

Fancy Dan screwed his face up in a grimace that seemed to say that this was all too wearisome.

'Mr Sullivan,' he said in a long-suffering tone, 'I am mindful of the fact that this trial is now into its eighteenth day and we have yet to conclude the Crown case. In the circumstances, I propose to proceed with the evidence-in-chief of the witness, but I will hear you on any further application you might have on completion of that evidence.'

'Thank you, Your Honour,' said Walker, rising to his feet. 'I call Lindsay Norman Stone.'

Sullivan turned to his instructing solicitor. 'I don't like the sound of this, Brian,' he muttered. 'You'd better find out from our fellow what he knows about this rooster.'

As Brian set off for the dock the orderly led in a thin, wiry man whose greasy black hair was slicked back off his prominent forehead and hung lank and straight at the back of his large ears and down onto his collar. His face was freshly shaven but the beard-line was so heavy that it gave his sallow face an unwashed look. He gave no hint of tension as he entered the witness box and took the oath.

'Your name is Lindsay Norman Stone,' commenced Walker. 'And you are currently serving a term of imprisonment at Her Majesty's Prison, Annerley Road, Brisbane. Is that so?'

'Yes sir,' replied the witness in a nasal drawl. 'I'm doing fourteen years for rape.'

The jury eyed him with distaste while Brian steeled himself for the bombshell this eleventh-hour witness would almost certainly deliver.

'Do you know the accused, John Edward Arnold, now before the court?'

'Yes sir, I know Johnny,' said Stone.

There was a slight disturbance in the dock, where Brian was struggling to control his client.

'Did Mr Arnold ever discuss with you the bombing of the poolhall known as Mickey's Poolhouse?'

'Yes sir,' said the witness. 'It all started when we was in the exercise yard and I was talking about a bloke that had killed his missus and two kids, and what a terrible thing it was and that like, and Johnny reckoned, "Yeah, but some people need killing, don't they?" And I said, "But they was just little kids" like, and Johnny got all upset, and he said like, "Yeah, at least I never killed no kids".'

With that there was an eruption from the dock and Arnold leapt to his feet. 'This is lies! I don't even know this man.'

Brian Leary quickly dragged his client back into his seat, and the disturbance was over. The courtroom sat in silence for several seconds before the judge said testily, 'Mr Sullivan, another outburst like that and this trial will proceed in your client's absence.'

Sullivan murmured a response and Walker resumed his questioning.

'Mr Stone, was anything further said to you by the accused at that time?'

'No, but later on I seen him again. And we was talking about blokes generally inside, and how they all reckoned they was innocent, and Johnny was saying how that was all just bullshit. And I just said to him, "Well what about you, Johnny, did you do what they reckon?" And he said to me, "What do think, Lindsay?" And like I just said, "Geez, Johnny, how should I know?" And then he just turned around and says to me, "Of course I did. I set that bomb all right. I blew them up". And then he seemed to get real cranky and he wouldn't talk no more.'

The jury was dumbfounded. Here was a confession coming, not from police officers keen to secure a conviction, but from a man who claimed to be a friend of the accused, a fellow prisoner, a partner in crime, one of his own kind, with no reason to lie and nothing to gain by coming forward. And this confession corroborated everything the police had been saying, that Arnold was the one who bombed the Poolhouse. The police had been cross-examined up hill and down dale for days, repeatedly called liars by the defence, but here was a fellow convict, nothing to do with the police, who had come to tell them that it was all true.

Walker could feel the power of that evidence consuming everyone in the courtroom, and immediately stepped in to interrupt the monologue. 'Did you ask him for any details of what occurred that night?'

'No, I never asked him nothing more about it like,' he said, then added, as if in support and exoneration of a friend. 'But he did say he didn't mean to kill no one, or nothing. He reckoned "I never meant to kill all them people, Lindsay. It was just meant to frighten the owners of Mickey's, that's all". That's what he reckoned.'

'Did he say anything about his lawyers?' prompted Walker.

'Yeah, he did. I said like "Geez, I feel real sorry for you, Johnny. You're in a lot of trouble, eh?" but Johnny reckoned "No, I'm not. I never signed nothing, see, and my lawyers reckon I'll beat this one easy".'

Walker watched for the jury's reaction. It was right on cue. A frown here, a raised eyebrow there told him this repulsive little man had them wondering whether they had been duped by the accused and his clever lawyers.

'I see. Did the accused say anything further about that?'

'Yeah,' replied Stone. 'He reckoned he was going to beat it, and he reckoned "When I do, this whole town is going to sit up and take notice of Johnny Arnold!"'

The chilling warning had the desired effect. The fear and revulsion that had gradually drained away from the jurors' faces over the past two weeks came flooding back.

Walker moved quickly to conclude the evidence, so the jury would be left with that ominous warning ringing in their ears.

'Witness, did you have any further contact with the accused in relation to this matter?'

'No sir, I never spoke much to Johnny again after that.'

'Thank you, witness.'

Howard Walker sat down in the stunned silence of the courtroom. Brian Leary had no idea how Sullivan might counter, but however he might strike back, he would have to strike hard, and strike true.

'I move for a mistrial, Your Honour,' Sullivan said gravely. 'I ask that Your Honour dismiss the jury and declare the trial a mistrial.'

Dan Everett was horrified. The mere thought of a mistrial after eighteen days of evidence made him ill. He directed the bailiff to take the jury out to the jury room so this troublesome suggestion could be disposed of.

'On what ground, Mr Sullivan?' barked Fancy Dan as soon as the jury were out of earshot.

'On the grounds, Your Honour,' commenced Sullivan, warming to the argument as he unfolded it, 'that this shabby piece of transparent fantasy — and I use those words advisedly — has been thrust before this jury in such a fashion as to deny my client any chance of a fair trial. This evidence was not opened, nor was the defence provided with a copy of this man's statement, nor were we even aware of his evidence until moments before he took the witness stand.'

Sullivan paused, ostensibly to take a sip of water, but using the precious moments to shape the argument in his mind.

'Neither I nor my instructing solicitor,' he resumed, 'has had the opportunity to investigate the truth, or indeed the plausibility, of this man's story. In such circumstances we cannot hope to cross-examine him effectively. And his evidence is of such central significance to this trial that if it is not effectively challenged through cross-examination based on detailed and thorough investigation, a grave travesty of justice may occur.'

Sullivan paused for another sip of water. 'Your Honour, the Crown has put us in an impossible situation, in that this evidence has just been sprung on the defence and thrown unheralded before the jury in a quite inappropriate fashion. We will need time, and substantial time, to investigate this witness and his evidence. However, any lengthy adjournment at this point can only serve to bolster in the minds of the jury the significance of this man's story to the prejudice of the accused.'

Sullivan was starting to like this argument, and his voice gained in force as he proceeded. Even Fancy Dan was troubled by the notion that an adjournment at this point could unfairly prejudice the accused, since the jury would no doubt see it as a desperate ploy by a defence unable to provide an instant response. The judge was feeling increasingly threatened; he wished he had allowed Sullivan time to consider Stone's statement before the evidence had been called.

'Mr Sullivan, we are now in the eighteenth day of this trial,' he said plaintively. 'Surely you're not suggesting we completely abort the proceedings thus far.'

'Your Honour, in my respectful submission,' Sullivan responded, 'it would be dangerous in the extreme to proceed with this jury in view of the reckless fashion in which this evidence has been thrust before them.'

Dan Everett's agonised expression made it clear he did not want to abort the trial and that he was desperately seeking some justification to proceed without any further interruption.

'What do you say about this, Mr Walker?' he demanded.

Howard Walker knew exactly what Fancy Dan wanted to do. All Walker had to do was provide him with an acceptable excuse to do it.

'Your Honour, with the greatest respect to my learned friend, I fail to see what he might hope to achieve from an adjournment of the trial. We recently heard the accused quite vocally deny any knowledge of the witness. In those circumstances, it's difficult to imagine that any length of adjournment would produce any meaningful instructions from his client about the conversation. As I understand it, Mr Arnold simply says that the conversation did not occur. That requires no clarification or investigation.'

Fancy Dan liked the sound of it. 'Mr Sullivan, does your client deny any knowledge of the witness Stone?'

Sullivan conferred with Brian *sotto voce* before responding. 'On my instructions, he has never met the man, Your Honour.'

'Well, if he simply says the conversation never took place, I can't see that you need to take instructions on the content of the conversation. I do not see that there is anything to be gained from adjourning the matter, and it follows from that that I decline any motion for mistrial. Mr Bailiff, bring the jury back in please.'

Sullivan jumped to his feet before the bailiff had a chance to move. His voice had a hint of desperation in it. 'Your Honour has ruled on my motion for mistrial, and of course I don't seek to traverse Your Honour's ruling in any way, but I must now formally apply on behalf of my client for an adjournment of the trial for a period of at least twenty-four hours to allow the defence to consider this new evidence closely. In my respectful submission, the interests of justice demand it.'

Fancy Dan squirmed at the mention of 'the interests of justice.' He shifted in his seat. 'Mr Sullivan, we have already detained the gentlemen of the jury for eighteen days on this matter,' he chided.

'If my client is convicted he will be detained for a good deal longer than that, Your Honour.'

The judge didn't like Sullivan's irreverent tone. He had lost face as a result of the intellectual arrogance of this man on more than one occasion, and that rankled. He was not about to have this upstart preach to him about the 'interests of justice'.

'Mr Sullivan, quite apart from the inconvenience suffered by the members of the jury, I must consider the very significant cost to the community in prolonging the trial. I don't intend to tolerate any further unnecessary delay in this matter.'

'With respect, Your Honour, this delay is entirely necessary.'

Dan Everett knew that counsel were not always sincere when they claimed to be submitting 'with respect'. The formality had a particularly hollow ring to it as it fell from Eugene Sullivan's lips and the judge reacted as though it were a gross insult.

'I'm against you, Mr Sullivan,' he snapped. 'If you wish to cross-examine the witness, I suggest that you proceed directly.'

Sullivan was stunned by the ruling. He had launched into the mistrial argument with little confidence of success and, although he had converted himself to the argument as he developed it, he had not been surprised when Everett lacked the courage to accede. But he could not believe the judge would allow evidence of this kind to be introduced with no forewarning and then refuse the defence an opportunity to consider it fully. He responded almost on reflex. 'Your Honour, this is not trial by jury, it's trial by ambush!'

'Mr Sullivan!' Everett snapped. 'That is quite enough! I warn you, I will not tolerate any further such comments from you.'

Sullivan curbed his outrage. He knew that to indulge himself in further protestation would risk being cited for contempt with no prospect of shifting the judge from his decision to proceed. As the jury were ushered back to the jury box, Sullivan scoured his notes of Stone's evidence hastily, endeavouring to decide on the correct line of attack.

The jury seemed bewildered and suspicious about why they had been asked to leave and, as Sullivan rose to cross-examine the witness, they looked to him for some explanation. He rose to his feet in a confident, self-contained manner, but Brian knew only too well the agony he was suffering. He stood perfectly straight and spoke quietly, with practised assurance.

'Witness, your evidence here today is a complete fabrication, isn't it?'

Sullivan had a magisterial way of putting such a proposition that created an air of expectation in the courtroom, and even Brian's hopes revived a little when Stone responded in an unconvincing whine.

'No, you're wrong there, sir.'

'What have you been promised?' said Sullivan, more strongly now.

Stone paused momentarily before answering. 'Nothing.'

'Early parole perhaps?' The acerbity of Sullivan's tone grabbed the attention of the jury. Their eyes swivelled to the witness, waiting for his response.

'Nope,' Stone drawled insolently.

Brian's hopes began to revive. Stone looked like a man with much to hide. If anyone could exploit that, Sullivan could. The jury would not find it difficult to suspect this witness's motives. Brian could sense that Sullivan had already sparked the interest of some of them. They would expect answers from Stone, not insolence.

Sullivan quickened his pace. 'I suppose Senior Sergeant Harris and Sergeant Wilson paid you a few visits out there at the prison, did they?'

Stone looked uncomfortable, and Walker seized the opportunity to halt the momentum. 'I object, Your Honour,' he said, leaping to his feet. 'My learned friend did not put to either Harris or Wilson that any such meeting took place.'

'Dear, oh dear,' mocked Sullivan, shaking his head incredulously. 'Your Honour, if my learned friend cares to recall the witnesses I'll gladly put it to them.'

'Recall the witnesses?' Fancy Dan recoiled in horror at the prospect of the trial being further extended. 'Mr Sullivan, the Crown has already been put to significant expense in these proceedings.'

Sullivan's exasperation turned to anger. You'd think Dan Everett was paying for this trial out of his own pocket. Here was the Crown producing a surprise witness at the last minute and withholding statements, without a word of criticism from the bench, while the suggestion of recalling a Crown witness had Fancy Dan balancing the State budget and moaning about the cost of the proceedings.

Walker's objection was unreasonable and ill-founded. It could have been answered unemotionally and logically. But it had been a long trial and a difficult one and Sullivan's reaction was spontaneous.

'Your Honour, with respect,' he commenced in a tone that suggested scant respect, if any, 'the Crown really ought not start these proceedings if it can't afford the expense of conducting them fairly and justly, and according to accepted procedures. But I shall gladly donate the sixpence necessary to pay Sergeant Harris's tram fare in from the Valley Station if that becomes necessary.'

The jury snickered, and the judge's ears burnt with anger and embarrassment. He was tempted to explode, but thought better of it, realising that Walker's challenge was unsustainable.

'I don't see that there is any need for Mr Sullivan to have put the proposition to the earlier witnesses,

Mr Walker,' he said grudgingly. 'You may proceed, Mr Sullivan.'

Sullivan pinioned the witness with his stern gaze. 'Is it the case, witness, that you and Harris and Wilson have been meeting recently at the prison?'

'No.' Stone fidgeted in his seat.

'Are you certain of that witness?'

'Yes.'

'And you deny having met with Harris or Wilson on any occasion at the prison?'

'No, I never.'

Stone looked uncomfortable. Sullivan, sensing he was close to a breakthrough, pressed on relentlessly. 'But it is the case, isn't it, Mr Stone, that you have been visited at the prison by other police?'

Stone, seemingly mesmerised, stared at his interrogator. Did this bastard know that Curran had been out to see him? Was there some kind of record of the meetings? What if he denied it and this bloke could prove it? He sat motionless, feverishly trying to decide which way to jump.

Sullivan, scenting blood, increased the pressure on his quarry. 'That's the case, isn't it witness? You have met with police at the prison in relation to this matter.'

The sight and sound of Sullivan in full, majestic flight, the courtroom hushed, the jury spellbound, the witness cowed and perspiring, irked Fancy Dan Everett beyond endurance. This was his courtroom, his province, and the sooner Sullivan was forced to acknowledge that the better. So when the point occurred to him, he decided to take Mr Eugene Sullivan down a peg or two.

'Mr Sullivan,' he interposed. 'Are you putting this, or are you asking it? Do you have positive instructions that there was such a meeting?'

Sullivan looked up at the judge. The vigour seemed to ebb out of him and he appeared somehow diminished, his voice now flat and weary. 'I have no instructions on the point, Your Honour.'

'Then *ask* it, don't *put* it,' said Fancy Dan waspishly, revelling in the opportunity to instruct this popinjay on the proper way to conduct a cross-examination. If one has positive instructions on a particular point, one is permitted to put those instructions as a positive proposition to the witness, but if one does not have such instructions, the correct procedure is simply to ask about the matter in question form.

Given the intellectual arrogance of the man, thought the judge, one would think he would at least understand such matters of basic procedure. It made Fancy Dan feel good to know he could still teach these younger chaps a thing or two about cross-examination.

Daniel P Everett, a man of somewhat limited ability, had rescued Lindsay Norman Stone and likely salvaged the Crown case. Stone was grateful, Eugene Sullivan emasculated, Brian Leary appalled and Howard Walker more than a little uncomfortable. Fancy Dan was oblivious to it all.

Now Stone knew Sullivan had been foxing and knew nothing of the meetings with George Curran. He also knew better than to be lulled again into the state of uncertainty that had almost trapped him.

Sullivan could do nothing but feebly ask the question, 'Were you visited in the gaol by any police?'

'No, sir,' came the unhesitating reply.

From that point on the cross-examination struggled lamely along. Sullivan made a fair fist of it, relying on his immense ability as a cross-examiner and outstanding talent as an orator to provoke some thought and raise some questions in the jurors' minds about this evidence.

But he was unable to drive a crack into the rock-solid carapace of Stone's story, much less prise through the tough surface to expose its falsity. He put on an impressive enough display, and in another trial he might have taken the decision on points. But no one knew better than Eugene Sullivan that this was not another trial. In this trial, nothing but a knockout would suffice.

His cross-examination concluded, Sullivan settled slowly into his chair and turned to Brian with a furrowed brow. 'We're in trouble, Brian,' he murmured.

Brian nodded his agreement, a hollow, sinking feeling gnawing at his stomach.

There'd be no prize for coming second.

8

Gordon Yates arrived at the Supreme Courthouse just before midday. He had intended to be earlier but Saturdays were never good for him. He could see as soon as he arrived that nothing much was happening.

One of the Channel 9 cameramen was stretched out on the hall seat in the corridor and another was propped against the wall beside him, reading a Phantom comic. Jack Young from the *Truth* was sitting just inside the press room, working on a crossword. The southern press had formed a circle around a desk and were playing euchre without much enthusiasm.

'Any word?' Gordon already knew the answer, which Young confirmed with a shake of his head.

Gordon stepped into the corridor. He eased the courtroom door open. Howard Walker's clerk was sprawled across the bar table, reading a paperback. The bailiff raised a lazy eyebrow, then returned to his newspaper.

Gordon closed the door, smiling. It was curious how quickly a courtroom that had been the scene of high drama seemed to turn into a place of utter peace the moment the jury retired. But Gordon knew this wasn't peace; it was merely quiet. And it was a quiet laced with the apprehension of every person who had played a part in the trial of John Edward Arnold.

Gordon Yates had covered the proceedings for the *Courier-Mail*. The Mickey's Poolhouse bombing trial had been the most sensational criminal trial in living memory in Australia, and Gordon's editor had had the good sense to recognise that it justified having someone of Gordon's seniority and experience in court every day to report on it. So Gordon had followed every word of the evidence. And he had no doubt that the evidence of the convict Lindsay Stone had marked the turning point.

Until then Gordon had started to wonder whether Arnold really was the culprit, even though he had undoubtedly predicted the tragedy in advance that morning in the Shamrock. But when that appalling creature Stone, one of Arnold's fellow inmates, came forward and told how Arnold had admitted it all and boasted about how he would escape conviction, it was clear that Arnold was just another vicious criminal who could not wait to tell the world about his exploits.

Arnold made no real mistakes in giving evidence, but the prosecutor had spent a long time taking him through his history of prior criminal convictions, and that had certainly convinced Gordon Yates that Arnold was eminently capable of violence and had no qualms about breaking the law.

No, Arnold hadn't made any mistakes, but he had not pulled anything out of the hat either, which he needed to do to counter the devastating effect of Lindsay Stone's evidence. In fact, it was probably a tribute to the way Arnold's legal team had knocked the police evidence around that the jury was still out. They had retired mid-morning on the Friday, and Gordon was disappointed when the message came through at about eight that they did not expect to reach a verdict that night. Gordon went directly to the Grosvenor where some very nervous-looking police officers were quietly keeping their own company.

At one o'clock George Curran appeared at the press room door and summoned Gordon into the deserted corridor. 'Looks like you mightn't get a story here today, Gordon,' he said.

'It's starting to look that way, isn't it?' Gordon was pleased to be sharing a confidence with a man of undoubted influence.

'I had a yarn with Mal Campbell this morning,' continued Curran. 'I gave him contact numbers for a couple of the victims' families. I think he might want you to do a story for Bob Evans at the *Sunday Mail*, since you're right on top of this thing.'

Gordon thanked him, pleased to be back on the inspector's 'mailing list'.

'Yeah, well it doesn't look like there's much happening here, does it?' Curran observed, then turned and walked back down the corridor and out of sight.

Mal Campbell, the *Courier-Mail* editor, had been picking up leads from George Curran for years. When Gordon rang in, Mal gave him the numbers and suggested he get started on it straight away, as it was looking more and more as though this might be the only Mickey's Poolhouse story they'd get for Sunday.

And he was right. The jury held out through the rest of Saturday and the whole of Sunday. Gordon knocked out a great little human interest story on three families whose teenaged children were tragically killed in the explosion. It was the page three lead, with a good-sized pic of a grieving mum at the graveside. A great little heart-tugger, and Gordon congratulated himself on a quality piece of journalism.

The jury brought in a verdict first thing Monday. The courtroom was packed, the atmosphere electric as the judge's associate posed the formal question: 'How say you, gentlemen of the jury, do you find the accused John Edward Arnold guilty or not guilty?'

'Guilty.'

The associate had not managed to get out the final formal inquiry — 'So says your foreman, so say you all?' — when Arnold exploded.

'This is lies! It's all lies!'

He was a caged animal, his face distorted with rage, his powerful hands gripping the dock's wooden railing so forcefully that he might tear it apart. The muscles in his neck and forearms bulged as he leaned menacingly towards the jury ... violent, threatening.

There was a collective sigh of relief. The right man had been convicted and he would now be safely locked away where he belonged, behind bars.

The prisoner was jostled and dragged from the courtroom amid turmoil in every quarter, as journalists packed into the press bench and scribbled furiously to record the guilty man's rabid protestations verbatim.

Gordon Yates was delighted with his front page story in Tuesday's paper. It carried the very headline he had suggested: 'MICKEY'S MURDERER ATTACKS JURY.'

Arch Robinson came down for breakfast in the dining room of the Mackay View Motel on that Tuesday morning at precisely 7.45 am, as was his invariable habit when he was on the road.

After twenty years as a sales rep, he didn't get the chance to get up to Queensland much these days, but he enjoyed it when he did. In fact, he liked nothing better than waking up in a nice laid-back town like Mackay and having a leisurely breakfast in the dining room before setting off on a day's work.

It was a lot better tucker than he was ever likely to get at home and, like every other motel known to man, the Mackay View had waitresses that were a damn sight more obliging and a whole lot easier on the eye than Arch's missus had ever been.

One such lady arrived at Arch's table with the six-line menu, a serving of small-town chat about the weather of late and a copy of the *Courier-Mail*.

Arch ordered sausages, eggs and baked beans, then settled back to take in the local news. The first thing he saw was the headline, 'MICKEY'S MURDERER ATTACKS JURY', and he realised immediately that the jury must have reached its verdict in that case about the poolhall bombing in Fortitude Valley, the one that had caused such a stir.

Then he saw a familiar face, one he couldn't quite place but certainly knew. The photograph bore the caption 'Convicted Murderer John Arnold' and Arch Robinson was at once troubled and intrigued to know how it was that the face of this convicted mass murderer was so familiar to him. He couldn't imagine where or when he might have met such a man, but Arch prided himself that he never forgot a face — in sales you couldn't afford to — and he knew it would come back to him sooner or later.

He had polished off two eggs, two sausages, and a swathe of baked beans, and was spreading Vegemite on his second piece of toast when it finally hit him. This was the young bloke he'd picked up hitchhiking on the highway near Surfers Paradise early that morning he'd driven straight through from Port Macquarie.

That's right, no question about it. When was it? June, maybe July. Some time in winter anyway. Arch knew that for certain, because he remembered how bloody cold it was that morning. Brass monkey weather. He'd picked the young bloke up just after dawn and dropped him off in Brisbane.

That's right, he'd felt like tossing him out of the car because the bastard slept most of the way and was no company at all. Hardly said a word. He was glad to ditch him at Woolloongabba, down near the Mater Hospital.

Arch Robinson shook his head, swallowed a gulp of tea and mused on his lucky escape from an encounter with a crazed mass murderer and the vicissitudes and unpredictability of life.

9

Saturday the ninth of February 1977 was a typically bleak winter's day in London. Michael Leary was nursing a thick head and a dry tongue, courtesy of last night's party, and at this stage the prospect of a walk to the news stand in the brisk morning air was unappealing. He did want to get the newspapers though, and he ought to check the British Rail times for the evening train to Brighton.

Since his escape to London almost two years ago, hardly a week went by without someone ringing or writing from Brisbane saying they, or their mates, or a cousin-once-removed or a friend of a friend would arrive at Heathrow the following week, occasionally the following day, and would good old Mike show them a few of the sights and provide a bed for a night or two. It had become a crashing bore. So when Tony Artlett rang the previous day to say his sister, Jennifer, and her old school chum would arrive sometime today, his first impulse was to plead a prior engagement in the Outer Hebrides.

To complicate matters he had been making modest progress in his efforts to convince his secretary Paula that he should get into her pants. Or vice versa. He was flexible to a fault in such matters. Paula was of part-Nigerian descent with *cafe au lait* skin, ebony eyes, a voice like clotted cream, and a body that could bring tears to a young man's eyes. When she laughed her broad pink tongue would slide across her full lips and drive him crazy. The thought of what that tongue might do was sometimes more than he could bear. Paula liked him, he was sure of that, but he wasn't yet sure whether her thoughts of him were as lustful as his of her. He'd much rather chase an answer to that intriguing question than become a wet nurse for the latest wave of Aussie tourists.

Besides, he'd never liked that mealy-mouthed prig, Jennifer Artlett. And any friend of hers was likely to be cut from the same prissy, strait-laced cloth. But he and Tony Artlett went back a long way, and so he'd felt obliged to say, 'Yes, mate. Of course. I'll be glad to.'

Glad to? Bullshit! If it couldn't be avoided he'd put them up overnight, steer them in the direction of Earls Court, take them for a pint or three at the corner pub and suggest — he'd primed his flatmate Nigel on the point; it would sound better coming from him — they might like to take a run up to Brighton that night on the train, and come back on the morning 'milk run', an in thing for young people to do on a Saturday evening. With any luck they might stay on a day or two in Brighton, by which time he should have something sorted out for them to get them off his hands and out of his hair.

He was halfway through his toast and coffee when Nigel raised a frowzy head from the doona on the sofa and groaned pathetically, 'I'm dying. No, in fact I think I'm probably already dead.'

'Self-inflicted wounds, mate. No sympathy,' Michael said. He knew from experience it would take Nigel a while to come around, and he would get no sense out of him until he did. He downed the rest of what served as breakfast and said, 'I'll go and get the papers. And check those train times while I'm at it.'

'Oh shit!' Nigel moaned. 'Yet another invasion of the dreaded Aussies Overseas! Does the entire population of that godforsaken colony have our address tattooed on their forearms?'

'No mate, only most of them.'

Michael set out briskly, his gloved hands thrust deep into the pockets of his overcoat. It was a good five minutes' walk to Victoria Station. Pimlico Station was much nearer but he always enjoyed the sights along the way to Victoria.

The smell of curry mixed with the sound of Supertramp engaged his senses. As usual, the Cockney vendor at the news stand outside the Pimlico tube station was taking cheap shots at passers-by. A few doors up, a quartet of black women chattered outside the laundromat, undeflected from their gossip by a long-haired, bearded man in flared jeans and high-heeled boots who strummed on a guitar while a pretty, peach-faced girl in an ankle-length skirt slapped a tambourine and belted out a Carly Simon number. All around were the sights and sounds and smells of the teeming, pulsating city. Michael couldn't help but smile; the Brisbane boy had left the bush behind!

Victoria Station reverberated with the sounds of a hundred different accents and the tramp of feet scurrying in a hundred different directions. Michael paused to check the times for the evening train to Brighton and the milk run in the morning, jotting the information on the back of an envelope. Then he elbowed through the crowd towards the well-stocked bookstand in the centre of the platform. The display stands usually carried at least one copy of a reasonably recent issue of *The Australian*, and occasionally Michael treated himself to a bit of news from home.

He reached into his pocket and drew out a handful of coins. After earning a pittance as a law clerk for nearly fifteen months, he enjoyed having a little spare cash now he was working as a solicitor.

Suddenly he stopped. A tightness gripped his chest. His eyes fastened on a quarter-page photograph on the folded front page of a week-old copy of *The Australian* in the top row of a display stand halfway down the aisle.

He gazed at it from a distance, mesmerised by it. Then he nudged his way along the aisle until he stood in front of it. Michael knew this photograph, recognised the man it depicted. He took the paper in his hands and studied that remarkable photograph closely.

It was taken back in 1972 by a television news cameraman from a helicopter hovering over the roof of the old section of Brisbane's Boggo Road gaol. It showed the final stages of the hunger strike staged by convicted mass murderer John Edward Arnold, who had spent sixteen days clinging to the corrugated iron rooftop of the old gaolhouse, without food, sustained only by rainwater scooped from the rusty guttering, protesting against what he claimed was his unjust treatment at the hands of the criminal justice system until fatigue and exposure finally forced his submission to the authorities.

The photograph showed the ragged figure of Arnold, half-crouched against the steepness of a vast expanse of corrugated iron, his arms above his head like a drowning man thrashing about frantically in his desperation.

Above the photograph a headline said 'BOGGO ROAD BIRDMAN BOWS OUT'. The first few paragraphs below read:

Brisbane Prison's most controversial inmate, John Edward Arnold, died in prison last night.

Arnold was serving a life sentence following his conviction on eleven murder charges arising out of the 1969 Mickey's Poolhouse bombing.

He was involved in a number of sensational incidents in which he protested his innocence.

In 1972 he earned the tag 'The Birdman' from fellow prisoners after squatting on the prison roof for sixteen days in an effort to draw public attention to his claims that he had been wrongly convicted.

Michael bought the newspaper and sat quietly on a nearby bench. John Edward Arnold and his intolerable, interminable, unwinnable case. He'd only laid eyes on the man once, but his family had lived with him and his case for longer than Michael cared to think and they had paid a terrible price for the association.

When Arnold was convicted in 1969, Michael thought he'd hear no more of him, but it was not long before Arnold's appeal to the Court of Criminal Appeal was all his father could talk about. Brian's office was crowded with boxes of transcripts, statements and other Arnold documents, and the file seemed to totally monopolise his time. When the CCA refused the appeal Brian simply increased the number of boxes and started planning the High Court appeal. Faint mutterings were heard around the office that Neil Doyle was less than thrilled that his partner was devoting major time to the file of a client who had long since ceased to pay his way. But Neil bit his tongue, and Brian forged on, Eugene Sullivan in his wake, to the High Court, and further failure.

It should have ended there, but it did not. In August 1971 a man by the name of Lindsay Norman Stone, who'd given vital evidence for the Crown at Arnold's trial, recanted, asserting that investigating police officers had procured him to lie. That set in train

Brian's much-publicised effort to convince the Court of Criminal Appeal to order a new trial on the basis of fresh evidence. By then Neil Doyle was becoming openly concerned about the burden this charity work was placing on the firm's resources.

And it was then that Cath Leary's brain tumour was diagnosed. Brian was diverted briefly, but soon he was back leading the Arnold crusade. Eugene Sullivan stuck with it as far as the Court of Criminal Appeal, but when the CCA refused the appeal a second time, it seemed even Sullivan accepted that enough had to be enough. He was suddenly unavailable when Brian started talking about a second run to the High Court. By then, too, the doctors had recommended surgery for Cath, and things were starting to get very scary.

Ugly visions of her lying in the narrow bed at Mount Olivet Hospital for the Terminally Ill flashed into Michael's consciousness. The starched veils of the nuns, the smell of disinfectant, the undertone of compassionate murmurings and whispered secrets.

He remembered the parchment pallor of his mother's face on the night she died, the feel of her withered hand in his, and that pathetic, plaintive sideways glance before she closed her eyes forever.

Michael felt a sharp sting behind his eyes.

In the end, when it really mattered, Brian Leary wasn't there. On the night his wife died he was in Canberra for the High Court hearing of the Arnold appeal. He knew how close the end was and yet he had left her to fight a hopeless case for a worthless criminal. When he arrived home the next day he cried like a baby, great shuddering sobs that could change nothing. And then he crawled into a bottle.

The doctors told them she had long since lost all cognitive processes. But Michael knew that on the night his mother died she had looked one last time for her husband, and he wasn't there. Only Michael saw that glance, and he would never forgive his father for it. Never ...

Those weeks of sitting by his mother's bed night after night watching her deteriorate, long after she had ceased to react in any way, had shattered him. Dan, too. But Brian had worked on, business as usual, Arnold, as always. He spent his nights at the hospital, but he kept working, obsessed with that stupid Mickey's Poolhouse business.

The rest was a nightmare. Dan came back and forth but he had just been posted to Cairns and he had his wife to get back to. And Brian had his work. So by the time Cath Leary died on the sixth of September 1972, the family was long gone. Michael never told his father what he had seen in his mother's eyes that night, but that questing look had built a lasting barrier between them.

The High Court refused John Arnold's application for special leave to appeal and that was the end of the road. Michael moved into a house at Toowong with Tony Artlett and another law student and, although he stayed on at Leary & Doyle until the beginning of his final year and saw his father almost every day, they rarely spoke and when they did it was only for work. When he left the firm in March 1974 to do his final year of articles with a Gold Coast practitioner, he gave two weeks' notice. No one organised a sendoff.

Brian Leary continued to be obsessed with the Arnold case. There was talk about an appeal to the Privy Council, but in mid–73 he dredged up some forensic expert who claimed to be able to prove scientifically that the evidence against Arnold had been fabricated.

Brian began mounting a new approach to the Court of Criminal Appeal, this time seeking a recommendation to the Governor for a pardon. Neil Doyle finally blew up and, when Michael left in '74, there was talk of a partnership split. It probably would have happened, too, had it not been for Neil Doyle's loyalty to Brian Leary.

In late March 1974, as the pardon application was gaining some momentum, a police inspector by the name of George Curran announced that Lindsay Stone had just admitted to police that in August 1971 Brian Leary paid him $500 to deny his evidence at the Arnold trial and give false evidence to support an appeal.

Brian was charged with perjury and conspiracy to pervert the course of justice. Stone was given an indemnity from prosecution for his part in the scheme. He gave much-publicised evidence against Brian at the committal proceedings in May that year. Neil Doyle stood by his partner but Brian's reputation, and his practice, withered on the vine as the case ground its way through the court process to its eventual listing for trial in September 1974.

When the matter finally came to trial the Crown's central witness Lindsay Stone failed to appear, and the Crown elected to proceed no further with the charges. In the *Courier-Mail* report of the matter, Inspector George Curran was quoted as saying, 'We consider that there was a very strong case for perjury against Mr Leary, but without Stone it cannot be sustained. Given the uncertainty about locating that witness we had no alternative but to discontinue the prosecution.'

Brian and his legal team celebrated the reprieve, failing to recognise that in the minds of the general public and Brian's precious legal fraternity, he had evaded justice only by a stroke of good fortune.

Through all this Michael spoke to his father only once, in a stilted telephone conversation in which he awkwardly offered his support; the offer proudly declined. He could not remember a single conversation with his father after that, except for a last brief call to say he was off to England, to be wished *Bon Voyage*, and to say, without meaning it, 'I'll catch up with you when I get back'.

Michael heard on the grapevine there was no more talk about Mickey's Poolhouse after that, and that Brian had moved away from crime, mainly into probate work and some of Neil Doyle's spillage in conveyancing. His credibility in the legal profession was gone, and with it his enthusiasm.

In the meantime, it seemed, though John Arnold struggled hard not to be forgotten, for the most part, he was. Newspapers regularly reported his antics — protests and hunger strikes, court outbursts, and the occasional violent incident within the prison. No doubt these pathetic, attention-seeking stunts served to reinforce the notion that he was a violent man who properly belonged where he was. But no one really cared.

And now, at last, the final chapter, thought Michael Leary, sitting on a steel bench in Victoria Station, gazing despondently at the black-and-white image of a tiny, tragicomic figure posturing on a rooftop.

He hardly seemed capable of all that destruction.

When Michael arrived back at the flat he could hear Nigel talking animatedly even as he climbed the stairs to the first floor.

'And here is the man himself,' Nigel announced when Michael opened the door. Jennifer Artlett's face broke into a broad, spontaneous smile, and she stepped awkwardly over the luggage in the hallway to throw her arms around him. Michael couldn't help but laugh and hug her tightly as he would a long-lost little sister.

He was suddenly aware how long he'd been away from home. Jennifer had turned into a real person. He disengaged himself then laughed again at the two girls standing in the narrow hallway, looking like Arctic explorers in thick pants and hooded parkas.

'You look like something from Ice Station Zebra!'

'Well, it's bloody cold out there!'

Jennifer was a pleasant surprise. She was attractive — pretty even — her round face, now flushed a becoming pink by the cold, stretched into a smile that lit up her intelligent, dark-lashed grey eyes. Artlett's ugly duckling sister had grown into a swan.

'Michael, this is my friend Colleen.'

Michael turned to the other Arctic explorer with a perfunctory 'welcome stranger' smile. 'Hi, Colleen. Can I take those for you?'

The face framed by the hood smiled back at him, with an incandescence that ignited the green eyes, crinkled the tip-tilted nose and somehow embraced and enfolded him. He suddenly felt awkward, staring open-mouthed, then wondered whether he looked as silly as he felt. He quickly stooped to gather up the luggage.

The four of them struggled out of the narrow hallway into the little living room. Jennifer unzipped her parka and stripped down to a woollen sweater, revealing a well-developed chest that came as a complete surprise to Michael. None of this, he noticed, was lost on Nigel, who was now hovering over the girls like a dutiful waiter, delivering cups of tea and biscuits.

They sat in the little living room, eating, drinking and talking. Jennifer did most of the talking, regaling Michael with home-town news. Naturally, she dwelt on Tony. One of the senior partners at his firm had taken him under his wing.

'A mentor, Tony says,' she explained. 'Can't get by without your mentor these days, it seems, and Tony picked his out in no time flat.' She wrinkled her nose deprecatingly. 'Which means he's got someone powerful pushing his barrow, his barrow being his all-important career. Which is all mapped out: a salaried partnership next week and an equity partnership — you know, a share in the profits — the week after that. Something along those lines,' she laughed.

'Couldn't happen to a nicer guy,' Michael said, most of his attention on Colleen. He couldn't take his eyes off her. Her tousled mop of long blonde hair and the golden glow of her tanned skin seem to brighten the drab room, reminding him of home. She was slim and beautiful, with gentle smiling eyes that conjured up a vision of happy, idle hours basking under a burnished sun. He imagined them somewhere on the sand together, laughing in the warm Australian sunlight.

'I call him Macbeth,' Jennifer said, capturing Michael's full attention.

'Macbeth! Why Macbeth?'

'Vaulting ambition. It's quite unnatural in one so young.'

Michael laughed. 'Macbeth, eh? Didn't he come to a sticky end?'

'That he did. But Tony won't. He's too smart for that.'

'Can't imagine Tony mixing it with witches.'

'Hey!' Jennifer teased. 'I don't remember you as a Shakespeare buff.'

'Only what stuck from Junior English, I'm afraid.'

'W-e-l-l,' she said, darting a playful, meaningful glance at her friend. 'You could say he's under the spell of one witch he fancies madly but, sad to say, she's not interested.'

Michael turned and looked at Colleen appraisingly.

She blushed and stammered, 'I-I hope we can take in some of the West End shows while we're here.'

'You must see *The Mousetrap*,' said Nigel. 'It's been running forever. I'll probably take my grandchildren to see it if the little blighters will push my bathchair.'

'I can arrange bookings,' Michael volunteered. 'We could grab a show together if you feel like it.'

'That'd be great, Michael.' Colleen smiled her gratitude. *That smile again. Can't win 'em all, Tony old mate. You pick your mentor and I'll pick mine.*

The girls went to ready themselves for an afternoon stroll through the city. When Michael returned to the kitchen with the empty cups, Nigel was waiting for him.

'So,' he accused, 'you didn't tell me about them bristols, did you?'

'You're an incurable romantic, Nige. You know that, don't you?'

'I'd have been a lot more romantic if I'd known what was coming. I would have scrubbed up a bit, wouldn't I?'

'Never mind. You'll just have to rely on your personality and charm, admittedly both in short supply.' Michael loaded the cups into the sink. 'Anyway, mate, those bristols were as much news to me as they were to you. I haven't seen Jennifer for about four years. I must say she's changed out of sight.'

Nigel flashed a cheeky Cockney grin. 'Sight for sore eyes, I'd say.'

Michael did his best to ignore his friend as he tidied the kitchen. He was thinking of Colleen. It seemed remarkable that the pair of them had grown up in the same city — he on the south side, she on the north — breathed the same air, but hadn't met until now, in a place so far from home. *One day the two of us will marvel at that.*

'So,' interrupted Nigel, following him around the little kitchen, 'do you still want me to suggest they head for Brighton tonight?'

Michael stopped tidying and looked over at his friend. 'I suppose it's only polite to have them stay here a couple of days first just to catch their breath, don't you think?'

'I most certainly do, squire,' agreed Nigel enthusiastically. 'I most certainly do!'

As Brian Leary pulled his Holden Premier into the main driveway of the Brisbane Prison on that humid Monday morning in February he had an uncomfortable feeling in the pit of his stomach. Coming back to Boggo Road brought such a garbled mixture of emotions it was hard to sort them out.

He pulled in to the gutter and dragged himself from the car, looking up at that cold, hard face with the familiar inscription 'H. M. PRISON FOR MEN'.

As he rolled up the car windows, rolled down his shirtsleeves and pulled on his crumpled suit coat, Brian thought about the last time he saw John Arnold. Almost three years ago to the day, in the close, steamy heat of a brick-walled cubicle in the legal interviews section. He had tried yet again to assure his client of the proposition about which his own confidence was flagging: that this was a just legal system, and justice would ultimately prevail. And he remembered clearly the words of his client, spoken despairingly in the squalor of that grimy sweat-box, 'There ain't no justice for me, Mr Leary, and that's a fact'.

Brian Leary looked down at the crumpled, week-old newspaper on the front passenger seat. When he read of Arnold's death, he initially felt nothing but relief. He had carried the burden of that man for so long.

And, in the end, he had carried it alone. The little public support they had in the beginning died quickly. Eventually Sullivan tired of it, and in the end, even Neil Doyle would go no further on it, so Brian had struggled on alone. Alone that is, except for his beloved Catherine. She walked with him every step of the journey, even after her death. She alone had given him the strength to go on as long as he had.

Brian reached across and took the folded newspaper in his hands. He opened it and his tired eyes rested sadly on the picture of that lonely, desperate figure on the corrugated roof. It was an image that had touched Catherine's heart as much as his.

He thought about that awful night, after the doctors had pronounced their death sentence. He and Cath had clung together like shipwrecked sailors to a spar, speaking softly of what was to happen and how and when they would tell the boys. And he remembered the strength of her voice when she refused to accept his decision to give up work so he could be at her side in the hospital when the time came. She had spoken passionately of his responsibility to 'all those people', and demanded, 'Who will help that poor man Arnold if you don't?'

His heart broke anew as he remembered how she'd admonished him. 'This hasn't been just your life, Brian Leary!' she'd said with a passion that surprised him. 'You haven't done it by yourself, you know. We did it together. I've helped these people, too! I've striven for them and worried about them, just as you have. I insist on a say in what you do with my life's work.'

He'd held her even closer, his vision blurred with tears.

'Don't you dare, Brian Leary! Don't you dare abandon that poor man! After all we've been through, don't you dare pull out now!'

At first John Arnold's death had lifted a great weight from his shoulders. After his own trial in September '74 he had told himself that if he were to help Arnold any further he would have to allow some time to pass to restore his own credibility and to regenerate some public sympathy. But for a lonely, broken man it became a convenient excuse to stay out of the limelight and away from the agony of this hopeless case.

Perhaps he was no longer the best one to help John Arnold, he eventually told himself. Perhaps it was a job for a younger man, someone more objective. But Brian had always known he was trying to deceive himself, and the guilt built up over the years. When he read that headline last week — 'BOGGO ROAD BIRDMAN BOWS OUT'– it was almost as though he had finally been allowed to bow out too.

But then the whole history of the Mickey's bombing and the developments since had started going round and round in his head until he could no longer endure it.

Brian took his briefcase, slammed the car door and strode off towards the gates. He was going to find out more about Arnold's sudden death. He had to. The official preliminary finding of 'no suspicious circumstances' troubled him greatly. Now he would do something positive about it. He would talk to a crim he should have spoken to a long time ago.

Billy Peters was intrigued to know who had asked to see him for a legal visit. No one from the Public Defender had been out to see him in a long time and he couldn't think of any reason why they might be out there now. As he trailed the warder through the courtyard towards the super's office, he wondered whether this might be the coppers out to speak to him again, and how he ought to handle it.

William Alfred Peters was in Boggo Road serving a life sentence for the murder of a racing identity known as Ronnie 'The Rat' Abbott.

When Ronnie disappeared from the Eagle Farm racecourse one Saturday afternoon in '74, he was in way over his head to every bookie in Brisbane, and a couple in Sydney as well. It wasn't surprising that he might have wanted to leave town but, although a body was never found, from day one the dogs were barking that The Rat had met with a sticky end.

Still, the police treated it as a Missing Persons file until February 1976 when Billy Peters was charged with the hit. Peters had been around forever, and everyone in Brisbane who wasn't worth knowing knew Billy had the tattoo shop next to the old Manhattan, and later down beside the slot-car centre at the 'Gabba. He was a well-known fence, and the word was that you could buy just about anything out of Billy's tattoo shop.

But he managed to stay pretty square with the coppers, right through until late '75, when he wrote a letter to a local newspaper under the heading 'The Wrong Man'. In it Peters claimed that John Arnold had been wrongly convicted of the Mickey's Poolhouse bombing, and that Mickey's had been blown up by four young hippies he called the Prince Alfred Boys. They were the nucleus of a group that had formed an association at the old Prince Alfred Disco, across from the National Hotel, and had existed by committing small break-and-enters and dealing drugs. Peters said they had been offered $500 by 'certain people' to put 'a scare through the owners of Mickey's Poolhouse'. He said that one of them had told him that the order to stand over Mickey's owners had come directly from 'a well-known identity' Peters called the Magician.

The editor referred the letter to the police, who raided Peters' studio and residence the next day. His claims were found to be 'without foundation', but the search turned up a bag of heroin under Billy's bed. He denied in court that he had ever seen the bag before, but he was ultimately convicted and sentenced to twelve months' imprisonment.

Three months into that sentence he was charged with the 1974 murder of Ronnie Abbott, on the basis of a confession he was said to have made to a fellow inmate in the prison. They never did find Ronnie's body and Billy Peters always denied he had anything to do with The Rat's disappearance, but the jury disagreed with him, and in August 1976 he was convicted and sentenced to the big one.

When Peters stepped into the interview room he recognised Brian Leary immediately, although the two had never met. Crims like Billy had a way of finding out things they might some day need to know.

'Hello, Mr Leary.'

'Hello, Billy.'

'It's funny, isn't it? I thought I might see you out here eventually.'

'I'm not here about your case, Billy.'

'I know that. You're here for Johnny.'

Brian stepped through it carefully, telling Peters how Arnold had spoken about being approached by Sydney interests regarding the games in Brisbane, and how he had heard that Arthur Nagel, a Sydney heavy, had arranged for a 'bunch of long-hairs' to stand over Mickey's, and how all that seemed to accord perfectly with what Peters had written in his letter. He told him he wanted to get to the truth of the Poolhouse bombing and he wanted to know what really happened to John Arnold.

'They give Johnny an awful flogging the afternoon he died,' said Peters.

'Who did?'

'Couple of screws. He deserved it though. He was playing up merry hell that day. You couldn't blame 'em for giving him a flogging. Some days it all just got too much for Johnny and he'd carry on like a bloody pork chop. I'd say his ticker's give way, that's all.'

Brian questioned the convict closely, but the more the conversation progressed the more it seemed an inevitable end to a tragic life.

'Johnny was big and strong. When he got like that there was nothing else they could do to control him. They give it to him all right but when they left him in his cell at about four he was okay. About ten o'clock that night he give out this enormous scream, and that was it. We never heard nothing more from him. He just give up, that's all.'

The description was so final Brian dropped the subject and moved on. 'Who's the Magician?'

Peters pursed his lips as if pondering whether to answer. Eventually he replied cryptically, 'He's the man that makes them disappear.'

'Is he Arthur Nagel?'

Peters shifted in his seat. 'Why would you want to know that?'

'Because I want to help John Arnold.'

'You can't help Johnny Arnold no more. He's dead.'

'Who's the Magician?' Brian repeated.

After a long pause, Peters shook his head. 'You don't want to know about all that shit, Mr Leary. It's ancient bloody history.'

Brian was so close he could smell it. 'You and I both know the wrong man went to prison, Billy. I can do something about it.'

Billy shook his head again. 'You've already done your arse, Mr Leary. If you weren't a lawyer they'd have you in here with me right now. I mean, it's like they say, "Life's a shit sandwich. The more bread you got the less shit you got to eat". So that's why you're out there and I'm in here.'

Peters stood up.

'You could help me do something, Billy,' pleaded Brian.

'There's nothing to do any more. Johnny's dead. That's it. It's over.'

With that Billy Peters turned and shuffled back across the yard towards the Super's office, never to speak another word about the Wrong Man or the mystery of the Mickey's Poolhouse bombing.

10

On Tuesday, the twenty-first of January 1986, Peter Cosgrove turned nineteen. It was no big deal, but it was an excuse to go out raging on a Tuesday night. Not that Peter needed an excuse, any more than he needed a leave pass. He did pretty much as he pleased these days.

The Cosgrove boys were born and bred in Newcastle where their Dad ran the biggest car salesyard in town. After he took off with his secretary their parents seemed to spend their whole lives in court arguing over who should get the houses and the boats and the cars and all the rest. Peter soon took off to Brisbane where his eldest brother Trevor ran the Naked City Nite Club. Trevor was nearly thirty-five but he had lots of babes and lots of bucks and he drove a Porsche Carrera.

Peter moved into Trevor's apartment on the river and life had never been sweeter. He worked four nights a week at the Naked City, played footy in the minor grades for Valleys every Saturday arvo, trained Thursday nights and otherwise did exactly as he pleased. When Trevor wasn't at the club he was usually at his girlfriend's place, which meant that most times Peter had the apartment to himself. And that meant nonstop party time!

He hit the city just after eight-fifteen that night. For about an hour he cruised around checking things out. He ran into some Valleys guys and played some pool, then got into a major shout upstairs at the Gateway. They met some girls they knew in Queen Street and wound up in the Moon Bar. Peter wasn't sure what time he left there, but as soon as he hit the night air he could feel the bourbon in his brain.

He hadn't seen Trevor all day so when he made it to the Naked City, he should have been surprised when Louie told him his brother hadn't been in to the club at all. But by that time he was pretty much past caring. Peter couldn't remember how long he stayed at the club, only that he got tired of waiting for Trevor to show up and decided to walk home.

God alone knew how he managed to stay upright or what time it was when he got home. All Peter knew was that when he woke up on the couch, the harsh noonday sun was streaming through the windows and searing his eyes. He blinked, winced and took his bearings.

He staggered along the hallway, through his bedroom to the *en suite* where he emptied the full bladder that had roused him from sleep. Then he returned to the kitchen and clicked on the jug. He paused and rubbed his face. There was a niggling distraction on the edge of his consciousness, a tiny pebble in the bottom of his shoe that would give him no peace until he dislodged it. Something was not quite right. Peter padded back into the hallway inspecting his surroundings carefully. There it was, midway along and to his right, less than a metre off the floor. A curious little dark-red splotch, an inexplicable intrusion on the stark white wall.

The young man examined it intently. It was a minute bubble. He nudged it gently and it burst, a tiny daub of bright crimson spilling out onto the wall below. Blood! Peter recoiled, struggling with a sense of grim foreboding. He studied the living room. Nothing seemed out of place. He inspected the kitchen. Nothing ... He looked down at his own hands and arms. Nothing ... Then something grabbed his attention. On the hallway leading to Trevor's bedroom was a line of black bubbles and a rust-brown smudge.

Heart thumping violently, he stumbled around the bend in the hallway. A crazy pattern of red-brown blotches and streaks was spattered across the walls and on the plush cream carpet leading to his brother's bedroom.

Horror drew him to that room, until he stood in the doorway gazing at the grisly bundle coiled on the floor. It was a man, a man whose hands and feet were roughly bound with surgical tape, lying in a crumpled heap at the foot of the bed, caked in a congealing crust of blood that led to a deep, black, glutinous pool on the floor beside him. There were at least four neat puncture marks in the torso and the throat was cut so deep that white flecks of sinew and muscle stood out against the dark red pulp. Dirty white surgical tape obscured the face but Peter Cosgrove knew beyond doubt he was looking at the corpse of his brother.

The young man pounded frantically on the door of the unit at the far end of the carpeted hallway. As the door swung open he blurted out the first words anyone heard him utter on the subject of his brother's death:

'Quick, you've got to help me! There's been a terrible accident!'

Accident? Blind Freddy could see this was no accident and as far as Inspector Barry Reilly was concerned, that was a pretty bloody strange thing for that kid to say.

Barry wanted an explanation for that comment and so far he hadn't heard one. He'd seen a flock of bullshit statements the uniforms had got from Cosgrove's grubby 'business associates' and a whole lot of fart-arsing around by the Scenes of Crime boys, but so far nobody seemed to have taken this investigation by the balls. There were no positive leads and no suspect. Yet here was this bullshit statement from the kid and no one had even put it on him to explain it. Typical. Bloody typical.

As the new Inspector in Charge of Homicide Barry Reilly was under a lot of pressure. The press had been bleating about 'an execution-style hit' and the southern papers had been running stories about escalating violence in the Brisbane club scene. The Commissioner was keen to get the whole thing bedded down as quickly as possible. The best way to do that was to make a quick arrest and all available manpower was on the job. The only problem was that half these young blokes didn't know shit from clay when it came to real police work and all they did was go round and round in ever-decreasing circles until they finally disappeared up their own arses.

Here was a classic example. They'd had the forensic boys back to the apartment five separate times, they'd run umpteen bloody emu parades over the area, they'd got statements from every man and his dog and they'd door-knocked every poor bastard in sight, but nobody had even thought to give the kid a touch-up about his bullshit statement. What this job needed was some good old copper with a few rings around his arse to come in and take the whole thing by the scruff of the neck.

Most of the good old coppers were retired now. Marty Nolan was still around, but as Assistant Commissioner he never left his cushy office. Gerry Walsh went down with 'the dancer', Bernie Doyle and Bill Potter were both retired. They were damn good coppers those blokes. And what about old Merv

Harris? He ended up upsetting a few blokes, but old Merv was a top detective in his day. He'd have cracked this job in two seconds flat.

Barry Reilly grinned as he remembered how, all those years ago, as a young detective in his first year at the Valley CI Branch, he saw old Merv pile-drive that grub Les Douglas. They were looking for John Edward Arnold and they never would have found him if it hadn't been for old Merv. They never would have tied up the Mickey's Poolhouse job if it hadn't been for the likes of Merv Harris. That's what Barry needed now. Coppers with a few good miles on them. The sort that could smell bullshit when it was pushed under their nose.

There was a lot at stake. His old mate Mick Staines was the Inspector in charge of Licensing and of course he had everybody up his ribs about this Cosgrove thing. So from Mick's standpoint the sooner it was cleaned up the better.

And it wouldn't do Barry any harm to wrap this one up either. Head of Homicide was a plum position, and there was no reason he couldn't go all the way if he was seen as a bloke who could get things done. Look at Tommy Wilson. Everyone was tipping him to be the next Commissioner. Frank Delaney had jumped into politics and was handed a safe National Party seat. Even Bernie Doyle had copped a cushy number as Chief Investigator for the Government Insurance Office and by all accounts he was earning a poultice. Yeah, there were opportunities out there all right and it wouldn't hurt to get this one cleaned up right from the jump.

The first thing he did was to get a few of the more experienced blokes around the table. The one thing they all agreed on was that there was no way in the bloody world they were dealing with a professional hit. Whoever knocked this bloke had five chops at him first, and a pretty messy struggle as well. Any bloke on an earn would be a lot tidier than that. That meant that, percentage-wise, wives and lovers were the most likely bet.

The ex-missus had a rock solid alibi, but they still had some work to do to check out the girlfriend.

On top of that Barry wanted them to get back around his mates and his club staff to check out whether Trevor Cosgrove had been rooting anything on the side. Then there was the kid. Barry had a real feeling about that kid, and he intended to get him back in and give him a touch-up about this 'accident' business. But first he wanted him checked out. What was he into, what was he rooting, what was he smoking, what was he up to that night, how did his story check out, how did he get on with his big brother? The whole catastrophe.

Every murder investigation needs a number one suspect and for Barry Reilly's money, this kid was it.

Michael Leary brushed away a single hair that had fallen onto the open page of the *Encyclopaedia of Forms and Precedents*. Evidence that his hair was thinning reminded him he was not getting any younger.

Here it was January 1986. He had been with Queensland's biggest and most prestigious law firm, Messrs Martin, Schubert & Galvin, for nearly seven years now, the last three as a salaried partner. He would be thirty-five next birthday and he still had a lot of ground to make up.

Michael wanted something more substantial than a big salary and a warm and fuzzy feeling. He was servicing some of the firm's biggest commercial clients and his personal following was reaching the stage where some of them would follow him if he decided to cash in his chips and move to another firm. The equity partners had to be aware of that and that put Michael in a pretty strong position to put his hand up for a piece of the action.

He had made a late start so he needed to catch up as quickly as he could. Most of his contemporaries had settled into equity partnerships years ago. Tony Artlett had been a full partner at MS&G for six years and he was so far ahead of Michael financially it wasn't funny. The gulf between him and his old friend in the firm's pecking order stared him in the face each time he parked his ageing Volvo in the bay opposite Tony's brand new Mercedes.

In some ways Michael regretted wasting so much time in Europe. London was great but he could have seen almost as much in a six-month tour as he had living and working there for nearly three years. Colleen insisted it was the experience of a lifetime, and in a way that was true, but it meant his career had got off to a painfully slow start.

And he rather regretted following Colleen to Portugal in the winter of '77. If he hadn't, she almost certainly would have returned to London to be with him for Christmas and that probably would have seen them both back home and married by March the following year.

He blamed Colleen for the full year they'd wasted drifting around Europe, including nearly three months at Chamonix working on the snowfields for a pittance. Michael could scarcely remember why he had thought it so much fun at the time. Now it was merely lost time he had to make up.

And he was doing his utmost to make up that time. Over the past five years he had averaged over ten billable hours a day, which meant he was putting in at least a twelve-hour day Monday to Friday, with weekend work the norm rather than the exception. He had long been recognised for his technical ability but in recent times he had concentrated on developing his skills as a commercial negotiator, a fertile field for maximising his indispensability to the firm's corporate clients and, of course, to the firm.

On that last day of January, Michael spent all afternoon with one of his major clients and an assortment of development and marketing consultants on site at a retail and commercial office development at Springwood and by the time he got back to the office it was well after seven. Still, he wanted to get the master lease settled that night so the marketing people could start nailing down expressions of interest from prospective tenants, and he had dived straight into the documentation on his return.

He was startled by the buzz of his personal line. When he looked up from his paperwork at the gold-plated desk-clock, he was surprised to see that it was nearly 10.15. This would be Colleen wanting to know when he'd be home.

'Yes,' he grunted.

'Michael, it's Neil here. Neil Doyle.' Neil's voice was a hoarse whisper.

'Neil, how are you?'

'Oh, Michael. I have bad news. Terrible news. It's about your dad.'

A sharp indrawn breath. 'What's happened?'

'He ... he had a heart attack this afternoon.' Neil's voice trembled and faded, then he quavered, 'He passed away ... about an hour ago.'

The conversation struggled on from there. It was painful to listen to a man he had known as strong and in command reduced to waverings.

Neil had tried to get hold of Michael earlier but he wasn't in the office and Neil didn't have his home number and directory assistance was no assistance at all because his was a silent number, so he had rung various people, even the Law Society, to no avail ...

The story went on and on pathetically until Michael broke in, 'Neil, there was no way of contacting me, I've been running around in the car since three o'clock, completely out of touch.'

That absolution seemed to help and Neil Doyle went on to say all the necessary and appropriate things before he hung up, to Michael's great relief.

As he put down the handpiece, Michael felt numb. He had hardly seen his father in the last six years and had spoken to him rarely in stilted, awkward conversations that were mercifully brief. The wall between them went up long ago and it never had come down. Brian's death changed nothing. He was a selfish bastard who thought only of himself. And now he was dead. So what?

Michael tidied his desk, took the lift to the carpark and settled into the comfort of the Volvo's supple leather. *Brian dead* ... He shivered involuntarily at the remembered chill of a cold, clear night by the sea, felt in tingling nerve ends the thrill of playing that big, wily mullet, his aching back wedged against the support of his father's body, Brian's voice urging him to be calm, to be steadfast, until, at last, that huge fish — outwitted, outmanoeuvred, outgunned — lay gasping on the sand. They'd capered on the beach, hugged each other in triumph, in joy, in — yes — in love that was unrestrained and unquestioning.

As Michael sat in the silence of the lonely carpark, sadness threatened to overwhelm him. He blinked the sudden mist from his eyes and kicked over the engine.

By the second of February Inspector Barry Reilly was convinced he was about to hit paydirt. Staff at the Naked City had seen the kid have heated arguments with his brother over Trevor Cosgrove's bimbo girlfriend Tamara. According to Louie, the wog barman, Peter Cosgrove thought Tamara was a complete bitch. And according to Tamara there'd been bad blood lately between Trevor and his 'spoilt brat' kid brother. Add to that the fact that after Phil Vincent had 'read him the Riot Act' about not bullshitting to coppers, the wog barman had finally let slip that on the day the body was found, Peter Cosgrove handed him a bag of dope that he claimed belonged to Trevor and had to be ditched so the coppers didn't find it. So far as Barry Reilly was concerned, the whole thing had a giant smell under it.

'So where do we go from here, Barry?' Phil Vincent asked the question everyone assembled in the Day Room wanted an answer to.

Barry gave the only answer he could think of. 'Now we get the kid in and put it on him.'

'It's a bit thin so far, isn't it?' said Vincent.

Christ! That Vincent was always a bloody negative prick. Reilly didn't know whether to abuse him or agree with him. Eventually he did neither. 'Let's just throw the cards up in the air and see how they land.'

They kept young Cosgrove waiting in an interview room for about three hours. Plenty of time to stew. Left alone for three hours in a room three metres square with no windows and the door closed, wondering what sort of shit was about to descend on him, a guilty man could come up with a real bad case of the Hail Marys, and from there on it was usually a Sunday stroll.

When the four detectives filed into the interview room, they all wore appropriately sombre expressions.

Young Brad Whelan, who had taken Cosgrove's initial statement, led the way, followed by Mark Bertoli and Phil Vincent, with Barry Reilly bringing up the rear. As they packed into the little room, Cosgrove started to rise apprehensively but Whelan pushed a hand against his chest and unbalanced him back into his chair.

'Sit down,' said Whelan as Reilly closed the door behind him.

Vincent walked to the back of the room and Bertoli, hands on hips, stood over the seated youth. Whelan stood in front of him, with Barry Reilly on his right, feet shoulder-width apart and hands thrust deep in his pockets.

Peter Cosgrove cast nervously around at their solemn faces looking for a clue. Eventually he addressed Whelan. 'What's going on?'

'We want to know what happened to your brother,' Whelan said coldly.

Cosgrove looked puzzled. 'I've already told you all I know.'

'No you haven't,' Whelan replied, a pained expression on his face. 'See, a lot of people have been talking to us about you, mate. We know all about it now.'

'All about what?'

'All about everything. About the dope you gave Louie, for starters.'

Cosgrove was as white as a sheet. 'What is this?' he said, jumping to his feet, only to be roughly pushed back by Whelan.

'I told you to sit down, Peter,' snapped Whelan.

Cosgrove sat bolt-upright in his chair, wide-eyed and open-mouthed.

After several silent seconds, Whelan said in a milder tone, 'Now, do you want to tell us all about it, Peter?'

Cosgrove sat motionless for several seconds, staring at Whelan, then glanced around at the other detectives. 'Look, I came in today because you said I had to sign another copy of my statement. I've been here for three hours. I'm getting sick and bloody tired of this!'

It was time for Barry Reilly to step in. He lunged forward, gathered a handful of Cosgrove's thick, curly hair and pulled his head back so that it almost touched the top rail of his chair.

'You're getting sick and bloody tired, are you, you little shit?' he bellowed. 'Is that right? You're sick and tired, are you?'

Reilly released his hold and the young man's head came forward, his mouth trembling, tears welling in his eyes. Reilly took a step back towards the door, then turned and took a wild swipe at the boy. As the open-handed cuff grazed the top of his head Cosgrove yelped, from surprise rather than pain, then buried his head in his hands as though expecting a further onslaught.

Reilly leaned forward until his face was within inches of the cringing boy. 'I'll show you sick and fucking tired! I'm sick and tired of you, you little arsehole! I'm sick and tired of hearing your bullshit! I've had a gutful of your fucking bullshit! I want the truth! Do you understand me?'

Cosgrove lowered his hands slightly and peered ashen-faced at his interrogator. His voice came out as a thin whisper. 'I've told you all I know. I came home ...'

'Bullshit!' Reilly slammed his open hand against the wall in explosive emphasis.

Cosgrove let out another involuntary yelp and quickly pulled his arms back over his head.

'That's bloody bullshit!' Reilly's face was only inches from the cocoon of arms and elbows around the boy's head. 'Now you listen to me, smart arse. If you think you can put one over on us dumb fucking coppers, you've got another think coming, sonny boy. You understand me? We know all about the arguments with your brother, we know about the dope, we know the whole bloody story. So we don't want any more bullshit from you, you little arsehole! Do you understand me?'

Cosgrove's head nodded comically behind its protection and Reilly straightened up a little before he continued, less stridently, 'I've been working for eighteen hours straight and I'm starting to get very tired. And when I get tired, I get cranky. And when I'm cranky, I can get very bloody nasty. Understand me, son? So I'm going outside now to calm down a bit and try to forget that you've been bullshitting to us and treating us like a bunch of fucking idiots.' Reilly paused for effect, then added menacingly, 'When I come back, you're going to give me some answers. And you'd better pray to God that I like what I hear.'

Reilly walked out, followed by Bertoli, who closed the door behind him.

Cosgrove lowered his arms gradually, revealing tearful eyes and quivering chin, then dropped his head onto his chest and sobbed.

Whelan gave an almost imperceptible wink in Vincent's direction then moved forward and laid a gentle palm on the boy's shoulder. 'You all right, Peter?'

Cosgrove sucked in a long shuddering breath and nodded.

'I'm sorry, mate, but we just can't control him when he gets like that,' Whelan said apologetically. 'The bloke's a madman.'

'But I don't know anything about it,' whined the youth.

'Mate, we already know you do.' Whelan sounded regretful. 'See, people have put you in, mate. We can't tell you all what they said but they've dead set put you right in it. We've got the whole thing in detail. We know you're involved.'

'But I'm not. I'm not involved at all.' The voice, little more than a whisper, sounded distinctly unconvincing.

Disappointment flattened Whelan's voice. 'Suit yourself, Peter. But, you know, we can only protect you so far. The boss'll be back in a minute and, dead set, I can't help you then, mate. There's no telling how he's going to react. But, bloody hell, I wouldn't aggravate him if I was you.'

'Can I ring my mum?' Peter Cosgrove pleaded.

The two detectives knew at that point they were about to hear a young man confess to the murder of his brother. He did it all right, they could hear it in his voice. And they could tell he was just about all finished denying it.

'No mate, not yet,' said Whelan sympathetically. 'You'll have to talk to the boss first.'

Cosgrove sat motionless, his head slumped on his chest, his shoulders heaving.

Whelan lay a soothing hand on the young man's shoulder. 'Come on, mate, you'll be right. Just tell us all about it and it'll all be over. Then you can ring your mum. Okay?'

Brian Leary's funeral was held on the third day of February 1986. The crowd at St Stephen's Cathedral for the eleven o'clock ceremony surprised Michael. There was a sprinkling of battlers, barflies and racecourse touts, a few of them self-consciously flourishing black armbands. But most were people of some consequence. Like old man Rowell, a former president of the Law Society and still on the Executive Committee of Tattersalls' Club, and senior heavyweights from the big Queen Street firms, such as Norris Mason and even Sir Frank Winter and Brian Cullinane, who might have made Attorney General if Billy McMahon hadn't toppled Gorton. Mr Justice Walker, Senior Puisne Judge of the Supreme Court, was there, and so were several retired judges. Tony Artlett couldn't make it but he'd sent a card and the partners of MS&G had chipped in for a wreath from the city's most expensive florist.

Michael wondered at the presence of so many highly respected members of the legal profession at the funeral of a disgraced solicitor from a two-bit two-man firm from the 'top end' of Elizabeth Street.

The Requiem Mass was unbearably drawn out and peppered with the usual painful cliches and, to make Michael's agony complete, Neil Doyle embarrassed everyone by breaking down halfway through the epistle reading, taking a full two minutes to compose himself before continuing.

When they finally filed out onto the cathedral steps Michael lined up with Colleen, Daniel and Sally and a phalanx of aunts and uncles to field the condolences and commiserations of an army of appropriately miserable-looking mourners. This was the hardest part of all, dealing with the well-wishes of a sea of unfamiliar faces and doing one's level best to share their profound regret.

Brian Leary was finally laid to rest in a brief graveside ceremony at the Toowong cemetery. Few of the mourners had seen it necessary to come. The circus was over and now, standing in that peaceful place while the priest droned on about everlasting life, Michael's mind drifted ...

The dark wooden coffin gliding into position over that dark hole gave way to the fishermen's huts on

Stradbroke Island. Their rough, unpainted timber was dark, almost black, and looked wet even when it was dry. He could see those long-forgotten huts so clearly.

They used to pass them every day walking down from the campsite in search of firewood and he could see the tall figure of his father striding ahead of them through the sand, cradling firewood in his arms and lecturing his sons on features of the bush and the rocky outcrops below and the history of the curious little black huts on the headland.

As the coffin jerked into the open pit Michael felt a yawning emptiness inside him. He had a sudden urge to halt the process, just for a moment, so he could collect his thoughts. The coffin lurched again and he sucked in a tiny breath to speak but quickly checked himself. He glanced self-consciously at the other mourners but no one seemed to have noticed. When he looked back the casket had disappeared. Brian Michael Leary was gone forever.

The subdued little entourage filed slowly back to the carpark and gradually disbanded with hugs and tears and handshakes. Daniel and Sally left in Colleen's Honda. Colleen had kissed him on the cheek then fixed her level green gaze on him and said, oddly, 'Take care.' It was not a phrase she used.

With considerable relief Michael dropped into the seat of his Volvo and pulled the door shut behind him. The engine sang sweetly as the vehicle swung obediently towards the gates. He nudged a cassette tape into the slot and a mechanical click gave way to the power and the glory of the London Philharmonic. Beethoven's Sixth, sonorous, majestic, life-affirming.

As the front wheels lurched gently onto the roadway, Michael rested his foot on the brake pedal and glanced back to where the final stages of his father's burial were being completed. He wondered why now, after all these years of estrangement, he felt so deserted by this man he hardly knew.

He turned away, then looked back again. Something odd in this lonely scene attracted his attention. There, half-obscured under the canopy of an ancient Moreton Bay fig tree, not more than twenty paces from the men working on the grave, was a tall, elongated scarecrow of a man.

Michael recognised Eugene Sullivan immediately. He had not seen him at the ceremony, or for many years before that. He was a frail shadow of the man Michael remembered but for all that, there remained a kind of strength. As he stared at old Mr Sullivan standing under the fig tree sheltering from the bite of the midday sun, he realised with a sense of valediction how very many years had passed since they last met.

Michael pulled out onto Birdwood Terrace, turned up the music and tried not to dwell on thoughts of his own mortality.

11

Peter Cosgrove was charged with his brother's murder on the second of February 1986. On the morning of the third he appeared in the Brisbane Magistrates Court and was remanded in custody for hearing of committal proceedings in March. He spent two nights in the City Watchhouse and was then transferred to the Remand Section at Boggo Road.

His family chipped in and their solicitors retained Queensland's leading young criminal law barrister Mr Charles Davidson. They made an application for bail to the Supreme Court and when bail was refused they even went so far as to appeal the bail issue to the Full Court. Davidson argued it brilliantly of course, but the Full Court held that the original judge had not misdirected himself, and confirmed the refusal of bail.

They brought a second application in early March based on medical evidence that the young man was suffering some emotional problems in custody but, not surprisingly, it was unsuccessful. So Peter Cosgrove was still in custody when his committal proceedings commenced in the Magistrates Court on the twelfth and, when the magistrate committed him for trial two days later to the April sittings of the Supreme Court in Brisbane, he remanded him in custody.

The enormous level of public interest originally sparked by the case had dissipated somewhat as soon as

Trevor Cosgrove's brother was charged, thus putting to rest speculation about gangland executions and vice wars. When it became just another family murder, the Cosgrove case went from page one to page seven, and by the time young Cosgrove was committed for trial, it hardly rated a mention.

On the twenty-fifth of April 1986 the Trevor Cosgrove murder case burst back onto the front page.

It was right on midday that Michael Leary's secretary buzzed him to say that Gerry Manetti and another gentleman were in reception to see him. Shit! Wasn't it just like Manetti to pick now of all times and today of all days to arrive unheralded and expect to see him without an appointment. Michael was up to his eyeballs in mining leases and he had been trying all morning to finalise the documentation.

He was tempted to send Manetti away, but he knew he couldn't. Manetti was the project manager and general right-hand man to Michael's number one client, the Gold Coast property developer Bruce Dawson. Dawson was fast becoming one of the biggest private developers in Queensland and last year alone he was worth nearly two hundred thousand in fees to the firm. He was a rough-at-the-edges house-builder turned developer who demanded service from his solicitors. And Michael made sure he got it. So when Dawson's man Gerry Manetti turned up in reception to see Michael, Gerry saw Michael.

'Hello, Gerry,' said Michael in a subdued tone that paid due respect to the understated opulence of the MS&G reception area. 'Listen, I'm afraid I've got a bit of a problem just at the very moment. Is there any chance we can get together this afternoon?'

'No mate, I've got to see you straight away. It's real urgent.'

He sounded like he had a million-dollar problem on his mind; suddenly Michael was very interested. 'Okay. Come through.'

Manetti gestured towards the man beside him. 'Michael, this is my father-in-law Merv.'

A strongly-built man with a puce complexion and short-cropped, ash-grey hair gripped Michael in a vice-like handshake. Michael almost winced in pain.

'Hello, Merv. Michael Leary.'

Merv grunted and then said, 'Merv Harris. How're you going?' He released Michael's throbbing hand and added, 'I think I knew your old man. He was Brian Leary, wasn't he?'

'That's right.'

'Yeah, I was a copper for over thirty years.'

'Oh right.' By that it was said, without it being said, that the two had not been friends.

'So what's the problem?' said Michael, as the three men settled around the boardroom table.

'It's my boy, Joseph,' Manetti commenced with an emotional waver in his voice, and then he stopped completely.

The man was on the verge of tears and it was a relief to Michael when his father-in-law broke in impatiently, 'The coppers come round to their house this morning. They're looking for young Joe over the Cosgrove murder.'

'Trevor Cosgrove?'

'Yeah.'

'I thought they'd charged his brother.'

'Too bloody right they did!' Merv's eyes flashed angrily.

Gerry Manetti had composed himself. 'Maybe you didn't read the papers this morning,' he said. 'A guy by the name of Paul Duncan — he used to be kind of a mate of Joey's — anyway, this guy Duncan got arrested yesterday for something or other, stealing I think it was. And the police found some of this fellow Trevor Cosgrove's credit cards and things on him. So they questioned him about it and apparently now this Paul Duncan says that the brother — what's his name? — Peter Cosgrove, he didn't kill his brother at all. He says he done it with some other boys.' Manetti paused for a moment and added weakly, 'H-he says Joseph was with them.'

'It's a dead-set bloody set-up, that's for sure!' Merv burst in. 'The bastards kicked their door in this morning with a warrant to search the place.'

Michael was still trying to take it all in. 'But, look, didn't the Cosgrove lad make a signed confession to the murder?'

'My word he did!' erupted Merv. 'Two bloody confessions! He wrote a signed statement and then he signed a Record of Interview.'

Gerry Manetti slid forward on his chair. 'Peter Cosgrove didn't do it, according to this guy Duncan. There was three boys there, including Joseph. I don't think the brother had nothing to do with it.'

'Maybe Duncan's making it all up,' Michael ventured. 'Maybe he's just trying to big-note himself.'

'Duncan's not bullshitting,' the father-in-law growled, shaking his head. 'I made a few quiet calls this morning to a couple of blokes who'll still talk to me. They reckon Duncan's as right as rain for it. He told the coppers things about the murder that they didn't even know themselves until they checked with Forensics. He done it all right.'

Michael sat wide-eyed at the table, trying desperately to think of something meaningful to say. 'So was Joseph arrested?'

'No.' Gerry Manetti was much more composed now. 'He's in Sydney working in my brother's restaurant in Mosman.'

'Do the police know that?'

'No. We told them we hadn't seen him.'

'How old is he?'

'Eighteen.'

'Have you spoken to him?'

'Yeah, I rang him from Merv's place.'

Manetti's eyes glistened with moisture. 'He says he was there all right. He drove these guys to Cosgrove's place. But he didn't know nothing until it was all over.' His voice wavered and halted, and he paused for a moment before adding, 'What do I do Michael? Joey wants to come home straight away.'

A few basic rules came trickling back. Rule No 1: Don't leave your client exposed. 'Well, I'd suggest you get him back here as soon as possible, and get him into a police station with a competent solicitor as a matter of urgency.'

'Too bloody right!' grunted Merv. 'So those bastards don't get a chance to stitch him up!'

Michael was at once surprised and relieved to hear this ringing endorsement of his advice from the older man.

Manetti nodded sagely as though he knew exactly what his father-in-law was on about. 'Okay, Michael, that's what we're going to do,' he said almost brightly, as though they had just settled another commercial deal. 'I want you to speak to the police for him.'

Michael was horrified at the suggestion. 'No, Gerry, no,' he quickly responded, shaking his head. 'You don't want me on something like this. I haven't done any criminal work in years. You want someone who's a bit more conversant with this sort of thing.'

He was unprepared for the desperation in Manetti's voice. 'Please Michael,' he said sadly. 'This is my boy, you know. I need you to do this for me. Please.'

The poignancy of the plea seemed missed by old Merv. 'If you're worried about the dough, you needn't be,' he said gruffly. 'We can pay. Up front if you want. I can even give it to you in folders if that's what it takes.'

Michael was already developing a distinct distaste for this man, but Gerry Manetti sounded desperate.

'Please Michael, you are going to do this for me, aren't you?'

'How soon could you get your son back up here?'

'Tomorrow morning, I guess.'

'All right,' said Michael, reaching across the table and pulling a foolscap pad over in front of him. 'You move on that and keep me posted. In the meantime, what are the names of the other fellows that are involved?'

As Manetti spelt out the names Michael wrote them onto the pad in front of him. *Paul Duncan ... Peter Lade*. They had both signed statements saying that they had planned to 'get square' with Cosgrove over money he owed Duncan. They went to his apartment that night intending to ransack the place and steal one of Cosgrove's cars.

From there the stories differed, but it seemed that they had not expected Cosgrove to be at home, and when they found him there the whole thing got completely out of hand. Lade claimed that Joey had stayed in the car, but Duncan had given a statement claiming that Joey was part of the plan and was with them when the killing occurred.

'I take it that they're both out at the prison by now,' Michael said, unclicking his ballpoint.

'Duncan is,' old Merv replied. 'They've got Lade here in the City Watchhouse. Word is they want to question him about a shit-load of other matters.'

'Well, that's handy at least,' said Michael, sliding his pen back into his pocket. 'I'll go down there and have a chat with him sometime today.'

Gerry Manetti drew in a full breath of air and then expelled it. He felt that things might be moving in the right direction. Michael Leary was a very smart lawyer, and Gerry was sure that Michael would be able to help. The whole thing was like a nightmare, but Gerry knew that Michael would sort it all out for them.

Merv Harris wasn't quite so sure.

12

Licensing Branch boss Mick Staines phoned Inspector Tom Wilson at home at about 11.30 pm and broke the news.

By the time he hung up even Tom could see that this was a disaster of biblical proportions. That afternoon a couple of the uniformed blokes out at Darra had picked up this fellow Duncan on a pissant car-stealing charge and locked him up in the Inala Watchhouse. When they checked his car out they found some of Trevor Cosgrove's missing credit cards in the glove box so they passed it on to the boys in the CI Branch.

A couple of detectives went straight over to the Watchhouse but in the meantime Duncan had been seen by a duty lawyer from Legal Aid.

So the CI boys interviewed him about the credit cards in the presence of his solicitor expecting him to say nothing but to everyone's surprise he breaks down and starts blubbering about having bumped Cosgrove. Duncan claimed he was with two other young blokes, Peter Lade and Joe Manetti. They went there to square off with Trevor Cosgrove about money he was supposed to have owed Duncan for some tiling work he'd done at Cosgrove's nightclub. Peter Cosgrove wasn't there and had nothing to do with it. Duncan had never met Peter Cosgrove. So far as he knew neither had any of the others.

Barry Reilly, Phil Vincent, Mark Bertoli and young Brad Whelan had all given evidence of the Peter Cosgrove confession. Mick Staines had a long yarn with Barry Reilly about it and Barry said they'd had to lean on the kid a bit to get the story out of him. Now it was starting to look like the little prick might have confessed to it just to get himself out of a flogging. That meant big trouble for Barry and the boys in Homicide, but it wouldn't stop there. The press were already going berserk and people were going to want to know what makes a nineteen-year-old kid sign a confession to his brother's murder when he had nothing to do with it.

Peter Cosgrove's solicitor had scheduled a press conference for the following day and that meant all kinds of shit was about to descend. This was definitely Royal Commission territory and the last thing they needed right now was a Royal Commission into police interview practices.

Tom Wilson didn't get much sleep that night and the next morning he was in the office early to meet with Barry Reilly and Phil Vincent. They had run every check known to man on the three blokes involved but they couldn't bring up any sort of concrete connection to Peter Cosgrove. The best they could do was that one of them, Joseph Manetti, had played Rugby League for Valleys at the same time as young Cosgrove, although they had never been in the same team together. The boys had checked that out pretty carefully but it looked like they didn't even know each other.

As soon as the others left his office, Tom Wilson picked up his private phone and punched in a familiar number.

'George, it's me again,' he said. 'I've just spoken to Barry and Phil. Looks like the best we're going to get is that one of them played footie at Valleys with young Cosgrove but they weren't mates.'

'That'll do,' came the gravelly drawl on the other end of the line. 'Which one was it?'

'Manetti. He's the only one we haven't got.'

'Well get him,' urged George. 'And when you do, make sure he's stitched up tighter than a fish's arsehole. Understood?'

'Sure.'

There was a pause then George growled again, 'You make sure those boys don't fuck it up again, Tom.'

'Right.'

'If they do the Government'll find it pretty bloody hard to resist the pressure to call an Inquiry.' George belted out a rattly cough then took a settling breath. 'I'll get on the blower to a few people.' He paused again then added, 'So long as your fellows can serve up someone with a link to the Cosgrove kid we can probably muddy the waters with a bit of speculation about a possible conspiracy involving Cosgrove. That should be enough to take the heat off the Government. But you've got to make sure you stitch that little bastard up!'

When Tom Wilson put down the phone he felt a whole lot better. Old George had all the strings in his hands and there was no doubt he'd pull the right ones at just the right time. There was no better man in a crisis. He knew how to fix things, did old George. He knew how and when to pull a rabbit out of a hat.

That's why they called him the Magician.

The fat sergeant leaning over the newspaper splayed across the front desk at the City Watchhouse eyed Michael Leary with obvious animosity. Nobody was happy about the day's developments in the Cosgrove case and today all lawyers were to be treated with more than the usual disdain, especially those who might be involved in the case.

'There are no interview rooms in here, mate. You'll have to talk to him in the holding cell,' the sergeant said.

'Where would that be?' asked Michael.

The sergeant waved his cup of tea in the direction of a cell opposite the front desk. It was a large open cell which, like the rest of the complex, was painted a drab grey. Michael squeezed onto a narrow bench and waited patiently for the prisoner to arrive.

People came and went. Wild-eyed women and unkempt, malodorous drunks, sickly-looking drug addicts and men with dead eyes and stony faces, seemingly inured to the misery of the place. Some came in handcuffs, some struggled and jostled, some moved submissively as though this was their normal routine.

Michael wondered how often his father had been part of this ugly picture. He glumly studied the filth collected in the indentations on the bench and wondered how much of the grime would leave with him on his new Cardin suit and how much of the pain and squalor of this place his father had taken away with him every day of his working life. This place was part of the world that had shaped his father's failure, and Michael cursed himself for coming here.

He was about to cancel his requested visit when he saw the cold blue eyes of Peter Lade for the first time. They were set in a face of fine, chiselled features bordered by a neat head of shining shoulder-length ash-blond hair. Michael felt a chill snake up from the base of his spine and he stayed riveted to his seat.

A fresh-faced young constable ushered Lade to the front desk and reported to the sergeant. Lade stood beside him, impassive, unconcerned. He was undeniably handsome, with the muscular frame of an athlete. His shoulders were broad and his forearms, linked behind his back, were thick, as though he'd done some weight-training at some stage.

The sergeant directed Lade to the holding cell, and he strolled over and sat on the bench beside Michael.

'Mr Lade, is it?'

'That's right.' The voice was cultured and relaxed.

'My name is Leary. I'm a solicitor.' Michael took a card from his wallet and handed it to the prisoner, who glanced at it briefly. 'I have instructions to act on behalf of Joseph Manetti.'

'Right.'

'I understand you've been charged with the murder of Trevor Cosgrove.'

'That's right.'

'Mr Lade, you don't have to speak to me if you don't want to. But my client hasn't as yet been interviewed about the matter and I'm keen to find out what you and the others might have already told the police.'

'I've told them all about it,' Lade responded promptly.

Michael was about to explain in detail what he had been told already and of his client's intention to return to have the matter cleared up, but the response came before he had the chance.

'I killed Cosgrove. I was the first one to stab him, and in the end I went back and cut his throat.'

Michael tried to hide his shock at this matter-of-fact recital. 'Who else was involved?'

'It was Paul's idea actually. Paul Duncan. Cosgrove owed him money and we were going to go and clean him out. We didn't expect him to be there. But he was. So we trussed him up like a Christmas turkey.' His mouth twitched in a humourless grin. 'The unexpected taxes one's ingenuity, doesn't it? Somehow he got his hands free and he grabbed Paul. So I thought "Fuck you" and stabbed him in the chest. Then Duncan went berserk and got stuck into him with a knife from the kitchen. Chased him down the hallway. Made an awful fucking mess.'

Michael felt deeply uneasy at sharing this dreadful confidence but Lade spoke on with only a pause for breath. 'When we left the building we realised we hadn't checked whether he'd actually carked it. He knew Paul Duncan so we had to make sure he was dead. I went back to finish him off. When I got in there he certainly looked dead enough.' He paused briefly before adding, 'But I slit his throat anyway just to make sure.'

Michael was sweating. 'Look, all I really need to know is what you told the police about Manetti.'

Lade turned his piercing eyes on Michael. 'Manetti?' He looked confused for a moment then continued in a dismissive tone, 'Manetti had nothing to do with it. He's just some jerk-off Duncan knew. We needed a car to get there because we hoped to take Cosgrove's Porsche. Paul told Manetti he needed a lift round to see a guy. We left him waiting in the car.'

Lade leaned forward, casually resting his elbows on his knees. 'He's a wimp. When he saw the blood on us he went to pieces. We had to threaten to cut his balls off if he said anything to anyone. We went to his house the next day and he had the shits right up him. He disappeared after that.' Lade looked at Michael intently. 'And you're representing him?'

'Yes.'

'Where did he go?'

'He left Brisbane.'

'Right.'

Michael spoke again to forestall another question. 'Paul Duncan told the police that Joseph Manetti was involved in the killing.'

'I know.' Lade looked puzzled. 'Fantasyland. I don't know what Duncan's on about. I heard this morning he told them he thought he saw Peter Cosgrove there. Absolute crap! Duncan's a complete spinner.'

'Spinner?'

'He's not all there. A couple of sandwiches short of a picnic.'

There was something very sick about this young man expressing opinions about anybody's mental state. More than ever Michael wanted to be somewhere else. He stood up abruptly and started to round off the conversation.

'All right, Mr Lade,' he said formally. 'As far as you're concerned Manetti knew nothing until it was all over.'

'I've already told them that,' said Lade. 'Obviously, Duncan's trying to do some deal with them but I don't know what it's all about. Manetti had nothing to do with it. He was just the cab driver.'

'All right. Thanks for your time, Mr Lade,' Michael said.

Before he could turn to leave Lade stood up and spoke again, this time with some urgency. 'Wait a minute,' he demanded. 'I want to know can you represent me?'

'No, I'm acting for Mr Manetti. There would be a clear conflict.'

'Not on the Cosgrove thing.' Lade looked concerned, which was surprising given that he'd just described his part in a vicious murder without any sign of emotion or remorse. 'I've told them all about Cosgrove. But they're leaning on me about some pro who was murdered in the Golden Gate Apartments at Surfers. They say I killed her and they're starting to get pretty heavy about it. They're coming back to see me later but I can't tell them anything about it because I had nothing to do with it.'

Michael couldn't find it in himself to sympathise with Lade's predicament. 'I'll contact Legal Aid and have them get someone over to see you,' he said briskly and turned on his heel.

As the heavy metal door of the Watchhouse clanged shut behind him Michael took a deep cleansing breath. Leaving that place was like waking from a disturbing, violent dream and he wondered why anyone would want to practise in this depressing jurisdiction. It was good to sink into the leather comfort of the Volvo and pull the door firmly shut behind him. The ignition kicked over and the big engine purred obediently as a steady flow of clean air filtered through and the cassette tape clicked into position.

He drew the selector gently back into 'drive' and nosed the vehicle smoothly into Herschel Street, the manoeuvre orchestrated in concert with the civilised and civilising strains of Vivaldi.

13

Merv Harris sat at the green laminex-topped table in his kitchen, a half-shot bottle of Johnny Walker his only company. He reached across and dragged the chipped beer glass in front of him, then sloshed a shot of whisky in. He took a gulp, grimacing as the neat liquor burnt a fiery path to his gut. It was much too early in the day for Merv to take a drink, but he desperately needed one.

Young Joe was in steep shit, make no mistake about it. He had been at the scene of a murder, and he had driven the murderers to and from the job. To any cop that made him a party to the murder. And this wasn't just any murder. This was a murder that had at least a half-a-dozen senior coppers with their balls exposed. And that meant a shit-load of trouble for a lot of others. On this one they'd be playing for keeps.

It was all very well for that lawyer to be spouting a whole lot of legal bullshit about there being no admissible evidence against Joe, and claiming there was no way he could be committed for trial unless there was evidence other than the say-so of his co-accused Duncan in a Record of Interview. But that wasn't the way things went round on the streets. Evidence could always be arranged. The coppers would all know there was way too much riding on this one for them to get it wrong.

Merv gulped down another painful swallow. Nobody in the world meant more to him than that boy did. A great surge of emotion welled up inside him, tightening his chest and the thick fingers encircling the glass. His hand trembled uncontrollably, his eyes glazed, his face distorted and the ache in his chest knifed deep. Just as the glass threatened to explode, the hand eased its grip. The glass dropped lightly to the table as Merv huffed and grunted for breath.

He couldn't let it get to him like this. The doc — that mealy-mouthed, shit-faced little faggot — had warned him his ticker was no good, and he couldn't afford to blow his stack. The last thing Joe needed now was for his grandad to turn belly up. The kid was going to need a bit of rat-cunning in his corner once the dirty tricks campaign swung into action, and his grandad looked like the only one likely to produce.

It certainly wasn't likely to come from that half-baked lawyer. Merv thought about the lofty way Michael Leary had dismissed his warning that the police might have bugged Gerry Manetti's phone and might swoop on Joe and verbal him in Sydney before they could get him back.

'Come now, surely you're being a bit dramatic there,' the smart-arse, know-nothing prick had said. 'I'll notify the police that Joseph will present himself with his solicitor at the police station tomorrow. They really can't do much before then.'

Bullshit they can't, Merv thought, and he felt doubly pleased he had already warned the lad to move out of his digs for the night and book a motel room in a bodgey name. Young Leary's old man would never have counted on the coppers playing by the rules like that. Old man Leary might have been a pain in the arse, but you had to work overtime to put one over on him. Thinking all the time, he was, with more moves than a maggot in a shit-tin. In the early days that was, before the Mickey's Poolhouse case. And before the piss got to him.

Merv's thoughts drifted over a lot of ancient history and mild regrets. When he closed his eyes he saw people he had chewed up and spat out along the way. He threw his head back and drained the last mouthful from the glass. No one meant more to Merv Harris than his grandson Joe. No one ever had, so far as Merv could think.

He had never known his mother much to speak of. She cleared off early in the piece with a rodeo bloke from Blackall, and Merv had grown up with his old man and his two older brothers in a two-bedroom shack next to the railway bridge at Buranda. His old man worked at the garage through the week, pencilled at Eagle Farm on a Saturday, and spent Sunday on the piss, so the boys didn't see much of him, even before he finally went permanently chocko one night in the public bar of the Chardon's Corner pub. Merv's eldest brother Charlie never came back from the war, and after their dad died, his other brother Tom went north looking for work, and settled somewhere outside Cairns, on all accounts.

After Tom left, Merv was on his own, and that's the way it was pretty much all his life. He only married Dawn because he got her up the spout, and even though they shared a house for twenty years, they were never really together. His two daughters never thought much of him, and fair enough. When they came along he was just a raging young bull, drinking piss, rooting molls, and chasing crooks. His days were spent in courthouses and police stations, his nights in bars and on the streets. His friends were all tough, hard-nosed slobs like him, and his associates were prostitutes and druggies, crooks and scumbags of every variety, who filled his life with shit, and his dreams with misery. Merv had never let his family into his life, but then they wouldn't have liked it anyway. It was no place for women and kids. He'd been a shithouse husband, and a shithouse father, and that's just the way it was. He couldn't change that now if he wanted to.

When young Margie got pregnant at eighteen Merv blew his stack and dished out a flogging to her long-haired wog boyfriend, but only because it was expected of him as the outraged father. Fact was he wasn't surprised and didn't really care, even when she married the wog. Merv had fathered Margie, and she had grown up under his roof, but they had never meant much to each other. There was no point in wishing it was any different, because it wasn't.

When baby Joe was born in '68 Merv was only thirty-eight, and the last thing he wanted to know about was grandchildren. In 1970 Dawnie finally plucked up the courage to leave him, and of course she took young Alison with her. Merv put on an almighty turn, again because it was expected, but deep down he didn't really blame her, and he didn't really care. He was on his own, just like he'd always been.

The greatest surprise of Merv's life came when that little kid got to be about five and, out of the blue, started ringing him up, pestering him about taking him out fishing in his boat, and always wanting to come over and kick the football, or work with the tools in his garage. Merv couldn't work it out. At first he thought Margie and the wog must have put the kid up to it, but when they blew up about the kid coming home with new swear words, he realised it wasn't their idea at all. For some reason no one could work out, least of all Merv, the kid just liked his grandad.

When Merv was suspended from the police force in '77 and had nothing to do with his time but crawl up the walls, the kid spent every weekend under his feet, and even bunked over in the school holidays. They painted Merv's house together that holiday, and the little nine-year-old really was a big help. It was probably then Merv realised, for the first time that he could remember, he had someone in his life he really cared about.

Joe was a good kid. Most kids these days had no respect, and they didn't know the meaning of hard work. But not Joe. Merv was always strict with him, and he copped a thick ear when he deserved it, but he grew into a good stamp of a lad.

When Merv made the jump from the Force in '78 and bought the bait shop at Wynnum, Joe used to help him out on weekends and sometimes after school, until his parents made the move to Mt Gravatt in '83.

Merv remembered the night several months back when Joe came to the house, shaking and whimpering like a baby. Merv had coached the boy in football, and he knew he had a heart as big as a whale, so whatever was worrying him was pretty bloody serious. Joe wouldn't tell him what it was about, only that he was in big trouble and his life was in danger, and no, it wasn't something the police could help him with. He couldn't tell his grandfather, or his parents, for fear their lives would also be in danger.

Merv guessed it was drugs, that the kid had welshed on a debt to some dealer, and so they'd put the shits right through him. He'd seen it happen to plenty of young blokes before. The best thing was to get him out of town and let the whole thing blow over. The druggies would soon find someone else to fall out with, and hopefully the kid would learn a bloody good lesson out of it. So he arranged for Joe to fly to Sydney and got him a room in a boarding house, and gave him a few bob to tide him over until he scored a job with his uncle down there.

Merv couldn't believe he'd got it so wrong. Thirty years a copper and he hadn't even got close. Maybe he should have leaned a bit more on the kid and got the truth. Still, what would he have done with it?

He threw back the last splash of whisky and wondered again where and when the arrows would start flying. Joe was due back from Sydney tomorrow morning, and that Leary bloke had already notified the police that him and his client would be at Police Headquarters by 10 am.

That meant one thing for certain: in some police station somewhere at this very moment a group of very concerned and very experienced coppers was sitting around making arrows. The question was, who was going to fire them, and where would they be coming from?

When the morning flight from Sydney arrived at the Brisbane Airport on Saturday the twenty-sixth of April 1986, Michael Leary and Gerry Manetti were there to meet it.

Michael's first sight of Joey Manetti was of a youngster, little more than a child, with light olive skin and dark curly hair, dressed in a T-shirt and Levis, legs rolled up to fit, toting an over-stuffed sportsbag across the tarmac. It occurred to Michael how very young eighteen was. As Gerry, on the verge of tears, embraced his son, Michael wished that he was somewhere else.

After brief introductions, the three moved quickly to the carpark. Michael was surprised no police were in sight, given that his firm had notified them by telex earlier that morning of the flight number and estimated time of arrival. They had also been advised that Joseph Manetti would go directly from the airport to the Police Station, and, reassuringly, it appeared they were satisfied with that. As Michael drove out of the carpark, his young client beside him, Gerry Manetti in the back seat, he launched straight into the matter at hand.

'Now, Joe, these other fellows claim you were with them on the night Trevor Cosgrove was murdered. One of them says you were involved.'

'No, that's not true, Mr Leary,' the young man protested. 'I was with them but I never knew they were gonna do nothing like that.'

'I understand that,' Michael said curtly. 'Just listen up for a moment. What these fellows have said about you in a Record of Interview is not evidence against you, and at the moment the police have no actual evidence you were even there that night.'

'I was there; I drove them there,' said Manetti, his voice shrill with emotion. 'But I thought they just wanted to stop to see some guy that Paul knew. I-I never thought they were gonna do nothing like that.'

Joe's eyes filled with tears and Michael broke in quickly to avert an outpouring of emotion. 'Yes, but the point I'm making is that it seems to me that at the moment the police probably have no admissible evidence whatsoever on which to found any charges against you. The only way they're likely to get any such evidence is if you give it to them by making admissions confirming that you were there.'

Young Manetti didn't seem to be listening. 'They come back to the car with blood all over them. I thought it was some kind of a joke until I seen the knife. There was blood everywhere!'

His voice fell away and he sat silently for a moment, his father's comforting hand on his shoulder. Then he sniffled loudly, and continued. 'Peter was all pumped up. He reckoned "The guy was bleeding like a stuck pig". And Paul goes, "Did you finish him off?" and Peter reckons, "Yeah, I cut his throat".' Manetti stopped abruptly and drew in a shuddering breath.

'All right ... well, we can talk about all that at a later stage,' said Michael. 'At the moment my advice is this: you say nothing to the police about the matter except to deny that you took part in the murder. It would then be up to them to decide whether they think they have enough evidence to charge you. Frankly, I don't think they do, and if they charged you simply on the basis of what Duncan said in his Record of Interview, you'd be discharged by the first court to consider the matter. Your best course is to decline to comment at all. Are you happy to proceed in that fashion?'

Young Joseph Manetti looked far from happy, but he nodded his assent.

When Michael Leary and his client walked into Police Headquarters the atmosphere was vaguely menacing. The constable at the front desk obviously knew who they were, and when Michael identified himself the stony-faced officer waved a dismissive hand towards a vinyl couch against the wall. 'Take a seat.'

Manetti sat on the edge of the couch, wide-eyed and terrified, while Michael paced back and forth in the small vestibule. He was nervous, and curiously intimidated by his surroundings, but he tried not to show it, and traversed the floor with a measured tread.

A human wall materialised in the corridor. Three huge men stood in front of Michael, one a bull-necked, barrel-chested hulk, his short-cropped ginger hair peppered with grey, the other two considerably younger but similarly imposing giants, all wearing plain clothes and a surly attitude.

'Mr Leary, is it?' said the red-haired man in a gravelly monotone. 'I'm Detective Senior Sergeant Darryl Batch. I wonder if we could have a brief word with you before we interview your client.'

'Certainly.' Michael followed them into a large, airy office on the fifth floor.

An older man — in his early fifties, Michael estimated — rose from behind a large desk positioned against the western wall and extended a hand in greeting.

'Gidday. Inspector Mick Staines. How are you?'

'Well, thanks. Michael Leary.'

'Yes, Michael. Take a seat, mate.' Staines pointed to the two chairs in front of his desk and Michael settled in one as Staines returned to his chair. Batch strolled to the Inspector's side and perched one buttock and a large thigh on the edge of the credenza. Michael knew the other two sections of the human wall were behind him, and he could almost feel them breathing down his neck.

'Michael, I was hoping we could have a quick chat off the record about this thing,' Staines said, shuffling the papers in front of him into a neat little pile. He inspected his handiwork briefly before continuing.

'The Attorney General announced this morning that further prosecution of Peter Cosgrove is to be suspended until charges against Duncan, Lade, and anyone else charged jointly with them, are prosecuted to finality.'

Staines shifted slightly in his seat and rearranged the little pile on the desk. 'That means that the charge against Peter Cosgrove is subject to complete review, depending on what comes out of this matter.'

Staines paused again as if searching for words and Batch jumped in impatiently, 'We know Peter Cosgrove was involved, even if he didn't actually do the killing himself. He set it up. We know that.'

'That's where all our information is leading us,' continued Staines mildly. 'And we're more or less hoping your fellow might be able to assist us in that regard.'

'Quite frankly,' said Michael, 'I don't think he can.'

'Well,' Staines replied quickly as if to forestall a too-hasty decision. 'We haven't got much against your fellow at the moment. And we don't necessarily have to charge him with anything over this. Particularly if he was seen to be assisting police with the matter, he might well be considered nothing more than an innocent bystander. Now Duncan says he took part in the murder, but of course at this stage it's just his word against your bloke. So we wouldn't necessarily have to charge your bloke. But obviously what we're looking for is a bit of a show of good faith here.'

Staines shifted in his seat then continued. 'We know your fellow knows Cosgrove. They were at Valleys football club together. Now if your fellow can give us some evidence to link Cosgrove to the murder or even just to these other two, we might be disposed to treat him as being just a Crown witness.'

'You mean no charge at all would be preferred against him?'

Batch answered for Staines. 'Provided he can tell us what we need to know,' he said, stressing the 'provided'.

Michael walked along the corridor to rejoin his waiting client, struggling to understand the full import of the proposal. He was shocked to think he might have correctly understood the proposition: provided Manetti could implicate Peter Cosgrove in the murder, the police were not interested in what his involvement might have been. However Michael examined and re-examined the conversation, that's what it amounted to.

He understood the crucial significance this offer might have for his client, now and in the long term. His task was to relay the conversation objectively, neither overstating nor interpreting the words spoken, and carefully avoiding a judgement of any kind.

The young man listened closely, then shook his head firmly. 'I don't know nothing about him, Mr Leary,' he said. 'Maybe the others knew him. I didn't.'

Michael needed to know the youth fully understood what was on offer. He chose his words carefully. 'Did you ever hear them mention his name in conversation? Think about that, Joseph. You need to give it careful thought, because from what I can gather, if you can tell them anything that would help them prosecute Cosgrove, they'd probably forgo any charges against you.'

Manetti looked directly at his lawyer and shook his head. 'I know what they're trying to do, Mr Leary,' he said. 'But I can't lie about him just to save my own neck, can I? That wouldn't be right.'

Michael looked into his young client's face and saw a noble heart behind those frightened eyes. 'No,' he agreed gravely. 'I guess you can't.'

As he relayed his client's instructions to Inspector Staines and the human wall, what had been an awkward atmosphere in the room became openly hostile.

'I suppose your bloke doesn't want to be interviewed,' Batch barked.

'That's right.'

'You know Duncan positively states that your bloke was involved in it, don't you?'

'At this stage that's nothing more than hearsay in a Record of Interview.'

Batch scowled, and then, opening a folder he was holding, produced a bundle of photographs which he half-threw, half-dropped on the desk in front of Michael.

'What about them? They're not fucking hearsay!'

The photographs were an assortment of gruesome images of human savagery. Contorted human limbs and dark pools of black-red blood splashed across the glossy snapshots. One glance shocked and revolted Michael. He wanted to look away, but he knew why the burly policeman had confronted him with those awful images, and he was not about to give him the satisfaction of betraying his revulsion. He picked the bundle up and leafed through them slowly, trying to give the impression he was studiously and clinically considering every detail. His stomach turned with each new record of the butchery chronicled.

First, the twisted, blood-soaked body of a man, hands and feet bound with surgical tape, the torn and stretched binding vivid testimony to the frenzy of his last agonised moments of life. Then close-up photographs of deep puncture wounds in his chest and abdomen, from which his lifeblood had oozed and spurted leaving speckled patterns over his clothing and the pale skin below. The sickening sight of the clean slice across his throat, dragged so deeply that the head was almost severed.

Michael flicked over the final photograph and lightly drummed them on the desk into an orderly pile.

'They don't constitute evidence against Manetti,' he said coldly, extending the bundle of photographs to Batch.

'Don't they?' snapped Batch, returning the photographs to his folder. 'We'll see about that.'

Joseph Manetti was charged that day with the murder of Trevor Cosgrove and lodged in the Brisbane City Watchhouse at approximately midday. On the Monday morning Michael Leary appeared in the Supreme Court instructing Mr Julian Parrish, barrister-at-law, upon an application for bail. The application was opposed but Mr Justice Knox took into account the applicant's voluntary return and surrender to authorities, and granted him bail subject to a hefty surety and a condition that he reside with his parents until his trial.

Peter Lade and Paul Duncan were remanded in custody.

Michael rolled and tossed in a restless, fitful sleep. Finally he sat upright on the edge of the bed. Moonlight filtered through the blinds onto the body of his soundly-sleeping wife. He turned his head and studied her, something yearning, something protective stirring within him.

The bedclothes hugged Colleen's waist revealing a slender torso, half-covered, half-exposed by a thin nightgown, gently rising and falling with the rhythm of her untroubled breathing. He dwelt briefly on each loved feature — the soft, ruffled hair, the broad forehead, the short, tip-tilted nose, the slender neck, the generous curve of her breast. How peaceful she looked ... and how defenceless.

An ugly image of a blood-soaked body flashed into Michael's mind and he blinked hard to dispel it. Groaning to his feet, he stumbled to the *en suite* and splashed water on his face. He studied his reflection. *You look terrible!* How could he be so tired and yet unable to sleep?

Michael squinted against the harshness of the living room light and adjusted the dimmer. He took a glass from the cabinet and placed it on the bar, then poured a nip of Scotch. Glass in hand, he eased into the comfort of his armchair and took a sip of his drink. As it rolled down his throat he felt the muscles of his back relax.

'Are you all right?' Colleen stood at the entrance to the living room blinking against the light. 'What time is it?'

Michael checked his watch. 'Almost one-thirty.'

She laid a gentle hand on his hair. 'What are you doing up?'

Michael thought of the million painful thoughts that had been bouncing around in his brain. 'Nothing really,' he said wearily. 'I was thinking about something for work.'

'At this hour? Tell me, Michael. Something's troubling you. What is it?'

Michael's troubles were all his own and would stay that way. His wife, so untouched, so innocent, so remote from the ugly underbelly of life, would not be burdened or distressed by them.

'I'm fine, sweetheart. Don't fret. You go back to bed. It has nothing to do with you.'

Colleen ignored the patronising tone. 'If it's to do with you it's to do with me. You know that.'

'What I know is that this has nothing whatsoever to do with you,' he said brusquely. It wasn't what he meant to say, or how he meant to say it.

Colleen Leary stiffened, withdrew her hand, smiled a fixed smile and, without another word, retreated to the bedroom. Once there she lay awake, feeling somehow rejected and alone.

Michael Leary poured himself another whisky and vowed to always shield his family from the ugliness that was keeping him from sleep.

14

Michael Leary could not remember the last time he had ventured to the 'top end' of Elizabeth Street. He rarely left his office during daylight hours, except by car, or to stroll the short distance up Queen Street for morning coffee or lunch at Milano's. Not that Michael avoided Elizabeth Street, he simply never had cause to go there.

Like most of the city, the 'top end' had changed almost beyond recognition. The boarded-up windows and dingy doorways Michael remembered had given way to trendy boutiques and novelty shops. Even the old Greek milk-bar was now an establishment calling itself 'The Healthy Habit', offering banana smoothies and freshly-squeezed fruit juices of every description.

Neil Doyle had rung to ask Michael if he would mind 'popping in for a yarn', and now, as Michael strode up to the narrow entrance of the old Forbes Henderson Building, he noted that the little foyer had been tarted up with double glass entry doors and a slate floor and that a new lift had replaced the old one.

When he stepped out at the first floor he realised the tarting up had been confined to a coat of paint and a new lift. Apart from the fact that someone had recently taken the Brasso to the BM Leary & Doyle sign, the corridor looked as dingy as it had been when Michael left all those years ago.

The girl on reception was a pretty young thing for all the jet-black spiky hair and heavy make-up, and obliging. On his entrance, she looked up from her computer screen, flashed a pleasant smile and said, 'Good morning, sir. May I help you?'

'Yes. My name's Leary. I have an appointment to see Mr Doyle.'

'Oh, Mr Leary!' The receptionist seemed overjoyed to make his acquaintance. She stood up and thrust out her hand. 'I'm very pleased to meet you. I'm Sharon. I'm the receptionist.'

'Really?' said Michael, shaking the proffered hand. He was not used to this level of familiarity from junior staff. Perhaps it showed because Sharon suddenly looked flustered. 'I'll tell Mr Doyle you're here,' she said. 'He's on the phone at the moment but I'll get him.'

With that, she scurried out of sight leaving Michael alone in the reception area, conscious that the main switch had been abandoned.

At MS&G there were two receptionists and another two girls on the switch and if the front desk had ever been deserted like this there would be hell to pay. He turned slowly, soaking up his surroundings. The walls were a different colour and some of the furniture had changed but the atmosphere was still the same. When he and Dan were little kids, they would sometimes play in this room on the weekends while their dad was tinkering around in his office. They would clack away on the big manual typewriter on the front desk and push the buttons on the shiny black telephones.

He moved to the edge of the reception area and looked across to the doorway leading to his old office, then nudged the door open. The room was empty but for a round table surrounded by four squat maroon-upholstered chairs. He stepped in and looked around.

For his last three years with the firm this had been his room. He had been proud to have his own office. In those days not every articled clerk could say the same.

'Michael!' Neil Doyle's voice startled him.

'Hello, Neil,' he said, flushing with embarrassment as he shook the older man's outstretched hand.

'Did I startle you, my boy?'

'I was miles away,' said Michael. 'It's a long time since I've been in here.'

'It looks good, don't you think? We've turned it into a settlement room.'

Neil Doyle swung the door open and led the way out. 'Come on through, Michael. I'll get the lass to throw the billy on. What will you have?'

'Just black coffee, thanks Neil.' Michael knew that in this office the choices began and ended with Indian tea or instant coffee.

'I see you're branching into crime over there,' smiled Neil, as he settled back into the leather chair behind the oak desk. 'I've been reading all about you in the papers. Must be the first criminal job your mob's done in a while.'

'This is a one-off. A favour for a good commercial client. That's all.'

Neil Doyle threw back his head and laughed. 'Be off with you! You Learys just can't help yourself. 'Tis the Irish in you.'

Michael felt a little uncomfortable at that and was glad to see the office junior arrive with a tray carrying two cups of coffee and a small plate crowded with an assortment of biscuits. She unloaded the tray onto the desk and withdrew.

Once she was gone Neil Doyle picked up a dog-eared document from the desk in front of him and pushed it across the desk. 'That's his will.'

'I beg your pardon?'

'It's Brian's will. Take a look at it.'

Michael looked down at the small folded paper. In the top corner were the words: *The Last Will and Testament of Brian Michael Leary*. It was written on light-blue will paper which was bent at the corners and creased in the middle as though it had been folded up and stuffed haphazardly away. Typical of Brian, he thought. Wills are important legal documents that should be secured in safe custody, not stuffed in the bottom of a drawer somewhere.

'I'm not interested, Neil,' Michael said. 'I don't want anything from him.'

The older man looked at him, sadness in his eyes, then leaned forward in his chair and studied his own hands which were cupped together on the desk in front of him.

'Well, Michael,' he said eventually, 'you may not be interested but I am — vitally interested. Have a look at the first page.'

Michael looked again at the little blue sheet, reluctant to touch it, then he reached out and unfolded it until the document lay flat. His practised eyes processed the contents. When he finished he refolded the will and pushed it away from him.

'He's left you his share of the practice, Michael,' said Neil Doyle. 'It's yours whether you want it or not.'

Michael raised his cup, sipped, then replaced it on the saucer deliberately. Neil was a fine man; he would not insult him for the world. 'I'm sorry, Neil, but I don't want it,' he said at last. 'You draw something up and I'll sign it over to you.'

Neil Doyle's bushy eyebrows met in a frown. 'You don't want to turn your nose up too quickly, Michael,' he said. 'This place might not be as flash as what you've been used to lately but at least it's all paid for.'

Michael could hear the injured pride in his voice.

Doyle waved a hand towards the door. 'There's over forty thousand in computers out there in the typing pool. We've still got one of the best probate practices in Queensland and there'd be well over two hundred grand's worth of work-in-progress in our litigation files alone. There aren't too many firms that can make that claim.'

Michael could readily think of half-a-dozen. The equity partners at MS&G would find such figures risible.

'Sorry, Neil,' Michael said, striving for a light touch. 'But I've no intention of ending your new-found career as a sole practitioner.'

'Now, just a moment, Michael,' the older man said stiffly. 'There's more involved here than whether all this happens to suit your career aspirations at the moment, you know. Your father and I spent the last thirty-five years building this firm. Until a few weeks ago, BM Leary & Doyle was the longest-standing partnership of original make-up in Queensland. In my book that's a record to be proud of! Certainly not one to be dismissed out of hand. To have a Leary in the firm again would continue a proud tradition.'

Neil Doyle stopped abruptly and adjusted his tie, embarrassed by his ardour.

'It certainly *is* something to be proud of,' said Michael patronisingly. He picked up his cup and sipped politely.

Neil drank from his cup too, and the two men sat for a time, saying nothing.

'Your Dad's had that office in there waiting for you to come back to for the last ten years,' Doyle said. 'He told me more than once, "Michael will get whatever's troubling him out of his system. He'll be back before we know it".'

He was wrong there, Michael thought.

'There's no way I can extend the life of this firm much longer. I've got another two years of practice left in me at best. After that she'd be all yours.'

'It's a lovely gesture, Neil,' Michael said, trying to select words that would not hurt a man he respected.

'You have a think about it,' the older man broke in, as if he didn't want to hear what Michael had to say.

'Sure.' Michael nodded thoughtfully as if there was something to consider and then, glancing at his watch, said, 'I'm afraid I really have to go.'

Neil Doyle led Michael through a quick tour of the office. When they returned to reception, he saw him off with the dignity of an elder statesman.

Neil was insulted, Michael could see that. A wall was going up and he wanted to dismantle it, but he did not know how.

When they shook hands in the reception area, the older man smiled warmly and said how good it had been to see him again. Michael walked out into the corridor, wishing he had not come at all. He had just pressed the lift button when he heard Neil call after him.

'Michael.' Neil was walking down the hallway carrying a small cardboard carton bound with pink legal tape. 'This is yours.'

Michael took the dusty carton in both hands and held it, careful that it did not brush against his expensive suit. Through a thin layer of dust appeared in bold print the inscription, THE PROPERTY OF MICHAEL JOSEPH LEARY — PRIVATE AND CONFIDENTIAL, written in black marker pen.

'Don't ask me what it is but your Dad had it packaged up like that. I don't know how long it's been there.'

Michael looked at the dilapidated package. Probably just loose papers and other rubbish he had abandoned in his desk drawers and behind the filing cabinets when he left the firm. Michael was about to suggest it be consigned to a rubbish bin in the office but thought better of it. He and Neil Doyle had already lost some ground that day; it would be better to find a bin somewhere else.

'Right. Thanks, Neil.' Michael nodded and Neil Doyle returned the gesture. 'Listen Neil, I, er …' Michael didn't know quite what to say to this man he had known all his life.

'Not at all, Michael,' said Neil, tapping him lightly on the shoulder, his fixed smile failing to disguise the sadness in his eyes. 'Not at all.' Then, as if help had come to him from an unexpected quarter, he added more cheerfully, 'Here's your lift.'

The door of the new elevator slid smoothly open. Michael stepped in, pressed the button, then turned to see the door slowly closing on Brian Leary's oldest and closest friend.

15

The Manetti case was the first real criminal matter Michael Leary had had anything to do with in over ten years. He'd handled a couple of drink-driving cases for some of the firm's commercial clients but had not come near a serious criminal case since he left Leary & Doyle.

Not that there would be much in this one. The only thing implicating Manetti in the murder was Duncan's statement to the police. Unless Duncan got into the witness box and repeated the statement in evidence, it was nothing but inadmissible hearsay. And Duncan was a defendant in the proceedings and so unable to give evidence for the Crown.

The committal proceedings were listed for hearing in the Brisbane Magistrates Court on the sixteenth of June. A magistrate would decide whether there was sufficient evidence to justify sending the defendants for trial before a judge and jury in the Supreme Court. There was plenty of evidence against Duncan and Lade but as far as Michael Leary could see, there was no admissible evidence against Manetti to justify his committal for trial.

He would make that simple point to the magistrate, who would undoubtedly react accordingly and discharge Joseph Manetti.

Michael was pleased to learn that committal proceedings had been simplified so that there was no need to call all of the witnesses. The prosecution could simply supply copies of the witnesses' statements to the defence before the hearing and if the defence agreed, the magistrate could accept those statements in lieu of oral testimony. If the defence wished to cross-examine any such witness, it could notify the prosecution accordingly and the witness would be made available for cross-examination at the hearing.

This suited him perfectly. He received copies of the police statements well in advance of the hearing, which allowed him to confirm that there was no admissible evidence against Joseph Manetti. Paul Duncan's confession implicated each of the other defendants and, curiously, had included an assertion that he had heard Peter Lade mention Peter Cosgrove's name in conversation and he thought 'they might have had some sort of business association'. He had also claimed that when the three of them left the murder scene together, he had seen a young man who looked like Peter Cosgrove standing on the balcony.

Peter Lade had made a full confession and had taken part in a video-taped interview with police in which he took them to various locations relevant to the incident and described in detail what had happened.

There was certainly plenty of independent forensic and other evidence to tie Lade and Duncan to the crime. Items of Trevor Cosgrove's property were found in their possession. Their fingerprints matched prints lifted from various locations throughout Cosgrove's apartment. Two knives had been reliably identified as the weapons that had inflicted the fatal puncture wounds to the torso of the deceased. These had been located in a storm drain by following directions Peter Lade gave in his police interview.

The only one against whom there was no confessional material or forensic or any other admissible evidence linking him to the murder in any way was Joseph Manetti.

When Michael read the police brief for the first time, he could not help but congratulate himself on the way he had handled this matter from the outset. His recent inexperience in criminal matters didn't seem to have handicapped him in the least.

If the police had been able to get to Manetti without his lawyer, Michael told himself, he almost certainly would have admitted being at the scene and that would have had him committed for trial on a charge of murder.

As it was, there was no confessional material alleged against Manetti and there was no forensic evidence to implicate him in the crime. Either Manetti had not been involved in the killing or, if he were involved, he had been careful enough to leave no tracks. To Michael it didn't much matter which. Either way this was a straightforward legal exercise involving a simple application of the evidentiary rules relating to the admissibility of hearsay assertions. Since the prosecution case against Manetti at the committal proceedings relied entirely on such assertions, the law was quite clear and its application quite simple: the assertions were not admissible evidence and there being no other evidence against Manetti, no *prima facie* of guilt could be established and the magistrate must discharge him. The question of his guilt or innocence did not come into it. There was simply no admissible evidence against him.

In this case, Michael told himself, the question of Manetti's guilt or innocence was irrelevant and so should be ignored. To do otherwise would require him to consider whether his client had participated in the butchery depicted in those awful photographs.

Michael Leary was happy to conclude that was not his function.

'Got a minute?'

Michael so rarely saw Tony Artlett in the office these days that he was surprised to see him peering around his door. Tony's office was on the next floor up — the Promised Land, as Michael thought of the equity partners' domain — and he rarely strayed into the underworld.

'Sure Tony. Come in.'

Artlett went to the 'conversation end' of the office, unbuttoned his suit-coat and seated his lean frame in one of the armchairs positioned around a long, low coffee table.

'You've been a busy boy lately. I've been hearing good things.'

'Yeah, things are happening,' said Michael, as he left his desk to join his friend. 'Should I order coffee?'

'No, I can't stay,' replied Artlett. 'I just dropped in to tell you there were some very favourable comments about you at the partnership meeting last night.'

'Really?'

'You've been doing some good figures lately.'

Michael liked the tenor of the conversation. 'Better still to come, I think. Bruce Dawson is starting to hit his straps. He looks like doing some big things over the next twelve months. And there'll be substantial fees in that Springwood development for Brentnalls, and in that Callide deal. So I expect to write some pretty big numbers.'

Artlett did not pursue it further. Instead he said, 'What's this I hear about you doing a criminal case?'

'Pardon?'

Artlett's smile had faded. 'A criminal case. Someone was saying last night that you've accepted instructions on a murder trial.'

The incredulity in Artlett's voice obliged Michael to justify himself. 'Oh, that,' he said dismissively. 'That's more or less a favour to Bruce Dawson. It's the son of his top man, Gerry Manetti.'

'You know this firm doesn't normally accept instructions in criminal matters. And I gather this one is likely to attract some media attention. We can do without that kind of publicity.'

'It couldn't be more straightforward,' Michael assured him. 'The young fellow's been charged but the evidence doesn't support a case against him. It will simply be a matter of a submission to the magistrate at the committal proceedings and that should be the end of it.'

'Still, it's not the sort of thing we should be involved in, is it? Surely we could refer it off to one of the criminal firms.'

'I recommended that but Gerry Manetti's very keen for me to stay with it, Tony. If I ditch him now it could well affect our relationship with Dawson.'

Tony Artlett wasn't satisfied. 'Do you want me to sound out Dawson for you?'

'No I don't!' The cheek! Michael knew what would keep his clients happy and the last thing he needed was Tony Artlett's silver tongue intervening.

The response was emphatic enough to convey his resentment and Artlett did his best to mollify him. 'I'm just trying to help you, Michael,' he said. 'I know you have aspirations to go further around here. In that as in other things, I'm your biggest ally. But some of the partners are very conservative and they don't want the firm's good name dragged through the criminal courts.'

Michael considered that. Tony Artlett was an old friend, not such a close friend these days, but, without doubt, his oldest friend. If anyone would help him enter the Promised Land, it was Tony. He was doing no more than warn him of the possible consequences of the course he had embarked on and for that he should be grateful.

'I'll make sure our involvement ends at the committal.'

'I'd rather see you out of it altogether,' replied Artlett as he slid out of his chair and moved towards the door. 'Got to go,' he said, glancing at his watch. 'Can't keep the big boys waiting.'

Michael straightened his legs and stretched his back against the soft leather. The bottom line is what really matters, he thought, and the bottom line was that the sooner he was out of this the better.

The whole thing shouldn't take more than about an hour. That was the view of Mr Julian Parrish, barrister-at-law. 'We go in, make our submission and get out. All very low-key.'

It sounded safe enough. And Parrish had no interest in prolonging the matter. 'The last thing I need is for people to think I've taken to crime,' he said with a shudder as they shared strong black coffee over Parrish's antique mahogany desk. 'But it really is quite a simple submission.'

It seemed straightforward enough and, after all, Julian Parrish was as eager as Michael to keep the Martin, Schubert & Galvin hierarchy happy. Most of Parrish's work came from the firm, mainly in commercial litigation and intellectual property work. He was not about to put any noses out of joint. Michael knew that and it made him feel secure and comfortable.

However, he felt decidedly uncomfortable when Parrish telephoned him two days before the Manetti committal was scheduled to start, to say he was caught up in a Federal Court matter that looked like spilling over for several days and he was afraid he might not be available to do the committal. He was most apologetic and offered to send over the summary of his intended submission but Michael felt vaguely uneasy about his late withdrawal and more than a little exposed.

The die was cast and there was nothing for it but to get the committal over and done with. He would appear himself without a barrister and in accordance with Parrish's advice, he would get in, deliver Parrish's submission to the magistrate and get out.

When he arrived at the Central Courts Building on the morning of Monday the sixteenth of June, Michael saw three television vans parked outside the courthouse and journalists, photographers and news cameramen milling around the steps of the building. The proceedings were to start at ten and he had hoped to avoid the press by arranging to meet his clients inside the building at nine but this morning the paparazzi were off to an early start.

Joseph Manetti was standing outside the lifts on the first floor, flanked by his parents. His pallor contrasted with the darkness of his suit. Judging by the way he tugged at his tie and fiddled with the buttons of his jacket it had been bought especially for the occasion. His parents looked no more at home than their son and the three of them huddled together in silence.

'I'll talk to Joseph alone if I may,' Michael said as soon as greetings had been exchanged. He led his young client into an interview room and closed the door.

They sat opposite each other at the table and Michael stepped through the details of the submission he would make to the magistrate.

When he finished, the young man shrugged his shoulders. 'I don't know about any of that, Mr Leary. I just know you'll do your best for me.'

'I will.'

'I never knew they were going to do it, Mr Leary,' the young man said. 'Whatever happens to me, I want people to know that.'

'You leave it to me,' Michael reassured him. 'I'll make them understand.'

16

Graham Worrell was prosecuting. Worrell had spent his whole career with the Crown, initially as a clerk and later as a barrister and Crown prosecutor with Crown Law and then as a senior prosecutor for the newly-appointed Director of Prosecutions. Committal proceedings were usually handled by a police prosecutor. The appointment of a prosecutor as senior as Worrell underscored the highly sensitive nature of the Cosgrove affair.

Since his release from prison, Peter Cosgrove had made several media appearances calling for a full judicial investigation into his arrest and prosecution. He claimed he had been beaten, threatened and bullied by police for hours until he finally agreed to sign a statement confessing to his brother's murder. The public were outraged that such a thing could happen and once the case was concluded there'd be no restraint on Cosgrove's complaints and accusations.

Duncan and Lade were both represented by Ron Forbes of the Public Defender's Office. Forbes had sought from the prosecution and received in advance copies of all statements and other evidence to be tendered at the hearing. He had subsequently announced prior to the hearing that he did not wish to cross-examine any of the witnesses at all. He would consent to the prosecution statements being tendered in evidence against both clients and would make no submission contesting their committal for trial.

Michael met Forbes for the first time outside the No 5 court at about five-to-ten. He was a short, rotund man whose green and gold tie clashed violently with his blue sports coat and brown slacks, which were unflatteringly slung below the widest circumference of his broad girth.

Forbes wasted no time in expressing his views on the case. 'No point in cross-examining anyone here,' he said. 'Complete waste of time. They've got signed statements, fingerprints, the works. These boys are ratshit. They might be able to deal for manslaughter upstairs but there's not much point in wasting any time here. What's your view?'

'I'm planning to make a submission on my fellow.'

'Yeah?' Forbes considered that for a moment then nodded thoughtfully. 'Yeah, I suppose there's not so much on your bloke, is there?'

'There's nothing at all,' said Michael coldly.

'Except that Duncan says in his statement that Manetti was in it up to his neck.'

'That's hearsay.'

'Geez, that's right, I suppose,' replied Forbes. He pondered on that for a moment and then conceded, 'Yeah, that's worth a submission.'

'I think so,' said Michael dryly then moved into the courtroom.

The three defendants were already in court. Manetti sat in the gallery with his parents, staring at the empty bench the magistrate would soon occupy. Handcuffed together in the dock sat Paul Duncan and Peter Lade.

Peter Lade sat bolt upright against the wall — a well-groomed, refined-looking young man but for the mocking, glacier-blue eyes. Next to him, Paul Duncan was in perpetual motion, shifting, turning, fidgeting, squirming at every development around him. He seemed delighted to be the centre of attention. Michael moved quietly through the crowd and whispered to his client to join him at the bar table.

Graham Worrell opened his case by calling Senior Sergeant Darryl Batch through whom he tendered the statements of the other prosecution witness and all the exhibits. It was purely formal evidence and as soon as the various items were admitted into evidence, Worrell resumed his seat.

'Cross-examination, Mr Forbes?' said the magistrate without looking up.

'No, Your Worship,' piped Forbes.

'Mr Leary?' mumbled His Worship.

Michael had not asked for Batch to be made available for cross-examination but now there were some questions he wanted to ask. He had promised Joe to 'make them understand,' and making a few points for the public gallery's benefit now would be a first step in achieving that aim.

'Senior Sergeant Batch,' he commenced, his voice by no means as firm and confident as he expected it to be. 'You first sought to question Mr Manetti on the twenty-fifth of April this year, didn't you?'

'The day we learned that he'd been in on the murder, that's right.' Batch had been in this game for over twenty years and with a full press gallery like this he wasn't about to miss the opportunity to score off a novice like Michael Leary.

'You mean the day Duncan claimed that to be so,' corrected Michael.

'Duncan and Lade both told us the same thing. Manetti was the look-out, the "cockatoo" if you like.'

The assertion could not be sustained on the evidence and if Michael had been more comfortable in his role he would have challenged it. Batch sat back and relaxed. It was almost too easy.

'All right,' continued Michael tentatively. 'You went to the house of Geraldo and Margaret Manetti and you told them you were anxious to speak to their son about the Cosgrove murder, is that right?'

'I wanted to do a lot more than just talk to him!' The line was delivered with great gusto for the amusement of the paparazzi who lapped it up with obvious delight.

'In any event,' said Michael quickly in a voice loud enough to drown the snickering, 'within twenty-four hours you were notified of Mr Manetti's whereabouts and of the fact that he intended to present himself to the police as soon as possible.'

'We were told that he had skipped to Sydney and that he'd decided to come back, yes.' Another cheap shot.

'Yes, and ever since then he has cooperated fully, hasn't he, in terms of presenting himself to police and so forth?'

'No, he has not.'

Michael had led with his chin and he ought not to have been so surprised when Batch struck it as forcefully as he could.

'I beg your pardon?'

'He most certainly has not cooperated. He refused to answer any of our questions. That's not what I call cooperation. He knew all about that murder and he refused to say a word.'

Michael could feel the sweat starting to collect on his forehead. 'He returned immediately and at his own expense from Sydney and presented himself promptly to Queensland police, didn't he?'

'I'd say he discovered that we'd tracked him down to his Sydney address. He knew we were right on his tail.'

Batch was most likely lying about having Manetti's Sydney address and for a moment Michael agonised over whether he should challenge him on it but then he retreated, letting another blow slide through to its target.

'When you interviewed Mr Manetti at Police Headquarters on the twenty-sixth of April,' continued Michael retreating to safer ground, 'he denied having been in any way involved in any act of violence to the deceased or in any plan to commit such an act. Isn't that so?'

Batch wasn't about to concede the point. 'He refused to answer any of our questions.'

Michael's handkerchief mopped up a few beads of perspiration from his forehead. 'That's not quite correct, is it? He declined to answer questions generally, but he did make a statement that he had not been involved in any violence to the deceased. Isn't that so?'

'He was there and he was involved,' Batch insisted. 'We already knew that from what the others told us. All your client did was deny the whole thing. That was after he had a chance to plan the whole interview with his lawyer. What would you expect?'

This wasn't going as Michael expected and he sought some reasonable point to escape on. 'Nevertheless, he did deny having been involved?'

'Yeah, he denied it.'

At last, an answer that didn't leave him reeling. 'And that's the only evidence you have against Mr Manetti in this matter, isn't it?'

Batch paused before answering and for one agonising moment Michael wondered what would come next from this belligerent man. To his relief, Batch answered simply, 'That's the only evidence I have, yes.'

Michael had suffered too much to allow the point to pass without some emphasis. 'A denial of any involvement?'

'Yes.'

'Thank you, witness,' Michael said then sat down. He tried to look cool and collected, ignoring the ache in his neck and back and the beads of sweat rolling freely behind his collar and onto his chest. He felt good about his last point but he felt as if he'd been through a wringer.

'Your Worship, I have one more witness,' announced Graham Worrell, rising to his feet again. 'It's proposed that he'll give full evidence.'

The magistrate seemed to be even more surprised by this announcement than Michael was and for the first time since the proceedings began he seemed to come alive and peered studiously over his glasses at the prosecutor. 'Have you canvassed with defence counsel the question of whether they would consent to the witness's evidence being received in statement form?'

'No, Your Worship,' said Worrell emphatically. 'I don't intend to give either of my friends a copy of the witness's statement. I intend to call him to give full evidence.'

A murmur rolled through the public gallery and the expectation of an unscheduled witness prompted a rustle of notepaper and a shuffling of feet in the ranks of the press. It was unusual these days for witnesses to be called to give full evidence at a committal hearing, and the fact that this one was unheralded suggested something significant was about to occur.

'I call Arthur Bruce Kent.'

The words boomed out with theatrical clarity, to the obvious amusement of Ron Forbes who, sprawled in his chair, quipped, 'What's this, Graham, a secret weapon?'

Worrell looked down briefly at his seated opponent with a grin that contained more venom than humour. 'Just a little surprise witness for you, Ron.'

Forbes slid over towards Michael. 'This sounds like a bit of a stiff-arm to me,' he whispered. 'It's got to be for your bloke. My two are already stitched up.'

Michael had no idea what Forbes was alluding to. He dismissed the comment, returning to the notes he had added to Julian Parrish's outline of argument. Yes, the punch was in the final paragraph — *for the purpose of assessing whether a* prima facie *case has been established the magistrate can act only on material which is admissible in accordance with the strict rules of evidence.* He underlined it with a red pen. As soon as the prosecution closed its case he would ask the magistrate to discharge his client.

Thus occupied, Michael did not notice the burly frame of Arthur Bruce Kent lumber past the bar table and climb into the witness box. He was a broad, rawboned man in his early fifties whose sun-ravaged, craggy face might have belonged to a man of the land. But when he spoke he had the hard twang of the city in his voice, a voice so belligerent that it captured Michael's attention immediately.

'My name is Arthur Bruce Kent,' the witness asserted, as if to challenge all comers for that title.

'You were an inmate of the Brisbane City Watchhouse on the night of the twenty-seventh of April this year, is that so?' said the prosecutor.

'I was,' the witness growled.

'During your stay in the Watchhouse, did you have contact with any of the three defendants now before the court?'

'Yeah, that bloke there I did.' Kent waved a thick finger in the direction of Joseph Manetti.

Michael leaned across to his client. 'Do you know this fellow?'

'I think so,' replied Manetti guardedly. 'He's the old bloke they put in the cell with me.'

Worrell continued, 'Did you have any conversation with the defendant Manetti at that time?'

'Yeah,' replied the witness.

'Would you kindly relate to the court to the best of your ability the conversation which you had with the defendant on that occasion?'

'Yeah,' replied Kent, leaning back in his seat and resting one elbow on the side of the witness box. 'We was in a cell together and I asked him "What are you in for?" and he said "Me and me mates knocked off that Cosgrove bloke".'

Michael's head was spinning. Here was a confessional statement directly admissible against Manetti and it had just hosed his legal argument right off the table. The liferaft he had totally relied on had suddenly sprung a leak.

He could hear Joseph Manetti's whispered protestations that it was not true, that he had said nothing of the sort to Kent, that he had told everyone in the cells he was on a drink-driving charge, but Michael was taking little of it in. His head was throbbing. He knew he had to do something, but what?

'I was kind of interested 'cause I'd read about it in the papers and that,' continued Kent as casually as if he were chatting over a neighbour's fence. 'And I said "I thought his brother was supposed to have knocked him" and he reckoned "Peter set it up, but they can't pin nothing on him".'

'Did he say how the murder was committed?'

'He reckoned that at first they were just going there to flog the bloke's car and do him over a bit. But when they got there they decided to knock him.'

'What did he say in that regard?'

'I just told you. He reckoned he was in the car at first and then one of his mates called out to him and he's run over and they've all just put the boot into the bloke. Simple as that.'

As the evidence rolled on Michael tried to collect his thoughts, to think how he should respond, what he should or could do to defend his client from here and — this was important — how to avoid total embarrassment to himself.

Joe Manetti was whispering urgently to him and although Michael was nodding and punctuating the outpouring with an occasional comment his thoughts were not synchronised with his actions but were running in other directions, trying to settle on an effective, or at least respectable, line of cross-examination.

Joseph Manetti would now surely be committed for trial and the only thing his lawyer could hope to salvage was his own self-respect.

'Thank you, Mr Kent,' said Worrell eventually as he resumed his seat and then glanced at his opponents at the other end of the bar table.

'No questions, Your Worship,' mumbled Forbes without looking up from his doodlings.

'Mr Leary?' said the magistrate, peering over his glasses.

'Ah, yes, thank you, Your Worship.'

Michael was on his feet, still with no idea where he would start. He could almost feel the hot breath of the gallery on his back fuelled as it was by the knowledge that this was a witness whose credibility must surely be challenged.

Unbelievable! A nice neat legal point had turned into a complete nightmare, and now all he wanted to do was to pass from public gaze with some semblance of dignity.

'Mr Leary?' repeated the magistrate.

'Yes, thank you, Your Worship,' replied Michael, prodded into action. Then, without further thought, he looked at the witness for the first time and asked his first question, 'Mr Kent, why were you in the Watchhouse?'

Kent said nothing for a moment but simply glared at Michael with an intimidating scowl.

Michael suddenly felt calm and focused. He returned the insolent gaze unwaveringly. This man was perjuring himself and Michael Leary was determined he would not get away with it. Lawyer and witness glared at each other until Kent finally looked up to the magistrate.

'The coppers picked me up on a warrant for breach of bail.'

'Bail for what?' Michael had forgotten the gallery. Now he wanted to know the answers.

Kent curled his lip and looked back at his questioner momentarily, then turned again to the magistrate to deliver his response. 'Just a couple of charges on some cheques I wrote.'

The more the witness avoided his gaze the more Michael was determined that his treachery would not succeed. 'You mean fraud charges, do you, Mr Kent?'

The witness addressed the judge, not Michael. 'I just wrote some cheques, Your Worship. They reckon I never had enough money in my account to cover them or something.'

Michael was angered by the man's dishonesty and his own passion surprised him. 'Fraud!' he snapped. 'That's what you were charged with, wasn't it? Fraud!'

Kent's eyes swung back to the lawyer. 'Yeah,' he said.

'How many fraud charges were you facing, Mr Kent?'

Now they were eye to eye again, the street-fighter scowling threateningly at the puny challenger facing up to him. 'I dunno. A few.'

Kent was sitting back in the witness box, his chin thrust forward pugnaciously. His eyes darted fleetingly from his interrogator to the gallery and back and a trained ear might almost have heard the cogs whirring in his brain. The practised survivor was searching for just the right moment to regain the ascendancy, as his young challenger surged forward blindly in his passion.

'A few? You must have some idea how many.'

'Mate, I told you. I wouldn't have a clue. You'd have to ask the coppers. They're the ones that charged me.'

A faint snicker of amusement rose from the public gallery, putting a tiny nick in the dialogue, a breach just big enough for Kent to get his toe into, and he recognised it immediately.

Michael paused momentarily, conscious once more of his audience. 'But you were there. Surely you know what you were charged with.'

'Mate, are you Perry Mason or something?' returned the experienced showman with perfect timing. 'I told you, I dunno.'

The response had the desired effect, with several audible chuckles from the back of the courtroom dissolving any tension Michael had established. They were amused by the apparently spontaneous objections of a colourful old rogue. Kent had instinctively homed in on his opponent's weakness — inexperience.

Michael blushed at the thought that his inexperience as an advocate was transparent to all in the crowded courtroom. He must sound like a novice mimicking the theatrics of a television drama. The whole public gallery must be laughing at him. Why did he ask such a stupid question? Michael's mind went blank and he leafed back and forth through the papers on the lectern searching for nothing but his own train of thought.

The witness's eyes narrowed as he watched the young lawyer squirming at the bar table. He had scored a direct hit and he knew it. He was on top of this young bloke now and he'd been around long enough to make bloody certain that he stayed there.

'Have you any previous convictions for fraud?' Michael said at last.

'No,' replied the witness without a moment's hesitation.

It was an answer Michael did not expect. He looked up at Kent disbelievingly, but the witness boldly returned his gaze.

'What? You have no prior convictions?'

'None.'

The answer was delivered with such conviction that it seemed to echo around the courtroom.

Michael blushed again, almost ashamed to have suggested such a thing and was about to lower his eyes to the lectern when he saw a tiny, almost imperceptible change in Kent's expression. The eyelids cramped closer just a fraction and Michael focused on them. Kent was perfectly still and Michael looked deep into his defiant eyes. The eyes widened slightly and then the corners of the mouth curled almost imperceptibly. Both men knew what game was being played.

'In any event, you've been charged with a number of fraud charges, haven't you?' Michael had forgotten the public gallery; it was one on one again.

'Yeah, I've been charged,' replied the witness. 'But I've pleaded not guilty to all of them. Because I'm not. A bloke's still presumed innocent until he's proved guilty, isn't he?'

Michael neither heard nor saw the reaction of the public gallery if there was one. All he heard was the answer and all he saw was the smug, self-satisfied look on the face of a witness he knew to be lying, a witness who would single-handedly see Joseph Manetti committed for trial on a charge of murder. The two men looked at each other. They both knew what game was being played and they both knew who had won this round.

'Yes. Thank you.'

As Michael sat down Graham Worrell climbed to his feet and declared the prosecution case closed. Darryl Batch sat at the end of the bar table next to him, his beefy shoulders merging into his thick neck. He caught Michael's eye and the corners of his mouth twitched in a derisive grin. Michael looked away. Batch was telling him it was his game they were playing and he made the rules.

Michael rose to his feet. 'Your Worship, could I ask that the witness Batch be recalled for further cross-examination?' he said almost without thinking.

Batch's grin faded.

Graham Worrell had no objections and the magistrate grudgingly ordered the witness recalled.

Batch strolled to the witness box, faced the magistrate to be reminded that he was still under oath, then settled back comfortably.

'Witness, you were aware of the evidence the witness Kent was to give in these proceedings?'

'I was.' Batch's cold stare was so intimidating it unsettled the questioner. When Michael spoke his voice had little of the strength he had hoped to muster.

'When I questioned you earlier you told me that Mr Manetti's denial was the only evidence you had.'

In contrast, Batch's reply was prompt and confident. 'That's right.'

'At the time you knew of the evidence of Kent?'

'Yes.'

'So you lied under oath?'

'No, sir, I would never do that,' returned Batch self-righteously. He appeared slightly bewildered and a little hurt, and then proceeded to explain. 'You asked me earlier if I had any further evidence,' he said. 'Obviously I can't give evidence as to what your client told other people in the Watchhouse. That would be hearsay, Mr Leary. I know I can't give hearsay evidence. I thought you'd be aware of that.'

With that the humourless grin reappeared. Batch had made his point.

Michael had come to these proceedings to teach the police a simple lesson about hearsay evidence but he had learned that nothing was quite that simple.

'I see,' he said limply. 'I take it you're not aware of any other evidence against my client?'

'I am.'

'I beg your pardon?' It was an answer Michael had not expected.

The witness adopted a more challenging pose. 'Your client was evidently very proud of his handiwork. He told several people in the Watchhouse about it.'

Joseph Manetti was whispering frantic denials to his lawyer but Michael pressed on. 'What people?'

'An undercover police officer for one,' replied Batch, glancing across to the public gallery where the members of the press were now frantically scribbling. 'Sergeant Reagan. I think he even got a tape-recording of their conversation. And Manetti told two other inmates as well.'

Suddenly Michael had doubts. Batch was talking about tape-recorded confessions and three or more people who would implicate his client. He turned to Manetti who was looking up at him imploringly.

'That's bullshit, Mr Leary,' the youth whispered, earnestly shaking his head and fighting back the tears welling in his eyes.

'What are the names of these other inmates?' Michael said to the witness, wondering whether he should ask or not.

'Let's see,' replied Batch, obviously enjoying himself, 'Well, one was Kent of course. And I think the other one's name is Rays. I didn't interview him myself but if I remember correctly it was Stanley John Rays.'

Michael was shell-shocked, not knowing whether to ask another question or not. Every time he opened his mouth the case against his client seemed to grow worse and he was suddenly haunted by the time-honoured warning given to fledgling advocates to avoid asking 'one question too many'. Michael had a sinking feeling he had badly breached that golden rule.

'Are these people to be called to give evidence here today?' he ventured at last.

'No sir,' said the witness. 'We don't have to call all our witnesses at this stage, as you would know, Mr Leary. We only have to make out a *prima facie* case. Your client will hear from the rest of our witnesses at trial.'

Batch's stare was now so powerful and overbearing that Michael was overwhelmed by the desire to end their exchange as quickly as possible. 'Thank you,' he said lamely and sat down.

By eight-thirty that night Barry Reilly was starting to feel a little uncomfortable.

The boys had been on the turps since they left court at about midday and most of them had piss dribbling out of both ears. Barry could see that Batchy had 'let go of the rope' and was going to have a big one that night, so things could get ugly. He had been on the rum all afternoon and now he was ordering doubles, standing at the centre of the group of detectives, propped against the bar, his glazed eyes ranging around the room looking for trouble. And, Barry Reilly knew, he'd find it soon enough.

Barry drifted towards the door waiting for an opportunity to slip out unnoticed. Half the Inala CIB was there along with a good few of the Homicide boys, and they were all as full as a state school hat-rack. All except young Mitchelson, who was just starting his first stint out of uniform, and looked about as comfortable as a ham sandwich at a bar mitzvah. Mitchelson didn't drink much so he had been hanging around all day like a stale bottle of piss waiting for the troops to drive back to Darra. He was perched on a stool nodding dutifully and trying to laugh at all the right times. No one really trusts a bloke who doesn't drink so Mitchelson would always do it tough in plain clothes.

Barry knew he wouldn't be missed so long as he slipped out quietly. The boys were getting very boisterous and now that Batchy had that look in his eye, Barry knew it was time to bow out. He had been in enough shit lately with this Cosgrove business and he could do without any more drama.

As he moved to the end of the bar, Barry looked back at the bull-necked redhead leaning against the bar. There wasn't a better copper alive than that big boofhead. What he'd done with this Cosgrove case was beautiful and now Barry was starting to hope that him and the others who had charged Peter Cosgrove might come through it unscathed.

All three defendants had been committed for trial that day and all the press could talk about was the fact that according to Duncan's story Peter Cosgrove was somehow involved in his brother's murder after all. That took the heat out of young Cosgrove's call for an inquiry and with a signed confession there'd be no chance of any charges being laid against any coppers out of it. The way it was looking now Barry and the others might just sneak through by the skin of their arses.

If they did they could thank Batchy for it. He had joined the Force later than Barry but they were about the same age. Batchy had stood out even when he was still in uniform. He was always fitter, and faster, and had more balls and natural rat-cunning than anyone in the job. And when it came to the dirty work out there on the streets, no one came within cooee of Darryl Batch. Barry put it down to his Army background. His old man had been a career sergeant in the regular Army for something like thirty years and probably Batch would have been too, except he got three of his toes shot off at Nui Dat and got shipped home from Vietnam in '67 with a medal and a medical discharge.

He was already twenty-one when he joined the police force which was considered pretty bloody old in those days but from day one he was totally committed. Sometimes he could get a little bit crazy but all those vets were like that. He was as staunch as they come and there was no better bloke to have in your corner when the heat was up.

George Curran saw it right from the start and took him under his wing. George had a way of recognising the blokes who understood what real loyalty was all about.

As Barry Reilly slipped quietly out through the front door he didn't notice the couple who caught the swinging door and forged into the little bar. Darryl Batch did. The girl was a long-legged, stringy blonde in her early thirties, her handsome features prematurely hardened by late nights and hot lights. Her shapely body was barely covered by a skintight mini-dress that advertised her profession as well as if she were carrying a neon sign on her back.

If anything, she looked more robust than her companion, a scrawny, spidery man wrapped in a leather jacket and black stovepipe jeans. His pasty skin contrasted with his black clothes and long, greasy hair. They stopped dead in their tracks when they saw the drunken policemen, then without missing another beat they made a beeline for the back door.

'G'day, Margie,' bellowed Batch.

'G'day, Darryl,' replied the girl without deviating from her path.

With that some of the others in the group hooted derisive comments but she and her partner continued steadily across the bar and out through the back door.

'Don't you stop to mag with your old chinas any more, Margie?' Batch shouted. 'Why don't you ditch the faggot and come and have a drink with us?'

Margie's companion fired back a frail token of defiance by holding up one grubby finger which he quickly withdrew as the door swung shut behind them. Batch pulled himself unstuck from the bar and leaned forward until his big red head was inches from young Mitchelson's face.

'Come with me,' he muttered then strode deliberately towards the door followed by the younger officer.

As Batch burst through into the long corridor leading to the toilets, Margie and her companion were hastening through the far door out into the alleyway at the rear.

'Oi!' barked Batch and the two stopped dead in their tracks, Margie one step into the alleyway and the spider framed in the doorway looking back at the advancing enemy.

As Batch strode down the corridor towards him, the spider said, 'Fuck off and leave us alone!'

A second later Batch struck. His head lunged forward and smacked against the spider's forehead with a sickening thud blasting him into the darkness of the alleyway where he landed in a bundle on the gravel. A neat pink slice appeared above his eye and the hands that clutched at it were soon covered in thick, red blood.

'What did you fucking say to me, you grubby cunt?'

The wounded man cowered, his knees bent to his chest and his arms wrapped tightly around his head. Batch raised his heavy boot and stomped it down on the bundle of arms, shoulders and head, bouncing his victim off the bitumen with a grunt.

'Don't you dare fucking talk to a copper like that, you little arsehole! You understand me?'

The package on the ground remained tightly wrapped and made no answer. Batch curled his lip and bared his teeth and kicked wildly at his prey.

Mitchelson stood wide-eyed in the darkness of the alleyway, every muscle in his body on edge, his chest pumping painfully. He did not like what he was watching and the grunt of each kick dragged him closer to the precipice until Margie intervened. She stepped forward, her rough, husky voice bathed in genuine concern.

'Come on Darryl, leave him, mate,' she said, reaching out towards Batch without touching him. 'He never knew youse was coppers.'

Batch stopped kicking and stood puffing in the darkness. 'Bullshit he didn't!'

He stood over the cowering bundle as if wondering what to do with it. 'Don't you ever talk to a copper like that again, you understand me, you little shit!' He emphasised his point with a final kick, then turned to the girl with a sneer. 'Is this maggot supposed to protect you when you're turning tricks?'

A tough, street-wise smirk drifted across Margie's face as she looked down at her cowering associate. 'He's nearly as useless as youse blokes. But I don't have to pay him as much.'

Margie had always been a little too half-smart for her own good but Batch liked that, and Margie knew it.

'He probably gets more snatch than we do though.'

'You've had your share.'

Batch's eyes moved hungrily over the woman's body. Margie could see Batch was pissed and he was angling for a free root. She was willing to accommodate him so long as he didn't want to look through her handbag. She and the spider had just hit up a little taste and she still had enough smack in her handbag to get them both in plenty of trouble. One hand settled on her hip and as the burly detective advanced on her she cocked her head at a flirtatious angle and held her ground. Without warning Batch spun around and swung a heavy kick that connected heavily with the curled-up bundle on the ground.

'Piss off, grub,' he grunted.

The spider scuttled into the darkness and disappeared.

'Let's have a look at those tits of yours,' he said pulling roughly at the press-studs on Margie's dress so that her ample breasts spilled out into the dim light of the alleyway. She was wearing no bra and the sight of those magnificent, naked, vulnerable breasts sent a tiny shiver of pleasure through Mitchelson, despite himself. He was standing back in the darkness wondering whether to step in and try to stop what was happening or sit back and enjoy the show.

Batch pulled the other studs free and slipped his hands on to the woman's naked hips, pushing and rolling her panties down over her slender thighs. Mitchelson shifted uneasily, part outraged, part stimulated.

'Hang on,' pleaded Margie, struggling to keep her footing. 'Bloody hell, don't rip them!'

Batch released her long enough to unzip his fly and in that time she stooped and slipped her panties off and into the handbag draped over her shoulder. Then he came at her again like a charging bull barrelling her back against the wall. She grunted as her back struck the tin cladding behind her and then he wrapped his big hands around the back of her naked thighs and hauled her abruptly and violently off her feet.

'Oh shit!' she groaned in obvious pain as he thrust forward once, and then again, and again, ramming her body against the rickety wall.

In the filtered light Mitchelson could see the big man's half-naked hips surging forward again and again, pumping mechanically like the piston-rods of a great engine.

Each time the girl grunted and groaned as if in acute pain. On and on it went until eventually her arms and legs hung limply around the detective's huge frame, her only sign of life the soft *o-o-f* she sighed each time her back slapped against the cladding.

Eventually Batch gave a long, loud groan followed by several short, sharp, violent thrusts ramming the woman's limp body heavily upward and back until she groaned again, the sound muffled against her assailant's chest.

Then they were still, their bodies propped against the wall. Batch released the woman's thighs but she remained oddly suspended against the wall, her legs wrapped loosely around his knees. Then he lifted and pushed her against the wall and stepped back, adjusting his trousers and zipping his fly as the girl slid down the wall and crumpled into an awkward squat.

Mitchelson watched him standing over the woman's misshapen body, her legs bent and spread, her tousled hair falling over her lowered face as she panted, trying to regain her breath. He felt immensely powerful, masterful.

As they stepped back into the lighted corridor Darryl Batch wrapped a heavy hand around the back of the younger man's neck. 'We own these fucking streets!' he growled with a look that paralysed his young companion. 'Not the fucking shithead lawyers. Not arseholes like that out there in the alley. Us! The coppers!'

They were standing so close that Mitchelson could feel the puff of the older man's rum-soaked breath on his face.

'Don't ever forget that. And don't ever let them forget it either.'

Mitchelson stood open-mouthed, mesmerised by the intensity of the moment.

'You understand?' asked Batch insistently.

The young man nodded eagerly. 'Yeah, I understand.'

'Good,' said Batch, straightening up and swaggering back down the corridor. 'Let's go and get pissed.'

17

'Frankly, I suspect he's as guilty as sin,' said Julian Parrish as he sliced a sliver of avocado fastidiously and placed it neatly in his mouth.

Michael looked up from his entree and waited patiently while Parrish carefully chewed, then swallowed gracefully.

'Two of his own friends say he was involved. This Watchhouse evidence confirms it, doesn't it?'

In the elegant surroundings of the restaurant it all seemed to make perfect sense. Michael placed another oyster on his tongue. It slipped down smoothly, chased by a cool wash of Chardonnay.

'I'm sure that Kent fellow was lying though,' he demurred.

'Perhaps,' Parrish conceded. 'But, even if he were, there appears to be no dearth of other evidence.'

Michael savoured the briny flavour of another oyster and took another mouthful of wine. 'What do you think I should do with it?'

'Frankly,' said Parrish, 'I think you should withdraw immediately.'

'Ditch him?'

'I wouldn't put it in quite those terms.' Parrish looked pained.

Michael helped him out. 'Terminate my involvement?'

'Precisely.' He held Michael's gaze for several seconds then renewed his dalliance with the avocado, speaking softly as he did so. 'After all, you took it on as a favour to his father because you genuinely thought the justice of the situation required it. But now that it's obvious the lad was in it up to his neck surely they can't expect you to remain in it.'

As Parrish placed another slice of avocado in his mouth and chewed precisely, Michael wondered whether he had ever considered 'the justice of the situation'. He could not remember having done so and he did not recall Parrish ever having mentioned it.

'I mean really,' continued the barrister, 'they've known all along that MS&G don't do crime. You were only going to take the matter on to get them through the arrest stage.'

That's true, thought Michael, and he began to compose the lines of the script that would explain his withdrawal to his client. *A very serious criminal matter ... it called for someone with considerable experience in criminal law ... It was only fair to his client that he refer the matter on to someone who practised regularly in that field.*

'In any event,' said Parrish, 'I should tell you now, make my position perfectly clear, I can't see myself getting embroiled in a lengthy criminal trial like this. I've got far too much on my plate.'

So Parrish was refusing the brief, as tactfully as possible of course, but refusing it nonetheless. This was Michael's first experience of a barrister turning down a paying brief, and Parrish was more acquisitive than most.

'No,' Parrish said. 'If this thing goes to trial as a three-header it could last a month.' He glanced up briefly to meet his companion's gaze then returned his attention to his plate, adding, 'You'd be well-advised to wash your hands of it.'

The waiter lifted the wine bottle from the ice-bucket and refilled their glasses.

Parrish was right. If the Manetti matter went to trial with three accused, it would take a long time and there was no way Michael could afford to be out of the office for an extended period. Gerry Manetti of all people should appreciate that.

In the sedate atmosphere of those elegant surroundings, amidst the polite hum of luncheon chatter, the subdued sparkle of heavy silverware and the faint rustle of starched napery, it all made perfect sense.

It was after nine when Michael arrived home. The afternoon had been unexpectedly hectic and by three he had started to regret those wines over lunch. A problem had blown up with the major tenant in the Springwood development and he had spent over four hours in conference with their solicitors and accountants trying to bed the whole thing down. By the time they adjourned for the evening his eyes were strained and weary and he had a slow, persistent throbbing in his forehead. A nip of Scotch had taken the edge off his tension but as he pulled into his driveway, his mind seemed overburdened.

Kent was lying; of that he had no doubt. He had seen it in the man's expressions and reactions. Seen it, sensed it, known it. And if Kent was lying, someone had convinced him it would be to his advantage to lie about Manetti. That humourless grin of Detective Senior Sergeant Darryl Batch left Michael in no doubt who that someone was.

He dragged himself wearily from the car and walked to the boot, opened it and pulled his heavy briefcase out. He was about to drop the lid when he noticed the small cardboard carton bound up with pink legal tape and bearing the inscription, THE PROPERTY OF MICHAEL JOSEPH LEARY — PRIVATE & CONFIDENTIAL.

He'd meant to dump it but it still sat in the boot, a load of rubbish taking up space.

He placed the briefcase on top of the box then lifted the combined bundle out, closing the boot lid with his elbows and forearms. As he staggered into the house Colleen looked up from where she was curled under the light of the lamp beside the family room sofa.

'Hi darling,' she said, closing her book over a forefinger. 'You're late.'

'Yeah,' he grumbled as he backed into the study, pushing the door open behind him. 'Shit of a day.'

He meant it. He knew the Springwood hiccup wasn't the main stress factor. He normally thrived on such situations, relished the cut and thrust, the adrenalin rush, the give a little here, take more than a little there, until resolution was reached. No, it was the Manetti thing, rumbling around in the back of his head all afternoon like distant thunder.

Ditching it really was the only sensible thing to do. It was getting terribly messy; he couldn't afford the time it would take and, most important of all, the partners wanted him out. It would be madness to rock the boat now when the equity partnership he'd been angling for these past three years was within his grasp. He couldn't think of a single rational reason to stay in it. And yet, for reasons unknown, his wretched brain refused to let it go.

Michael dropped the box on the floor in front of his desk and returned to the family room. He bent over briefly to kiss his wife then collapsed into his favourite chair.

Nods and grunts and an occasional comment acknowledged Colleen's recital of the daily news while his brain followed its own wayward course. Colleen was talking about a function at the tennis club next weekend but Michael was thinking about that derisive grin on the face of Detective Batch and Arthur Kent's truculent glare. He heard himself saying to his pathetic, frightened client, confidently, hearteningly, reassuringly, 'I'll make them understand'. What on earth possessed him to say that?

Colleen was on her feet heading for the kitchen. Yes, thanks, he'd love a cup of coffee.

He closed his eyes and breathed a long deep breath that eased the tension in his neck and shoulders. He was suddenly bone-weary ...

His mind drifted away, back to the Camp Hill house. He was sitting on the back steps, whimpering from the thrashing he'd copped from the Farrow brothers for having tried to stop them bullying little Denny Ryan from next door. He recalled his mother's gentle comforting. And then Brian, climbing the steps in his rolled-up shirtsleeves, his grey felt Akubra perched on the back of his head, asking what had happened and listening gravely to the reply. Then taking his right hand in his, shaking it, man-to-man, and saying, 'Two of 'em, eh? Well done, lad. Well done.'

Michael's eyes opened at the sound of a clinking spoon.

'There was something about that Cosgrove thing in the paper today,' Colleen said, as she delivered a cup into his waiting hand.

'Did you keep it?'

'Yes,' she called. 'It's on your desk.'

Michael quickly digested the article. Following 'revelations made' at the committal proceedings of three men accused of the murder of Trevor Cosgrove 'it is believed that senior police are now considering whether to recommence prosecution of the dead man's brother, Peter Cosgrove, for the murder'. According to the article, 'senior police' now believed there was sufficient evidence to charge Peter Cosgrove jointly with the other three men, 'as a party to the offence'.

Michael tried to make sense of it. Were they serious, or was this just newspaper talk or another tactical ploy to take the edge off public outrage about the Peter Cosgrove allegations?

His brain sagged under the weight of it. It was a complicated game they were playing and the rules seemed to change from day to day.

'So, did you decide whether you're going to do the trial?' said Colleen, her hand on his shoulder.

Michael sat back in his chair. His foot brushed against a cardboard carton bound with pink legal tape. 'No way in the world,' he said wearily. He propped his heel against the carton and pushed it against the wall, neatly out of sight and out of mind.

The Springwood development conference reconvened at 7.30 the following morning over coffee and croissants and by ten they had tweaked the numbers, crunched the deal, and everyone was happy. All that was needed now was for the lawyers to 'wrap paper around it', and it was agreed that Michael would shoot the draft amendments through to the tenant's solicitors that afternoon. He emerged from the boardroom feeling good — in control, doing what he did best.

As he dropped into his chair he reached for the phone with one hand and for his telephone messages with the other. He leafed quickly through the messages as he waited for his secretary to answer his call. He'd ask her to ring Gerry Manetti and make an appointment for him and his son to come in for a conference. But as his secretary answered Michael flipped to a message that stopped him in his tracks. It read 'Mr Forrest would like you to meet him for lunch in the beer-garden of the Spring Hill Hotel at 1 pm today. He has some information for you regarding Arthur Kent'.

'Noela, who's this Mr Forrest?'

'He says you acted for him some time ago. He rang several times while you were in conference. Finally, he left that message and said that if you could meet him for lunch he had some information about some fellow. His name should be on the message.'

'Kent, yes.'

Intriguing. Michael could not remember a client called Forrest. 'Did he leave a telephone number?'

'No, he just said he was in town and he'd like to meet you for lunch if you could make it.'

Michael trudged up Edward Street and asked himself why he was doing this. Lunch with a long-forgotten client, especially one who professed to be an associate of Arthur Kent, was sure to be a painful experience. He'd been around long enough to know better. He asked himself, too, why he had postponed arranging the appointment to end his relationship with the Manettis. He just had to know more about this whole affair. But curiosity can be a dangerous thing for a young man going places.

Michael had never been in the Spring Hill Hotel before but he expected it to be much like any other older-style inner-city pub and it did not surprise him. It had that yeasty smell and the noisy chatter of a knockabout crowd that casually leaned on anything upright.

'Hello, Mr Leary. Johnny Forrest. Remember me?'

Forrest was a bloated bullfrog of a man, not tall but with a massive barrel chest and a solid potbelly flanked by two powerful forearms splotched with faded tattoos. His ginger-grey hair was cropped so short he looked almost bald. He appeared to be in his late fifties but his podgy face and beady eyes had the impudent look of a mischievous schoolboy.

'No, I'm afraid I don't,' said Michael, accepting the extended hand.

'John Francis Archibald Forrest,' the man replied pumping Michael's arm in a vigorous handshake. 'Receiving stolen property. *Circa* 1972. Me and Kevvy Howe were pinched for a boot-full of Windsor Smiths. Remember?'

'Oh, yes, Mr Forrest,' Michael replied struggling with a vague recollection of the man as one in the endless procession of seedy characters that filed in and out of his father's office. 'You were one of my father's clients.'

'That's right, God love him,' said Forrest. 'But drop that "Mr Forrest" shit. That was my old man and he's long gone, poor bugger.' Forrest laughed infectiously. 'Me, I'm just plain John, mate.'

'Yes, John,' Michael said politely and then added, somewhat reluctantly, 'Call me Michael.'

'Good on you, matey.'

Forrest called to the bar attendant, 'Hey, Nance. Can't complain about the service, love. What's your poison, Michael?'

When Michael Leary drank alcohol over lunch these days it was usually the right wine to complement fine food. He decided on a beer.

'What'll it be, darl?' asked the middle-aged bottle blonde behind the bar.

'Love, I'll have two beers, a kiss on the lips and a coupla quid from the till, thank you very much.'

He erupted into a volley of laughter and Nance cackled in harmony. 'You'll have to settle for one out of three,' she said as she grabbed two glasses and moved to the taps.

'The story of my life, love.' Forrest turned back to Michael. 'Yeah, Mike, I was with your Dad a lot of years. He pulled me out of some shit too, I can tell you.' His voice was reverent. 'By the way, matey, I heard about his passing and I was very sorry to hear it. He was a champion little bloke, your old man. One of God's own.'

With that the beers arrived and Forrest bounced back into his banter until Nance moved on to another customer.

'Here's luck,' said the big man, tipping the glass back until almost half the contents drained away. Then he smacked his lips and added, 'Yeah, he was a mighty little bloke, your Dad. Ten stone dripping wet but a heart the size of the Story Bridge. Never once saw him take a backward step.' He thought about that for a moment and added approvingly, 'He beat that receiving blue for me. Remember?'

'Yes,' lied Michael, sipping his beer.

'That silly old bastard Rolly Penthurst pinched me for it,' Forrest chuckled. 'He dropped the biggest brick since the Fall of Rome on me, fair dinkum. And didn't your old man give him some curry in front of the magistrate!'

Forrest's big frame shook with laughter at the recollection.

'You were with my father for quite a while then, were you?'

'Oh, yes mate,' said Forrest. 'I was a terrible fucking tea-leaf as a young bloke, before I went into the Navy, like. When I come out in '58, mate, the coppers just wouldn't leave us alone. That's when I first came across your dad.'

'What business were you in then?' Michael regretted the question as soon as he had asked it. But Forrest didn't seem at all fazed by it and continued without missing a beat.

'Oh, a bit of this, that and the other,' he said. 'I come up the hard way see. Learned how to spot an opportunity, sort of thing. Had a gift for it. I've sold the Opera House to a couple of blokes in my time. But, mate, I never dudded any bloke that wasn't dead set begging to be robbed. Greed, it's a bloody beautiful thing, old mate.'

Forrest erupted into another great burst of open-mouthed, body-shaking laughter, so contagious that Michael had to join in despite himself.

'Truth is, the best quid I ever made was out of the SP, and let's face it, that's just about legal. Only problem was, I couldn't stand them whinging bloody punters. Mate, couldn't some of those bastards put on a performance if they lost. Enough to drive a bloke back to thieving!' He thought about that for a second then looked up from his beer and rattled off another peal of laughter.

Michael chuckled along with him, genuinely amused by the performance of this big, brash, bullfrog of a man. He wondered how his father had reacted to him, how he would have handled the man's theatrics and his unabashed opportunism.

As Forrest chatted on, and talked about his skirmishes with police, and with the punters, his days at the track, and out on the road 'selling success', his exploits in the clubs and restaurants and the courts of law, the question of legality seemed largely irrelevant, except in so far as it meant a court appearance or the possibility of a night in the Watchhouse. Michael wondered how this had sat with Brian Leary's fierce commitment to the law and all things legal. And yet there was a kind of fundamental morality about this man that seemed to have something to do with 'coming up the hard way', and being loyal to those who had done likewise, which Michael fancied might have struck a chord with Brian. Forrest spoke reverently of Brian as a man who 'fair dinkum took time for the little bloke' and Michael guessed that he had thereby fitted neatly into a morality of loyalty to those who had 'come up hard'.

At Forrest's suggestion they decided to 'swerve the sit-down job' and opted instead for a steak sandwich at the bar. The big man chatted incessantly, regaling his companion with stories of how his father had 'stuck it to' some policeman or other or stood up to some magistrate or judge. Michael was intrigued by Forrest's picture of his lawyer, a dimension he had never factored into his own conglomerated picture of the man who had been his father.

From time to time they were interrupted briefly by passing patrons who would slap Forrest on the back and rattle off a quick-fire 'G'dayJohnnyhowy'goin'mate?' or stop for a short exchange about 'a sure thing on Saturday at Eagle Farm' before moving on. Everyone, it seemed, from the publican to the bouncer, from shady-looking characters with tattoos and gold bracelets to the natty salesmen in pink shirts and leather ties, knew Johnny Forrest and liked him.

They had been together more than half-an-hour before Forrest came to the point. 'I see where that grub Kent dropped a brick on some young bloke for the Cosgrove murder.'

'Do you know Kent?'

'Mate, he's as low as they come. He'd dead set get under the two of clubs, that bloke would.'

'What do you know about him?'

Forrest curled his lip. 'I know he's a fucking dog.'

Michael remembered enough about prison jargon to know a 'dog' was an informant and considered to be the lowest of the low.

'He's been giving blokes up with bullshit for years. Why do you think the coppers had him in the Watchhouse that night?'

'Do you think he was planted there?' It was a thought that wouldn't have occurred to Michael a week ago.

'Mate, I wish I had a certainty like that for the Melbourne Cup.'

'Has he given evidence before?'

Forrest scoffed at the question. 'Listen, matey,' he confided. 'Kent dropped a remand yard verbal on Jimmy Friar for the bookie heist back in '72 and pulled himself a deal on some major fraud charges. When he's landed back in Long Bay a couple of years later on another fraud blue, he was that scared of getting bashed for being a give-up that he's lagged a couple more blokes just to get himself out again. He can't afford to go back inside.'

'But he said under oath he had no prior convictions.'

That prompted another hearty laugh before Forrest controlled himself sufficiently to say, 'Mate, he's appeared more often than the Virgin Mary. That arsehole Batch would have set it up. The coppers are in shit up past their eyeballs over that Cosgrove thing and they'd figure on using Kent to drag them out of it. That city lockup must have looked more like a kennel than a Watchhouse that night, there was that many dogs in there, dead set!'

When Forrest had exhausted his store of information he promised he would 'put out a few feelers' and see what else he could find out. When they shook hands on the footpath shortly after 2.15, Michael felt obliged to offer to pay Forrest something for his assistance but the big man shook his head vigorously.

'Turn it up, mate,' he said. 'No, mate, I'm here because of a bonzer little bloke called Brian Leary. He done me a lot of good turns. If Johnny Forrest can ever help you or yours, just give me a yell.'

As Michael Leary walked back down Edward Street to the city that day, he turned over in his mind some very interesting information about Arthur Kent, and about a man called Brian Leary. He also thought how very dangerous curiosity could be for a young man going places.

Michael was not surprised when Tony Artlett dropped into his office for the second time in a week. Ostensibly he'd come to have a friendly chat about the likelihood of MS&G expanding their equity base within the next quarter by bringing in at least one new equity partner. But soon the subject turned to the Manetti case.

'I hear you've decided to refer it on to one of the criminal firms.'

'Who told you that?'

The response seemed to surprise Artlett. He raised his eyebrows. 'Julian Parrish, as I recall.'

'When?'

'Last week. I happened to run into him in Queen Street.'

Michael had spoken to Parrish only yesterday and he did not recall telling him he had made a definite decision.

'And what did he say about it?'

'Nothing of consequence.' Artlett's eyes examined Michael's tie, then raised to meet his. 'He simply said he'd decided he wasn't going to do it and that he didn't think you should either. Naturally I agreed with him.'

'Naturally,' said Michael dryly.

The equity partners were suddenly showing a lot of interest in this case. All this fatherly concern from Tony

Artlett was wearing a bit thin and Artlett's uneasy shifting in his chair did nothing to dispel Michael's suspicion that he was not getting the full story.

There was a prolonged, embarrassed silence.

'And why might that be, Tony?' Michael said eventually in a tone that did nothing to disguise his scepticism.

The pregnant pause persuaded Artlett it was time to put his cards on the table. 'Look, I'm not going to beat around the bush,' he declared. 'As far as I'm concerned the whole Cosgrove thing is a disaster waiting to happen and we should be out of it, right out of it, this minute.'

The belated rush of candour seemed to spur him on and he continued with even more vigour and conviction. 'You know as well as I do that if that Cosgrove person succeeds in his push for a Royal Commission to investigate his allegations, it's going to be a major headache for the government.'

'So what?' The offhand reply was calculated to inflame his companion.

Artlett's fingers drummed a tattoo on the armrest of his chair. 'Do you have any idea how much the state government pays in legal fees to this firm every year?' he asked. 'It's vital to preserve that connection. I've spent hours in the past few weeks down at the Premier's department massaging the Callide deal and I can tell you unequivocally they're all extremely sensitive about this whole issue. Extremely sensitive.'

Michael could not quite see the connection. 'Fair enough,' he acknowledged. 'But the Cosgrove allegations are a separate issue. Manetti has no connection with Cosgrove. He says he's never even met the fellow.'

Artlett shook his head patronisingly, then leaned forward. The thick bifocals enlarged the calculation in his hazel eyes. 'Michael, get it firmly in your head: the whole thing's a time-bomb and if it goes off, anyone within a bull's roar of it is likely to get his bloody balls blown off!'

Tony wasn't given to such colourful language. He was obviously convinced that there was a great deal riding on this thing.

'Anything from this trial that vindicates Peter Cosgrove spells deep trouble for the police and that means deep trouble for this government.' Artlett studied his fingernails for a moment before continuing less vehemently. 'They've held power all these years on the law-and-order platform. They can't afford a Royal Commission into the police force. If we're seen to be supporting Cosgrove in any way — and representing Manetti will be seen as support, make no mistake about that — we can kiss goodbye to any more government work.'

Each one of us must choose a side. The words sprang unbidden into Michael's mind. He brushed them aside to consider the import of what Tony Artlett was saying.

He was making sense. The Cosgrove allegations had been extremely damaging to the government already. People wanted to know what was really happening behind police station doors.

The whole controversy had reinvigorated perennial allegations of corrupt police practices. It had even dredged up a lot of ancient history, like the allegations made by the prostitute Gaye Welham in the sixties that certain police were operating a protection racket for prostitutes and SP bookmakers. Gaye Welham might have gone away but her story hadn't, and the Cosgrove affair had brought it crashing back into the press, along with a myriad of other allegations embarrassing to the police and, consequently, to the Government. The Opposition was having a field day in Parliament, even going to the extreme of suggesting the current Commissioner might be less than squeaky clean. It had all been very damaging to the government, mainly because of its strong support for the police force, and vice versa. So the Cosgrove affair was as much an embarrassment for the politicians as for the police.

The power-brokers in the government had undoubtedly breathed a sigh of relief when the Kent evidence hit the headlines, and there was no doubt it had taken the real sting out of the push for a Royal Commission. Now that it appeared that Peter Cosgrove might have been involved in the murder after all, the Opposition had dropped off him completely, at least for the time being, undoubtedly waiting to see what might come out of the evidence at trial before hitching their wagon to a cause that could blow up in their faces.

The talk in the press about the possibility of Cosgrove being recharged meant that no one, the Opposition included, was likely to touch the Cosgrove allegations with a barge-pole, at least not until the trial was over and the dust had settled. A moratorium had been unofficially declared, thanks to Arthur Kent's evidence. Cosgrove and his lawyers were still agitating for an inquiry but the political wind had gone out of their sails and unless the current cloud of suspicion hanging over Cosgrove as a result of the statements of Kent and Duncan could be blown away, the impetus would never return.

Kent's evidence had been a masterstroke, a solution to deficiencies of proof and at the same time a panacea to the problems of both police and politicians.

Michael knew Tony Artlett was right. Anyone who did anything to discredit the Kent account would be seen as an enemy of the government. The government power-brokers would staunchly resist any move for an inquiry that could well topple them and they would curse anyone who added fuel to the Opposition's fire.

Tony Artlett had a fine nose for a political wind as well as the intellectual skills to master a situation and turn it to his advantage. He had made his point forcefully and Michael was convinced.

But if Artlett lacked anything it was the ability to factor in irrational emotion. It was probably that failing that caused him to continue now when he would have been better served to hold his tongue.

'I took the liberty of speaking to Bruce Dawson,' he said. 'I told him I want you out and he doesn't have a problem with that. He's happy to see Manetti referred to another firm.'

Michael felt a stab of resentment. Artlett had elected to teach him how to suck eggs, even if that meant going to Michael's best client behind his back. The master negotiator had stitched it all up and all his non-equity partner had to do was flick the kid on to another solicitor.

'Well actually,' Michael said evenly, his face a mask, 'I'm not sure Manetti wants to change solicitors.'

Artlett was white with suppressed anger. 'We can't terminate our retainer without his consent,' he said tersely. 'But I want you to persuade him as a matter of urgency, Michael. I want us out.'

Artlett stood up and walked, stiff-backed, out of the room without another word.

Michael fumed. How dare Artlett go around orchestrating the affairs of one of his clients behind his back? What about the interests of the client? What if it just so happened that the kid was innocent?

He dragged his *Legal Directory* in front of him and flipped it open to 'Barristers', skimming down the list, looking for names he might recognise as knowing something about crime. The first thing he had to do was work out where this bloody case was heading and that meant talking to someone who could give him and his client some reliable advice.

He ran his finger down the list, occasionally jotting down a name and number. He flipped to the last page and scanned it in a single glance. His eyes bounced back to the name at the top of the page. It read 'Sullivan, E P'.

Michael remembered a tall, imposing figure, a mellow, compelling voice and an agile mind. He held the page open, weighing up a dozen different considerations. Then he reached over and picked up the telephone.

'Jesus, Frank, the problem's solved,' said Tom Wilson as he stuffed another prawn into his already crowded mouth and continued munching.

Frank Delaney MLA had not touched a morsel on his plate. He was known in political circles as a ruthless head-kicker who could handle anything the Opposition threw up at him, but today he looked vulnerable.

'I can see that, Tom,' he whispered hoarsely. 'But how long's it going to stay solved?'

Delaney glanced around the riverside restaurant. Waiters were scurrying back and forth and the clink of plates and cutlery and buzz of the lunchtime crowd assured their privacy. Still, Frank Delaney was far from happy. He slipped a monogrammed handkerchief from his pocket and mopped his brow. As an ex-copper he knew that a crowded restaurant was as discreet a place to exchange confidences as any on earth but since he had taken on a ministerial portfolio he had not been comfortable with these public meetings with high-ranking police and his old mate George Curran. He had to protect his public image and certain inferences could be drawn from meetings with such companions.

George Curran swallowed a mouthful and said mildly, 'Why don't you let us handle that, Frank?'

'Listen, George,' Delaney continued, 'we can't leave it to a Coroner. If even a sniff got out we'd all be fucked! You know that, don't you?'

George Curran was sawing carefully through a choice eye fillet. He shovelled a morsel into his mouth, his cold grey eyes skewering Delaney's.

'What's that you've got there, Frank?' he said, still chewing. 'Chicken, is it? Looks good.' He swallowed and then pushed another piece of steak into his mouth. 'Why don't you eat your chicken, Frank?'

Delaney turned to Wilson. After all, he *was* a Minister of the Crown. 'Tom, I don't care how many blokes you put on it, you've got to pinch somebody for this one as soon as possible.'

George Curran looked mildly irritated. He put his knife and fork down on his plate with a decisive little clatter. 'Frank,' he growled malevolently, 'Tom just told you. The problem's solved.'

Frank Delaney looked at old George Curran and knew the topic was closed. Whatever the solution was, and right now George was probably the only one who knew, it was all in hand. He had seen that look in George's eyes a hundred times before and he knew exactly what it meant. The problem was solved.

Frank lifted a gleaming silver fork and sank it into the soft white chicken breast.

18

As Eugene Sullivan settled into his chair he could feel every bone in his body creak. He stretched one arm across his desk and tore off several calendar sheets until he settled on Wednesday. This was his first day into chambers this week and when he saw the date on the little sheet he smiled wryly. *The twenty-fifth of June, 1986.* Exactly forty years to the day since his admission as a barrister-at-law.

He looked around the book-lined walls of the little room in the Inns of Court he had owned since 1965 and tried to recall the names of those admitted on that day with him. *Let's see — Charlie Carlisle, Brandis, Horrie Allen, Maxted, Dinny O'Grady, Ambrose Freeman — half of them dead now; the rest retired.*

Sullivan opened a packet of Craven As, dragged the silver foil cover strip from the box, rolled it into a ball and lobbed it into the metal wastepaper bin in the corner.

As he clicked on his lighter and dragged in that first long, longed-for breath, he opened his first brief in three weeks, in the matter of *R-v-Manetti*.

Eugene Sullivan had forgotten more than most of the young fellows would ever know about the criminal law but he was no longer fashionable, it seemed, and, though highly regarded, he was rarely briefed. The work that did come almost invariably came from the Public Defender's Office, the hardest cases done for the worst clients at rates that barely covered the rent. And at Sullivan's age, it was getting harder and harder to stoke the fire in his belly.

He leaned back into the worn leather of his chair and glanced around at the thousand dusty books that had been his friends and family and had kept him poor, he told himself, for all these years. Every man has his day in the sun, he mused, and the sixties were the years when Eugene Sullivan could have made some real money, just like these young fellows did today.

His best years, when he was undisputed leader of the criminal bar, were now two decades gone. The bitter memory of the painful years since then pushed uninvited into his mind ... his son's death, the divorce, those ugly, hurtful arguments tearing at each other's dignity and emotions and the lost days and nights on the drink or immersed — enmeshed — in the misery of others. His later life had been a disaster. He knew it and so did just about everyone else in town. He had married badly and he had divorced publicly. In the law it was forgivable to be a drunk but not a public embarrassment.

'Sully, what are you doing in here?' The greeting came from Colin Robinson, a tubby fellow who had been a member of their chamber group for several years now and whom, despite his relentlessly cheery disposition, Sullivan rather liked. But not first thing in the morning.

He glanced up briefly at the man at the doorway, then returned to reading the brief. 'I keep chambers here,' he said dryly. 'Have done since 1965. Hadn't you noticed?'

Robinson was far too agreeable a man to be put off by Sullivan's crusty response. He chatted on about the news of the last few days and eventually settled one fat buttock on the edge of the older man's desk. Sullivan looked up for a moment, his face pained, and then returned to his reading.

Robinson stemmed the flow. 'Are you in court today or something?' he ventured cautiously.

'I detect a note of incredulity,' said Sullivan. 'I do get the occasional brief, you know.'

Robinson stood up, embarrassed. 'Have I offended you, old chap?'

'Not at all,' Sullivan said, looking up from his brief. 'I'm simply feeling particularly crotchety this morning, having bounced off the last three stairs of the upstairs bar at the Majestic last night.' Then added, as something of an afterthought, 'Pissed, of course.'

He looked up through his imposing eyebrows and said, 'And the answer to your first question is also no. I'm not in court but I have a conference with a solicitor starting at nine and I've yet to read the bloody brief.'

'Fair enough,' Robinson said, backing out the door. 'I'll get out of your hair. And I'll let Mrs Martin know you'll have your morning coffee.'

'Right,' said Sullivan as Robinson retreated, closing the door gently behind him.

Michael Leary arrived at the Inns just before nine and having announced himself to the receptionist, sat on a rickety chair in the poky little reception. It had been years since he had been in this squat little three-storey building which was soon to be demolished and replaced by a high-rise commercial office building. Michael looked around at the general shabbiness and thought that redevelopment of the site was long overdue. With CBD prices climbing every day it was madness for this prime site to be so hopelessly underdeveloped. The barristers he briefed were mainly up in the newer, more fashionable MLC Building.

'Michael Leary, is it?'

After the deep resonance of his voice, the sight of Eugene Sullivan in the hallway was positively disappointing. His light-grey trousers were fractionally too short and they badly needed ironing, and the hand extended in greeting revealed a frayed shirt-cuff. But as Michael followed him into his chambers, he noted that Sullivan's upright carriage still gave him an imposing dignity.

'Bring us two coffees, would you please, Mrs Martin?' Sullivan said as he passed the receptionist. He eased himself into his swivel chair, then slipped a packet of cigarettes from his shirt pocket, flipped the lid open and held it out to his guest, who politely declined, then leaned back in his chair, delving into a trouser pocket for his lighter.

'Looks like they're trying to brick your fellow in well and truly,' he said as he drew the open brief to the edge of his desk. He studied it for a moment, then lit his cigarette.

'Batch, eh?' he said absently. 'Verballing bastard.'

There was something mildly encouraging about the distasteful way the barrister eyed the brief and at intervals shook his head and grunted disapproving comments.

Michael sat silently as Sullivan leafed slowly from page to page, occasionally reading aloud a phrase or sentence for no apparent reason, all the while drawing on his fast-disappearing cigarette.

The coffees arrived. Michael sipped one while Sullivan ignored the other, until finally he leaned forward across the desk and ground the butt of his cigarette firmly into a large glass ashtray already piled high.

'What do we know about these roosters in the Watchhouse?' he said, taking cup and saucer in hand and settling back in his chair.

'Not much. I have a patchy history on one of them.'

'We'll need more than that.' Sullivan swallowed some coffee and then continued as if dictating to a secretary while Michael scrawled notes. 'First of all, get in touch with the Crown and tell them you want a copy of their statements and their criminal history sheets. If the Crown tries to bugger you around take out a subpoena returnable at the next standover in the Supreme Court.' Sullivan's eyes focused on the far wall. 'We want to know where they've been in custody, whether they've given this sort of evidence before and whether there's any sign of any of them doing a deal with the Crown.'

'How do I do that?' Michael interrupted.

Sullivan, surprised, turned and looked at his instructing solicitor appraisingly.

'How? Start with the court records, of course,' he said testily. 'Court files, bench charge sheets. I want copies of everything you can lay your hands on relating to the charges that landed these fellows in the City Watchhouse that night.' He sipped his coffee and added, 'Plus anything about any bail applications they've made. If any of them applied for Supreme Court bail, search the registry and get copies of their supporting affidavits.'

Michael scribbled busily.

'And get hold of the prison records, subpoena them if you have to. They'll tell us if any of these fellows has received any visits from the boys in Homicide. I want to get inside these fellows' heads.'

Michael had not been dictated to in a long time but his initial mild resentment was overcome by relief at the prospect of some progress at last.

'What about this undercover fellow that taped Manetti in the cells?' said Sullivan, setting the cup and saucer on his desk. 'Do we have the tape?'

Michael welcomed the opportunity to make an intelligent contribution. 'Oh, it turns out there was no tape,' he said, rustling through his briefcase and producing a two-page document. 'I got a copy of his statement from Crown Law late yesterday afternoon. It doesn't mention any tape-recording, only a verbal confession.' He handed the statement to Sullivan.

'Reagan,' Sullivan mumbled. 'Reagan — he's with BCI if my memory serves me correctly.'

The statement was by a Detective Sergeant Andrew Phillip Reagan, an experienced detective who had spent a short stint with the Special Branch and in recent times had been involved in several major homicide investigations. Sullivan knew the name — he was sure he had cross-examined him at some stage — but at the moment he could not put a face to him.

The statement claimed that on the afternoon of the twenty-seventh of April 1986 he had attended a briefing session at Police Headquarters, and from there he had proceeded to the City Watchhouse, where he was lodged in one of the cells as an undercover operative.

It continued:

Shortly after 6 pm the defendant was lodged in the same cell, and after several minutes I engaged the defendant in general conversation. The defendant told me that he had been living in a harbourside unit in Sydney, and he then commenced to complain about the conditions in the Watchhouse. I then said to the defendant, 'What are you worried about? You're probably only here for the night. I'm in for armed robbery. There's no way I'll get bail.' The defendant then said, 'Bullshit, mate, I'm in for the big one.' I said, 'What, murder?' and the defendant replied, 'Too right. Me and two other blokes knocked that Trevor Cosgrove.' I then said, 'The nightclub bloke? Didn't they pinch someone for that ages ago?' The defendant replied, 'Yeah, that was his brother Peter. He's another mate of mine. But they've got nothing on him.' I then said, 'How did the cops get on to you?' The defendant replied, 'One of the blokes that was with us put us all in.' I said, 'Bullshit, what a dog. What about the brother, did he grass on him too?' The defendant replied, 'No, he never even knew about him. Peter just helped organise it with me and another bloke.' At this point our conversation was interrupted by a uniformed police officer who removed the defendant from the cell for fingerprinting.

Sullivan mumbled and grunted his way through the statement, then placed it on the table. 'No tape-recording my foot! Reagan's with the Bureau of Criminal Intelligence. They do all the phone taps and electronic monitoring. The only reason Batch would call in the BCI would be to use their surveillance equipment.'

He pondered for a moment and then rattled off more instructions. 'Take out a subpoena *duces tecum* on the Commissioner of Police requiring production of documents at the next standover. Put in the usual direction for all relevant documents, and then add this:

Including in particular, but without limiting the generality of the foregoing, all originals and all copies of all tape-recordings made by Detective Sergeant A P Reagan and/or any other member or members of the Queensland Police Force or any other person or persons whomsoever of all conversation had by the said Detective Sergeant A P Reagan with Joseph Leo Manetti at the Brisbane City Watchhouse on the twenty-seventh day of April 1986, and further including, but without limiting the generality of the foregoing, all originals and all copies of all tape-recordings of any other conversation in the Brisbane City Watchhouse on the twenty-seventh day of April 1986, made by any member or members of the Queensland Police Force or any other person whomsoever, as part of and incidental to the police investigation into the murder of Trevor William Cosgrove.

Michael scribbled furiously, filling in the gaps he had left along the way while Sullivan drank his coffee. That done, he looked up at the older man and cautiously inquired, 'Don't you think I should check first that they've definitely got a tape before I subpoena the Commissioner?'

'Definitely bloody not,' snapped Sullivan. 'If we ask them if there are any tapes they'll tell us they aren't. If we tell them there are tapes and we want them, they'll wonder how we know that, where our information is coming from, and that means we might have some chance of getting them.'

'But what if there aren't any tapes?'

'There are,' said Sullivan firmly, taking another sip of his coffee.

Michael was still confused. 'Do you think it's possible Manetti did make some kind of statement to Reagan? Do you think they might be planning to spring the tapes on us at trial?'

'No,' said Sullivan. 'I don't think so. They're trying to bury them. And we need to find out why.'

The conference went on for more than an hour, with Michael jotting notes, feeling like an eavesdropper on an old man's conversation with himself.

Not a single word of social conversation passed between them. It was a new experience for Michael, who was used to being feted by young barristers with an eye on where their next brief might be coming from. With Sullivan he felt like an apprentice taking directions from his master. Still, for some reason it seemed appropriate coming from this man and as Michael rose from his chair when the conference ended, instead of feeling slighted, he felt vaguely privileged.

He was halfway out the door when Sullivan observed as something of an afterthought 'You're Brian's Leary's son, aren't you?'

'That's right.'

The old man stood behind his desk gazing off to one corner of the room as if grappling with another thorny problem.

'Yes,' he said. 'A good man, Brian.' He seemed about to say more, but didn't, and they stood for several seconds in the silent room, before Sullivan looked up and said decisively, 'Right!' as if to declare proceedings finally closed for the day, then added, 'You'll get back to me on all that then, will you?'

Michael stepped out of the building into Turbot Street, feeling much had been achieved.

Eugene Sullivan might be past his prime, but Michael was convinced he had what it would take to do the job.

When the subpoena lobbed on to Darryl Batch's desk he was as shitty as all get-out. He'd been cranky with himself ever since the committal for having thrown in that bullshit about Reagan having got a tape-recorded confession. He'd only done it to stick it up that pisshead lawyer in front of the press but he realised right away it was a bloody stupid thing to do. And now he had a subpoena to contend with. The question was what to do with it.

'By the look of it, they know we wired the place.' Andy Reagan looked worried. Several of the other detectives in the Day Room mumbled their agreement.

'Bullshit!' Batch barked. 'They're just fucking trying it on. They've seen the BCI involved and they're taking a punt on the tapes. I say we just tell them there was no bloody tapes. How would they know?'

Phil Vincent shook his head. 'Shit, Darryl,' he droned in his annoying bloody whine, 'how easy would it be for one of the uniform boys in the Watchhouse to have let it slip to some journo or something?'

As Batch thought about that proposition he turned a deeper shade of puce. 'Mate, if they have,' he growled, 'I'll get down there and kick some fucking freckle.'

The little group pondered in silence for a moment as Batch lumbered around the room huffing and snorting.

'The tapes don't really hurt us anyway, Darryl,' Vincent said eventually.

'They don't fucking help us, that's for fucking sure!' Batch erupted, standing aggressively over the seated Vincent, who gave no reaction at all. Vincent was no Einstein but he was a cool customer. He never let anything faze him and that more than anything else shitted Darryl Batch right up the wall. He set off again, stomping around the room and the group waited silently for the big man to pace out his frustration.

Eventually he turned and faced the group. 'How much of it can we bury?'

'Probably most of it,' said Reagan. 'The only real problem is the first tape I did. It's been transcribed, which means it's been all over the office. There'd be at least two typists that have listened to it. Maybe even three.'

One tape was not going to be a major problem. It wouldn't help but it wouldn't be fatal. They could work around the one tape, provided they could ditch the rest. The BCI boys had a bug in the ceiling of Manetti's cell as well as the wire Reagan had taken in with him and if anyone got hold of all the tapes they would soon work out that Reagan's story was bullshit and, unless they had a better ear than Darryl Batch, they wouldn't recognise any of the conversation that Kent and Rays were talking about either. Those two grubs had served up a crock of shit but as a matter of caution he got the BCI boys to work on the tapes to see if they could pick anything up. Of course they couldn't. Now the tapes were nothing but a liability.

'Right, here's what we do,' he announced. 'Andy, you ring Crown Law and tell them you only got one tape. You and I'll do up a statement to explain it. The rest of them we flush down the dunny.'

As the group dispersed, Darryl Batch made a mental note to find out who was this half-smart little shit that was issuing these subpoenas.

19

Johnny Forrest looked about as comfortable in the plush reception area of Martin, Schubert & Galvin as a butcher at a vegetarians' convention, and his usual patter was lowered to a reverent whisper. Michael had been in conference all morning, and was surprised to receive the message that a Mr Forrest was in reception and would like to see Mr Leary for just a moment 'to give him some information he's been waiting for'. Michael decided to make time to see him.

'Mate, I won't keep you,' Forrest whispered as they shook hands. 'I just wanted to give you these. Thought they might come in handy.'

He thrust some rolled-up sheets of paper into Michael's hands, which he recognised as the criminal history of Arthur Bruce Kent (aka Arthur Stevens, aka Garry Smith, aka Francis Burnett, aka Garry Sommers). He wondered how and where Forrest acquired the document, but thought better of asking. He decided not to mention he had already obtained a copy from the Crown.

Michael was happy to hear his visitor's assurance that he would definitely come up with the 'good oil on that shifty bastard Kent', and expected in the next couple of days to meet with 'an old china who'll give us all the drum'.

'By the way,' muttered Forrest as they shook hands outside the lift, 'that Rays is in SOBS out at Boggo Road.'

'SOBS? What's SOBS?'

'Special Observations. It's like a protection yard. That's where they put the dogs and rock-spiders.'

'Rock spiders?'

'You know, kiddie fiddlers.'

'You mean child molesters?'

'That's it,' Forrest shrugged. 'Same dog, different doodle. Anyway, that's Rays' caper — he's a rock-spider.'

'Has he been convicted of it?'

Even Michael with his limited court experience could see the value to the defence of a crucial Crown witness with prior convictions for indecently dealing with children. This might explain why to date, try as he might, he had been unable to get either a statement or a criminal history on Rays from the Crown.

'Oh yeah, I'd say so,' rumbled Forrest. 'Apparently that's his go. And they reckon he'll talk to you too if you get out there. He'll talk to anyone who'll bloody listen, apparently. Word is he's got a few roos loose in the top paddock.'

Michael interpreted this to mean that Rays' mental stability was questionable and it occurred to him that that might be a good reason to get out to the prison and get a statement from Rays as soon as possible.

When he got through to Sullivan with the news, the barrister's response was, 'Get out there straight away, and take a tape recorder with you.'

It was Michael Leary's first trip out to the Brisbane Prison in over thirteen years. Boggo Road Gaol was as stark and imposing as he remembered it, and the bleak wintry wind whistling through the main gates added to the overall air of misery pervading the place.

Michael could see other solicitors interviewing seedy-looking characters in other half-glass interview rooms. He hoped none of his colleagues would recognise him in such a place, but then none of the lawyers he knew was ever likely to set foot in this godforsaken place.

As the minutes ticked by he ran his thumb over the 'Record' button of the tape recorder in his pocket. As each new face arrived at the warder's desk by the entrance he eased the button down, and as each one went elsewhere, he clicked the button off.

Finally a man who even in this deviant company looked decidedly odd appeared at the desk. He was painfully thin with long, lank brown hair tucked behind prominent ears. The lenses of his horn-rimmed glasses were as thick as Coke bottle bottoms. His ugly face was further disfigured by a nervous tic. Periodically one eye would squint, causing his glasses to slide forward on his nose, prompting him to push them back with one finger and simultaneously twitch his shoulder.

The warder pointed in Michael's direction and the convict squinted, adjusted his glasses, twitched and then walked towards the room.

Michael's right hand moved to his trouser pocket and fumbled with the tape recorder, his thumb searching for the 'Record' button. As the oddity poked his head into the room, Michael found the button and pushed it down.

'Mr Rays, is it?'

'Yeah,' said Rays loudly, then squinted, pushed and twitched and sat down.

Michael asked himself, not for the first time, how and why he had ever got involved in this whole sordid business. All he wanted to do was get through this meeting and get away from this benighted place.

'Mr Rays, my name is Leary. I'm a solicitor acting for Joseph Manetti, one of those charged with the Cosgrove murder.'

Rays stared at Michael as if he were a visitor from another planet.

'I've been told you've made a statement about a confession Mr Manetti is said to have made to you in the Brisbane Watchhouse.'

Rays tilted his head to one side, as if he were translating the words into another language.

'You're not obliged to speak to me if you don't want to,' said Michael. 'You can tell me to go away if you wish, and I will.'

Rays executed another grimace. 'I'm certainly willing to speak the truth, sir,' he said. 'The question before us is whether you are open-minded enough to listen, intelligent enough to understand and brave enough to act on what I say.'

He seemed to become more agitated, launching into a series of squints and twitches. Without hearing another word, Michael knew it would be a serious mistake for the Crown to rely on his evidence in court.

'Well, yes,' said Michael, anxious not to excite the man further. 'I am interested in finding out the truth.'

'Very well,' said Rays. 'But know now, that when the truth comes out, this state, this nation...' He slapped the table so hard Michael jumped. The warder turned his head, saw it was just Rays, and returned to what he was doing. '...will never ever be the same again! Great will be the fall from grace of some prominent people. Heads will roll, my friend, heads will roll!'

Michael did his best to steer the man back to the subject of Manetti, with little success. Rays lapsed into a long, agitated diatribe about how he had been arrested in New South Wales on numerous charges of indecent dealing with a minor, the outcome of a 'wide-ranging criminal conspiracy' between high-ranking officers of the New South Wales Police Force and 'certain powerful Federal politicians who must remain nameless for the time being' but who had been out to get him for some time.

'Charges brought against me by a ten-year-old girl who has known connections with the Communist Party!'

How the hell do I end this conversation and get out of here? thought Michael. 'Mr Rays,' he said abruptly. 'Did you speak to Manetti in the Brisbane Watchhouse?'

'No sir, I did not,' Rays shot back, and then he grimaced an added, 'I thought I did. But I didn't. It was another man, and it was somewhere else. I made a statement and they were going to get me out on bail. But then I saw the photos. I told them I knew that girl. She wasn't who they said she was. I told them that. I knew that girl a long time ago. She definitely wasn't who they said she was.'

Rays was making no sense and Michael had heard all he needed to. He pushed the chair out noisily and stood up, whereupon the strange creature opposite him fell silent.

'Thank you, Mr Rays,' said Michael.

Rays's face twisted into a hideous squint as Michael stepped past him into the doorway and out into the corridor.

'Yes,' said Stanley Rays alone in the empty room as the lawyer nodded to the warder and disappeared around the corner. He squinted, pushed his glasses back, twitched and flicked, then stood up and headed back to SOBS.

When Michael clicked off the tape recorder Sullivan groaned and sat back in his swivel chair.

'All right,' he said. 'If we assume they won't call Rays — and I'm sure they won't — what else have they got?'

It felt good to have Sullivan asking him for information, and even better to be able to report some progress. He now had the full criminal history of Arthur Kent and despite what the man had claimed under oath at the committal, he had a list of previous convictions as long as his arm, including thirteen separate appearances for offences of dishonesty.

'Ah, that's helpful,' mused Sullivan as he studied the record. '*April, 1973, Ipswich Magistrates Court — Living off the earnings of a prostitute.* The jury won't like that.'

In the last two years Kent had given evidence of remand-yard confessions in three different trials, two in the south and one in Brisbane. Michael was still chasing more details on those matters. Meanwhile he had dug up some interesting information on Kent's visit to the City Watchhouse. Kent was charged in Cairns in late January with thirty-four charges of false pretences relating to the use of a stolen Bankcard. He had been remanded to appear in the Cairns Magistrates Court on the fifth of February, 1986. When he failed to appear, the local magistrate had issued a warrant for his arrest. The bench charge sheets on the court file showed him to be residing at an address in Jane Street at West End, and the arrest warrant was received at the Woolloongabba Station in mid-February.

The local police took no action on the warrant until early on the morning of the twenty-seventh of April, by which time Manetti had been lodged in the Brisbane Watchhouse awaiting a Supreme Court bail application. At about 6.30 am on the twenty-seventh, three police cars, one marked, two unmarked, went to Kent's house in Jane Street and he was delivered to the Brisbane City Watchhouse at about 7.30. The Watchhouse records showed he was arrested by a uniformed constable by the name of Johnson, but Michael had spoken to the neighbours in Jane Street and they remembered that there had been mostly plain clothes officers at the scene that morning, one of whom fitted the description of Darryl Batch.

When Michael relayed that piece of information, Sullivan raised his eyebrows and smiled. 'We'll make a criminal lawyer of you yet, Michael,' he said. Michael interpreted it as a compliment.

Kent first appeared before the Chief Stipendiary Magistrate on the morning of the twenty-eighth. Bail was opposed by the police prosecutor, who asked for the matter to be remanded for further mention in the No 1 court in two days' time because there was a possibility of further charges being laid. Two days later, Kent again appeared before the Chief SM. This time there was no mention of any further charges. The prosecutor consented to his being released on bail with no surety, and he was simply ordered to appear back in Cairns on the fifth of May.

'In the meantime he's given Batch a statement implicating Manetti,' said Sullivan.

'His statement's dated the twenty-ninth.'

'What about the charges in Cairns? Do we know what happened to them?'

'They're still in the Magistrates Court. The police keep asking for them to be remanded for further mention.'

'Mmm ... No doubt they'll disappear once Kent's done what's required of him.'

The whole thing had a peculiar smell about it and as Eugene Sullivan leafed thoughtfully through the documents in front of him, Michael Leary felt a flutter of excitement. He could almost hear the old man's thought processes planning out the battle strategy.

Despite himself, he could not help but think how sweet a victory would be.

20

On Wednesday George Curran lunched with Frank Delaney at Milano's. On the following Monday Frank Delaney lunched at the Sheraton with his good friend Steve Wallace from Corley & Tuite, Surveyors, and Steve's mate Bruce Dawson.

Steve's firm had been doing surveying work on some of the big government jobs recently, and it was felt that Dawson might well be able to handle some proposed government projects as main contractor. The lunch went well and it was agreed that Frank would speak to his people 'on the ground', so to speak, and get back to Bruce.

The next day Delaney rang Dawson. It was very awkward to have to verbalise it, he couldn't be more embarrassed, but, well, he had just been told that Bruce's project manager was tied up in that dreadful bloody Cosgrove business. That was all very messy and well, really, the government couldn't afford to have a Cosgrove connection to one of its major contractors. Most unfortunate when the potential was there for Dawson to become a major government contractor. What could be done to make that happen? Well, it all boiled down to the project manager thing, didn't it?

Less than a fortnight later Gerry Manetti came in to see Michael Leary. He would be finishing up as project manager at Dawson's at the end of the month. Cash flow had become super-tight so Bruce Dawson had decided to get 'hands-on' himself and shed a couple of the management boys. Gerry had only been on salary for a bit over twelve months so it was only fair he would be first off. Bruce had promised to feed him plenty of contract work, but things were still going to be a bit tough, at least at first.

Michael digested that information. It didn't ring true to him. No one knew better than Dawson's lawyer that his business was on a roll, expanding rapidly and financially sound. It was inconceivable he would be reducing upper management at this stage. At a time when one would expect him to be hiring, not firing, Dawson was dispensing with his tried and true lieutenant, a key man. Michael wondered why.

The one thing really worrying Gerry was the legal fees for Joey. He had applied for a second mortgage on the house, but without a steady income now, he had serious doubts the bank would advance him much or even come to the party at all. What Gerry needed to know was how much all this likely was to cost.

Michael and Gerry went through the estimates together, Michael careful to talk 'fat figures' to cover all eventualities. At the moment all three accused were to be separately represented at the trial. Duncan and Lade would be represented by the Public Defender's Office, which would brief a separate barrister for each of them, and so, if the matter proceeded as a joint trial, as the Crown was proposing, each prosecution witness would be cross-examined three times, which meant the proceedings were likely to be lengthy. Each accused had the right to apply for a separate trial, but the trial judge was unlikely to grant that. In any event, such an application could not be made until the first day of the trial, so at this stage they had to budget on a three-header, one likely to take every bit of four weeks. All in all, they would have to budget for costs of $45,000 minimum.

That was a lot of money, and Gerry would have a hard time raising it. His father-in-law Merv had offered to kick in but Merv couldn't have much, just a police pension and maybe a bit saved. He didn't really understand the extent of it. And Merv was not really making enough out of the bait shop to justify a bank advance of that kind of money either. Gerry would have to put his thinking cap on.

By the time Gerry Manetti left his office Michael had an uneasy feeling about the whole affair. Even if the Manettis came up with the money to fund the trial, which was doubtful, how did Bruce Dawson really stand on the matter?

He did not wait long for an answer. The following day Bruce Dawson phoned saying he was about to tender for two new government schools to be built in the western suburbs.

'I had to let Gerry go,' he said as the conversation neared its end. 'Not that I wanted to. But all this business with his kid would reflect on the business sooner or later. Especially now we're in the running for some government jobs.'

It was a vaguely familiar line and Bruce Dawson didn't have to spell it out for his solicitor to realise that his biggest client was distancing himself as far as possible from the Manettis.

Michael felt profoundly sorry for Gerry Manetti, but he really couldn't blame Bruce Dawson. Business was business and, in business, it was the bottom line that counted.

The bottom line for Michael Leary was that the Manetti brief was becoming a definite liability. He was well aware that Tony Artlett, and, no doubt, the other equity partners, were losing patience with his defiance of them in continuing to act in the matter. He'd been foolish to persist this far. And for no good reason — simply a stubborn, childish reaction to Artlett's deviousness and an outlet for his frustration with being kept dangling in his quest for equity partnership. But this new development put things in a different perspective. Maintaining his involvement in the Manetti case could now jeopardise his relationship with Bruce Dawson. And without Dawson as his rock-solid, mega-fee-producing client his standing in the firm would plummet along with any hope of an equity partnership.

Michael hastily revised his strategy, self-preservation his highest priority. The cavalier approach he had adopted with Tony Artlett must be urgently reviewed, for fear that his current course might leave him not only isolated within the firm but also with a client base so seriously depleted as to make his bargaining power virtually nonexistent.

Dawson relied heavily on Michael's technical advice and negotiating skills, but if he became even a remote liability to Dawson's business empire, he would be jettisoned without compunction. After all, look what happened to Gerry Manetti. And there was little — virtually nothing — further he could do for Joseph Manetti. He had provided Eugene Sullivan with as much material as he was ever likely to get. Joseph Manetti's own statement was now complete, as were those of the various other potential defence witnesses, and all had been included in Sullivan's brief. Their client's detailed comments on the prosecution statements and evidence given at the committal proceedings had also been provided to Sullivan.

In addition, Michael had compiled dossiers on each of the main Crown witnesses, including all information on their background, copies of criminal history sheets, and all documents relating to their time in custody and applications for bail. They'd had several pre-trial conferences with Joseph, and even the potential witnesses had been carefully proofed in conference with counsel.

In short, the matter was fully prepared for trial, Sullivan was briefed and ready to go. Michael had made his contribution, and from here on in it was up to Sullivan. What difference would it make if he withdrew from the matter and handed it on to another firm of solicitors? Provided Sullivan stayed with the matter, Joseph Manetti would have lost absolutely nothing. Joseph was now unemployed and would undoubtedly be eligible for Legal Aid.

If Eugene Sullivan would conduct the trial on a Legal Aid retainer, Michael would be doing the Manettis a big, big favour by withdrawing and handing the matter on to the Public Defender. And, at the same time, it would solve his own problems with Bruce Dawson and the partners at Martin, Schubert & Galvin.

Michael made some discreet inquiries. He confirmed that Joseph Manetti would have no problem getting Legal Aid through the Public Defender's Office. He was relieved to discover that on a big matter like this, the Public Defender would almost certainly retain the barrister already briefed. He also learned that Sullivan regularly did work for the Public Defender.

The best solution, he told himself, was to persuade Joseph Manetti to apply to the Public Defender for legal assistance at his trial.

Yes, that was obviously the best, perhaps the only, solution. He had his secretary arrange for Gerry and Joseph Manetti to come to see him 'to sort out the funding issue'.

Joseph's grandfather, Merv Harris, came along to the conference, and though he said little, his very presence was off-putting. He sat back, seemingly distrustful of every word, every motive, and Michael felt the weight of the old man's scepticism dragging heavily on his every proposition.

'So that simply means,' said Michael, choosing his words carefully, 'that if Legal Aid is granted, the Public Defender would probably want to take the matter over and handle it in-house.'

Gerry Manetti shook his head. 'No, Michael,' he said. 'We want you to handle it. We have confidence in you.'

'Well,' said Michael, 'the Public Defender may ask this firm to do the trial as his agent, in which event…' Michael paused, ever so briefly, to structure his words precisely, '… in which event, I am sure the firm would give due consideration to that request.'

Michael looked up at the three men facing him. Gerry and Joseph seemed confused, Merv Harris suspicious and distrustful.

'But even if I don't continue in the matter,' Michael continued, 'Mr Sullivan has been fully briefed and he would certainly be retained by the Public Defender to do the trial.'

From there Michael launched into the arguments he had already used on himself, and as he spoke he found it increasingly easier to advocate that the course he was proposing was the only sensible, logical way to go. Apart from anything else, the family would save at least $45,000, money that once outlaid could never be recovered, even if the defence were successful. Such a debt would be a permanent burden on the family, and this was really the only way to avoid it.

Joey Manetti ultimately made the decision. Michael was surprised to hear him speak up confidently, without any reference to the others.

'I want to go for Legal Aid,' he said in a voice so firm and final that no one questioned or challenged him.

Michael produced the Legal Aid application form and took him through it, filling in the formal details himself. Minutes later Joseph signed it.

'Will you still come to the trial if we need you, Mr Leary?' Joseph asked.

Michael was touched by his young client's faith in him, and somewhat shamed by it. After all, he had been largely inept so far. He had gradually come to believe in the boy's innocence, and he had done his best to help him, but his best had been far from good enough.

'I promise you I'll provide whatever assistance I can,' replied Michael.

'And you think Mr Sullivan will handle everything okay, do you, Mr Leary?'

'Of course,' said Michael. 'I guarantee it.'

Merv Harris grunted, unconvinced.

Eugene Sullivan winced when his first paying brief in months became a Legal Aid job. Nonetheless he agreed to continue in the matter, and expressed his regret that he and Michael would not be doing the trial together.

When Michael told Bruce Dawson the Manetti brief had moved on, the awkwardness that had strained their recent conversations evaporated. Tony Artlett was so overjoyed Michael had belatedly come to his senses he suggested they have lunch together some time soon to celebrate. Michael agreed without enthusiasm that, yes, indeed, they should do just that some time soon, quite soon.

His withdrawal was undoubtedly the best thing all round. But for some reason he could not quite rid himself of a vague, irrational notion of betrayal. Or the memory of the contempt on Merv Harris's tough old face when they parted company. Or of a taunting echo of his undertaking to 'make them understand'.

The Public Defender's Office assumed the conduct of the Manetti matter on the twenty-ninth of July. Within a week Ron Forbes from the PDO rang Eugene Sullivan to confirm that he had all the material he needed for the trial, which he did, and invited him to contact the PDO if he wanted anything further. The trial of Joseph Manetti was listed to commence on Monday, the first of September 1986.

When Michael Leary withdrew, Eugene Sullivan felt curiously bereft. The Manetti brief sat in a corner of his chambers gathering dust. Sullivan could not think of a single reason to open it. Strange really, when it had kept him and Michael Leary so fully occupied until now.

As the first of September approached Sullivan expected someone from the PDO to ring him, but no one did. He thought about what he should ask Ron Forbes to get for him, but could think of nothing.

When Sullivan left his chambers for lunch, just before 1 pm on Friday, the twenty-ninth of August, he still hadn't heard from the PDO. There was no particular reason he should, none he could think of, but he wished someone would contact him. He restricted himself to two beers over lunch and was back in chambers by 2.30, in case he was needed for a conference that afternoon.

Mrs Martin handed him a message slip that said Mr Ron Forbes from the PDO had phoned to say he would be in Mr Sullivan's chambers with the client at 9 am on Monday morning.

That was it. No more conferences. Straight into it, first thing Monday morning. Sullivan mentally processed the trial strategy. One, maybe two civilian witnesses to be attacked directly. Totally destroyed, or Manetti was sunk. Then Reagan, the police officer. Again a direct attack. No room for Reagan to be mistaken; the jury had to be convinced he was perjuring himself. So it had to be boots and all. If Sullivan scored anything less than a direct hit on any one of them, his young client would be sentenced to spend the rest of his life in prison.

Well, that was it for the afternoon. Nothing more could be done now. Sullivan picked up the folders marked *R-v-Manetti* and tucked them into his briefcase.

He would work on the brief at home. In the meantime, he thought, why not drop in at the Majestic for a few minutes to have a couple to settle the nerves?

On Sunday afternoon at about two o'clock, in the kitchen of his modest New Farm unit, Sullivan opened first a bottle of claret, then the Manetti brief. By 8.30 he had decided on his opening address to the jury and most of his closing and was now striding a lurching path around the cramped living room reciting the hallowed words of the great Robert Emmet's speech from the dock.

'Why did your Lordships insult me?' he slurred, as he staggered and swayed through the room, making theatrical flourishes with one hand, the other clamped around a beer glass half-filled with Galway Pipe, which occasionally slopped onto the carpet. 'Or rather, why insult justice, in demanding of me why sentence of death should not be pronounced against me?'

He gestured dramatically and lost his balance so that he stumbled and fell backwards, his ribs thumping painfully against the faded Genoa couch, yet managing to salvage much of the port in the glass held aloft in his right hand.

He lay still for a moment, groaning with the pain knifing at his kidneys, then settled back against the couch. He tipped his head back and drained the last of the port, then closed his eyes. His head was spinning, his mind clouded.

'You're drunk, you old fool!'

Sullivan peered through the mist to discern a man in a blue pin-striped suit sitting in the armchair opposite. 'Is that you, Brian?' he quavered.

Brian Leary turned a disdainful head away.

'You're in no shape to do a murder trial,' said a new voice, soft yet powerful, that filled every corner of the room. In the other armchair sat a grey-haired man whose face the old barrister remembered well.

'Dan? Is that you, Dan?' Sullivan cried, his vision blurred behind a film of tears.

'One client at a time,' the melodious voice intoned.

'One client ...' Sullivan repeated.

'You have to be prepared to go the distance, Sully,' said Brian Leary. 'You have to have the courage.'

Sullivan closed his eyes again and a single, maudlin tear rolled down his wrinkled cheek. 'I'm sorry, Brian,' he slurred. 'So very ... '

The glass slid from nerveless fingers, and toppled onto the carpet. Eugene Sullivan, barrister-at-law, lying crumpled in a deep sleep on his living room floor, had found temporary refuge from his demons.

It was impossible to concentrate. Michael Leary reread the third paragraph of an article on Section 260 of the Income Tax Assessment Act and prepared to wade through it yet again. He had brought the latest issue of the *Law Society Journal* home because he had been meaning to read that article for several days. But his mind refused to absorb its contents.

It was not that the movie Colleen was watching on the bedroom TV disturbed him. She was wearing headphones, and Michael was used to reading while she sat beside him in bed glued to the Sunday night movie. Nor was her flimsy nightgown a distraction, though it had slipped off one rounded shoulder to reveal even more of her lithe curves. Not so long ago that would have been more than enough for him to abandon his reading, to revel in the yielding warmth of her body. Now there were more important things than sex to consider.

He resolutely turned his attention to the article, but almost immediately his thoughts strayed. It was the eve of the Manetti trial. Michael cursed himself for dwelling on it, for constantly wondering what his father might have done in his shoes. Surely anyone with a grain of nous would do exactly as he had.

He thought about the back stairs of the old Camp Hill house, holding his bloodied nose and whimpering. 'Well done, lad,' Brian had said to him. Cath was livid — 'He needs comfort and advice on how to avoid such situations, not encouragement'. She was probably right but Michael had felt a kind of pride, had wiped his bloody nose, stifled his tears, stood erect and walked a little taller. He believed then that there could be honour in defeat. *But that was then ...*

Michael Leary flipped the journal closed and studied the glossy cover portrait of an eminent member of his noble profession. In the real world you have to have your eye on the bottom line, working all the angles to your own advantage. He thought about the precious years his father had wasted on the Mickey's Poolhouse case, how he had destroyed his practice, and his life. Brian Leary had been too stupid, too out of touch with reality to even know there was a bottom line. A born loser.

Colleen had slipped the headphones from her ears and switched off the set with the remote control. He realised now that she had been sitting silently watching him.

'I think it's time we talked, don't you?' she said.

'About what?' he said shortly.

'About us.'

He winced and shook his head. 'Please, Col. Don't start this now, okay? I've got so much on my plate right now I can't think straight. I don't need this shit.'

She sat in the glow of the lamplight, her cheeks flushed, her brow knitted in a frown. He had hurt her, and that was the last thing he wanted. He clasped her hand gently.

'I'm sorry, baby,' he whispered.

The frown faded and, after a quick, impenetrable glance at him, she pulled her hand away and clicked off her lamp. He loved this woman and to see her like this made him ache inside. He wanted to make all the problems disappear, flush away the heartaches and the complications so that it was just the two of them again, together. But somehow he just couldn't. Everything was so mixed up he couldn't even think where to begin.

He switched off his light. When he leaned over to kiss her she proffered a cool cheek. Her skin was soft and fragrant with the familiar night-time scent of her. One hand moved to her breast, the other slid down along the curve of her hip, his intention unmistakable.

Colleen swiftly rolled on to her side, her back a wall between them.

For a long time, they both feigned sleep.

21

Eugene Sullivan arrived in chambers at precisely 8.45 am on the morning of Monday the first of September 1986.

With the assistance of a damp tea-towel, he had ironed a stiff crease into the trousers of his good grey suit and had matched his freshly-ironed, best white shirt with the navy-blue Bar Association tie the boys in chambers had so kindly presented to him to mark his forty years in practice. He looked an impressive sight indeed, he thought, befitting his role as learned counsel. Over the years, Eugene Sullivan had mastered the art of looking better than he felt.

Sullivan opened the Manetti brief over a cup of black coffee shortly before 9 am. As his eyes focused on the first page, he felt a soft *whoosh* of anxiety. His hands trembled slightly as he turned the pages of his notes to 'Kent — Cross-examination' and began running his eyes down the page, underlining words as he went or scribbling page references in the margin. Yes, his brain was ticking over precisely. Some things become second nature so that one can go through the motions more or less automatically, he thought, and almost convinced himself of that.

As he ran through the points on the page he visualised the attack step-by-step. Whenever a doubt crept into his mind he dismissed it, casting out all but his own forward motion. At ten-past-nine Mrs Martin knocked and announced that Mr Forbes and Mr Manetti had arrived. Sullivan wondered why he felt nervous. This was all routine.

'Show Mr Forbes through, would you please, Mrs Martin,' he said. 'Oh, and more coffee too, if you don't mind.'

Ron Forbes, relaxed and smiling, greeted him with a casual wave. 'Ah,' said Sullivan awkwardly, standing behind his desk as his visitor placed his briefcase on one chair and his fat rump on another. 'You're instructing me on this trial, are you, Ron?'

'If it goes to trial, Gene,' replied Forbes, leaning across and rummaging through his bulging briefcase.

Sullivan eased himself gingerly into his chair and straightened up to see his instructing solicitor toss a folded statement on his desk. It landed with a slap in front of him.

'Duncan's done a deal with the Crown,' said Forbes as Sullivan opened the document. 'They dropped his charges back to manslaughter on the basis that he give evidence against the others.'

It was not totally unexpected but it was news Eugene Sullivan could have done without that morning. Now he had four crucial witnesses to contend with, and this one was potentially the most damaging. He was a co-offender with a direct account of the incident.

Sullivan quickly picked through the document and read that Duncan had repeated the allegations made in his police interview that Manetti had planned the murder with the others.

'They ran him through on Friday afternoon,' said Forbes. 'He pleaded guilty before the Chief Justice and drew six years.'

Sullivan's eyes shot up from the page. 'Six years! On his own word he's as round as a hoop for murder!'

Forbes shrugged. 'The coppers really wanted him on side because he puts Peter Cosgrove in it. They've obviously leaned on the Crown to offer him a deal.'

Sullivan shook his head incredulously. A self-confessed murderer permitted to plead to manslaughter in order to put out a political fire, and here was the Crown and the Chief Justice himself allowing themselves to be used to add respectability to the whole grubby farce by sealing it with a curial stamp of approval. Unbelievable!

He was trying desperately to shape his thoughts on the whole issue, knowing he now had to formulate an attack on the run. He had precious little to go on with Duncan and though he could ask for an adjournment to investigate the deal that had been done he might not get it, so he had to prepare himself immediately for an effective attack on this extremely damaging piece of evidence.

His brain was sluggish, veering erratically from one idea to another and settling on none. The chaos of his thoughts panicked him further. He hardly heard the words of his instructing solicitor as he chatted on casually.

'Our fellow will be duckshit with this sort of evidence against him, of course,' said Forbes. 'And it looks like Lade's decided to nod to it.'

Here was another bombshell. Peter Lade would plead guilty to the Cosgrove murder. It was rare to see anyone plead guilty to a murder.

'Anyway,' continued Forbes, 'Graham Worrell's prosecuting and I know him pretty well. I've been talking to him this morning and he reckons that if he got an indication that Manetti would nod to manslaughter, he'd drop the murder charge.

Drop the murder charge! The words came as a reprieve. If the murder charge were dropped, all the pressure was off. Instead of a four-week trial fighting tooth and nail against every witness, with the odds stacked as high as they got in this game, a plea of guilty required simple submissions to the judge in mitigation of penalty, in circumstances in which the penalty was unlikely to exceed six years, given that that was the sentence that Duncan had drawn.

Sullivan tried to conceal his immense relief. 'What does our fellow say? Will he plead to manslaughter?'

Forbes looked surprised. 'Well, I haven't spoken to him about it yet. But he'd be mad not to, wouldn't he? I mean, he's just about a living certainty to go for murder if they push on with it. God, they've got three bloody confessions on him. And now they've got Duncan as well!'

For an instant Sullivan was inclined to remind his instructing solicitor of the quality of some of the evidence and the work that had been put into preparing the defence. A remote corner of his brain was not entirely comfortable with the way this gross little man was so summarily dismissing the advocacy skills of the great Eugene Sullivan. But he had long ago learned to swallow his pride and hold his tongue.

'Well,' he said, 'I suppose we'd better bring him in and speak to him.'

Ron Forbes did all the talking. He went carefully through the Crown case, explaining the strength of the confessional evidence and how they would have to destroy that evidence completely to have any chance of securing an acquittal. Then he told the young man that Duncan had done a deal with the Crown and showed him the statement.

Sullivan listened and said nothing. As Manetti read the Duncan statement his face looked greyer and more drawn but he said nothing.

Forbes waited for the right moment and then announced his 'good news'. He explained that Duncan had been sentenced to six years' imprisonment and that Forbes had been able to get the Crown to agree to a similar deal for Manetti, provided he pleaded guilty to manslaughter. Duncan got six years and he did the actual stabbing. No one could say for sure what a judge might give Manetti but surely it could not be more than six. Forbes's guess was that he would draw four or five.

Joey Manetti protested, 'But I didn't do anything. Why would I plead guilty to something I didn't do? I was just driving the car.'

Forbes smiled condescendingly. 'Driving the getaway car is as good as sticking the knife into the bloke,' he chided. 'You're a party to the offence.'

Sullivan could hear the desperation in Manetti's voice. 'But I didn't even know what was going on until they got back to the car and Peter had blood all over his hands.'

'That's not what Duncan says. He says you were part of the whole plan.'

'He's lying!'

Forbes shrugged his shoulders and the young man turned to his barrister. 'Mr Sullivan, you know he's lying.'

Sullivan looked decidedly uncomfortable. He swung around to face the young man, about to respond. But his instructing solicitor took up the cudgels again.

'Well, it's a matter for you,' Forbes said, shrugging his shoulders. 'That deal's available now but it definitely won't be once the trial gets under way. Duncan drew six years on manslaughter and I can't see a judge giving you any more than that. Would you agree with that, Gene?'

Sullivan was uneasy about being drawn into this process but considered the proposition and then answered honestly, 'Yes, I'd agree with that.'

'So it's just a simple matter of mathematics,' Forbes continued. 'How old are you, Joseph?

'Eighteen,' whispered Manetti.

'Fair enough. Eighteen,' said Forbes, as if that were the ideal number for his equation. 'If you pull six years you'll probably serve four, so you're out when you're twenty-one or twenty-two. Still a young man.' Forbes's satisfied smile suggested it was almost too easy. 'But if you plead "not guilty" and the jury slots you,' he continued, 'you go for life. That's it. The judge has no discretion. If you're lucky you might convince the Parole Board to let you out when you're about forty, but there's no guarantee of that.'

They were impressive mathematics, and the impact of them drained the blood from the young man's face. He was rigid while Forbes explained that if he signed a statement for the Crown acknowledging that the contents of Duncan's statement were true and correct, the Crown would accept a plea of guilty to manslaughter in full discharge of the indictment. That meant no murder charge and a virtual guarantee he would be sentenced to no more than six years' imprisonment.

It was nearly half-past-nine and he had until ten to make up his mind. After that the deal was probably not available.

'B-but Mr Leary said he'd make them understand that I was innocent. He said we could win,' Joseph Manetti faltered.

'Did he now?' scoffed Forbes. 'If you're convicted of murder it's you that goes to gaol for life, not Mr Leary.'

Eugene Sullivan sucked hard on a cigarette and held his tongue.

Michael Leary always intended to make an appearance at some stage at the Manetti trial just to demonstrate moral support. Other business took him to the MLC Building early that Monday morning, so when he was finally free he crossed to the Supreme Court building to watch the proceedings get under way.

He arrived shortly before eleven and was surprised to find the Manetti matter had been transferred to a court other than the one scheduled. With the court bailiff's help he tracked it down quickly enough, so that he stepped quietly into the hushed courtroom just on 11 am, bowed to the judge and took a seat at the edge of the public gallery.

The first thing he noticed was that the jury was out and he assumed counsel had raised a question of law for consideration in their absence. He glanced along the rows of gallery seats and spotted Gerry Manetti and his wife. Margaret Manetti was openly weeping and Gerry looked close to tears. Beside them sat Merv Harris, dressed in an unaccustomed suit, his anguished gaze fixed on his grandson.

Something was wrong. Terribly wrong. Michael sensed it immediately. As soon as the prosecutor spoke, he knew what it was.

'Your Honour will see that the new indictment is in respect of a charge of manslaughter,' said Worrell, handing a single-page document to the court bailiff who delivered it to the judge's associate, a fresh-faced young blonde sitting demurely behind the long, low desk below the bench. The associate stood up, turned to the judge at the bench behind her and handed him the document. The judge skimmed the document before handing it back to the young woman.

'Very well,' he said gruffly and then, turning to his associate he added, 'Arraign the accused on that indictment please.'

The associate turned to face the dock and read from the sheet of paper she held in front of her. 'Joseph Leo Manetti, you stand charged that on the twenty-first day of January 1986 at Brisbane in the State of Queensland you did unlawfully kill one Trevor William Cosgrove. How say you, Joseph Leo Manetti, are you guilty or not guilty?'

Michael Leary's heart was pounding. From where he was sitting in the gallery he could see only the back of Joseph Manetti in the dock, his narrow shoulders slumped forward so that his meagre frame looked even smaller. His lawyers sat at the bar table awaiting his response but the pause lengthened for what seemed an eternity until it became an embarrassing silence.

Ron Forbes hastened to the dock where he engaged in a whispered monologue. Joseph Manetti listened, then nodded his head. Forbes resumed his seat

'Repeat the question,' the judge said to his associate.

'How say you, Joseph Leo Manetti, are you guilty or not guilty?'

In a voice no louder than a whisper Joseph Manetti replied, 'Guilty.'

'Guilty, Your Honour,' said the pretty young associate.

The judge nodded and smiled kindly at her as she resumed her seat.

In assessing penalty in the case of Joseph Leo Manetti the learned sentencing judge took into account that on the facts agreed as between the Crown and the defence, the accused had entered into a criminal concert with two other men to go to the residence of the deceased and there to perpetrate acts of physical violence upon him.

It was not alleged by the Crown that the accused intended that death or grievous bodily harm would be inflicted upon the deceased but it was clear in all the circumstances that the accused must have known that his accomplices, Peter Lade and Paul Duncan, were at the time armed with offensive weapons, and therefore the possibility of some harm befalling the deceased must have been apparent to him at all material times. In those circumstances his involvement in the killing that ultimately occurred could not be considered to be other than most central.

His Honour took into account that the accused was not said to have taken any actual physical part in the attack which ultimately occurred on the deceased but by driving what was in fact the getaway car he had facilitated the commission of this horrendous crime and in the end it was perhaps little to his credit that he was happy to have others perpetrate the actual violence on his behalf.

His Honour noted that the person Duncan had pleaded guilty to a similar count last Friday and was sentenced to six years' imprisonment for his part in the incident. On the one hand it might be said that this accused's involvement was relatively less than was Duncan's in that Duncan was said to have physically taken part in the acts of violence perpetrated on the deceased. However, for reasons that His Honour had already expressed that was perhaps little to the credit of the current accused.

On the other hand, Duncan had cooperated fully and immediately with investigating authorities and it had been conceded by the Crown in Duncan's case that the police might never have solved the Cosgrove case without his assistance.

Mitigation of that kind was not available to the accused in this case. This accused had declined to submit himself to interview by police or to assist police in any way with their investigation and while that was his right, his reliance on that right excluded him from sharing in the mitigation from which Duncan had benefited in that regard. It was a mitigatory factor which in His Honour's opinion entitled Duncan to a substantial discount of the sentence to be imposed, which discount, for the reasons His Honour had already explained, was not available to the accused in this case.

His Honour took into account all of the matters put forward in mitigation on behalf of the accused by his counsel Mr Sullivan. He accepted that the accused was a young man of previously unblemished record and that he had strong familial ties and support. He also took into account the fact that the accused was only eighteen years of age at the time of the commission of the offence and that he had been previously a young man of apparently good character.

Weighing all the facts, including the accused's personal circumstances and taking into account the need for punishment and strong deterrence in such cases, His Honour concluded that it was appropriate that Joseph Leo Manetti be sentenced to imprisonment with hard labour for a period of ten years.

Michael swallowed a mouthful of Scotch and felt it warm a path to his gut. He had never had a drink in the public bar of the Plaza Hotel before today. But the Plaza was the closest hotel to the courthouse and today was different from any other.

He had slipped out of the courthouse at about a quarter-to-one, immediately after the judge had passed sentence, careful to avoid the Manettis. He'd felt bad about that but he couldn't face them.

He wondered why it had hit him so hard, why a client's fate had affected him so deeply.

'Hello, Michael.' Eugene Sullivan placed a frosted glass of beer on the bench and with a muffled groan settled his bony frame on the stool next to Michael. One hand plunged into the pocket of his suit coat and pulled out a crumpled packet of cigarettes. Retrieving the last survivor, he completed the job of crumpling it and dropped it into the large tin ashtray on the floor.

Michael sat silent and uncomfortable, an irrational anger welling up inside him.

Sullivan sucked in a draught of smoke, then picked up his glass and inspected it as he exhaled. 'Here's luck,' he said, and then drank.

Michael tried to respond, but found he couldn't. *Luck! Talk to Joe Manetti about luck!* 'I see they dropped the murder charge,' he said eventually, the words half-choked on his resentment.

'He pleaded to manslaughter. Had to, really,' said Sullivan. 'There was too much stacked against him to go to trial.'

Michael had an overwhelming urge to abuse this weak-kneed incompetent. He drained his glass and placed it on the bench. 'I have an appointment,' he lied, rising to his feet. 'Might catch up with you some time.'

Eugene Sullivan sat alone. Alcohol was no remedy for the pain gnawing at him but it was the only one available, the only one he knew. He ordered another beer.

22

At 6.15 am it was stinking hot. Considering it was only late September this had to be one of the hottest spring days Stan Morrissey could remember and as he lumbered across the quadrangle towards B-wing he could feel the heat of the sun even at this hour. He was breathing hard from the exertion of the walk as he shuffled his keys and turned the lock to the heavy steel compound door. He stepped through, clanged the door shut behind him and strode purposefully across the stone floor.

Stan Morrissey had been a prison warder for over thirty years and as the senior prison officer on duty at the time, he knew it was up to him to make sure this business was sorted out quickly.

Laurie Coogan was coming down the narrow metal stairs.

'Stan, did they tell you?' said Coogan as they neared each other. 'We've got a swinger upstairs.'

'Yeah, I know,' said Morrissey glumly.

Coogan turned and fell in behind him.

'Who is it?' Morrissey asked Coogan.

'Manetti.'

'I thought so.'

For a big man like Stan Morrissey it got harder every day to climb the long central staircase that divided the two long lines of cells in B-wing and as he hauled himself up in the unseasonal heat of this spring morning he decided, not for the first time, he was getting way too old for this sort of crap. These young blokes were trouble with a capital T and it was only ever going to be a matter of time before this Manetti kid went off, one way or the other. Stan Morrissey was sick to shit of pulling twenty-year-old corpses out of this place.

'Has the GMO been notified?'

'Shit no.'

'Good.' Stan didn't want the Government Medical Officer under his feet just yet, not until he and the boys had had a look around and worked out what was what and who was paying the rent. No use complicating things with any embarrassing details. He already had a fair idea what this one was all about.

Manetti had been nothing but trouble since the day he arrived. When he first came in there was talk that he was a dog and had signed some statement for the Crown putting in the other grubs charged with him. The gaol heavies had taken a dim view of that.

Stan had first got wind of the whole thing the day after Manetti arrived when some arsehole threw a cup of hot coffee over the back of the kid's neck and he spent the night in the infirmary. At that stage the super had offered to put him in SOBS full-time until he could get himself declassified to a protection prison like Wacol B. But the kid wouldn't come into it presumably because someone had clued him into the fact that going into SOBS was like making an open admission that you were a dog, and doing ten years as a dog was a hard way to do time.

Manetti had claimed he hadn't informed on anyone and that he only signed the statement to have his charge dropped to manslaughter but that was never likely to cut any ice with the prison hardheads. As far as they were concerned he was a dog and he would be treated like a dog.

The word was out he was in for a major flogging and Blind Freddy could see there wasn't much he'd be able to do to stop it. There was that incident in the mess and some silly bastard had emptied a piss-bucket through the vent in his cell door a couple of times, but the kid had held up pretty well at first. Then some bright spark in the Crown decided to call him as a witness for the coppers in Peter Cosgrove's civil damages trial.

Even then, he showed some balls, no risk. Word was he refused to take the stand until the judge threatened to tack a few more years onto his sentence for contempt. Then he gave evidence and he tried to say his statement was all bullshit but the Crown tendered it in evidence. When news of that got back to some of the crazies, Stan knew there'd be trouble.

And there was. On Manetti's first day back some rock ape king-hit him and broke his jaw in three places. Then on the day he got out of the infirmary the real fucking loops got hold of him. Gave it to him in their own special style.

As they reached the upper level Stan saw Jim Greer standing in the walkway outside Manetti's cell with his hand over his nose and mouth. As he got closer he realised why.

'Jesus, what's that bloody smell?'

'Some arsehole's got him with the shit-bucket again,' responded Greer.

There was a putrid film of slime splashed across the floor at the front of the cell and a single thick, grimy rivulet ran towards the back wall and pooled against the leg of a wooden chair lying on its side in the middle of the floor. Suspended above the chair was the twisted body of a slender young man hanging like a carcass in an abattoir. His neck was bent at a crazy angle and his head screwed away to one side, his wide-open eyes staring coldly into eternity.

'No one got at him?'

'No, he was under lock and key. This one was all his own work.'

Morrissey nodded. It didn't surprise him one bit. When these young cleanskins copped the kind of treatment this bloke had — particularly what those sick mongrels had dished out to him the day before yesterday — they were always a chance of necking themselves and Stan had been half-expecting this one.

He'd write it up as another routine suicide by a young buck who couldn't face the prospect of hard time; no use complicating things with any of the other details.

'Hose this bloody cell out properly and then call the GMO.'

As Morrissey turned to leave, one of his shiny black boots squelched into a soggy lump of human excrement.

'Arrgh,' he groaned, scraping his boot against the steel door frame. He shook his big grey head and lumbered out into the walkway.

'I'm getting too old for this sort of crap.'

23

The equity partners of Martin, Schubert & Galvin held their first formal meeting for 1987 on the ninth of January. One of the main topics of the meeting was the impressive performance of Michael Leary.

For the last quarter of '86 he had averaged a remarkable sixty-five billable hours a week and his fee output had been consistently higher than that of anyone else in the firm.

With these figures he was clearly entitled to come knocking on the door for an equity share and without doubt the equity partners would have to give serious consideration to his claims.

At first Tony Artlett was delighted. There'd been a bit of tension between Michael and him over that murder case but thankfully Michael seemed to have flushed all that out of his system. Just as well, since it turned out the client was actually guilty and had pleaded so in the end. Then he proceeded to commit suicide in prison which would have been most upsetting for Michael if he had still been acting for the man. Tony had still been a little concerned. A stressful thing like that could affect a fee-producer's output but it turned out that Michael was not in the least concerned by it. He had dealt with the whole thing professionally. His work had not suffered in the slightest. If anything, his output had increased.

Artlett thought fleetingly of Colleen. She must never see Michael. She must feel shamefully neglected. He filed that away for future reference and returned to the matter in hand.

Lately he was starting to feel a little disturbed. He knew full well that Michael had been working for years to arrive at a position where he could stake a legitimate claim for equity partnership but now he had arrived there, there was not so much as a peep out of him. All he had done was churn out work and say nothing about his legitimate aspirations. Artlett hoped he was merely allowing his deeds to speak for themselves but when he effectively invited Michael to test the waters by broad hints of the partners' delight with his December figures, he had evinced no interest.

Something peculiar was going on and Artlett did not like the smell of it. There was no doubt Leary had ditched that Manetti thing in order to shore up his relationship with Bruce Dawson, and now he didn't seem interested in anything but churning out work, mainly for Dawson who had recently struck a mother lode of government contracts.

To Tony, that had all the hallmarks of a big fee-producer who was about to jump ship to whichever of the other big firms had lured him with promises of equity partnership or to set up his own firm on the back of clients like Dawson, filched from MS&G.

Tony Artlett prided himself on being a master tactician and he was not about to let Michael Leary steal a march on him. Even if he stayed on with the firm and took up an equity share, Tony wanted to be sure that in the negotiations the existing partners would be dealing from a position of strength.

The first step was to nurture his own relationship with Dawson and then to somehow monitor Michael's correspondence to make sure he had not entered into any arrangements with any clients. These things were notoriously difficult to control but a skilful operator like Tony Artlett could always find a way around it.

For Colleen Leary the past few months had been a seemingly endless repetition of the same unrewarding day. She could not pinpoint when or how her life had changed but she knew it had become tedious to the point of being near-intolerable. The children were a joy and her days were busy, but for all the golf and tennis and concerts and art galleries and charity work, life was somehow empty and unrewarding and she yearned for those happier days when there had been plans, and dreams, and shared aspirations.

She was alone, stranded. Michael was forever at work, often gone before she woke, often home after she was asleep. And when he was home he was withdrawn, uncommunicative, consumed by what seemed to be an inner rage that was blighting both their lives. It was unendurable.

And that odd call from Tony Artlett this afternoon suggesting they meet for coffee and a chat — 'I think you need an old and trusted friend to talk to ...' *Old friend? Trusted?* He was the last person she'd confide in. In any case that would be disloyal to Michael, on his part as well as hers. Ugh! She'd always found something about him repugnant, despite his initial doglike devotion and, even now, something within her recoiled when they met, mainly at MS&G functions, and she felt his appraising eyes fixed on her as if she were unfinished business not yet relegated to his inactive files.

Sleep had not come and when she heard Michael quietly close the boys' bedroom door and tiptoe down the corridor, she switched on the bedside lamp and squinted against the light. Her watch said 11.30.

'You're late,' she groaned sleepily but with enough bite in her voice to get the message across.

Michael was bone-weary. He was glad to be back in the safe cocoon of his home. One part of him wanted to hold his wife close and forget the troubles of the day in her arms. But the bite in her voice scraped over an exposed nerve and he responded aggressively.

'Yeah. I've working my butt off so we can live in the manner to which you've become accustomed,' he said sourly, slipping off his tie and flicking on the light in the walk-in wardrobe.

There was a charged silence, and as he undid the buttons of his shirt, he steeled himself to counter any criticism. It's all right for you, he thought, you've probably been in bed for the past two hours after a hard day at the golf club. Or was it tennis today? Or a work-out at the gym? Or yet another onslaught on the credit card in some trendy boutique?

As Michael moved through to the *en suite* he imagined all the selfish, unreasonable things his wife would say, and he answered them, one by one, in his mind.

When he returned to the bedroom, the bedside light was still on but he ignored Colleen and adjusted the alarm on the bedroom clock, his resentment simmering. He would make another early start tomorrow and no doubt be criticised by his wife for doing it. She carped about his never being home but she was quick enough to spend every cent he earned. Where did she think the money came from? Out of thin air?

Colleen broke the silence. 'Got a lot of work on?' It was a cautious appeal that said she didn't want to fight, that she wanted to talk, to understand.

Part of him responded. But there was a tightness in

his chest, a hollowness in his heart, that crippled him emotionally.

'Yeah,' he heard himself say in a voice laced with so much venom he wished he had not spoken.

Michael heard the bedside lamp click off, and he stood alone in the darkness, the alarm clock ticking steadily.

By 8.15 am Queen Street was a scramble. Michael liked the assault of sounds and sights that hit him as he left the office for his morning walk downtown to get the paper and a takeaway cup of cappuccino.

As usual he had been in the office since just after six, and as usual he had achieved more in those two quiet hours without the phone, the clients, and the hundred-and-one other interruptions than he was likely to do for the rest of the day. As soon as he heard the first faint stirrings of life outside his office door he knew that MS&G was groaning into action for another day, and as the army of clerks, typists, paralegals and lawyers filtered through the office to take up their battle stations, Michael, as usual, headed in the opposite direction for his ritual walk downtown amid the morning frenzy of sights of the city, in search of coffee and fresh air.

He felt marginally better now that he was out of the office. There was a warm familiarity about this city sidewalk, and as he drifted past Tattersall's Arcade he recalled Sunday mornings in the city years ago. Straight after Mass at the cathedral it was off to Christies' Cafe down by Her Majesty's. Brian and Cath, unlikely sophisticates, drank those newfangled Italian cappuccinos in the upstairs section, while he and Dan sat down below sucking chocolate malted milkshakes through striped straws. So long ago ...

As usual, Michael was back in his office by 8.25 and as he plopped the newspaper down on his coffee table and placed the cardboard cup on top, he eased into the comfortable armchair and willed himself to relax.

A knock on the door dragged him back abruptly. His secretary entered, greeted him, deposited his mail on his desk and promptly withdrew. Every file looked like a mountain whose peaks reached into the clouds. He felt depressed to the point of tears. Days like this had come and gone for months.

He could not recall when he first came to the conclusion that all the things he had spent his adult life chasing were illusory. He simply knew he had. And he knew the only thing that stopped him from walking away from it was that there was nowhere else to go.

The power he had craved no longer held appeal. But nothing else did either. There was no other power, no other appeal. There was no righteousness, or justice, or salvation, as Brian Leary would have claimed. Only lies, and avarice, and ambition. There was no Camelot, no Promised Land. All his life he had been working to become a man who had never really existed. Somewhere along the way he had convinced himself that self-interest and greed were the only human virtues worth relying on. Now he knew they produced only empty, hollow men. But he was trapped. He had no options.

He snatched up the newspaper and scanned it, hoping to dispel the dark thoughts that were troubling him. His eyes darted blindly across each page, looking but not seeing, as a mild anxiety started to take hold of him. Suddenly a familiar name reached out and captured his attention.

COSGROVE KILLER FOR TRIAL was the headline over a twenty-line report that was all but hidden in the far right-hand column of the newspaper.

Self-confessed murderer Peter Lade was yesterday committed for trial by magistrate Barry Andersen in the

Brisbane Magistrates Court on a further charge of murder.

Lade, who in September last year confessed to the murder of Brisbane nightclub boss Trevor Cosgrove, is now charged with having murdered Shirley Anne Probert, 46, in February last year.

Probert's body was discovered in the living room of her high-rise unit in the beachfront Golden Gate Apartments at Surfers Paradise.

Michael's eyes skimmed quickly down the column and fell on to another name.

Reginald Davey gave evidence at the hearing that while he and Lade were both inmates of Brisbane Prison, Lade confessed to him that he had broken into Probert's unit and strangled her.

Reginald Davey ... As Michael read the name he recalled that hot day in early spring when he had finally plucked up the courage to go back to Boggo Road and see his former client, to speak to him, and help him if he could. As he filled out the visitors book, scratching his name into the column marked 'Visitor', he'd noticed the name of Detective Senior Sergeant D Batch written in above and he quickly scanned across to see if he had been to visit Joe Manetti. He hadn't. In the column marked 'Prisoner' was written the name 'R Davey'.

The name meant nothing to Michael then but it stayed with him, as had all the events of that stifling September day. That was the day a very pleasant warder had told him cheerfully that he couldn't see Manetti ''cause he bloody died this morning, mate, didn't he?'

Reginald Davey ... Michael wondered who he was and what it was he and Darryl Batch had found to talk about that morning.

He thought, too, about another conversation in another prison, with a blond killer whose cold eyes had chilled him to the marrow. Peter Lade had spoken of his vicious handiwork with frightening detachment and Michael remembered how his cultured voice had betrayed no emotion until he said, *They're leaning on me about some pro who was murdered in the Golden Gate Apartments at Surfers ... I can't tell them anything about it because I had nothing to do with it.*

That was what Lade had said in the depressing squalor of the City Watchhouse, and Michael had not doubted the truth of those words coming from that sick young man for a moment. *I can't tell them anything about it. Because I had nothing to do with it.*

He had dismissed Lade's plea but he hadn't forgotten it. Now he couldn't help but think that yet another trap was being set and would be sprung. Reginald Davey would provide evidence to convince a jury beyond reasonable doubt that Peter Lade had killed again. Michael Leary knew it wasn't true. Still, did it really matter?

It all swam around in Michael's head throughout the day and although he did his best to strike it from his mind, the name of Peter Lade kept drifting back and the vision of that handsome, well-groomed butcher poisoned his thoughts and destroyed his concentration. Reginald Davey was another miserable survivor contracted by Batch to produce a result that had nothing whatsoever to do with justice or truth, and once again a jury would be fed a lie that would do no more than calm public outrage and quell public fear.

As the day wore on Michael thought, too, about Joseph Manetti, a child sucked into a crazy whirlpool of politics and powerful men who had slaughtered him to protect themselves. He had failed the boy. He'd tried to convince himself he hadn't, but he knew he had.

He thought about a man called Sullivan, and another one called Brian, and the tragic, lonely look in a dying women's eyes, all those many years ago. The ghosts came back to haunt him as the day went on and his depression deepened by the hour.

As the clock above the bar in the upstairs lounge of the Embassy Hotel clicked onto eight o'clock, Michael Leary looked up from his glass. He wondered how he had come here, and when, and why. He told himself he should be home with his wife and children. Then he thought of how painful that would be, Colleen tight-lipped and unsmiling.

The dimly-lit lounge was empty except for a couple perched on stools against the bar, he an ageing Elvis, she an overblown rose long since plucked. Piped music played discreetly and the lone barman drifted back and forth behind the servery linking this bar and the one next door. He had been gone so long Michael tired of waiting. He stepped to the bar and peered across to see the barman serving drinks next door.

There was a larger crowd in there and the barman was attending to the orders of a group of men — in real estate or insurance, by the look of them. Darkened corners were peopled with ones and twos having a quiet one to finish up the day. As Michael stood slumped against the bar, his eyes wandered to a lone figure huddled over a stand-up table in a far corner. He recognised that man, and there was a flutter in his chest as he pondered his next move.

'Same again, sir?' said the barman.

'Thank you,' Michael replied as he pulled a note from his wallet. Then he added, 'Oh, and a pot of beer too, thanks.'

With a drink in each hand Michael made his way to the darkened corner.

'Hello, Merv.'

Merv Harris lifted an eyebrow. Then, without speaking, he continued his contemplation of the contents of his glass.

'I was hoping we might talk.'

'Piss off, will you?' growled Merv. There was no anger in the voice, only bitterness and contempt.

'I've got to speak to you about Joseph,' Michael said.

'What's there to talk about? How you fucked up his case?'

Michael stood there, stripped of all dignity, a dull ache behind his eyes. 'Yes,' he said simply. 'That's what I want to talk about.'

Merv Harris raised his eyebrows. 'Is that beer mine?' he said and when the younger man nodded, he scooped it up. 'Pull up a pew.'

Harris had been drinking for most of the day. That much was obvious. His voice was thick and laboured and his movements were deliberate.

Michael Leary settled on a stool, the two men cradling their drinks and saying very little until eventually Michael said, 'I know I let him down.'

'Bullshit!' said Harris. 'You done the right thing.' He poured a long draught of beer into his mouth then wiped the foam from his lips with the back of a hand. 'No, you done the right thing.'

The right thing ... It made no sense. Michael suddenly felt foolish to be seeking enlightenment from a drunken man. He was about to climb to his feet and walk away when Harris added, 'They'd have just fucked you like they did your old man.'

Michael stared at the top of the man's head, slumped forward over his beer. 'Who's "they"?'

Harris's brows knit into a frown. 'They?' he echoed. 'The Magician for one.'

'Who's the Magician?'

The response came in a deadpan monotone. 'The Magician? He's the master of illusion.'

Michael watched Harris pour another long flood of beer down his throat and wondered why he was persisting with this inane conversation.

Harris burped loudly and said, 'He's the one that saw your old man off. And yours truly, too. And now young Joe.'

'What are you talking about?'

Merv Harris stared at the empty beer glass cradled in his hands. 'Tell you what, mate,' he said wearily. 'See that? That's an empty glass.' He placed the glass carefully on the table. 'You fill that up and I'll tell you a story worth hearing.'

Michael ordered a jug of beer and two ten-ounce glasses, and as soon as both glasses were filled Merv Harris poured most of the contents of one down his throat, then said, 'I joined the Force as a cadet in 1946. Shit, that's forty fucking years ago! I was only fifteen years old, for Christ's sake! I've been a copper almost all my bloody life.'

Michael waited in silence, expecting him to continue, but he did not. 'You knew my father,' he prompted.

'Yeah, course I knew him. Back in the sixties your old man used to act for every grubby bastard in town.' He raised his glass and swallowed again. 'He was a little prick, he was. But he didn't deserve what he copped.'

'What did he cop, Merv?'

Harris shrugged. 'He got in the way. And they ran right over the fucking top of him!'

'Who did?'

Merv Harris hesitated, like a man with ten toes over the edge, wondering whether to jump. And then he did.

'The coppers have been running this state for as long as I can remember. Back when I first came into the job the Masonic push was pulling the reins. In them days you just didn't get a look in if you weren't a goat-rider. They controlled the perks from gambling and prostitution, so they pretty much had things by the balls. Course, all the Paddies that were on the outer didn't fucking like it.

'The bloke that changed all that was George Curran. He was a big Irish Mick and he's the bloke they come to call the Magician. Meaning he always had something up his sleeve. George got the Paddies in the door and later on he just become the all-round Mister Fixit in the Force. He's retired now, but he's still running things, no risk.

'Anyway, coppers have been taking a sling out of the punters, and the sly-grog joints, and the molls, since bloody Adam was a lad, and no one's really bothered much about it. And, shit, why should they? Everything was kicking on all right. Most of us never copped an earn but we knew the smart boys in Licensing did, and good luck to them. The rest of us could always chalk up a free root or a drink on the arm so, what the hell, life couldn't be sweeter.

'But then a few of the boys went a little crazy. A whole lot of garbage was talked about how the coppers down south had arrangements with the big boys in the Sydney crime scene so that they copped a kick off every job they done. According to the talk — and who knows whether it was fair dinkum — they franchised certain areas to certain crooks and they were pulling out a squillion.

'If a bloke in the know wanted to pull a job, he'd just square it off with the right coppers first and then he'd be sweet so long as he come up with a cut of the take when the job was done. Covered everything from housebreaking to drugs. They reckon they even had pickpocket franchises going. If some crook had the

Randwick contract, he'd be sweet to work the track provided he kicked to the right cops. Who knows?

'Anyway, I never got into that sort of shit. I mean, up here we'd pick up the occasional bit of lolly if it come along. If we pinched a druggie with a wad of cash, we'd divvy her up, stuff like that, but I was never in on any of the organised jokes going round with the casinos and the brothels. I wasn't interested in doing deals with any of them grubby bastards.

'I think old George Curran knew that, because even though we was good mates for a lot of years, he never offered me a guernsey with the big boys. George once asked me if I'd be interested in a spot in Licensing, which I think we both took to mean did I want a piece of the action. I just told him I wasn't interested and he said "Fair enough", and that was it.

'Anyway, it was common knowledge that a few blokes were making a shilling out of licensing and gambling. And molls, of course. And I guess that was fair enough. It was a dicky area anyway. No one was interested in shutting down the sly grog shops and the illegal games, much less the dirty girls. The last thing the government wanted was to stamp them out. Shit, there would have been a bloody revolution!

'So old George got the whole thing running like clockwork through the sixties until just about every sleazy hole in the Valley was hitting the tin, and a fair few other joints as well. It's a bloody good system really because it keeps all that shit clean and under control. The coppers know who's in the business and what they're up to, so at least it's them that's in charge of the jungle, not the fucking apes. George liked to tax the arseholes out there, to tell 'em when to jump, and how high. Most of the troops don't get a piece of the action but the action helps make 'em kings of that fucking jungle! So long as they stick to one another there's no one that can touch them.

'Old George, he's a copper first and always and he'll stick to his boys like shit to a blanket. If you're a copper and you're staunch, the Magician'll look after you. Unless you put old George's nose out of joint and then you're in the shit, no risk. That's what happened to me in the end, but I deserved it, I guess.

'Yeah, it was the Magician who pulled every bastard's bacon out of the frying pan back in '67 when that silly slut Gaye Welham went to the papers and tipped buckets on every copper in town just about. We were all shitting ourselves because even if you weren't taking a sling from the molls you were at least copping the occasional freebie off them. And, anyway, if the house came down, everyone would suffer and we all knew it.

'But George Curran got to Gaye Welham and scared the shit right out of her, no risk. She withdrew her allegations because she worked out pretty quick that the Magician doesn't piss around.

'There was a lot of talk about just how far he'd go, but personally I had no doubt. I'd been out there with him and I'd seen him do what sometimes needed to be done. If some grub needed doing, George would do him good and proper.

'Anyway, after that Welham bullshit blew over there was this feeling round like we were all bullet-proof and a lot of blokes started to run red-hot, so that even George had to put out the word to a few blokes to pull their heads in. And it was round about then that Mickey's went off. You'd know all about the Mickey's Poolhouse bombing because your old man ended up in the middle of it. What you wouldn't know is what I didn't know either at that time.

'I suppose it was sort of like the joke — if you started to suspect something was a little hot, you just blanked it out and went about your business. Anyway, I was Chief of Homicide in those days and so I got the guernsey to investigate it. I suppose I knew something was on, the way the Magician had his snout in it from day one, but I just put it down to the fact that Johnny Morris who run Mickey's had been shelling out for years.

'George had his finger on that arsehole John Arnold right from the jump. He was a grub that Arnold. He'd slit his mother's throat for two bob. He blued like shit for years over being done for it and now I know a little more about it, maybe he had good reason. Not that it matters. He was just a grub anyway and he ended up where he belonged.

'Old George brought up two heavyweight Sydney d's for the bust. I couldn't work out why. It all fell into place later on. Anyway, Tommy Wilson dropped a brick on Arnold and the rest of us backed him up. Me and Frank Delaney and Gerry Walsh. Tom's a heavyweight now, of course, and Frank's a pollie, a fucking Minister, no less. That arsehole Batch was in on it too. He was only a bit of a kid then but old George was dead-set keen to have him in on it. George was a cunning old bastard. He knew that once you put your name to something like that you're locked in forever.

'I didn't see it at the time, but that one was so big there was no way out for any of us once we signed that Record of Interview. George knew then that Batch was crazy enough to be a lot of use to him, provided he had a good grip on his balls, and that was how he did it. It's easy to see why he wanted Tom and Frank in there. He had plans for them. I never really understood why I was in it. Maybe he was getting worried about what I knew.

'Fact was I didn't know diddleyshit. I knew it was a verbal, of course, and none of us believed for a moment the bullshit that faggot Lindsay Stone came up with. Stone was the rock-spider that trotted out the good old remand yard confession on Arnold. It was a bloody joke really, but that's what got us there in the end. Arnold was a grub all right, but he wouldn't have shared the time of day with a dog like Stone, much less his darkest secrets.

'Gerry Walsh filled me in years later. Poor old Gerry's gone now with the Spanish dancer, but before he went he worded me up. Apparently George Curran and a few of the other big boys had been talking to some Sydney coppers about them setting up a similar sort of deal up here, with the local coppers in charge. The Mickey's Poolhouse job was a part of all that.

'There was a bloke in Sydney by the name of Harry Tipple. He was just a jumped-up, two-bit fucking hood, but in those days he fancied himself as a bit of an Al Capone and he had a big tie-up with the Sydney coppers. Tipple controlled all the illegal gambling in Sydney and of course his mates in the New South Force were skimming off the top. That's where the Sydney d's came in. Wallace's carked it now but in them days he had the whole scene humming down there. Dent was his offsider.

'Anyway, Tipple went to Wallace, and Wallace and his mates squared it off with the Magician, so that when Tipple's boys came up here the heat would be off of them. The plan was to move in on all the games in Brisbane and have them all shell out to Tipple. They were just going to make a couple of threats and maybe get some local boys to start a couple of harmless fires to put the frighteners through the owners, then sit back and collect the money.

'George Curran even supplied them with the fire-starters, and that's where he fucked up badly. He put them on to a bunch of young hoods he'd been doing business with. I remember the little shitheads. They were just petty crims, half-crazy on drugs most of the time. Anyway, according to Gerry Walsh, they were the blokes that bombed the Poolhouse.

'So the whole thing was set up by the big boys, and according to Gerry Walsh, this was to be the start of a major link-up between Brisbane and Sydney. The Mickey's Poolhouse thing was just supposed to be a blown-up rubbish bin. But when those silly bloody pricks nearly blew the joint to Thargomindah, all hell broke loose. Arnold had been getting around the town saying it was on so of course he was the perfect fall guy.

'Anyway, that's what I didn't know and I don't think your old man did either. If he had he might have had the sense to walk away from it. He went on banging the drum for that low-life Arnold for years after that. If he'd known what was at stake he just might have had the sense to realise that Johnny Arnold wasn't ever going to see the light of day and anyone who tried to help him out of that shit-hole was going to get pulled right in there with him. Frankly, I never really could understand why he'd want to make the running for a grub like Arnold. Guilty or not, that bloke was never any good.

'I never liked your old man, I make no bones about it. He had a bit of heart, I'll give him that, but he was an annoying little prick and I couldn't cop him. Still, I didn't like what I saw old George get up to through those times, particularly once I had the drum from Gerry Walsh.

'They done a lot of things to bury what they done with Mickey's and they buried a few people along with it. Your old man for one, but at least he probably had a choice. If he'd have had an ounce of brains he'd have got out, just like you did with young Joe. After all, you don't have to be a bloody genius to read the fucking writing on the wall. But there were others they just chewed up and swallowed and I felt like I was standing right beside them when they done it.

'Them druggies had some sort of a bust-up in '74, and started killing each other off. One of them ended up on the Mt Gravatt tip with a hole in the back of his head. Next thing his brother's going round saying he's going to spill the beans about the Mickey's bombing. So the brother's car gets booby-trapped and it blows up in the face of the eight-year-old kid who lives next door. Eight years old — just an innocent little kid, for Christ's sake. That put a whole lot of people offside.

'That's when Billy Peters wrote that silly fucken letter to the editor half-pie giving up these druggie blokes. Next thing Peters gets a visit and he's done for Ronnie Abbott's murder. Peters was another worthless arsehole but he didn't knock that Ronnie Abbott. Everyone knew that. George's boys stitched him up tighter than a fish's arsehole, and I knew then and there it was all just to cover what we done to Johnny Arnold.

'So that's the sort of shit your old man got himself sucked into and that's why the Magician eventually had to make him disappear. They nearly put him off for good, you know, and I reckon if he'd gone again for Arnold, they would have. Your old man was just dead-set lucky Johnny Arnold kicked the bucket when he did.

'As for me, I kept my trap shut and stayed right out of it, but old George knew I wasn't happy. He pretty much kept away from me and we rarely spoke for years. But he knew I was staunch and I'd have gone along all right except that I let myself get led by my dick into a head-to-head with him in '77.

'I was rooting this sheila by the name of Marsha Reynolds — she was a junior detective, one of them new unisex jobs. Anyway, she got all fired up about corruption in the Force and got it in her head she was going to clean it up.

'I kept telling her it didn't exist, but she was dead-set out for Curran. Of course she got herself arrested. They found four ounces of smack in her car and a junkie crim who claimed she'd been supplying him. Surprise, surprise ...

'Anyway, I was stupid enough to go to bat for her and we ended up with proof that the bag of smack was lifted from the Exhibit Room at Herschel Street when Marsha was out of town on court duties in Toowoomba. They had to drop the case, but it caused a major stir. You probably read about it in the papers.

'As usual, George had it all bedded down quick enough, but he didn't forget my part. I think he sort of figured that I'd turned and was out to get him, so he got me first. Within a couple of months I was up on charges of assault for belting a grubby bastard down in the cells one night — which I did, of course — and they suspended me on full pay.

'I spent nearly twelve months sitting on my arse waiting for a trial and then the grub absconded, so they dropped it. I didn't know whether that was just George's way of warning me or whether the grub pissed off of his own accord, but it was plain as day I wasn't welcome any more. So I cashed in the super and bought myself the bait shop. Like I said, you don't have to be a genius to read the writing on the wall.

'That Cosgrove business was potentially every bit as big as the Gaye Welham thing, or the Mickey's Poolhouse bombing, or any other bloody thing that's come along, and old George Curran would've seen that straight off. When you got a nineteen-year-old kid confesses to a murder he didn't do, people want to know why. And when they start asking questions about serious shit like that, everybody suffers. Next thing you've got yourself a Royal Commission on the Police Force, and from there anything can happen.

'The Magician knew that. Old George would have gone to work on it, no risk, as well as others. They needed Joe's arse on a plate and they were always going to have it. And that's why you were always going to drop him. It made good sense.

'Right from the start I tipped you were a lot smarter than your old man ever was. I guessed you were in it for No 1, not some nobody little kid. And I was right. You ditched him, just like I thought you would.'

Harris interrupted his monologue occasionally to drink from his glass or to refill it but otherwise he droned on as though he were speaking to no one but himself. Michael listened in silence, processing the torrent of startling information as it issued forth, stunned by events that had unwittingly shaped his life. He could not yet react to it; he was numb and he wondered where he fitted in it all. Was he a villain, a pawn, a victim, or simply an irrelevance? He didn't want to think about it, and as he sat, and watched, and listened, and drank, he tried hard not to think at all.

But as old Merv droned on and on, Michael saw his father working late at night, slumped over transcripts splayed across the kitchen table. He recalled how he'd slept fitfully one night, and when he wandered bleary-eyed out into the kitchen, the old tin clock showed quarter-past-eleven. He remembered Brian's gentle smile as he looked up from his papers.

'Hello, Mikey.'

'Hi, Dad.'

'Can't you sleep?'

'No.'

The fridge light made him squint and the cold smooth surface of the bottle chilled his fingers as the milk tumbled into the glass.

'Court tomorrow?'

'Yep. I've got a fellow on a break-and-enter.'

'Did he do it?'

'He says he didn't.'

'Yeah, but *did* he?'

'I don't know.'

'Will he get off?'

'I doubt it.'

That made no sense at all to a sixteen-year-old. 'So why are you defending him?'

In those days Brian had a warm, contented smile that had a way of putting all the world in order and perspective. 'That's my job, Mikey. That's my job.'

When Michael Leary spoke at last, Mervyn Harris raised his head, startled, as if he had thought he was alone.

'What did *you* do for him, Merv?'

Harris stared back through bloodshot eyes. 'What could I do?' he said. 'He might as well have been run over by a train. There was nothing I *could* do.'

Michael felt an overwhelming sense of waste, and a flood of bitterness stung his eyes. 'Why didn't you speak up before?'

Merv looked helpless. 'Because it wouldn't have made an ounce of fucking difference, that's why.'

Michael climbed to his feet. He was drunker than he thought. He steadied himself with one hand on the table and looked down at his companion. 'You wouldn't know, would you?' he accused, 'because you didn't even try.'

With that he turned carefully and deliberately, and made his way discreetly to the door.

24

There was a dry, bitter taste in his mouth and a hammer was pounding in long, reverberating thumps behind his eyes. The bedroom curtains were closed so that daylight struggled in through cracks and crevices in streams of light. It was late.

Michael tried hard to focus on his watch. Ten-past-nine. His queasy stomach gave a warning lurch and he scrambled out of bed and made it, in the nick of time, into the *en suite*.

He couldn't front up at the office today. Not yet anyway. He showered, dressed in casual clothes, then crept gingerly into the empty kitchen. It was 'kindy day', he remembered, so Col was no doubt dropping off the boys.

He swallowed two aspirin, then a handful of Vitamin C, and tottered to the phone. His secretary was reassuring: his wife had rung already to say he was feeling ill so all his appointments had been cancelled. She would ring him if anything urgently requiring his attention came up, but in the meantime he should relax and recover.

'You sound awful, Mr Leary,' she commiserated. 'Is it that flu that's going around?'

'Something like that,' he croaked.

It was the first time Michael had ever rung in sick and he was almost disappointed by the lack of fuss his absence caused.

He slumped on the couch in the family room. He had no energy to do anything but lie there motionless while the aspirin slowly took effect ...

When he woke again he felt marginally better. The tension had eased in his neck and shoulders and the hammer in his head had subsided to a bearable dull ache. His stomach would have to be handled with care but the queasiness had dwindled to a general malaise. With a bit of luck he might survive.

Colleen was moving back and forth in the kitchen. He watched her through half-closed eyes — graceful, still with that same softness in her pretty face, she moved efficiently about the room

'Do you want coffee?' she said sharply as she flicked off the boiling jug.

And in the blue corner ready to come out fighting ...

'Yeah. Thanks.' Michael sat up, and stretched.

'You were home late,' she accused, handing him the cup.

'True,' he said defiantly, preparing for the confrontation.

'Where were you until four this morning?'

'Out.'

There was a charged silence. It suddenly occurred to him that she might think he was with another woman, and he wanted to deny it, to tell her that he'd never looked at another woman since he'd first laid eyes on her.

'Have we got a problem here?' Her voice was steady and controlled. She might as well be asking him to pass the salt. And this from Col, who sobbed her way through sad movies and over the plight of starving kids in Ethiopia. Now the mobile face was flinty.

'Problem?' he repeated, as if the word were new to him. There was a long silence before he looked up and saw the tremor in her lips. She reached out cautiously, and a single finger touched his shoulder. It was like a painful shock that drove straight to his aching heart and he quickly grasped her slim fingers. He held them tightly, like a drowning man.

'I've got a problem, Col,' he admitted.

'And am I that problem?' Her eyes glittered with unshed tears.

Michael stood up, gathered her in his arms and held her close. 'No, Col, no,' he said urgently. 'Never you.' He pressed his cheek against the softness of her hair. 'I don't know how to explain it but my whole life is upside down right now. I don't know what I'm doing, I don't know where I'm heading, I don't even know who I am any more. But the one thing I do know, that I've never ever had any doubt about, is that I love you, Col. I'll always love you.'

They stood in silence, clinging together in a desperate embrace. Each could feel the other's anguish, and now the love between them flowed through their touch and healed them.

'Do you know where I woke up this morning?' Michael said at last, in a trembling whisper. 'I was in the carpark of the cemetery. In my car. I shouldn't have been at the wheel. I don't even remember going there.' His voice was husky. 'Why the hell would I go out there?'

Colleen slipped her hand onto his cheek, and kissed him softly on the neck. They moved down onto the couch, and she held him close as he gazed through tear-filled eyes at old and bitter memories.

'I hated him,' he said breathlessly. It was painful, scarifying, but if he didn't say it now he never would and it would fester inside him until some vital part of him withered away, leaving just a hollow, empty shell.

'I hated him for what he did to Mum. He let her down when she needed him most. And I hated him even more for what he did to me. I grew up believing in him. He was always the decent, honourable man. When I stopped believing that it was like I lost my whole identity, everything. That old bastard! When the crunch time came, he just completely dropped the ball. And I swore I'd never do anything like that to any human being. Never.'

A single tear broke free from Michael's eye and ran down his cheek.

'I dumped that poor kid, Col,' he said at last. 'If it hadn't been for me he'd be alive today.'

'That's not true,' Colleen answered quickly, holding him even closer.

Now that the words were said they seemed to open up a door somewhere inside him, and through it came a bitter, long-caged emotion. His mouth and eyes were filled with salty tears as he drew in a long, relieving breath that cooled his throat and restored his composure.

'You did your best to help him, Michael.'

Michael shrugged. 'But I didn't help him, did I?'

'You tried to. That's what counts.'

'The fact that I tried isn't much consolation to him, is it?' he said bitterly

'No, but it should be to you.'

'I dumped him when he really needed help,' Michael whispered, his voice strained by the intolerable guilt.

Her gaze was compassionate. 'You did what you thought was right at the time.' She gently placed her palm on his cheek. 'You ask too much of people.' Her voice was soft and calming. 'You're not perfect, any more than your father was.

Perfection. Was that what he'd demanded of his father? Of himself?

'We're all human, Michael. No matter how hard we try, we don't always measure up to expectations. Our own, other people's. The important thing is that we try, isn't it? That we keep on trying.'

It sounded vaguely right, comforting at least. His confession had brought a kind of release to his troubled mind.

His thoughts now drifted aimlessly, back to his first confession, nervously peering through the grate to the half-hidden priest. The guilt of impure thoughts, of undiscovered disobedience, profanities offensive to the Lord our God. 'Go in peace, my son.' Go in peace. Three Hail Marys and a pure white soul...

Michael opened his eyes, unsure of how long he'd slept. He stumbled into the kitchen and checked his watch. Nearly two. There was no sign of Colleen but the note on the bench told him she had gone 'to buy some groceries and pick up the boys'.

His stomach grumbled, telling him it needed sustenance so he retrieved a terrine from the refrigerator, sliced it and a tomato and made an unaccustomed cup of tea. Brian had loved his tea. The cup that cheers but not inebriates, he used to say. Some old-hat advertising slogan that caught his fancy. Michael tried to pinpoint when and why he'd abandoned tea for coffee.

Cup and saucer in one hand, plate in the other, he moved to the desk in his study. He usually felt at ease there but today the journals lined up in the bookcase and the neatly stacked papers made him edgy. His work seemed pointless, unimportant. If he could walk away from it right now he would. But with a wife and two young sons his options were limited. He felt hopelessly confined within the boundaries of his own potential.

His eyes focused on a small, dusty cardboard carton

against the wall. He moved over to it, lifted it onto the desk and read the inscription: PROPERTY OF MICHAEL JOSEPH LEARY — PRIVATE & CONFIDENTIAL. He wrested with the pink tape, lifted the cardboard flaps and studied the contents.

On top was a bulging foolscap pad. Below it was a dog-eared court transcript, the front page bearing the title: *Regina-v-John Edward Arnold*. It hit him like a sledgehammer and he wondered how it was that, today of all days, his father mocked him from the grave.

For the accused, Mr E P Sullivan of counsel, instructed by Messrs BM Leary & Doyle. Michael dropped the document back so that once again he was looking at the cover of the over-stuffed pad.

Why would Brian leave him this? How was the transcript of the Arnold trial now the property of Michael Joseph Leary? He carefully removed the foolscap pad and turned back the cover.

The first page bore the title *'The Property of Daniel Thomas Leary and Michael Joseph Leary'*. Michael recognised his father's neat, compact hand, even remembered the fountain pen he had used. Someone had more recently deleted Daniel's name by ruling through it, this time with a biro.

Inside the pad was a patchwork of assorted newspaper clippings, dried, yellowed and rippled, some stuck firmly on the pages, others either loose or lightly holding their position. On the top left-hand corner of the first yellowing page was a clean white patch that corresponded with a narrow little clipping lying loose against the spine. Michael deduced that this had been the first insertion in the scrapbook.

Under the white patch his father had written the inscription: *Courier-Mail*, 19.5.1953. It was a newspaper report about a retired army sergeant who had 'assaulted the publican and several patrons with a bar stool' and broken three windows in the public bar of the Grand Hotel.

His solicitor, Mr BM Leary, told the magistrate his client greatly regretted the affair, which had resulted from 'excessive drink' and was sparked by some 'derogatory comments passed by another patron concerning His Majesty King George'. After thirty-two years of army service, the soldier, who was forty-eight years old, had been wounded in Malaya then discharged as medically unfit.

The magistrate imprisoned him for seven months.

The same faded blue ink appeared in careful notations on the first few pages. The dates were in the 1950s and the clippings came mainly from the *Courier-Mail*, with several from the *Telegraph*, the *Sunday Mail* and the *Truth*. They told of petty cases concerning apparently insignificant people from every walk of life charged with mainly unremarkable offences.

The common thread was Mr BM Leary, solicitor, appearing for his clients. Soldiers, sailors, prostitutes, shoplifters, tradesmen, salesmen, barmen, stockmen, shearers, painters, dockers, footballers and fighters. As Michael turned the pages, moving on through the 1960s, he saw a long procession of motley remnants of humanity filing endlessly through the courts.

Somewhere in the sixties a biro replaced the fountain pen but the clippings went on and on and on. And through it all the little man in the double-breasted suit was there beside these sometimes reprehensible people, fighting for their rights. His role was constant, unquestioning and uncompromising.

Michael turned the page to the rippled newspaper photograph of a black man's face. Under it his father had inscribed, *Injustice anywhere is a threat to Justice everywhere. Martin Luther King, Jr. 1963.* He had heard his father speak of 'justice' many times. It was a word lawyers used as some men use profanity, to punctuate their sentences. But he suspected that most had no more than a hazy notion of what the abstraction meant. Here, in these tattered clippings was the definition Brian Leary gave it. For him, it was no high-flown concept of an unachievable ideal; it was a simple, practical precept that dictated that every person was entitled to be heard, and judged on merit. No more, no less. *That's my job.*

The log jam that followed was made up of scores of clippings of various shapes and sizes pushed randomly into the book at a point towards the back. The earlier articles had been carefully cut out for pasting but it was clear that somewhere along the road his father's fervour had subsided or been diverted, and the later articles were simply torn from newspapers and the occasional magazine and jammed into the scrapbook. Michael thought about those terrible months of his mother's illness and, for the first time, had a glimmering of understanding of how hard that must have been for Brian Leary.

Michael opened the transcript of the trial, *R-v-Arnold* and began to read. He read for hours. He read about the horror and the outrage, the anger and the hatred of that trial. And, between the lines, he read of courage and commitment. He felt the hope and the determination, the disappointment and frustration. He could see the little man in the double-breasted suit persisting doggedly, faithful to his task.

Brian Leary's son was conscious of a growing sense of pride. He understood now why this case had meant so much and why it had changed their lives forever.

When Colleen Leary returned with the children and a clutch of supermarket carry bags it was close to four o'clock. The boys tumbled in yelling 'Daddy! Daddy!' and hurled themselves at him.

'And where have you been, pal?' he said, ruffling Simon's hair and then tossing Daniel in the air.

Simon's little eyes were bulging. 'We went shopping. We bought milk and ice cream and lots of stuff. And Mummy rode us in the trolley.'

'Except we didn't go very fast,' chimed in Daniel.

'No, well you're not allowed to speed in supermarkets, are you, pal?' Michael said, taking the boys by the hand.

Colleen unpacked the bags and stowed away their contents while Michael made the most of his sons' company. Then Colleen called to them, gave them a glass of milk and apple wedges and despatched them to the backyard swings, as Michael bundled up the papers littering the floor around him.

'What have you been reading?' she asked, glancing at the musty transcript in his hand.

'A morality tale.'

'Interesting?'

'Instructive.'

'Really? What did you learn?'

'I'm not sure yet,' Michael said reflectively. 'Maybe that sometimes you don't have to come first to be a winner.'

'Really?'

'Yeah, really.'

'Worth learning, I'd say.'

He dropped the transcript and slipped his arms around his wife. 'Yes, it is,' he smiled at her. 'It's like a great woman once said: the important thing is that we try.' He held her slender body close to his.

Whatever was illusory, this was real. Whatever was wrong, this was right.

25

'Did you murder Shirley Probert?'

Michael Leary had mentally rehearsed the words so often that now they sounded melodramatic, a line straight out of a cheap novel.

Peter Lade said nothing. Even in the stifling closeness of the interview room he looked cool and detached. His ice-blue eyes assessed the lawyer unwaveringly. 'You know I didn't,' he eventually said.

It was the answer Michael had expected, and now he considered the import of those words.

The handsome young killer stared at him unflinchingly across the table and it seemed to Michael that Lade was peering through his skull right into his brain. It was discomforting, mesmerising. Those penetrating eyes bored into him like twin drills, and he asked himself again whether he really had to walk this road.

'Did you have anything to do with her death?' he asked.

The glacial eyes narrowed slightly and the faintest smile tugged at the young man's lips. 'You know I didn't,' he mocked. 'Otherwise you wouldn't be here.'

'Reginald Davey says you did. He says you confessed to him.'

Lade gave a contemptuous 'huh' and sat back in his chair. His eyes fixed on Michael's, aware of the discomfort they caused. For a long, intimidating moment, he said nothing and when he finally spoke, the cultured voice was arrogant and contemptuous.

'Don't talk fucking bullshit to me, man.'

Michael struggled hard to remain calm, to mask his loathing, returning Lade's cold stare in silence, until the killer spoke again.

'You don't believe Davey's bullshit fucking story! So don't come here and insult me, man!'

The last words were spat out with some passion. A pulse throbbed in Lade's cheek.

The Ice Man is angry; finally displaying a human emotion, Michael thought, taking courage from it. He returned Lade's stare and said evenly, 'I didn't come here to insult you. In fact, I came to ask if you'll accept my services as your solicitor.'

Lade's lip curled as if he saw some irony in the statement. He spat back, 'Why should I? Your track record doesn't recommend you. The last person you represented is maggot shit already. I don't want to end up in your dead files section too.'

The shaft hit home and Michael winced at the pain of it. He forced himself to speak. 'There's perhaps one small thing in my favour,' he said stiffly. 'I'm the only person on earth who thinks you might not be guilty.'

Peter Lade sat upright in his chair, clinically assessing what was happening. Finally he jerked his head back arrogantly. 'Then I accept your services,' he said. 'Provided, of course, that you're prepared to work for nothing.' His mouth stretched in a mirthless smile. 'What do you lawyers call it? *Pro bono publico* — for the public good.'

The public good ... The mocking words conjured up the bloodied image of a dead man's face obscured by masking tape, his throat sliced back to sinew. Michael shuddered in revulsion but the look in his new client's eyes said it all — right now Michael Leary needed him much more than he needed any lawyer.

'All right,' Michael said. 'Let's get started.'

The Volvo had been cooking in the January sun for several hours and it was not until he had driven as far as the Story Bridge that the air-conditioning overcame the stinging heat trapped within the vehicle.

Michael thought about what he had just been told. Peter Lade knew nothing of the Probert murder and he had repeatedly told the police as much. Coming from a man who had already pleaded guilty to murder and was serving life for it, the denial was compelling, and Michael Leary believed him. As much as he despised the man, he could not accept that he was Shirley Probert's killer — and that meant someone else was.

Comforting as it might be to the public to have Peter Lade blamed for this murder, it was not the truth. Michael was convinced of that. And right now the truth was very important to him.

The other thing Michael had recently been told was that Senior Sergeant Darryl Batch was the arresting officer. Somehow that was very important too.

'Princeton' was a handsome redbrick building trimmed with white stucco and adorned with leadlight glass and carefully crafted iron railings, a fine example of the ordered little 1930's apartment blocks that predominated in the near-city suburb of New Farm.

Michael stepped into the grey terrazzo-floored foyer and was agreeably surprised by the coolness of the stairway. On the second floor two solid cedar doors confronted him. The one on the right bore a tarnished brass '4'. He pressed the button below it and soon heard unhurried footsteps approaching. The door creaked open.

'Hello, Gene,' Michael said.

'Michael!' Eugene Sullivan responded, clearly surprised. His shirtsleeves were rolled up to the elbows and he wore an apron that looked to have recently sustained a flour bomb attack. He paused for a moment, then said, 'Come in.'

He led the way to a cosy living room.

'I'm baking scones,' he said. 'They should be done by now. Have a seat while I check.'

Michael smiled at this unexpected activity, then studied the cluttered room. It was furnished with solid Victorian pieces and decorated with mementos and bibelots accumulated over many years. Royal Doulton figurines and framed photographs — some studio portraits, some casual snaps — formed an orderly row along the wooden mantelpiece. In the centre stood a framed black-and-white photograph of a much younger Eugene Sullivan with flashing white teeth and a full head of hair, one hand proudly holding aloft a good-sized fish, the other resting on the shoulder of a fair-haired boy. His son, Michael guessed. The boy had died young. Leukaemia, perhaps? The pair were standing by the old pavilion on Kirra Beach, both dressed in baggy swimsuits, Sullivan strong and athletic-looking. A long time ago ...

Beside it was a vaguely familiar portrait of a rawboned, thin-faced man with gentle, honest eyes.

'Do you know who that is?'

Michael turned as Sullivan, minus the apron, re-entered the room. 'The face rings a bell, but ...'

'That's Dan Casey, back when he was at the height of his career. He was my master when I started at the bar.'

Michael remembered the old man now. His name was still revered in Queensland legal circles as a kind of doyen of the criminal bar. He was supposedly a drinker and a fighter, a lifelong bachelor who, in his younger days, had spent many an alcoholic night curled up on a tramstop bench. But he was admired as a fervent champion of the underdog and was still revered as the first and only popular hero of the Queensland criminal bar. The thought of Sullivan as the fresh-faced apprentice to a brilliant, alcoholic master fitted easily in Michael's mind as did an accompanying sense of human tragedy.

'He was the best of us,' said Sullivan wistfully, studying the old portrait. It occurred to Michael he was talking about much more than just old Mr Casey.

'They said you'd given up your chambers,' Michael said to change the subject.

'Decided I'd go fishing for a while,' Sullivan said more cheerfully as he replaced the photograph. 'And bake some scones.' The old man bared his nicotine-stained teeth in a smile. A brief embarrassed silence passed between them before he added, 'Would you like a drink?'

'No,' said Michael. 'I'm here on business actually.'

'Ah!' Sullivan reached into his trouser pockets and produced a cigarette packet from one, a lighter from the other. 'I didn't expect to see another brief from you.'

Such candour made Michael a little uncomfortable. He pretended to have understood the comment differently. 'Well, as you know, I don't do much criminal work.'

Sullivan lit his cigarette and inhaled deeply. Behind a thin veil of smoke his narrowed eyes held Michael's. 'I never had Dan Casey's brilliance, Michael. Nor your father's courage.'

Michael looked this stranger in the eye and for the first time felt like he was speaking to a friend.

'Brilliance ... Courage ... They're pretty limited commodities, Gene.'

Sullivan nodded. 'Yes,' he said. 'Indeed they are.'

'I'm here about the Probert murder.'

'Why?'

'Because I don't believe Lade's right for it.'

'It's a dreadful brick they've dropped on him. Who's the arrester?'

'Batch.'

The old man's face paled to a wrinkled, parchment grey. 'They never bloody stop, do they?'

'I'm afraid there are no fees in it.'

'A crying shame,' Sullivan smiled ruefully. For the first time in a long while, he could feel some fire in his belly. 'When do we start?'

'As soon as you tell me where to start.'

26

Michael's first instruction was to get whatever material the Crown Prosecutor had to give them on the matter. That meant the transcript and exhibits from the committal proceedings in the Magistrates Court as well as a copy of the prosecution witness statements tendered to the magistrate.

Then he should deliver a letter to the Crown asking for any earlier or other statements made by the prosecution witnesses and check them for any inconsistencies against their final statements. He should also ask for all statements provided to police by anyone who did not give evidence at the committal but who would, or might, give evidence at the trial, and also those the Crown had elected not to call. He should get copies of all reports compiled and entries made by all investigating police in any notebook or diary as part of their investigation, and copies of the investigation running sheets and court files prepared for the initial bail hearing.

He should get copies of this material to Sullivan and if he ran into any opposition from the Crown, issue a subpoena *duces tecum* requiring the Commissioner of Police to produce the records to the court at the next standover.

The next thing was the newspapers. There was bound to be something about this murder in the papers at the time. Such stories invariably mentioned something about the leads and theories police were working on. That material could be crucial. It could raise questions about alternative suspects — why they weren't investigated or why they were eliminated. Sometimes it would include descriptions of suspects later eliminated by police merely because they did not fit the accused. He should review the papers as a matter of priority.

Then he should get down and inspect the scene as soon as possible. The trail was nearly twelve months old and would be pretty cold, but it was still worth going there and seeing it first hand. Speak to the dead woman's neighbours, to anyone he could find who had lived there at the time or who might have seen or heard anything on the night. Find out how the body was discovered, who, if anyone, went inside the apartment before the police arrived, and what the police did when they got there. Nosy neighbours were often the most reliable source of such information.

Michael's first stop was the office of Graham Worrell, the Deputy Director of Prosecutions. Worrell was a big man with a chubby face, capable of great charm or great boorishness, depending on his mood.

'Why doesn't he plead guilty and save us all a lot of gut-ache,' growled Worrell as he dumped a bundle of dog-eared documents on his desk and leafed through them, retrieving an occasional document from the pile. 'He's rooted anyway. Davey's evidence shoots him down in flames.'

Michael bridled. 'Davey's evidence is a crock of shit.'

Worrell's head jerked up from the papers, scowling at the brusque response.

'Doesn't matter if it is,' he returned. 'Once Davey gives evidence of that confession, your grub has to get into the witness box and call him a liar. And you know what happens then — the Crown gets to cross-examine him on his prior convictions. Once the jury knows your hero is already doing time for murder, it's all over Rover.'

Michael flicked through the papers impassively. 'We'll see,' he said evenly.

He took out the statement of Reginald Bruce Davey and skimmed through it. It was dated in November 1986 and in it Davey claimed he had first met Lade in the May of that year when both were prisoners at Boggo Road. He said Lade would often talk about the crimes he had committed, mainly break-and-enters in Brisbane and on the Gold Coast, and on several occasions he had told Davey that he would not fight the murder charge he was facing at the time.

Davey continued:

He said that he had murdered Peter Cosgrove. He said his mates had given him up on that and the coppers had him cold, so he would just plead guilty. He said that if he pleaded guilty and pretended to be remorseful he would get out on parole eventually. I said it must be a big burden for him to cart around, knowing that he'd killed someone and he said, 'Bullshit. I enjoyed it. I've killed before. It's fun. I necked a bitch in Surfers they don't even know about.'

That seemed a very strange comment for Peter Lade to have made in November 1986 when police had already interviewed him at length about the Probert murder. Michael knew that from the conversation he had with Lade in the City Watchhouse back in April. Why would Lade be saying the police knew nothing of the murder?

I asked him what had happened and he said he had broken into a unit in the Golden Gate Apartments down at Surfers Paradise. He reckoned he had broken into units there before and there was heaps of cash and jewellery, especially in the holiday season. When he got in there was no one there, but the woman who lived there came home while he was inside, and he was hiding in the lounge room when she came inside.

He said at first he was going to wait until she went to bed and then sneak out. But she sat down in the lounge room for a while. He said she was sitting at the dining table eating oranges so he came out and he knocked her down, and then he tried to rape her. He said that he got on top of her and he was sitting on her stomach. He tried to pull her pants down but she was holding on to them with one hand and he couldn't get them off. He said she was really strong. I said, 'But why did you kill her, Peter?' and he said, 'Because the slut bit me on the finger, that's why. So I belted her and then I put my hands round her throat and choked her.'

The statement went on to say how Lade had said that after killing the woman he was worried someone might have heard them struggling, so he left the apartment straight away without taking anything.

'There's the photos of your hero's handiwork,' said Worrell, lobbing a small pile of photographs on the desk. 'You can keep these copies if you like.'

There were nineteen glossy colour photographs. The top one showed a general view of the living room of an apartment. The first thing Michael registered was how neat and tidy it was, not at all what one would expect from the scene of a murder and attempted rape. Nothing in the room seemed dislodged. The furniture looked in place. The flowers on the sideboard and cheap ornaments on the television cabinet seemed undisturbed. Even three glossy fashion magazines were artfully displayed on the coffee table.

The only sign of violence was a naked foot protruding from behind the living room couch, so tidily positioned its owner might have simply stretched out on the carpet for a nap. As Michael flipped each photo over and slipped it to the bottom of the pile he nerved himself for the inevitable close-ups of the body. They must be at the bottom of the pack, perhaps put there by Worrell to maximise their effect.

Then it came. A woman lying face down on the floor, her arms and shoulder-length brown hair spread on either side as though she had been dropped from the ceiling. Her head was turned to the right and her open mouth and one rounded cheek could be partly seen through the screen of outspread hair. There was no blood, no laceration, no abrasion — only stiffness, finality. It was a woman as much devoid of violence as the fashion magazines, shaped into a perfect fan.

The next one was a closer shot showing the head and shoulders from a different angle. It might have been the picture of a woman fast asleep except that one eye was partly open and a little piece of pupil peered out, glazed and distant.

The woman looked as though she had fallen or been thrown face down on the floor. Her fitted knee-length shirt was hardly creased and the hem lay in place behind her knees. Her lightweight knitted top was still tucked into her skirt, neat as a new pin.

These photographs didn't fit the story.

'Michael, have you lost your senses? Have you gone completely insane?'

Michael was becoming accustomed to Tony Artlett's sorties to his office these days but this unceremonious entry took him by surprise. The door had burst open and Artlett stormed in, flushed and uncharacteristically flustered, a lock of his usually impeccably-groomed hair falling down onto his forehead.

'I've just this minute come from a meeting with the Natural Resources Minister, Frank Delaney,' he panted. 'He tells me — he tells me, mind you, not you — that now we're acting for that homicidal bloody maniac, Peter Lade.'

Michael had three fingers stuck in various sections of Volume 10 of the *Encyclopedia of Forms and Precedents* and his nose buried in *Chitty on Contract*, but now his train of thought was hopelessly derailed. The visit was inevitable, of course, but Artlett usually took a less direct approach. Michael felt his hackles rise. Tony Artlett stood in front of his desk, his hands propped on his hips like a teacher remonstrating with an errant schoolboy. Bloody cheek!

'Did you knock?' he asked coldly.

'What?' snapped Artlett.

'I didn't hear you knock before you entered.'

'Knock!' he fumed. 'What the hell's got into you, Michael?' Artlett's patience was exhausted. 'First it was that damned Manetti business — and what a debacle that turned out to be! Now it seems you've put out the welcome mat for every psychopath in town. What are you trying to prove? The minister has made it crystal clear. This government doesn't want its lawyers acting for these kinds of people.'

'What kinds of people, Tony?'

Tony Artlett had broken all his golden rules of people management. Michael Leary was insulted and had moved into defensive mode and it would take a very different tack to shift him. Artlett blamed his lapse on the stressful meeting he had just endured, fielding Frank Delaney's endless questions about how and why the firm had taken up the Probert murder case, where the fees were coming from and was it likely to proceed to trial. He'd had as much as he could take of the aggravation Michael Leary and his clients were causing him and on this hot summer afternoon it had become too much to bear.

Now he regretted his short temper because that wasn't the way to bring Michael Leary to heel. The only way was to appeal to his intelligence and his business sense. After all, he had eventually seen the light on the Manetti thing.

'Look, Michael, I'm sorry I blew in here like that.' As he settled on the edge of a client chair Artlett's tone was conciliatory. 'It's just that competition's tight for this government work. You know that. And the state government is this firm's biggest client. We can't afford to go upsetting anybody over there.'

It all made perfect sense, and Michael knew it.

'The fact is, Michael, we're in business. We can't afford to go around championing people's causes.'

Championing people's causes ... The very thought of it was distasteful; you could hear it in Artlett's voice.

Michael studied his old school friend and saw a high-powered businessman with all the answers, one of those very important persons on the podium at legal congresses, on the boards of all the biggest blue-chip companies. The kind who knew just how to get a good commercial outcome. Championing causes didn't enter into it.

Suddenly Tony Artlett didn't look like anyone Michael Leary hoped to be. An image came of that frantic night at the university so many years ago when he had marvelled at his friend's apparent courage and conviction. *Each one of us must choose a side* ... It was true. Michael understood that now. But his side would not be Tony Artlett's.

'Funny,' he said. 'I used to think that's what lawyers were for — championing causes.'

Artlett pushed up from his chair and strode to the door. He'd had a difficult day already and his time was too valuable to waste on pandering to the sensitivities and misdirected ideals of his professional staff. 'I don't give a rat's arse what you used to think,' he said curtly. 'I want us out of that Lade case immediately. Do you read me?'

The door slammed shut.

I read you loud and clear, Michael thought.

27

The Probert unit in the Golden Gate Apartment block at Surfers Paradise, now rented short term, was vacant at the moment. The agent told Michael new tenants would move in on the Friday so he could make arrangements to be shown through immediately. They agreed to meet on site at midday but Michael planned to be there by eleven to scout around and speak to neighbours and the like if he could.

The drive from Brisbane to the Gold Coast tourist strip took not much more than fifty minutes on a double highway that weaved through satellite suburbs, past small farms, virgin bush, burgeoning developments and garish theme parks. As he drove, Michael's thoughts turned to Colleen. As they lay in bed last night, bathed in moonlight, she had confronted him.

'I want to hear it all. You need to tell it all,' she'd said.

She was right, of course. He had been hinting cautiously, breaking his decision gently, to her and to himself. He needed to verbalise it, to share it with someone. With Colleen, his wife, his lover, his friend.

It came out haltingly at first. Then in an onward, inexorable tide he told her of all that had happened since Gerry Manetti had come to see him; told her about his doubts and fears and inadequacies; about his guilt and where it all had led him. He finished by telling her that he was committed to the Lade case and meant to see it through, even though it meant he would have to leave MS&G. The trial was set to start in March, so he would resign immediately and then take time off to prepare the case.

He waited, flinching internally, for her response. He expected her to object, to weep perhaps, to remind him of his responsibilities to his family and his duty to the firm, maybe even issue him with an ultimatum.

Instead, she asked, her eyes intent on his, 'And is Peter Lade worth all this upheaval?'

'No, he's not,' he replied, verbalising for the first time the reality that had plagued him for days. 'But this isn't about Peter Lade.'

'What is it about then?'

It was hard to put it into words. Maybe he still didn't know the answer. 'Peter Lade didn't kill that woman, Col. I'm sure of that. And if he didn't do it there's someone out there walking free who did. No one seems to care about that. That Batch character is quite happy to sell this lie of Davey's just so the police can close their books on it. It's just not right, Col. I don't know, it just seems that someone's got to make a stand.'

'All right,' Colleen said calmly. 'Go for it.'

'You don't mind?'

'Of course I don't mind.'

'It will mean some major changes for us. I'll never make the kind of money I could have if I'd got equity at MS&G.'

'So what? We'll get by — we always have.' Her voice was confident, reassuring. 'You know, Michael, what worried me most over the past few years was watching you turn yourself into another Tony Artlett.'

Michael was about to protest but he couldn't deny it.

She went on, 'From the day I met you I knew you were a better man than he could ever hope to be. It scared me to death to think that you were making him your role model.'

'Me? Turning into a Macbeth?' he groaned in mock horror.

She grinned at him, remembering. 'Yeah. A Macbeth.'

He leaned across to her and whispered, 'In that case, witch, my burning ambition is to make love to you until you beg for mercy. To no avail of course.'

'Call that justice?' she dimpled, her eyes dancing.

'Your just desserts, I'd say.' He slipped the flimsy nightgown over her head and tossed it on the floor.

'I'll accept that,' she gurgled happily as her pliant, eager body accommodated itself to his.

The Golden Gate Apartments building was a giant concrete structure by the sea, one of a line of high-rise sentinels that stretched along the beach at Surfers Paradise.

The corridors were wide but circuitous, the front doors of the units discreetly separated from their neighbours. The Probert unit was on floor 4, its front door entered from a stretch of corridor that could not be seen from the lifts or from the front doors of other units. The rendered block walls would be near enough to soundproof, Michael thought.

The only way in was through the solid wooden front door which, like all the front doors of the units in the block, was fitted with a deadlock. An intruder would have to cope with that or come in from the ocean side, four storeys off the ground.

Someone could easily get there from the balcony of an adjoining unit, but Michael had already checked with management who assured him that there had been no reported break-ins to the building on the night in question. The Scenes of Crime investigators had found no mark or damage on the front door. If Lade were the murderer he had managed to pick the front door lock without leaving any sign of it. If he had entered by the open door or windows on the ocean side, he had shinnied up four levels on the outside of the building in full view of traffic on the southbound Gold Coast highway. Unlikely ...

Michael knocked on the door of the nearest neighbouring unit, No 405. An eye came to the peephole and then withdrew, and he heard the lock turn. A suntanned, craggy face peered out from behind the safety chain.

'Yeah, mate,' said a gravelly voice in a broad Australian accent.

'Hello, my name's Michael Leary. I'm a solicitor. I'm involved in an upcoming trial concerning Shirley Probert, the woman who lived in the unit next door.'

'Oh yeah.'

'I'd like to ask you a few questions about anything you might have seen or heard at the time.'

'Yeah,' the man answered doubtfully. 'You with the police, are you?'

'No. I'm acting for the fellow who's been charged with the murder.'

The door closed momentarily while the safety chain was rattled open, then it swung back open to reveal a man wearing a pair of shorts and a singlet that looked even whiter than it really was against the leathery brown skin.

'Les Burrows, mate. How ya going?' He held out his hand and Michael shook it. 'Come on in.'

Les Burrows had owned unit 405 for about ten years and lived there with his Filipina wife, Maria. He was a builder by occupation, and these days most of his work was in Darwin and in Cairns. He'd been in Cairns when 'all this happened'. He said he'd had a bit to do with Shirley Probert, and he liked her, even though she was a pro. She sometimes came in for a drink if they were having a few mates over, but otherwise kept quiet enough and didn't cause Les any grief.

'There were blokes comin' and goin' all the time, of course,' said Les, sprawling back on the living room sofa, his bare feet resting on the coffee table. 'But that never bothered us. You'd hardly know she was there like.'

His wife Maria dutifully arrived with two tall glasses filled with orange juice and ice cubes, deposited them on the coffee table, and then withdrew.

'Shirl'd only been up here about twelve months or so,' Les said as soon as he had gulped down half his drink. 'I think she come up from South Australia in early '85.'

'Did she have any close friends or relatives up here, do you know?'

'Wouldn't know, mate.' Les drained the rest out of his glass and then rattled it until a cube of ice slid down into his mouth. 'Her only china that I knew was a sheila by the name of Rita. She was on the game as well, I think.'

'You wouldn't know her surname, would you?'

'No. She lived in Brisbane though. She'd sometimes come down and stop with Shirl for a couple of days like. They'd usually go into Surfers.'

'Rita from Brisbane' was not a lot to go on, and Michael tried to think of any other detail he could get that might assist.

Les struggled to his feet. 'Hang on,' he said, as he waddled out of sight into the hallway. He reappeared carrying a photograph album.

'Yeah, I thought I had a snap of her somewhere,' he said settling back on the sofa, this time close to Michael's armchair. 'That's her and Shirley there,' he said, a callused finger indicating a slightly out-of-focus photograph of two smiling, suntanned women lounging on that very sofa.

'That was Christmas '85. They come in for a drink with us.'

Shirley had a pleasant, friendly look about her, not glamorous at all but attractive in a girl-next-door way with none of the artificial glamour Michael expected of a woman in her line of work. Her round face was lit up by a cheeky grin. He had not seen her face before, only glimpses of a drawn, grey mask, featureless and drained of all expression. The picture of this laughing, animated face surprised and touched him.

Rita was a handsome woman but there was a wariness in her smile that suggested she had seen more than her fair share of trouble in her life, and expected more to come.

'Did Shirley ever visit Rita in Brisbane, do you know?'

'Wouldn't have a clue, mate.' Les slumped back into the comfort of the sofa. 'Tell you what though, I think they used to work together up in Brisbane. Apparently Shirl was up here years ago and they used to work together in the Valley.'

'Whereabouts in the Valley?

'Turn it up, mate. I wouldn't know.'

Michael smiled to show appreciation for his host's assistance to this point.

Les sat back on the sofa idly studying the album on his knees. 'I'd say Bob would know though, that's for sure,' he said, somewhat absent-mindedly.

'Bob who?'

'Bob. The bloke she used to live with.'

'Shirley Probert had a man living with her?'

'Shit yeah! Bob.'

'Bob...' Michael said reflectively. 'I don't think he did a statement for the police.'

'Well, he was gone when all this happened, wasn't he?' said Les with a note of irritation in his voice. 'He left just before I went back to Cairns. That was in the January like.'

Shirley Probert was murdered in the February. Until January she had been living with a man who was not mentioned in any of the Crown material, nor was he mentioned in any of the press reports or police despatches. If the police had known about him he surely would have been questioned, but there was not one word about him in the investigation running sheets. Incredibly, it seemed as though the investigators were not aware of him.

'They weren't married, were they?'

'Shit no!' said Les, as if horrified by the thought. 'No, mate, I think they were just good mates so far as I could see. They had some blow-up in the end and he took off.'

'You wouldn't know his surname, would you?'

'No mate. Just Bob was all I knew him as. Little short pommy bloke he was. Built like a brick shithouse though. Used to reckon he was in the pommy SAS as a young bloke. He might have been too, by the look of him.'

'Would he be in there at all?' said Michael, indicating the album resting in his companion's lap.

'Not a bloody snowball's chance in hell,' said Les emphatically. 'Bob'd run a mile from a camera.' A dusty chuckle crackled out of Les's throat. 'Fair dinkum. I seen him do it here one time. He dead-set didn't like getting his picture taken. Shirley used to reckon he was dodging Immigration. She could've been right.'

Michael stepped out of Unit 405, shook Les Burrows' hand and thanked him for his time and assistance and for the loan of the photograph of Shirley Probert and her friend, which he promised to return within the week.

As he walked along the empty corridor he thought about the photographs Graham Worrell had shown him and recalled how neat and tidy the living room of Shirley Probert's apartment was that night.

Surely anyone who had broken into the unit that night would have left some trace of the intrusion. Surely if Shirley had surprised an intruder there would be some sign of a struggle, even something as minor as a carefully-arranged magazine knocked askew.

Perhaps the killer had simply walked right in and been welcomed by the victim. Perhaps Shirley Probert was expecting a visit from an old friend.

Fortitude Valley's Shamrock Hotel was better known for its green beer on St Patrick's Day than for its fine cuisine. It was a place Michael Leary would never have chosen for a meal, but when Johnny Forrest said he had to 'see a man about a dog' that day down in the Valley and suggested they meet over a 'steak sanger' at the Shamrock, Michael was happy to go along. If anyone could provide him with the information he needed it was Johnny Forrest.

They met in what was loosely called the beer garden, a cramped outdoor enclosure at the side of the hotel in which plastic chairs and metal tables competed for the meagre space available. Michael sat down at an unoccupied table and took off his jacket. It was hot and steamy.

'Hello matey,' Forrest barked as he thrust one large forearm forward and lowered his roly-poly body into a chair. Michael took his hand, trying not to wince as Forrest shook it energetically.

'Isn't this a bloody bonzer day?' the big man said. 'Fair dinkum, you wouldn't be dead today for quids, would you?'

Michael smiled at the sight of Forrest, splayed out in the sun and grinning broadly like a well-fed ginger cat.

'This is a pleasant spot for lunch, John.'

'It is. But listen, matey, I'm afraid I can't stop for lunch as it turns out. I have to meet that bloke at one o'clock so we might just have to settle for a beer.'

'That's fine,' said Michael, relieved rather than disappointed he would not dine at this establishment. 'I only wanted a quick chat with you.'

'That's what I reckoned, mate,' said Forrest. 'Anyway, eating's cheating when you're drinking, isn't it?'

Michael went to the bar and returned with two ten-ounce glasses filled to overflowing. They wished each other luck, then Forrest poured most of the contents of his glass steadily into his mouth. His mighty neck expanded and contracted rhythmically as the contents quickly disappeared. Finally he relented and smacked his lips contentedly.

'Ah, nectar of the bloody gods!' he said and then rolled the frosted glass across his shiny brow, closing his eyes to savour the experience.

Michael slipped the colour photograph from his breast pocket and placed it on the metal table.

'I was wondering if you know this woman,' he said, pointing to Rita.

'That's Rita,' Forrest said immediately. He scooped the photo up with one hand as his other delved into his pocket and eventually produced glasses which he held, unopened, up against his eyes.

'I was told that's her name,' said Michael. 'What can you tell me about her?'

Forrest's smile had faded and his eyes were evasive. 'Where'd you get this photo from?' He paused, then demanded, 'What's this all about?'

There was suspicion in his voice, and uncertainty, and something else — something that sounded like fear. The transformation in his happy-go-lucky companion took Michael by surprise.

'I'm acting for Peter Lade,' he said. 'He's been charged with murdering a Gold Coast prostitute called Shirley Probert in February last year. She's the other woman in the photograph.'

'Shirley who?'

'Probert. Shirley Probert.'

Forrest held up the photograph and squinted at it through his folded glasses. Then he unfolded them, slipped them on and studied the photograph minutely.

'How'd she cop it?' he asked.

'Strangled.'

'Strangled ...'

'They've verballed Lade for it,' Michael added. 'The perfect fall-guy. But I'm sure he didn't do it.'

Forrest leaned his head towards the lawyer and peered out over his glasses. 'Who pinched him?'

'Batch.'

Forrest dropped the photograph as if it were too hot to hold. 'Drop it, matey. Leave this one alone.'

Forrest leaned back in his chair and poured another draught of beer down his throat. His interest in the photograph seemed to have evaporated.

'Why? What do you know about it, John?'

'Nothing, mate,' Forrest said emphatically. 'I don't know nothing. OK? I'm just telling you to drop it.'

'How do you know Rita, John?' Michael insisted.

Forrest flicked a sideways glance at Michael. 'That Lade's an arsehole, Michael. He won't be missed, not by anyone. He's not worth getting people killed for.'

'What's that supposed to mean?'

Forrest drained the contents of his glass and placed it firmly on the table. 'It means drop it, matey,' he said and rose up to his feet. 'You get your head right out of it.'

He held out his hand and Michael took it. 'Sorry I can't help you, mate,' he said. 'My shout next time.'

Michael smiled thinly. 'I'm going to track down this Rita woman eventually, you know John.'

Forrest shook his head. 'Don't make the same blue your old man did,' he said in a voice that barely rose above a whisper. 'That nutcase ain't worth it.' He held Michael's gaze for several seconds, as if to emphasise his message, then added, 'I'll catch you for that beer some time.'

With that John Forrest turned and left.

Michael leant back in his chair and swallowed a mouthful of beer. Lying on the table was the photograph of two suntanned ladies of the night, posing for a Christmas snapshot. He wondered what it was about these ladies that had spooked a tough old campaigner like Johnny Forrest.

Something had, without a doubt.

28

Michael Leary and Eugene Sullivan strode along the George Street footpath towards Herschel Street at the slow deliberate pace dictated by Sullivan's unhurried progress. Little conversation passed between them. Sullivan seemed disinclined to talk. He ignored or dismissed Michael's every opening gambit until Michael, too, fell silent.

They had spent the morning in the office of the State Government Health Laboratories talking to Neville Barton. Barton was the forensic scientist assigned the task of conducting scientific tests of the exhibits and had been more than helpful in explaining the tests he had done and their results. His findings were largely unremarkable, perhaps because no foreign blood or hair had been located at the scene.

Sullivan had closely questioned Barton about the samples he had received for testing. A scraping had been taken from the woman's fingernails but, when tested, it revealed no tissue or other matter of significance. In Barton's view that was somewhat surprising given that the allegation was that there had been a violent struggle between the deceased and her attacker. It was not completely inconsistent but it was certainly unusual.

Barton had not been told the details of the prosecution case before. He had simply been provided with material for testing. But when he heard from Sullivan details of the allegations made in Davey's evidence, his reaction was immediate.

'That doesn't seem right,' he said.

His notes confirmed that he had checked the woman's clothing and discovered nothing of significance. There were no blood or semen stains and the only pubic hair discovered belonged to the deceased. More significant now was the fact that there was almost no fabric damage to the clothing.

Barton retrieved the garments from a large sealed plastic bag, and spread them across his desk to prove his point. He explained that when a vigorous struggle occurs such as in a rape, it is usual to find some signs of fabric damage.

The only damage he could find was a stretching of the fibres at the front of the woman's cotton-knit top, just below the neckline. The garment wasn't torn but the fibres had been pulled with enough force to stretch them. The knee-length skirt was intact, with no observable damage to the fabric. But more significantly, the woman's underwear showed no sign of trauma whatsoever. That, it seemed to Barton, was quite inconsistent with Davey's claim that Lade had tried to forcibly remove the woman's pants and she had violently resisted.

'If you look closely you'll see this undergarment is made of a quite delicate fabric,' Barton observed. 'The lacework at the edges in particular would be highly susceptible to damage if pulled with any force.'

Michael was sure there was something quite obscene in three men so coldly examining intimate items of a dead woman's apparel; nonetheless the conclusions that were surfacing were dynamite. In Barton's considered view the incident could not have happened in the way

Davey had described it, not without some clearly observable damage to the fabric of the panties.

When they walked from Barton's office, Michael rejoiced at this new support. But Sullivan counselled caution. Scientists, he said, saw life in terms of black and white; juries rarely did. The clothes looked inconsistent with the Davey story, but anything was possible and it would take more than Neville Barton to swing this jury.

'I've known Doug Netting for over thirty years,' Sullivan huffed wheezily as they began to mount the staircase to the office of the Government Medical Officer. Halfway up he halted momentarily, caught his breath, and added, 'Doug's always been a bloody fascist!'

Shirley Probert's Life Extinct Certificate had been completed by Dr Douglas Netting, who had been the GMO in Brisbane for longer than most people could remember. Netting had been on the Gold Coast on another matter at the time the body was discovered and the police had called on him to certify the death.

According to Sullivan, Netting knew his stuff and would certainly have made a careful note of all the relevant features he'd observed.

'There was no struggle to speak of,' Netting said conclusively, eyeing the lawyers sitting opposite him at his desk as if daring them to challenge the veracity of that statement.

He was a big man with a thatch of snow-white hair and a deep, booming voice of great authority.

'The woman was attacked suddenly, and from behind.' Netting closed his notes as if to declare the subject closed.

Michael added another credit entry to the defence ledger.

'According to the Crown case,' Sullivan said, 'he was trying to rape her.'

'Huh! Then he chose a rather deviant direction of approach,' said Nutting scornfully.

'It's said he was on top of her trying to rape her and then, unsuccessful in that despite, shall we say, his best endeavours, he strangled her.'

'Nonsense!' said Netting emphatically. 'No, the woman wasn't strangled. Not in the true sense of the word.'

'The Crown witnesses say she was choked,' persisted Sullivan.

'Bullshit!' snapped the doctor. 'When we talk of someone being choked to death we are dealing with obstruction to or restriction of the airway so that the vital flow of oxygen to the lungs is interrupted, ultimately leading to asphyxiation.' Netting reopened his notes and flicked through them. 'When that happens you will almost certainly find damage to the windpipe and the larynx. The trachea is made up of fragile cartilaginous rings. With strangulation, you will quite often see the larynx completely crushed. Here there was none of that.'

Sullivan seemed unconvinced. 'But it's possible, isn't it Doug? It's possible he applied sufficient pressure without causing such damage.'

'No! No! No!' barked Netting. 'There's no indication at all that a ligature was used and yet you find no thumb-mark bruising, and the hyoid bone is totally intact. That doesn't happen in a violent struggle with a man's hands around your neck.'

Sullivan sat back and slipped his cigarettes from his breast pocket. 'So what do you say killed her, Doug?' he said.

'I know what's going to kill you.' Netting indicated the No Smoking sign on the wall. 'I've told you to give those things away.'

Sullivan growled and slid the packet back to his pocket. 'Did I ever tell you you're a bloody fascist, Doug?'

'Yes you did. Many times. Have you got Fred Arrowsmith's report?'

Dr Frederick Arrowsmith was the forensic pathologist who had performed the autopsy. Sullivan passed the autopsy report across the table and Netting quickly leafed through to the last page.

'There, you see,' he boomed. 'It's all in here. The post mortem findings confirm it. Significant petechiae in the tissue of the brain, and Fred Arrowsmith ascribes the cause of death to cerebral ischaemia.'

'Cerebral ischaemia,' repeated Sullivan. 'That's a lack of oxygen to the brain.'

'Exactly! To the brain! Not the lungs!' roared Netting triumphantly, flourishing the report aloft. 'Sustained pressure properly applied to the carotid arteries on either side of the neck will cut the flow of blood — and therefore oxygen — to the brain, and can produce a loss of consciousness within ten seconds. If the pressure is maintained, irreversible brain damage and ultimately death will occur within three to five minutes.'

'Without damaging the trachea?'

'If the pressure is skilfully applied the only obvious signs of trauma will be minor bruising, externally and internally, to the neck. Such bruising was present in this case.'

'On what you're saying, this all suggests a specific intention to cause death.' Sullivan said it tentatively as if it were altogether too confusing.

'Yes. And whoever did it had some practice at it,' said Netting, closing his notes and looking as smug as a man whose judgement has been questioned and then vindicated had a right to do. 'That hold is known as a

Gurkha Headlock. Left arm round the neck, with the elbow bent around the Adam's apple, then the right hand applies the pressure so the left arm closes like a pair of scissors on the neck, and cuts the carotid artery on both sides. Much more efficient than asphyxiation. The Brits taught their commandoes how to use it during the last war.'

'I dare say they would teach it to the SAS as well,' Sullivan said.

'Undoubtedly.'

Shirley Probert's flatmate Bob had just become a prime suspect.

After midnight the Valley had a dangerous feel to it. Its streets took on a surreal glow that seemed designed to hide the true identity of those who walked its pavements and the buildings kept their secrets behind closed doors and darkened windows. Bohemians in exotic garb, and weirdos draped in black with heads shaved on one side and hair down to the shoulder on the other, joined sailors, skinheads, transvestites and gays on the dingy footpaths. Above the awnings flashed dilapidated neon lights that flickered unrepaired. Half-hidden figures lurked in doorways and at every street corner the night people of the city's underbelly collected. Michael Leary had forgotten just how weird this place could be.

'You want coffee? We got beautiful cappuccino.'

The waiter was a swarthy brute but he was friendly enough, and he controlled the little restaurant with his noisy presence, so that it seemed a relatively safe refuge from the streets outside.

Michael had been there now for an hour or more. The pizza had been first-class and he was glad to stay a little longer, positioned by the window, from which he could keep an eye on the passing parade outside.

The best, most recent lead they had was Rita. If anyone could put a face to Bob, maybe even an address, then surely Rita could. She was sure to know Shirley's flatmate Bob. The Gold Coast letting agent could remember 'a little English fellow with tattoos down both arms' who had come in to pay the rent once or twice, but he'd paid in cash and never waited for a receipt, so the agent knew nothing more about him. Neither Les Burrows nor his wife, nor management, nor any other neighbours could be of any further help.

So that left Rita.

Michael knew what Rita looked like, that she was probably a prostitute, and that at some stage she had worked the Valley. That meant there was really only one place he could start to look, and he had been cautiously examining the sleazy night-time streets of Fortitude Valley for several nights now, hoping that the woman might appear. A longshot but, as Sullivan had said, the best shot they had.

Michael had arrived in the Valley at half-past-nine and walked around the infamous 'Sin Triangle' so many times that by half-past-ten the loiterers had stopped approaching him and were eyeing him suspiciously. It was easy to convince himself he should move on further down to Wickham Street. He stood near the intersection of Brunswick and Wickham until he excited the interest of a muscular young man wearing a spotted tank-top and a leather cap. That decided him to adopt a lower profile, and the little pizza cafe fronting Wickham Street seemed the perfect spot.

'A cappuccino, thanks,' said Michael, and then leaned his head against the cool glass window. Figures moved past on the footpath. Some looked alive and interested as if they had a place to go; others shuffled aimlessly, drifting through the darkness. There were faces painted with a hunger for excess, and drunken men, and hoboes, and lost and lonely people with vacant eyes that stared down at the dirty city pavement.

'Bruno, give us a packet of Marlboro Reds, will you, darl?'

Michael turned to look at the woman with the rasping voice. He recognised her instantly as Rita, Shirley Probert's closest friend. He had not noticed her come in through the door, but as she leaned against the counter under the light above the Pepsi sign, he knew that this was the woman in the photograph.

'Thanks, darl,' she said as Bruno flipped the cigarettes onto the counter. 'I'll catch you up later on for them. Okay?'

'Okay,' said Bruno.

Then she was gone. Michael ran out onto the footpath. There she was, in a short skirt and stiletto heels, drifting off into the darkness.

'Rita!'

The woman stopped mid-stride and turned. In the jaundiced glare of a yellow street light her haggard face was chalky white. She clutched her handbag against her breast as if it were a shield. She was clearly terrified. Her head flicked to one side, then the other, as if trying to decide where to run. Then she faced Michael with a look of abject terror.

'That's not my name,' she wavered.

Michael tried to think of an approach that would ease her fear. He had to act quickly before she bolted.

'I'm here about Shirley Probert,' he said.

The woman shrank back like a cornered animal. 'Don't hurt me,' she pleaded.

'I just want to talk to you, Rita,' Michael said. 'I'm a lawyer. I'm acting for the man who's charged with Shirley's murder. All I want is information.'

With this the woman froze completely. The fear in her eyes became a look of total shock.

'They don't know about me,' she said urgently. 'Please don't tell them!'

'I'm looking for Shirley's flatmate Bob,' Michael said.

'He'll kill me! Just like he killed Shirley.'

'Hey mister!' The swarthy pizza man was on the pavement. 'You don't want your cappuccino?'

Michael knew he could not afford to take his eyes off Rita for an instant. 'Rita, please help me,' he pleaded. 'I want to find the guy who really killed her.'

'Hey, mister, you gonna pay your bill?' the pizza man was growing impatient.

Michael didn't dare move his gaze from the woman. She was his only chance. He pulled his wallet out and, slipping out his Law Courts ID card, thrust it towards the woman.

'I'm a lawyer,' he repeated.

'Hey, mister lawyer, you gonna pay your bill or what?' The pizza man was standing beside Michael, as Rita cautiously stepped forward.

She took the card and cupped it in both hands. As she did so Michael pulled a fifty dollar note from his wallet and held it out in the direction of the pizza man who quickly took it and waddled back into the restaurant.

'Her diary,' said Rita, holding out the card to Michael. 'It's all in the diary.'

She stepped quickly to the kerb and hailed to a passing taxi.

'Wait a minute! What do you mean?' cried Michael as the woman walked towards the slowing cab. 'What's in the diary?'

Rita opened the rear door and started to climb in. 'It's all there,' she whispered breathlessly. 'All you want to know.' Her chin began to tremble and her painted, world-weary eyes were wet with tears. 'It's all in the diary.'

With that she clambered in and slammed the door. The taxi was soon swallowed up in traffic and disappeared in the direction of the city. Michael stood wondering if he should follow her, but there was no other cab in sight and the opportunity passed. He thrust his hands into his pockets and walked back to the restaurant wishing the cappuccino he was about to drink was something much stronger.

'What diary? I don't know anything about any diary.'

Graham Worrell's reaction to Michael's inquiry about a diary having been found by police in Shirley Probert's unit was decisive. As far as he was concerned this was an open and shut case. The trial was nothing but a formality and he was not about to go wading through the police exhibit room searching for a diary that probably didn't exist. With great forbearance he had pointed out to Michael that there was no mention of a diary on the court exhibit list and therefore it was irrelevant, whether it existed or not.

Michael feared then that he might have come to a dead end. But Eugene Sullivan had been dealing with the likes of Worrell for a long, long time. 'Put it in writing,' he barked. 'Get a letter over to Worrell today.'

Then he leaned back in his chair, sucked on his cigarette, and without further warning launched into a rapid dictation, on the apparent assumption his instructing solicitor would record every word.

We note that the trial is listed to proceed in less than three weeks. In order to satisfactorily prepare a defence of the matter we require a comprehensive inventory of all property located by police at the scene of the crime. It may be that we will wish to inspect some or all of the items contained on that list, and it may ultimately be necessary to have an item or items examined by an independent forensic expert prior to the trial. In the circumstances we require the list as a matter of urgency. We hope that you will respond accordingly since, if we do not get the list within sufficient time to satisfactorily carry out such examination or inquiry as is necessary, we shall have no other alternative than to seek an adjournment of the trial. In our respectful view, every effort should be made to avoid such inconvenience to the court. Et cetera, et cetera, yours faithfully.

'Have someone stick that up Worrell's nose today.'

Worrell was a career public servant who had been around long enough to know not to expose himself to unnecessary judicial criticism. That letter had 'Adjournment Application' written all over it and if the defence came along to court complaining they had been denied information or material they were entitled to see, and asked for an adjournment on the strength of it, there would be some harsh words from the judge for whoever was responsible. Worrell would not risk that. All he had to do was pass on the request to the police concerned.

The list appeared within three days. But it contained no reference to any diary.

'Perhaps she kept the diary somewhere else,' Michael ventured wearily.

They had been sitting there at Sullivan's dining table for hours, poring over the exhibits, and the statements, and the other material, that all seemed to raise more problems than solutions.

On every issue Eugene Sullivan would pause and ponder, crosschecking with the evidence and reflecting carefully before he took a view. He never spoke merely to fill a silence, and it seemed to Michael that he did not seem to know what 'small talk' was. He did not think aloud and seemed to disapprove of those who did, believing that 'the correct sequence is to first engage one's brain, and then one's tongue'. As a result, their conferences were punctuated by long silences during which the old man read and sometimes mumbled faintly to himself, while Michael struggled not to lose the thread.

'What about the photographs?' said Sullivan at last. 'Have you looked for any sign of a diary in them?'

'No, there's nothing like that in the photos. You've got a copy of them there in your brief.'

'I have the ones that were exhibited, but what about the other photographs?'

'What other photographs?'

Sullivan opened the cover of his brief. 'It's in the investigation logs. You've read them, haven't you?' he said tartly, then leafed slowly through the document. 'Here it is. The body was discovered by the uniformed police at 9.05. *0908: Scene secured. Call to radio room. Request assistance CIB. Scenes of Crime Officer notified.*'

He scanned to the bottom of the page and then turned it over. 'Then here, you see, *0933: Constable First Class Garfield at scene.* That's Roy Garfield. He does most of the Scenes of Crime stuff down there. Photographs and that kind of thing. He was there by 9.33. He must have taken photographs. The Homicide fellows are there by 10.15 and their forensic people photographed the scene. But there'd be a lot more photographs than we've seen, that's for sure.'

He leafed through the photographs in his brief. 'There are only nineteen photographs here. Garfield would have shot off at least one roll of film and so would the Homicide fellow. Get hold of Worrell and tell him we want to see the rest of the photographs.'

When Michael rang him Worrell sounded more compliant but also much more condescending than before. Yes, there were some other photographs in the police material, and, no, he had no objection whatever to allowing access to them. In fact, if Michael wanted to, he could borrow them provided that they were returned before the trial. Was there anything else they wanted? If so, they only had to let the prosecutor know and he would have it attended to.

'By the way,' said Worrell, almost as an afterthought, 'I suppose your client's going to say he wasn't even in the Probert place that night. Is that right?'

Michael did not feel inclined to telegraph the defence case to Worrell but the prosecutor did not wait for a reply.

'And I suppose he reckons Davey's lying?' Graham Worrell clearly had a punch line to deliver. 'Let's see — what did Davey say? That's right, he claimed that your bloke said he was hiding in the unit watching Probert eating oranges. Two oranges I think he said, didn't he?'

'What's your point, Graham?'

'Well, Michael,' the prosecutor drawled. 'My point — an excellent one, I think — is that I've just received a further statement from Fred Arrowsmith, the pathologist. You can pick up a copy when you come to get the photos.' Worrell paused for effect. 'Seems he did a check on all the stomach contents, and you'll never guess what he came up with.'

Michael heard the sound of turning pages. 'Here it is. He found, I quote, "The undigested remains of at least one, and possibly more than one, orange".'

Worrell's voice was triumphant. 'Now isn't that an extraordinary coincidence?'

29

As Michael sweltered in the stuffy little room and watched the warder at the desk meticulously pick his bulbous nose, he tried to quell his uneasiness. If Lade did not tell Reginald Davey he had seen Shirley Probert eating two oranges before he attacked her, how could Davey possibly know that?

Arrowsmith's report confirmed what Davey claimed Lade had told him. There was no way Davey could have known that unless he was there when Probert died (which he wasn't — he was serving time in Etna Creek for a Bankcard fraud) or unless he was told about it by someone who had been there. Suddenly his story sounded very plausible.

All this meant Lade was lying, and had been lying from the start. For some perverse reason he had lied about the Probert case even at their first encounter at the City Watchhouse. He had readily confessed to Cosgrove's murder but had unaccountably chosen to deny the Probert killing. Even when he had confessed to Davey in the prison, it seemed he had opted for a version of the facts that could not be true.

He was obviously there when Shirley Probert died and there seemed no doubt he had killed her, but not in the way he had described to Davey. He did not break in to the apartment and he did not try to rape his victim; he did not sit on her stomach and he did not put his hands around her throat and strangle her. He came at her stealthily, from behind, and he slipped a lethal headlock round her neck and squeezed until her brain expired. On the medical evidence it could not have happened any other way. Peter Lade did not kill Shirley Probert in an act of lustful frenzy. He simply executed her, coldly and efficiently. Why?

Michael rubbed his weary eyes. It didn't matter any more. To wonder why a brute like Lade would kill another human being was a waste of effort. The police had told the press he was a 'thrill killer' who murdered solely for the sense of power it gave him. That was enough to answer any questions one cared to ask about his motives.

For whatever reason, Peter Lade, it seemed, had murdered Shirley Probert.

Which meant Michael had derailed his life for an illusion. He had believed Lade was not the killer, that Davey's story had been fabricated. Arrowsmith's report had changed all that. Only the murderer saw the victim eating the oranges. Only the murderer knew about that. Peter Lade had told Davey he saw her doing it. Which meant Lade was the murderer.

Michael wondered what he should do. The thought of turning back to MS&G was unacceptable. He would not do that. He had backed the wrong horse but he had done it for the right reason and he had made the right decision.

As Peter Lade approached the warder's desk, Michael steeled himself for their meeting. Being with this strange, amoral young man was never pleasant but today would be more difficult than usual because today he would confront him with the guilt he had chosen to deny.

When the warder waved him through, Lade focused his eerie eyes on his lawyer sitting behind the glass petition of the legal conference room. He walked forward mechanically, and Michael steeled himself for the encounter.

'That's a new report from Dr Arrowsmith,' Michael said, passing the doctor's statement across the wooden table.

Lade didn't bother to so much as glance at it so Michael summarised its damning contents: Davey made his statement to police in November '86, and in it he claimed Lade had told him the woman had been eating oranges immediately before her death. The original post mortem report made no mention of the stomach contents except to say no drugs or alcohol had been detected in them. But at the time of the autopsy Dr Arrowsmith had included in his notes a reference to the undigested remnants of one or more oranges. Davey did not know about that, and neither did the police, nor anyone else for that matter except, of course, the murderer.

Arrowsmith had not shown his notes to anyone but kept them locked in his desk drawer. They were still there when Michael went to inspect them earlier that day. He had read the reference to the oranges — there was no doubt it was genuine — and Dr Arrowsmith confirmed that no one knew about the stomach contents until a week ago when the prosecutor asked him to check the point specifically to see if they could confirm Davey's story of her eating oranges.

And there it was in the notes. Davey was in gaol when Probert died so the only way he could possibly have known about the oranges was if he had been told by Peter Lade, as he claimed he had.

Lade listened impassively. When the recital was finished, he picked up the statement from the table in front of him and slapped it back across the table.

'They're lying.'

'Who's lying?'

'All of them. The police, Davey, Arrowsmith, every one of them.'

'You'll have to do better than that, Mr Lade.'

'I've told you before. I didn't kill her.'

'Yes, I've heard all that. Trouble is, it doesn't square with the evidence.'

A derisive smile crept onto the young man's handsome face. 'That's your problem. You're the fucking lawyer.'

Lade was actually enjoying this, savouring the sport as Michael flailed about, damping down each new fire as it broke out. The outcome held no real interest to him. He was in for life, so the jury's verdict could neither help nor harm him. He seemed amused rather than concerned by evidence that pointed so conclusively to him.

As Michael walked towards his car parked opposite the prison, he pondered on the mystery. Why would a man in Peter Lade's position steadfastly maintain his innocence in the face of such compelling evidence? Why had he lied to Davey about how the murder had occurred? What, if any, connection did he have with Bob, Probert's flatmate? And why was Rita so afraid?

The tarnished brass lettering bolted to the brick wall beside the Volvo read 'United Nations Club' and since the day was all but spent, Michael pushed in through the twin glass doors and made his way into the empty bar. A young man stacking chairs moved behind the bar to serve his only customer. With a ten-ounce beer in hand, Michael settled at a table in the corner.

This was the perfect place to think about a mystery and reflect on human foibles, his own mistakes and aspirations, and how perhaps sometimes the greatest triumph was achieved by simply struggling on against the odds.

It was nearly six o'clock when Michael left the UN Club. The three beers had relaxed him and it seemed less crucial now to come up with the answers there and then. He was so relaxed he didn't even notice the police patrol car that pulled in behind him as he steered the Volvo into Annerley Road.

The siren wailed for a second then droned into silence. The driver pointed to the kerb and Michael pulled over in compliance. He counted how many drinks he'd had. Three beers couldn't possibly have tipped him over the legal limit he reassured himself.

A thickset policeman dragged himself from behind the wheel and strolled towards the Volvo. Michael watched him in the rear-view mirror and heard the crunch of his approaching footsteps on the roadside gravel. The sleeves of his short-sleeved summer shirt could barely stretch across his bulging biceps and the manner of his swagger seemed distinctly threatening. Michael's pulse-rate quickened.

'Licence.' The voice was so gruff that Michael abandoned any thought of conversation. He slipped his driver's licence from his wallet and passed it through the window.

'Did you know you crossed the centre line back there on Annerley Road?' the policeman grunted.

'I don't think so, Constable.' In the rear-view mirror he could see another uniform moving through between the two parked cars.

'Have you been drinking this afternoon, sir?'

'Yes, I've had a couple.'

The policeman took a roadside alcotester from his pocket. 'I now require you to undergo a roadside breath test.'

The officer rattled off an unfamiliar formula which amounted to an instruction to blow firmly and without interruption into the testing device. A small, black instrument was thrust into Michael's mouth. He blew hard. The device was snatched away. He heard the policeman saying he had failed the test, and he tried to clear his thoughts enough to comprehend the formal requisition that he accompany them to the station to provide a specimen of his breath for analysis on an approved breath-testing device.

What was going on? He had been drinking, but how could he possibly have failed the alcotest? Surely it took more than three beers in that time to go over the legal limit? Why was he pulled up anyway? Did he really cross the centre line?

'You'll have to accompany us to the police car now please, sir.'

'I'd like to see the result,' Michael said. The words were breathless, not nearly as steady as he would have liked.

'Sir, if you do not accompany us to the police car immediately, we'll have no alternative but to arrest you and place you forcibly in that vehicle.'

The response sparked a rush of indignation, and Michael spoke with more authority. 'Look, it so happens I'm a solicitor. And I want to see that alcotester.'

The burly officer placed two hands on the frame of the open window then bent forward until his scowling face was almost inside the car. 'I know what you are, cunt,' he snarled. 'Now if you don't get yourself into that car right now, I'm going to ram that fucking alcotester right up your arse sideways. Do you understand?'

From that point on events were a jumble. Michael was aware of being frogmarched to the car, the grip around his elbow so tight his arm seemed near breaking point. A heavy hand shoved him into the rear seat, and he sat behind the two policemen in a daze, wondering what was going on and where these men were taking him.

He watched the road ahead, half-expecting the car to veer off in an unfamiliar direction. As they crossed the bridge towards the city he became aware that his toes were curled up in his shoes, his teeth were clenched, and every muscle in his legs and shoulders was as taut as piano wire.

As the police car swung into Herschel Street he breathed easier. They were simply taking him to police headquarters for testing as they had said. His fears were irrational. He was being brought in for a breathalyser test, no more than that, and he should give some thought to how he should respond.

But what had that officer said to him back there? Did he really threaten him like that?

The iron grip was on his elbow again and he was walking between two tall men across a carpark, down a corridor and into a lift. The officers said nothing, but simply stared ahead impassively as the lift slowly climbed. It droned and jolted to a halt and they walked into another corridor, one man in front of him, one behind. The first man stopped beside a door and opened it.

'In there.'

Michael walked into a room three metres square, enclosed by four blank walls and furnished only by a table and two chairs.

'Sit there until someone comes to get you for the breathalyser.'

The door slammed shut and Michael was alone in the claustrophobic silence. He was to wait there for the breathalyser to be readied for the test. That seemed in order. There was no need for concern; it seemed quite regular procedure. But as he waited, his mind kept jumping back to what that officer had snarled at him back at the car. He could not be mistaken about that. The muscles in his stomach ached from being held so tensely for so long.

That man had threatened him with violence. No doubt about that. And how could the Volvo possibly have crossed the centre line in Annerley Road? He had just pulled out from the kerb. And surely three beers in that time would not tip the limit. Why would that officer have an alcotester in his pocket at the ready?

He told himself to be rational. He had been picked up on a suspected Traffic Act offence, and like any other suspect he must wait his turn for testing on the breathalyser. It amounted to no more than that. The officer's comment was a sorry example of how some police threw their weight around instead of dealing with the public appropriately, but it was no more sinister than that. But what did he mean when he said he knew what Michael was?

The handle on the door dropped down and as it opened slowly the space was filled with a looming giant. Detective Sergeant Darryl Batch stepped into the room and closed the door. His face and arms were moist with sweat and his shirt, unbuttoned at the collar, stuck in damp patches to his chest.

'Hello Michael,' he said.

'Hello.' Michael tried to hide his apprehension but his voice betrayed him with a squeaky whine.

Batch's mouth curled into a sneer. 'Had a few too many tonight, did you, Michael?' he said.

'I had a few.' It sounded apologetic. Michael cleared his throat and added in a firmer voice, 'Whether it was too many, we'll find out when I'm breathalysed, won't we?'

Batch shook his grizzled head. 'Don't worry about that. I fixed it up for you. You just blew under the limit.'

'I beg your pardon?'

Darryl Batch dragged the vacant chair across the floor, clearing a pathway to the door. 'We don't like to see you legal blokes get in this kind of shit.' He turned and opened the door. 'Come on, I'll take you down and see you get a taxi.'

Michael followed him down the narrow corridor towards the lifts. Was this some kind of setup? Or was Batch genuinely trying to help him? He certainly did not seem too concerned about his prisoner. When he reached the lift doors he pressed the button, then leaned against the wall, as though he did not care where Michael went. They stood at the liftwell in a silence broken only by the rhythmic sound of Batch's laboured breath.

'It's all just a big game, isn't it?' he said at last. 'We fight like shit in court, but at the end of the day, we all sit down and have a beer together. If you can't do that you don't last long in this game.'

Michael attempted a polite smile.

'We don't like to see you blokes get into strife, you know. You're just like us. You work your arse off round the clock and then when the whistle blows, you let off a bit of steam, that's all.'

Batch turned and looked at Michael with a face devoid of all expression. 'But you've got to be careful these days, Michael. Some of these young blokes will pinch you for nothing much at all. Half of them would love to get their hands on a solicitor.' His lips curled into a humourless smile. 'As you well know, that sort of thing can ruin a career.'

With a shudder and a jolt the lift doors slid apart. Batch stood aside and motioned Michael to go in. The doors slid together. Batch jabbed a button and the letter

'G' lit up. The lift lurched, then droned downwards. Michael studied the numbers of the floors as each one lit up in turn measuring their progress. With each floor Michael felt his pulse rate slow a little and the muscles in his neck relax.

'I hear you're acting for that bloke Lade.' In the half-light Batch's features seemed grotesque.

'That's right.'

Batch shook his head contemptuously. 'He's a fucking grub of the lowest order, that bastard. He's a bloody psychopath. He's probably better off locked up for his own protection. There's a lot of people with the knives out for him you know. You'd want to be getting well paid to take that bastard on.'

Michael kept his vision firmly on the lights.

'Yeah, well if you're not,' continued Batch, 'you want to have a think about it. I know his old man's dumped him. So if you're counting on Dad for your fees I can tell you now he won't be coughing up.'

The lift eased to a gentle stop and the doors slid open. Michael stepped into the well-lit foyer, deserted except for two uniformed constables at the central desk. He walked towards the exit doors, the echo of Batch's footsteps just behind him. He controlled the urge to sprint the few remaining paces and out the door.

Then they were walking down the steps to the footpath. A taxi slipped up to the kerb and stopped in front of him. Batch stepped forward, pulled the rear door open, then stood back courteously. A sweaty hand dropped onto Michael's shoulder.

'Michael,' Batch rumbled in a low, conspiratorial murmur, 'I knew your old man pretty well. That's why I don't like to see you make a mistake that you'll regret. People get emotional about evil bastards like Lade. Sometimes they start saying silly things.'

He was leaning so close that Michael could smell the cigarette smoke and the stale sweat on his clothing and could feel the puff of his sour breath on his face.

'Because I like you, Michael, I'll tell you there's been some whispers around the station here and you're not real popular. I even heard a couple of them young blokes saying something about you being tied up with drugs.'

Batch paused, his fingers tightening their grip on Michael's shoulders. 'Now you might enjoy a little puff of the old "wacky baccy" every now and then. I don't know. Don't want to know. But if some of these young blokes get their noses out of joint over you fronting for an animal like Lade, there's no saying what might happen. Understand? You're much better off to keep your head down. You with me?' He released his hold and tapped Michael's shoulder with a friendly little slap. 'Now you get straight home and sleep it off. Okay?'

Michael dropped down into the rear seat and Batch closed the door.

'Take this fellow home, will you driver?' he said, then peered into the taxi. 'He lives at 24 Carella Street, Coorparoo.' He paused for a moment then added, deliberately, 'It's the house with the little picket fence.'

Batch looked back at the passenger and smiled. 'By the way,' he said, 'I really like that antique clock, the one in the main bedroom. Your missus picked it out, I bet. A class act, your missus. Colleen, isn't it? I'd really like to make her acquaintance. Must do something about that real soon.'

With that he slapped the car's roof in dismissal. As it pulled away into the darkness Darryl Batch felt sure he'd made his point.

30

The waters of Wynnum harbour were as still and shiny as glass and the morning sun reflected off their surface in a thousand glittering diamonds. The distant chug of a faraway trawler, accompanied by squawking seagulls overhead, beat time with the rhythmic slap of waves against the sand. Along the narrow esplanade a row of fibro cottages was already bathed in the warm, orange glow that follows dawn.

Mervyn Harris jogged beside the lonely roadway, his canvas running shoes crunching on the gravel edges and squelching on the dew-soaked grass setting battalions of tiny soldier crabs scurrying across the muddy flats. He huffed and grunted as each footstep fell mechanically and his breath blew puffs of steam into the crisp morning air.

Merv Harris figured that for a bloke with a dicky ticker, he was still fitter than most blokes half his age. Ever since Dinny Conlan had trained him up for Golden Gloves back in the forties, he'd kept up his roadwork and his daily sessions on the bag. Dinny had taught him he had to do it to survive, and so he did it. It was harder now than ever but the pain in his body and the smell of his own sweat had a familiar, comforting feel about them. Doing what you had to do was never hard for Mervyn Harris. Life was only painful if you thought you had some choices.

He could feel the drops of sweat suspended in his eyebrows as he plodded up a gentle slope, his lungs pumping in time with his aching legs. He had run a lot further than usual this morning but he had to think, and this was the best way he knew how.

Merv wasn't sure why that young Leary bloke had phoned him last night. He had rambled on for half-an-hour about that bludger Peter Lade and how and why he thought Lade wasn't right for the murder of some sheila on the Gold Coast and how he had been trying to track down a couple of lost faces that had a familiar ring to them. But it all sounded like a load of shit to Merv until he heard about that boofhead Darryl Batch and the stunt he'd pulled on Leary down at City Station. Then it had a whiff about it, and every time Merv took a sniff he could smell George Curran.

Once Leary told him of Batch's threat, Merv listened very carefully. It was a load-up job on Lade for sure. So what? It was just another murder off the books and that grub wouldn't be missed by anyone.

But that didn't explain why Batch would try to put the frighteners through a solicitor. Why would any copper stick his neck out that far on a routine load-up? It didn't make a bit of sense. And furthermore, this stunt was far too subtle for a bonebrain like Batch. This had George Curran written all over it.

So what the hell was going on? The 'Rita' he was looking for was probably that brainless slut that used to work for Kranic at the 'Wet Touch' massage parlour years ago. Obviously 'Bob' was Pommy Bob from New Farm. But Merv had never heard of Shirley Probert and he couldn't think of why the coppers would be so interested in getting her off the books that they would take the risk of going around threatening lawyers. One thing was certain: if George Curran had his finger in this pie, there was a bloody good reason for it.

Young Leary sounded shit-scared on the phone but he didn't sound like a bloke about to quit. Maybe he had balls after all.

'I was hoping you might be able to give me some insight as to what this fellow Batch is on about,' he'd said.

Whatever it was, this kid had Buckley's chance of stopping him.

'Sounds to me like he's just talking shit as usual.'

There was silence at the end of the line and for half-a-second Merv almost felt sorry for the bloke. He was standing where a lot of blokes had stood before him and he was in way over his head. His old man had been there and he never made it out.

'You don't happen to know this woman Rita, do you?'

Whatever it was all about, why would Mervyn bloody Harris want to get involved? 'No.'

'Bob? What about Bob? Do you have any idea who he might be?'

A second's silence passed before the answer. 'Wouldn't have a clue.'

That conversation had stayed with Merv through the night and now it gnawed away at him as he trudged up to the dilapidated picket fence that lined the footpath in front of the weather-beaten little cottage that was home. He was breathing hard as he trudged the final footsteps to the gate, and suddenly he thought about his dream the night before.

His brother Charlie was standing at the front gate of the old Buranda house decked out in his Army clobber, off to war. Funny the stupid bloody things you dream about. He hadn't thought about Charlie in over thirty years. He couldn't even remember what he looked like.

Merv Harris pushed the front door open and strode across the creaking floorboards to the poky little kitchen. As he held the kettle underneath the kitchen tap he thought how Charlie had been more a father to him than his old man had ever been. The last time Merv saw him was the day he pushed his way out through the old front gate, all done up in khakis and a slouch hat. He stood on the footpath and shook Tom's hand. Then he turned and gave a big salute to his little brother Merv. And then he left. And that was it.

Merv eased himself onto a kitchen chair and dropped his elbows onto the table as the electric jug rumbled softly in the background. It had felt good to see his brother in that uniform. That was the first time in his life he could remember feeling really proud about anything.

What a silly bloody notion! Charlie Harris didn't last twelve months in the war. Not much to be proud of.

For some reason George Curran had his snout in that Lade business. What the hell was going on? The question had been going round in Merv's head all night and he just couldn't put it down. What interest did that old bastard have in stitching up a grub like Lade?

He remembered the first time he laid eyes on Curran. It was his first week in the job and he was just a hairy-arsed provo with absolutely no idea. All he knew was that he was a policeman. He'd made it through and for the first time in his life he felt like someone special. It didn't matter that his old man was a drunk and his brother Tom was a mug-lair spiv. Merv Harris was a copper and he wore a copper's khaki uniform and cap, and he was as proud as bloody punch. When he walked out in the street in that uniform people showed respect, and that made young Merv feel a whole lot better than he could ever remember feeling in his life. He was there to uphold the law and to protect the people, and that made him very proud.

That's when he first met Sergeant George Curran, a tall, good-looking bloke with a friendly smile and a ready wit. George was already fourteen years a copper then and he knew everything there was to know about the job. And he taught young Harris plenty.

George always took the best young blokes aside and showed them what was what. It was George who taught Merv what real police work was all about and how to stick close to your mates and how to get things done. From George he learned that things weren't always cut and dried, that sometimes you had to break some rules and that some rules weren't worth keeping. Somewhere along the line — when it was Merv couldn't quite remember now — he eventually came to learn that the game just wasn't quite fair dinkum. Somewhere along the line he learned that he had nothing much to be proud of after all.

A whistle from the kettle brought him round and he climbed back to his feet and flicked the switch off at the wall. He scraped around inside the cupboard for a moment, emerging with an empty Lipton's teabag box, which he cursed and squashed. Out of bloody teabags! Merv grumbled, then reached out for the saucer on the sill above the sink where a pile of soggy teabags sat slumped together in a rusty pool. He pulled three bags away and dropped them into his cup, pouring the boiling water over them. He jiggled energetically until the water turned brown enough, then removed the bags and tossed them in the sink.

George would be pushing seventy now, the old bastard. He'd bought so many souls, thought Merv, as he gulped the hot tea. He'd pulled them all together in a brotherhood that didn't mean a bloody thing. They were supposed to stand for law and order but all they stood for was themselves. They bent so many rules in the name of law and order that in the end they were the law and they gave the orders.

And when George Curran turned he took the whole lot with him, even those who, like Merv Harris, didn't know the real caper.

That was bullshit and he knew it. In truth Merv Harris knew the caper from the start, even though he tried hard not to know. Like a lot of others he had looked the other way. There was no more law and order, only mates, the job, and loyalty, and what was 'in the interests of the Force'.

Merv Harris had let George Curran take from him the only things he had ever cared about. And he had let him do it without a fight, without a word of protest. George had taken his ideals, and in return he gave him nothing back. And he had taken Joe ...

Poor Joe. Merv felt the sting in his eyes and tasted the bitter bile in his throat.

He sucked in another mouthful of tea and swallowed hard. George Curran was an old bastard and his grubby paw prints were all over this business with young Leary. The question was why was George and his mates so interested in that arsehole Peter Lade? Or was it the dead sheila they were on about? The one thing Merv could say for sure was that when a copper stuck his neck out far enough to threaten a solicitor, there was something on the go and the stakes were pretty bloody high. So what was it?

The dead sheila wasn't saying, and that boofhead bloody lawyer wasn't likely to find out. There wouldn't be too many coppers interested in turning over any rocks. And Pommy Bob was not about to put his hand up. The courts would cop whatever Curran served them up, and no one else was interested.

So that left Mervyn Henry Harris.

Merv rose and strode through the back door, down the steps and out to the metal garden shed tucked away in one corner of the backyard, half-obscured by unruly shoots of crimson bougainvillea. Inside it, he knelt down and reached into the far right corner and dragged a half-dismantled outboard motor off a rough-cut square of dirty carpet. He pushed the motor against the wall and flipped the carpet back.

With both hands he scraped away the earth below until his fingers traced the edges of a solid wooden box. He eased it out onto the earth floor beside him and instinctively glanced over his shoulder to the doorway before he prised it open. The lid popped up and Merv was pleased to see the contents, tidily arranged just as he had left them. He pushed the three thick wads of banknotes to one side and pulled the pistol out from underneath.

Merv Harris rolled his fingers on the handle of the gun and lightly touched the trigger. Sooner or later someone was going to have to kick their bloody guts in. And even with a dicky ticker, Mervyn Harris backed himself, odds on.

The Shirley Probert murder trial was set to start on Monday, March the sixteenth, 1987.

On that morning Eugene Sullivan rose early. By seven-thirty he was fully dressed and striding back and forth across his living room, muttering instructions to himself and planning the journey ahead, step by step. He had a cup of thick black coffee in one hand and a saucer in the other and from time to time he stopped and sipped and pondered for a moment, then resumed his pacing. He ignored the nagging alcoholic ache he had awoken to as usual and the aroma of strong coffee stirred his brain and focused it on what was to be done.

The Crown would certainly call Davey early in the prosecution case, to give the jury ample time to forget what a loathsome wretch he was before they finally retired to consider their verdict. So Sullivan would have to tackle him head-on, and soon.

He carefully considered every point he had to make. Reginald Davey had to be discredited. He would have only one shot at it and that would start when he rose to his feet to cross-examine and finish when he sat down again. If Davey was not totally destroyed by then that was it — the trial was lost. And even now, after thirty years of practice at the bar, that was a terrifying prospect. But Eugene Sullivan believed he could totally discredit Davey. Even now, that was exciting.

He stopped again, and put the cup and saucer on the dining table.

He could handle Davey. But then what? He could make the jury doubt that anything Davey said was true but then the Crown would call the evidence about the stomach contents. Then what? The defence had no explanation of how Davey could have known about those oranges, none that Eugene Sullivan could think of.

He pondered on it for a moment. What did it mean? Could it be that Reginald Davey's story was entirely true, that Peter Lade had really confessed his guilt to him? That would certainly account for the mystery of the oranges, but what about the rest?

There were so many things about this Crown case that didn't add up. A lifetime in the criminal courts had taught him that the truth was so elusive it was oftentimes irrelevant or at best incidental to the process. The Crown was looking for a culprit and the defence was searching for a doubt. No one wasted time or energy looking for the truth. It was dangerous to let such things distract you.

Sullivan looked up at the portrait of old Dan Casey on the mantelpiece.

'There are cases and there are causes, Gene,' the old man had once told him. 'We have to have the brains to know one from the other, and the courage to respond accordingly.'

Cases and causes ... It was a simple sentiment and one that, in his younger days, Eugene Sullivan had sometimes quoted. But not for many years now.

Sullivan thought about Brian Leary. The little man had always had such courage. He felt ashamed as he remembered all those months when he had found excuses, then lies, to avoid his friend Brian Leary and the Arnold case and the soul-destroying exercise of desperately fighting a losing case with all the world against you.

Brian Leary had always clearly understood what old Dan meant about the courage to fight causes and ultimately he had learned that Eugene Sullivan did not. Brian had eventually stopped calling.

Sullivan's long black robe, bar jacket and horsehair wig were draped across the dining table. He ran his fingers lightly across the yellowed bristles of the wig. He had bought it new in 1956, manufactured by the London firm of Ede and Ravenscroft and imported to order for the young Mr Eugene Patrick Sullivan, newly admitted member of the Queensland bar. It had been with him ever since and it had held up well. It had lost some hair, thought Sullivan, and it was stained and weathered, but, like its owner, it was still functional.

Howard Walker was to be the trial judge. Some young wit at the junior bar had christened him Maxi after the former Test bowler Maxwell Walker, because of Howard's tendency to use a heavy hand in sentencing. The name stuck. If anyone on the Supreme Court bench was likely to mete out the maximum sentence it was Walker and despite a spate of successful appeals against his sentences in the Court of Criminal Appeal, Maxi Walker continued to live up to his name.

Walker was generally disparaged by the young luminaries of the Bar Association who loved to cite his lack of experience in civil and commercial work when he was at the bar and seemed to think that disqualified him from adjudicating on their learned arguments. Eugene Sullivan did not share their disapproval on that count or any other. Although he'd had many disagreements with Howard Walker over the years, both as prosecutor and judge, Sullivan respected him. Howard had a good mind and, more importantly, he was intellectually honest. In Eugene Sullivan's opinion that was a quality all too rare in the judiciary.

When Howard Walker made a ruling he always made it because he believed it to be the correct one, not because it was safe, or politic, or palatable. He was a man who fervently believed that every man ever charged with an offence was guilty but that never stopped him from insisting on a scrupulous application of the presumption of innocence in his court.

So Peter Lade would get a fair trial. If either side could find the truth, this judge would make sure the jury saw it.

The truth ... Eugene Sullivan turned to peer across the mantelpiece at the face that looked back from the mirror. It was an undistinguished, unimpressive face, an old man without the energy to find what was, after all, only incidental to the process.

He reached over and lifted his wig, slipped it onto his bald head and looked again. There he was, that fellow who had haunted Eugene Sullivan for thirty years. That man who could fight and could protect, the man who could dredge up whatever energy it took. It was the man Dan Casey had believed he could be, the man Brian Leary had expected him to be.

Sullivan thought of the many things about his life that he regretted, the many things he'd missed out on, the many things he'd thrown away. And then he looked in the mirror, and saw that man. There were some things that he wouldn't change, even if he could.

31

Merv Harris hated Sydney. It was full of faggots, and half-smart arseholes, and spivvy-looking wogs, and chows, and druggies, and jumped-up smart arse shitheads who ponced around as though they owned the joint. So far as Merv could see this town had every kind of ratbag, deadbeat and drongo that ever drew breath, and the worst of them got flushed up here on Oxford Street after dark.

It was still dark but the night was all but gone. The street music had stopped blaring and the flashing lights of clubs, and restaurants, and bars, had died out completely or just limply flickered on, spotlighting the debris of the night.

Merv Harris tramped along the footpath, scowling sullenly at the occasional body slumped and crumpled up against a doorway, as he tried to formulate his plan.

Robert Albert Pitchers, also known as Pommy Bob, had murdered Shirley Probert and Batch was or might be trying to protect him. Merv Harris wanted to know why. He would only get one chance with Pommy Bob. If that grub got time to think about it he would clam up tighter than a fish's arsehole, so Merv had to get the jump on him. That wouldn't be easy, because Pitchers was as cunning as a shithouse rat, and twice as dangerous.

Finding him had not been hard. Merv still had a couple of contacts who could get him into Social Security records and he knew he would find Bob Pitchers in there somewhere. Pitchers was a pom with a deportation order on him following a conviction for living-off-the-earnings and he'd been dodging Immigration for the past two years so he was hardly likely to be collecting benefits under his right name. But Merv knew he'd be claiming under at least one bogey name. As an ex-British Army bloke, he knew just how to lurk the system.

He was also known as a fairly clever forger and his go was mainly bogey licences and passports and some low-level fraud, so Social Security scams were bread-and-butter work for him. They were a lot more his style than murder and Merv wondered what might have made a bloke like Pitchers neck that sheila. He had a reputation as a bar-room pug and he had a face that would scare a bulldog out of a butcher's shop but he wasn't known for violence and Merv had always found him reasonable to deal with. He wasn't the hothead type.

Predictably, Social Security records turned up nothing under Pitchers. The Golden Gate address showed an unemployment benefit to Shirley Probert but there was nothing for a bloke at that address. That meant that Pitchers' dole cheques must have gone somewhere else, so Merv put some feelers out at the Broadie pub where Pitchers used to drink. He soon learned that Pommy Bob had left the Coast and no one knew where he'd gone. But they would ask around.

In the meantime Merv had done his best to track down Rita but that seemed pretty hopeless. He had spoken to the dago at the pizza place where Leary spotted her a couple of weeks ago but the dago reckoned he hadn't seen her since that night. He thought she must be in some kind of trouble because the police were in the restaurant a few days later looking for her too. Funny that. Merv checked around with some of her old mates but they all said the same thing: Rita just took off a couple of weeks ago, and no one had heard a peep from her — the cops were looking for her too, and they had told them the same thing.

In two days the barman at the Sportsmens Bar came up with the information that before he went away, Bob Pitchers had been living in a flat in Whelan Street. He didn't have a number but the block of flats was called 'Koumala'. Merv had that address run through the Social Security computer as at January 1986. Until early February last year, three unemployment cheques were going out to Unit 10 there. All three pensioners were male and all three were still receiving pension cheques which now went to an address in Paddington, Sydney. Bingo! Unless Merv Harris was very much mistaken Robert Pitchers was cashing those three cheques.

Merv left the lights of Oxford Street and squinted in the darkness of the narrow, dingy backstreets. All those years as a copper had taught him that if you were going to go calling the best way to make sure your hero was at home was to drop in just before the sun came up — anyone who was coming home would be home by then. The question was, where did he go from here? He had to get inside and crawl all over Pitchers' peace of mind before he had a chance to think, but he had no badge and no back-up to help him do it.

He slipped his hand under his sweater and checked the safety on the pistol pushed into his trousers. It would help him get in the front door all right, but what if Pommy Bob was armed, and what if he had mates there?

Finally Merv stood opposite an ugly old terrace house crammed in between two other dumps in a squalid little lane. It was a narrow, two-storey terrace house with an upstairs verandah boarded up in fibro. That meant it had a sleep-out and possibly a second bedroom. Which meant Pitchers might not be alone. Somehow he had to find out just how many heads there were inside that joint before he made a move.

Merv sat down on a crumbling brick fence outside the dilapidated shell of an old house that was obviously deserted. It was across the road and three doors up from the house Merv was carefully assessing.

A battered Combi van slumped against the gutter just in front of him provided useful cover as he sat and waited. He could sit there till daylight and get Pitchers alone if and when he finally emerged. But then what? Or he could walk in right now and hope that Pitchers was alone. But if he wasn't? If he had some other rock-ape living with him, then the whole thing could get very bloody nasty. No, the only thing was to try and find out who was in there.

Merv eyed two empty beer bottles standing like faithful sentinels beside the rear wheel of the Combi. He slipped his jumper off and rolled it up into a tight ball. Then he pulled the pistol from his belt and pushed it up inside the roll. In the darkness the package would look like a drunk's home supplies tucked under his arm. He placed the bundle carefully beside the Combi's rear wheel and selected a beer bottle. Then he crossed the street and approached Pitchers' house.

The roof was made of corrugated iron — which was good and bad. It would make plenty of noise, enough to rouse whatever occupants there were but it might also wake the neighbours, which could mean trouble. But Merv figured this might be the kind of neighbourhood where people weren't too keen to get themselves involved in disturbances that didn't directly concern them.

He threw the bottle high into the air. He heard it crash down on the iron roof and roll and rattle across the corrugated tin sheets until it hit the guttering and jumped it, spilling off towards the patio below. As it hit the tiles it smashed into a thousand pieces.

Merv was back crouching beside the Combi. A light flicked on upstairs and muffled noises grumbled from behind closed doors. Just one light. No light in the sleep-out but someone was pulling at the sliding window. A head appeared followed by two shoulders and a bulging upper torso that hung out at right angles over the patio below.

'What the fuck?'

In the early morning stillness the Cockney twang was unmistakable. Pitchers, without a doubt. Merv pulled the rolled-up jumper under his left armpit and thrust his right hand deep into the bundle until his fingers felt the reassurance of the pistol butt.

The head and shoulders disappeared and then more noises bumped around the house. Still only one light. It looked to Merv like Pitchers lived alone.

A downstairs light came on and then the front door opened. A stocky little figure stumbled forward onto the unlit patio. Merv couldn't see his face clearly but it was Robert Albert Pitchers, no mistake.

'Shit!' Pitchers spat the word out angrily as his rubber thongs crackled on the broken glass, and he peered aggressively out into the street, first one way, then the other.

Merv waited for a moment, to be doubly sure no one joined him at the door. Pitchers moved towards the front gate, still searching for a culprit. No more lights, no noises from within, no one else appeared. Pitchers was home alone.

Merv snatched the second beer bottle from the footpath and lurched out from behind the Combi, staggering towards Pitchers. Bundle tucked against his chest, he waved the bottle in his right hand and meandered up the middle of the lane, mumbling incoherently.

When the little Cockney saw him, the muscles in his neck and shoulders flexed for action.

'Oi!' he yelled, striding towards the staggering drunk. Merv Harris stopped and, swaying slightly, dropped the bottle and slipped his right hand inside his jumper. He waited one second more. He wanted Pitchers close enough to touch him.

'Robert Pitchers!' he said as he whipped the pistol out and aimed it at Pitchers' heart. Pitchers propped as if he had been snap-frozen.

'I've got a thirty-eight here, sport. Make one move and I'll blow your bloody balls off!'

Ten minutes later Bob Pitchers was sitting on a chair in the centre of the unlit lounge room, his head covered by a pillowcase loosely fastened at the neck.

'I'm telling you, I don't know nothing about her!' Pitchers could hear his captor moving around behind him in the blackness and he was starting to feel very bloody scared. They had finally caught up with him. He could feel the muzzle of the pistol pushed against his temple and then from time to time the barrel lightly tapped against his ear, as his unseen tormentor urged him in a hoarse whisper.

'We know you killed her. I want to know why.'

They had been there for half-an-hour and Merv Harris could see that it was starting to get to Pitchers. Whenever the silence continued for more than several minutes his hands would shake and he would suck huge gulps of air in through the pillowcase. But still he wasn't talking. It was time to up the ante.

'I'm starting to get tired of this,' Merv said. 'I get paid the same for retribution as for information.'

He eased the hammer of the pistol back until it clicked loudly in the early morning silence, sending a shudder through Pitchers' upper body. He shifted in the chair.

'I know who you are, you bastard,' he spluttered. 'You and your arsehole mates killed her, everyone knows that. And there's plenty of proof of it around, don't think there isn't. You pull that trigger and you're all gone.'

Harris digested the curious response. 'What arsehole mates?'

'Get fucked, Harris!' spat the angry pillowcase. 'Do you think I don't know you? I know your voice, you arsehole. I know they sent you after me.'

Something about the way this low life pommy scum spat out his name made Merv see red. Before he knew what he was doing he was squatting face to face with Pitchers, the cotton pillowcase dragged up across the man's face and sitting across his forehead like an Arab headdress, his face distorted with the pain of the pistol pushed against his cheek.

'That's right, you pommy prick,' seethed Harris. 'Mervyn fucking Harris! Take a good look, because I'm going to blow your fucking brains out if I don't get some straight answers right now!'

It was a stupid, risky thing to do and Harris realised it too late. Pitchers, with lightning speed, snatched for the gun and gripped it in a strong hold, his powerful legs clamped around his captor's waist. One stubby thumb had prised two fingers loose already. The pain in Merv's right hand was almost unbearable and though he had his left hand lending what support it could, he could feel his fingers slowly giving way under the excruciating pressure.

The two men tumbled heavily onto the floor, locked in a static hold centred on the struggle for the gun. In the semidarkness Merv could see the blanched white skin of his blood-drained fingers grasping the metal. His grip would not last and once it gave way his fingers would be wrenched out of their sockets and his right hand incapacitated. If he lost this struggle he was a dead man.

They lay there for what seemed an age, their hands and forearms quivering with exertion, until finally the two fingers started moving slowly back. Merv pulled his left hand quickly from the contest and, almost in one motion, slammed his elbow back against Pitcher's face. It struck so hard that it sent a piercing pain right up through his forearm but his opponent did not react in any way.

Merv could see Pitchers' burning eyes fixed on the gun, his bared teeth locked together and the muscles and sinews in his face strained to breaking point. His grip was unrelenting and Merv's right hand was gradually peeling back, as two black blobs appeared in Pitchers' nostrils. The blood spat out of Pitchers' nose as Harris jerked his elbow quickly forward, then back again with every ounce of strength he could muster. It crunched down on the target with a splintering thud and Pitchers grunted.

The grip around Merv's fingers faltered for a moment and he wrenched his hand away so frantically that the pistol slid out of his sweaty palm and disappeared into the gloom of the room.

Then they were standing toe-to-toe, each with a handful of the other's shirt, swinging punches with the other arm. Merv felt his fist and forearm slide across a sweaty shoulder and then *whack!* Whiteness flashed across his eyes as something struck him with the power of a brumby-kick on his left cheek and then another banged flush on his left ear and left it ringing like a church bell.

He tucked his head down deep into his shoulders and held on tight as a wild two-fisted barrage smacked and slammed against his head and shoulders. Each one hit with force enough to knock him off his feet but he hunched against their impact, trying hard to clear his head.

This bloke could hit all right but he was short on puff. He was slowing up already and Merv could hear him blowing hard. One break was all Merv needed, and he knew that break would come. He peered up through his squinting eyebrows at his blood-spattered opponent and lined him up.

As the last punch slammed down on his forehead like a bludgeon, Merv crouched and when the Englishman moved forward for a kick, he made his move. He lunged up and forward as he released his right hand from the shoulder, driving it straight and hard with his whole body-weight until it smacked with thundering force into Pitcher's face. It struck his mouth and bloodied nose square on, with such force that both men recoiled backwards, jolted by the impact. Pitchers buckled at the knees and staggered forward. He fell into a crumpled, twisted heap and Harris kicked and flailed at him with both fists until he was completely still, curled up and groaning on the floor.

Merv flicked on a lamp and scooped the pistol up. He was panting heavily, his head still spinning from the battering. He fell into an armchair and sat there sucking in deep breaths of air. The pistol was trained on Pitchers, who was gradually coming round.

'I want to know what happened to Shirley Probert,' Merv Harris gasped. 'And why.'

Pitchers pulled himself into a sitting position on the floor. With the back of his hand, he wiped the thick red ring from around his mouth. 'What the fuck's your caper, Harris?'

'I want to know why you killed that woman and why Darryl Batch is trying to protect you.'

Pitchers raised one blood-encrusted eyebrow and looked genuinely surprised. 'Batch?' he said. 'Protecting me?' He looked at Harris with a quizzical expression. 'You really don't know what it's all about, do you?'

Harris raised the pistol up and peered down through the sights at Pitchers. 'That's why I'm here, killer,' he growled. 'To find out.'

Pitchers stared back. 'You got the wrong boy, Harris.'

'Bullshit!'

'No bullshit.' Pitchers wiped his mouth again. He hesitated for a moment, as if considering whether to say more, then said, 'It was your copper mates what done it. Not yours truly.'

Merv Harris was struck dumb by the shock of it. 'What are you talking about?' he said eventually.

'I'll tell you what I'm talking about.' Bob Pitchers wiped his mouth again and shook his head. 'I met Shirley up in Surfers when she first come to the Coast. She was doing street tricks and she was after a place to stay. I had a couple of dirty girls on the game for me in Surfers at the time so I set her up in the Golden Gate on a 60–40 split. I paid the rent and all the business phone calls.

'That was the deal. And it went okay for a while. Then she just went off the boil. She was bringing naff all in and suddenly the exes have gone through the roof. I was getting phone bills I couldn't jump over. I jerried she must be stinging me for calls she's making to her mates back home in Adelaide so I went and got a printout of the calls from Telecom. It turned out I was right, but that's not all I learned.'

On all fours Pitchers made a move towards a paint-chipped chest of drawers against one wall but Harris quickly straightened up and shook the pistol threateningly.

'Hey!' he grunted tensely.

Pitchers froze, then motioned to the cabinet. 'There's a *Penthouse* in the bottom drawer. It's got some papers in it.'

Harris kept the pistol trained on him while he pulled the drawer open and rummaged round until he pulled the magazine out and dropped it on the floor. Dropping back into the armchair Harris leaned forward and flipped it open. There were several folded sheets of paper in it, the uppermost of which was a sheet of double-sided colour photocopies of fifty dollar notes. He picked it up and inspected it.

'Not that,' said Pitchers quickly and shrugged his shoulders. 'Just trying to make a quid.'

They were pretty ordinary counterfeits but they would probably pass offshore.

Harris eased the hammer of the pistol down, flicked the safety on and pushed the gun into his belt. Then he slipped the sheet back into the magazine and, closing it, he lobbed it onto the carpet in front of Pitchers.

'What do you want to show me?'

Pitchers flipped the magazine open and pulled out three folded sheets. He opened them and held them up for Merv to see. They were itemised Telecom accounts showing lists of numbers called.

'There's where me money was going,' he said, running his finger down one column. 'These calls were all to South Australia. All a half-an-hour and more. No wonder I was going broke.' Pitchers turned to the next page. 'And then I noticed she was also ringing

Brisbane a fair bit. Only small amounts but when I looked closely at the numbers she was ringing, I fair shit meself.'

Pitchers pushed the pages towards Harris. Merv scooped them up and ran his eye down the column until he saw the prefix code 07, indicating a Brisbane telephone number. He recognised the number that followed the code. He had rung it many times. Queensland Police Headquarters, Herschel Street. There it was again, and again. Merv felt sick.

'At first I figured she was a police informant,' Pitchers said. 'So I snuck in when she wasn't there intending to turn the joint over. I found her diary, so I checked it against the dates when she made these calls to the coppers. That's when I really shit meself!'

'What are you talking about?'

'See for yourself.' Pitchers unfolded another little bundle of dog-eared photocopies and pushed them across in front of Harris. 'When I read this shit I nicked the diary and I took it back to my place. I was going to front her with it. But then I thought about it, and I thought "Shit, mate, you don't want to know". So I ran it through the copier, and then I put it back. These are the photocopies of the pages from the diary.'

As Merv Harris read the photocopied pages he understood what they were telling him. In her untidy hand Shirley Probert had chronicled a deadly game:

Monday, 3rd February 1986. 10.15. Wilson. First call. Told him I have Pollard statement and letter to G Y. $500k by Friday or copies go to all papers and TV. He will 'consider'.

Tuesday, 4th February 1986. 11.00. Wilson. Speaking to others. Cannot raise cash within time. Needs more time. Bullshit!

Tuesday, 4th February 1986. 3.15. Batch — abusive. Have till Friday. In future only deal with Wilson.

'The silly bitch was trying to blackmail the old Bill!' Pitchers said incredulously.

There were two further entries scrawled in on the Tuesday, and when Merv Harris saw them he snatched up the Telecom accounts. There they were: two calls to the same number. It was the phone number of a private residence Merv had been to many times.

6.30. Mrs C. George out, ring back later.

7.45. Big George. I have Pollard statement. Can prove you got it. George making threats. Fuck you. By Friday it's all over.

Merv Harris could hardly believe what he was reading. This was an attempt to extort five hundred grand from George Curran and his band of merry men. And if George had been sufficiently upset to be making threats over the phone that meant this sheila must have had some pretty heavy goods on someone. No wonder she had wound up dead.

Wednesday, 5th February 1986. 9.45. Wilson. No answer yet. Has scheduled meeting with G C and all the others 1 pm.

The next call was to Wilson's phone at home.

Wednesday, 5th February 1986. 9.30. Wilson. Meeting positive, but will need a week to get cash. Extension to next Weds. No calls at home. Ring office tomorrow.

Merv could see immediately that the trap had been devised at the meeting on the Wednesday. They were stringing her along and had kept her ringing regularly to headquarters where the opportunity of tracing calls was maximised.

This woman had been big on balls, but short on brains.

The final entry was on Tuesday, February 11, 1986.

11.30. Wilson. 500k will be deposited in nominated account this Friday 10.30 am. When confirmed all copies of Pollard statement delivered to HQ in sealed envelope.

Merv Harris shook his head in disbelief and looked at Pitchers who shrugged his shoulders once again and shuffled through the remaining papers.

'What's this Pollard statement?' Harris said. 'Do you know anything about that?'

'I never heard her mention no one by that name and there weren't no statements there that I could see.' Pitchers produced a single sheet. 'The only mention of a Pollard was in this old letter here.'

He handed it to Harris. It was dated February 24, 1970, and was addressed to a Miss S Pollard at the Bombora Holiday Flats in Coogee Beach.

'I figured Pollard maybe used to be her name,' suggested Pitchers. 'It's from a bloke called Yates, whoever he is.'

Merv's eyes slid down to the bottom of the page, where appeared the words

Yours faithfully, Gordon W. Yates

'He was an old pisshead journo with the *Courier* years ago,' Merv said as he went back to the text. 'He carked it about ten years ago.'

The letter was a total mystery to Merv. He read it, then read it again and wondered what it really meant. For some reason someone had seen fit to hang onto it for over sixteen years, and that meant that they must have thought that it was pretty bloody important.

The letter didn't say exactly what it was that Miss S Pollard of Coogee had had to say all those years ago but whatever it had been, it seemed to Mervyn Harris that it had upset old George Curran. Someone obviously had thought it was every bit important enough to kill for.

Frank Delaney MLA stared at the ceiling of his spacious bedroom through the blue light of early morning. His young wife lay curled beside him, sleeping soundly under the satin sheets, and through the window he could see the pre-dawn light collecting on the horizon. He had tossed and turned all night and now he knew he would not get back to sleep. He was thinking about the things he once thought he had put behind him, and what a lucky bastard he had been, and how just one thing could root a bloke's whole life.

The meeting at Tom Wilson's place the night before had been a short one, but it had unsettled Frank because it had made him face the awful truth. You don't just walk away from the past; you've got to kill it if you can, stone dead, and bury it, if you really want to sleep at night. Old George had always said that, and he was right.

The meeting had been sombre as the typed one-page report was passed around the little group, each ashen face reflecting the knowledge that their whole lives were on the line. Unless they made the right decisions here their careers, their reputations, perhaps even their liberty, were up for grabs. Everything they had built up so carefully could come tumbling down around them.

When Frank read the report it was all too much for him. 'Jesus, Tom, what the bloody hell is going on out there? First we find out that Brian bloody Leary's kid has gone in to bat for Lade, and now you tell us fucking Merv Harris is out there in the Valley looking for the girl. What the shit is going on?'

Tom Wilson had learned to handle pressure in recent years but he had looked very nervous. 'Calm down,

Frank,' he counselled. 'We don't know that they know anything yet.'

'Bullshit, Tom, wake up to yourself! Merv Harris knows every pimple on our collective bloody arse. And he's not looking for the girl just to inquire about her health!'

George Curran sat there quietly throughout the meeting, listening to the others speak their minds, perhaps assessing how much pressure each was under, and how well each one might withstand it. As Frank got up and tramped around the room, waving the report around and lecturing the meeting, the old man simply listened to Frank's ranting.

'Christ, Tom, it's one fuck-up after the other. You tell us after the bloody event that Darryl Batch has virtually stood over that solicitor. What the hell does he think he's doing? You just can't do that sort of thing in this bloody day and age! Batch is off his bloody cruet. And I want no part of it. If he's going to start that sort of crap I'm out!'

When old George interrupted Frank his voice was quiet and controlled but it carried enough venom to kill a grown man instantly.

'Sit down, Frank,' he had growled. 'You're not talking to your voters now.'

When George Curran spoke to you like that, you listened. In his rising panic Frank had hesitated but only for a moment. When his eyes met Curran's the defiance evaporated and he resumed his seat obediently.

'Nobody's out,' Curran said. 'Nobody will ever get out.'

It sounded like a death knell.

George waited while they soaked the message up. 'We all started out together and we climbed up on each other's shoulders, and we propped each other up, and that's why we've built something here. We're a human pyramid. Just like when we were all mug cops together. Some of you might think you're pretty fancy fellows now, but you're just a little higher on the pyramid, a little higher off the ground. And that means you've got a whole lot further to fall. And you could do yourself a lot more damage. If one of those boys on the ground falls over every one of you falls as well. Don't anyone forget that.'

Those words had floated round and round in Frank Delaney's head all night, and now, as he lay awake, he realised why they had disturbed him so. He had money, power, influence, even a new wife, so many things he'd dreamed of having. He'd come a long, long way. But in a sense he hadn't moved an inch. He was still a crooked copper doing crooked deals.

Frank thought of Mervyn Harris, out there somewhere, asking questions about a missing prostitute called Rita. Just like in the good old days, before things got to be so bloody complicated. How much did Merv know? What did he think he was looking for?

Poor bloody Merv. Old George had issued a directive that he be surveilled to find out if he was on to anything. Frank sincerely hoped he wasn't. Merv had already copped enough. He'd always been a good policeman and if he'd had the brains to be more flexible he could have come up through the group like the rest of Curran's chosen few.

But Merv always was pig-headed. He was always black and white. That was what Frank liked about him really — you knew exactly where you stood with him. But Merv had never really understood self-interest. That was why he had ended up on the bones of his arse. That was also why he really didn't deserve the kind of shit that would descend on him if he stuck his head into all this business.

Frank Delaney looked down at his beautiful young wife. George Curran used to say that once you chose your course you had to stick to it and see it through.

And that was true. For better or worse Frank Delaney MLA had set his course a long, long time ago.

32

'I swear to tell the truth, the whole truth, and nothing but the truth. So help me God.'

Reginald Davey was not at all what Michael had expected. He was a handsome, well-built man in his early forties, whose wavy brown hair, peppered by becoming streaks of grey, was cut short and neatly groomed. The gold-rimmed glasses contributed to an air of studious respectability. He stood erect and took his oath with clear voice and steadfast gaze. In his conservatively striped tie, crisp white shirt and well-fitting suit he looked more like a middle-ranking bank officer than a prison dog.

Michael glanced at Eugene Sullivan, beside him at the bar table, and wondered what was going through the old boy's head. Sullivan was staring at the witness, his eyes narrowed in concentration.

The first two hearing days had been fairly undemanding of him, taken up with the selection of the jury and the opening Crown address, followed by some largely uncontentious evidence about the discovery and location of the body. But on the third day Davey's evidence was expected to be called and Michael could sense the barrister's rising tension as the court rose on the afternoon of the second day.

Now, as Michael watched Davey give his calm, coherent evidence, he was starting to get worried. This was a murder case, and a particularly hard one to defend. Their client was a self-confessed murderer, with no alibi and an alleged confession to a so-called independent witness backed up by the scientific findings. And, as fine an advocate as Eugene Sullivan might have been twenty years ago, his best days were long gone.

The jury listened carefully as Davey told how Peter Lade had boasted of his deeds. He was certainly convincing, even to someone as aware of the inconsistencies as Michael was. If Davey's glib story was raising some doubts in his mind, the jury would be finding it compelling.

Graham Worrell took Davey step by step through his evidence, and even had him list his prior convictions which, although numerous, somehow seemed diminished by Davey's frank admission of them. He admitted to a history of dishonesty, and yes, some violence too. Nothing to be proud of, but he seemed sincere and genuine in telling what he knew of Peter Lade. By the time the prosecutor resumed his seat, Davey had the jury eating from his hand. He was no angel — he'd freely admitted that — but he had no time for murderers and was as appalled as anyone in the courtroom by Lade's degenerate behaviour.

When Sullivan stood up he seemed a frail, unlikely challenger. His hands trembled visibly and as he reached across to move the lectern into place in front of him on the bar table, his folder flipped shut so that he lost his place. He reopened it, obviously at the wrong page, and proceeded to leaf through the brief in search of his lost place.

There was a murmur from the jury but Mr Davey showed no sign of impatience and waited courteously for Sullivan to begin his cross-examination.

'Mr Davey, you first made a statement to police about this matter in June last year, is that correct?' said Sullivan, still leafing through the brief.

'No.'

Sullivan stopped his search and looked up from the brief. 'Didn't you make a statement to police in June last year?'

'No sir,' said Davey evenly. 'I didn't make a statement till December.'

'I see,' the barrister said. 'I see. December.' He sounded relieved to have that tricky point made clear. He resumed his search.

Michael stared at the bar table, and as he heard the interminable flicking of the pages in the silence of the courtroom, his ears began to burn.

'You had this conversation with Mr Lade some time in December, did you?'

'No, sir. As I said before, I had that conversation in April last year.'

Davey spoke with due respect, obviously trying to assist the befuddled cross-examiner, who once more interrupted his search to peer at Davey.

'So you remained in gaol from April until December, did you?'

'No,' said Davey, as one might speak kindly and clearly to a backward child. 'I was serving a sentence in April and then in mid-October I went back to prison on remand. Then I gave a statement just after I was released.'

'In April?'

'No, December.'

There were snickers from the jury. They variously looked amused, impatient or embarrassed. Mr Davey gallantly suppressed a patronising smile. Sullivan looked bewildered.

Mr Justice Walker leaned forward. 'Mr Sullivan,' he said helpfully. 'As I understand Mr Davey's evidence, the conversation with the accused occurred in the prison in April last year while Mr Davey was serving a term of imprisonment. He was subsequently released but then went back to prison in mid-October on remand. He was then released from the remand section in December, whereupon he made a statement to the police.'

'Thank you, Your Honour,' Sullivan said. Then turning to Davey, 'Is that it? December?'

'That's what I've been telling you all along, sir.'

'I see. I do beg your pardon.'

Davey's patience was a credit to him. He had handled this frustrating little episode with due respect and dignity throughout, and it had only served to reinforce his image as an honest, helpful witness.

Sullivan, his standing shot to pieces, had gone back to leafing through his brief. He stopped and fell completely silent, as though the complexity of settling on a time frame had exhausted his powers of concentration.

Michael Leary's scalp crawled. Eugene Sullivan was dying on his feet and the whole defence case was dying with him. He closed his eyes, wishing he could be somewhere, anywhere, but here. He tried to think of something to say to prompt Sullivan, but nothing came to mind.

'Why did you ultimately make a statement to the police, Mr Davey?'

Sullivan's quiet voice still had a resonance that could fill the corners of a silent courtroom. Coming after that long silence, it captured the full attention of the jury, whose eyes flicked back to the plausible Mr Davey for his answer.

He raised his eyebrows, wrinkling his suntanned forehead, and carefully considered the question. 'I suppose,' he said, 'I was shocked by what he'd told me. I didn't think he ought to get away with a dingo act like that, if you know what I mean.'

It was the reaction of any decent person, and Michael noticed some of the jury nodding in agreement.

Sullivan continued, almost sympathetically, 'You were disgusted by the callousness of the man, is that it?'

'I was.'

There was silence for a moment, and then Sullivan continued in a slightly louder, firmer voice.

'Incensed?'

Davey looked a little less relaxed, and hesitated for an instant before answering. 'Yes, I suppose so.'

'Outraged?'

The last word boomed theatrically into the courtroom with such power that several of the jury gave a start.

Davey, no longer relaxed or patronising, stared back at his inquisitor from the witness box. Then he answered. 'It was a pretty low act, by any standards, Mr Sullivan.'

With that one question — 'Outraged?' — the atmosphere had suddenly changed. It was charged with tension, and the jury hung on the next question, expecting an attack of some kind.

Now that he had their full attention Sullivan returned in a quiet, unemotional tone, 'By your standards, Mr Davey?'

'Yes.'

'I see,' said Sullivan as he carefully turned over one more page of the brief and flattened it beneath his palm. 'Well, let's look at that, shall we?'

Sullivan was standing upright with his hands firmly anchored to the lectern, looking every inch the cold inquisitor. Every eye in the courtroom was glued on him and every ear was waiting for his next word. He had assumed absolute control of the proceedings, and he had done it with two one-word questions and the power of his voice.

'When the accused first told you of this vicious murder in April of last year you were filled with outrage; is that so?'

'Of course. Anybody would be.'

'That's right, anybody would be — if they had been told such a dreadful secret. But I suggest you were not told anything of the sort by Peter Lade.'

The jury's eyes flicked back to Davey.

'Yes I was. He confessed the murder to me.'

'And you were outraged.'

'That's right.'

Sullivan paused then leaned forward on the lectern. 'But you controlled your outrage remarkably well, didn't you, Mr Davey?'

Davey looked uncomfortable and pushed his chin up slightly as if to release it from a cramping collar. 'I don't quite understand what you mean,' he said.

'I mean,' said Sullivan, 'that throughout the remainder of your stay as a sentenced prisoner at Boggo Road, you didn't mention this alleged confession to anyone, did you?'

The jury waited for an answer.

'No. That's true.'

'Not a living soul, is that so?'

'Yes.'

'Not a fellow inmate, nor a warder, nor a welfare officer, nor a chaplain?'

'No.'

'Never said anything about it to any friends or relatives who visited you during that period?'

'No.'

'No one?'

'No.'

'Having been so outraged by this revelation, you never mentioned it to anyone throughout the three-month period from April through until the end of June when you were finally released?'

'No.' Davey shifted in his seat and squared his shoulders, but now he did not look quite so impressive. The jury eyed him with distrust.

'Even after your release you were able to control your rightful outrage and disgust to the extent that you said nothing to the police or anybody else about the matter at any time from when you were released in June until your rearrest in mid-October.'

'No.'

'Is that right, Mr Davey?'

'That's right.'

'Despite the fact that during that period of freedom you were detained by police on no fewer than four occasions and on each occasion you were questioned in relation to alleged offences, and subsequently released.'

'Yes.'

'If you were so outraged by what you claim to have been told, why didn't you mention it during one of these interviews you had with the police?'

The courtroom fell completely silent. Now all the jury looked like inquisitors.

Davey shifted in his seat. 'I don't know really,' he faltered.

'Don't know!' Sullivan mocked. 'Well, your outrage did not prevent you from committing acts of violence yourself during this particular period, did it, Mr Davey?'

'Er ...' Davey hedged and hesitated. 'I'm not sure I follow you sir.'

'Oh, surely you do, Mr Davey,' Sullivan countered. He waited for the witness to respond, the jury's interest building as the silent seconds ticked away.

'No, I don't,' said Davey.

'On the thirteenth of October 1986 you were arrested following an incident in which you attacked a young woman in her home, partially stripped her, indecently assaulted her, tied her to a bed and threatened her with a firearm, isn't that so?'

Davey glared back at his tormentor. 'Yes.'

The facade he had built had been demolished and the jury eyed him with a combination of surprise and disappointment. A surly look had now replaced his earlier good humour.

'You pleaded guilty to that offence?'

'Yes.'

'You weren't too outraged or disgusted to commit that offence, were you?'

'No.'

'And when you were apprehended you gave the police information concerning your actions?'

'Yes.'

'And you gave them information about the man who had supplied you with the firearm. True?'

'Yes.'

'So tell me, Mr Davey, while you were handing out all this information, why didn't you mention to the police this vicious murder that you say you had been told about?'

Davey shrugged his shoulders. 'I don't know.'

'"Don't know" again!' Sullivan paused, eyeing Davey with palpable disdain. Then in a grim, accusatorial monotone he resumed. 'I suggest it was because you had been told nothing of the sort.'

'That's not right.'

Sullivan turned to a new page in his brief. 'Mr Davey, you initially had some trouble getting bail on the October charges, is that so?'

'Yes.'

'At the first court mention the police opposed bail and the magistrate refused you bail.'

'That's right.'

'You made a second bail application a week later but again the police opposed and once again bail was refused.'

'Yes.'

'Yes, and your matter was listed for a committal hearing on the nineteenth of December. Correct?'

'Yes.'

'But in the meantime you received a visit at the prison from Detective Senior Sergeant Darryl Batch, the arresting officer in this case. Isn't that so?'

The jurors switched their attention back to Davey, eager for an answer. But the witness simply stared at his interrogator. One could almost hear the machinations of his brain as he searched for the right answer. Finally, he made the wrong decision.

'No, I never met Detective Batch until after my release.'

Sullivan's voice trumpeted, 'On the twenty-seventh of October 1986 Detective Batch came to the Brisbane Prison and interviewed you. Isn't that so?'

Davey hesitated once again. 'No,' he said at last.

'Have a look at this document, please witness,' said Sullivan, turning and looking directly at the jury, his outstretched hand flourishing a single sheet of paper in the direction of the witness, until the bailiff whisked it from his hand and delivered it to Davey. 'That's a photocopy of a prison pass, isn't it?'

After little more than a glance, Davey placed it on the witness box in front of him, as if reluctant to read what it said.

'Yes,' he answered.

'And it shows that Batch had an official visit with you on the twenty-seventh of October 1986, doesn't it?'

'If you say so.'

'Please tell us, Mr Davey,' said Sullivan silkily. 'Did Mr Batch visit you at the prison that day?'

'Yes.'

'Why did you tell us a moment ago he didn't?'

'I must have forgot.'

'Forgot!' Sullivan's voice expressed his astonishment that Davey should expect the jury to be gullible enough to believe him. 'Or was there something discussed that day that you don't want the ladies and gentlemen of the jury to hear about?'

'No,' said Davey.

'So what did Mr Batch come to see you about that day?'

'I don't remember.'

Sullivan's powerful voice boomed through the courtroom. 'Did he come out there to enlist your assistance in putting together a case against Peter Lade on the Probert murder?'

Davey shook his head. 'No,' he said.

'Nevertheless, the very next day you applied for a job in the prison mess.'

'That's right. So what?'

'You knew Peter Lade worked in the mess, didn't you?'

'Yes, I knew that.'

'Your outrage wasn't so pronounced that it precluded you from working with the man then?'

'Not really.'

'You applied for that position in the hope you might be able to get close to Peter Lade, didn't you, Mr Davey.'

'No.'

'In case he might say something to you that you could use against him and to your own advantage.'

'No.'

'And when you were refused a position in the prison mess you approached the Superintendent asking for a transfer to the same yard as Lade.'

'Yes.'

'Why?'

'I had a few mates in that yard.'

'Name one.'

'Ahh ...' Davey turned a bright crimson. 'I can't remember all their names.'

'One will do,' persisted Sullivan.

Davey shrugged. 'I-I only knew their first names,' he mumbled. 'I think one bloke's name was Ron.'

The unimpressive answer brought an audible reaction from the jury. When Sullivan spoke again it was obvious he knew he was preaching to the converted.

'Following your meeting with Detective Batch on the twenty-seventh of October you did everything you could while you were in remand to get close to Peter Lade but you were unsuccessful in your efforts.'

'I didn't end up in his yard, no.'

'You didn't get within a bull's roar of him, did you?'

'No.'

'But Mr Batch came back to see you at the prison on the second of December and you had another chat, didn't you?'

'That could be right.'

'What did you talk about this time, Mr Davey?'

'I can't remember.'

Sullivan halted and let the whole room fall silent. Every eye was on him as he leaned forward on the lectern and then quietly inquired, 'Could it be, Mr Davey, that by now you had decided that instead of going to all the trouble of trying to get close to Peter Lade, you would simply say he had confessed the murder to you all those months before, when you were a sentenced prisoner?'

'No.' Davey shifted uncomfortably in his seat.

Sullivan turned over a page of his brief and pressed it flat. 'Two days after your second meeting with Batch the police brought you back before a magistrate. Correct?'

'Yes.'

'You represented yourself and made another application for bail. Correct?'

'Yes.'

'This time the prosecution did not oppose bail.'

'That's right.'

'And you were granted bail on your own undertaking.'

'Yes.'

Now Sullivan was accelerating the momentum. 'And you went directly from the Watchhouse to Brisbane Police Headquarters where you gave Detective Batch a signed statement alleging that over seven months previously Peter Lade had confessed to you the murder of Shirley Probert.'

'Yes.'

'A statement which was entirely false!'

'No.'

Sullivan boomed, 'A total fabrication by you, intended firstly to get you out on bail, which it did, and secondly to secure some leniency on your sentence! Isn't that so?'

'No.'

'And that second goal was achieved in January this year when the Director of Prosecutions recommended that you be spared a further prison sentence.'

'He agreed I should get probation, yes.'

'For a violent and indecent assault on a defenceless woman in her own home!'

'Yes.'

'Yes. And that completed your reward for bringing this foul piece of fabrication before the ladies and gentlemen of this jury, didn't it?'

'Well, I object,' said Worrell, somewhat feebly.

'I withdraw it,' Sullivan said disdainfully, and then added with a flourish, 'No further questions, Your Honour!'

When Eugene Sullivan sat down he knew that the first defence objective of this trial had been achieved, absolutely and completely.

As Michael Leary looked along the bar table, his heart beating wildly with exhilaration, he knew that behind the deadpan expression on the old boy's face a celebration was going on.

Sullivan turned his head a fraction towards his instructing solicitor and, without any other change of expression, winked one eye. He then turned back to his notes.

33

Light rain was falling softly on the dark, deserted backstreets, the only sign of life at this hour of the morning the rattle and gargle of water dribbling from rusty guttering. Bob Pitchers did not mind the drizzle — it reminded him of home.

The whisky had numbed his head and blurred his vision, and as he looked up to the streetlight ahead he could see dozens of glistening diamonds forming, drifting, merging. Pretty it was.

Bob knew he'd had far too much to drink and he'd regret it in the morning, but he wasn't sorry now. It had calmed him enough to think things through.

For the last two days he had been worrying whether it had been wise to tell that Harris geezer what he knew. He'd jumped at every shadow since, fearing every stranger that walked past him on the street. But the grog had helped him put it in perspective. Harris could have shot him there and then if he had wanted to. And there was no mistaking the shock on his ugly mug when he first saw those diary pages. No, Harris wasn't sent to knock him, and he'd had no idea what Shirley had been up to.

Bob stumbled towards the gateway up ahead. Merv Harris was an arsehole copper but he was always square. The more Bob thought about it, the more he was convinced Harris wasn't down here doing errands for the likes of Curran. He was running his own little show, just as he had always done, and now Bob had given him the lowdown, Robert Pitchers could wipe his hands of it. If the coppers had killed Shirley Probert, then they now had that arsehole Harris on their case, and Bob didn't envy them that.

As he staggered up the stairs onto the landing, Pitchers fumbled in his trousers pocket for his house keys. His head was thick with whisky and the task of opening the door preoccupied him. He did not hear light footsteps or see the flicker of reflected streetlight on the barrel as it came up behind his ear.

A metallic 'ping' spat softly through the silence of the empty street and a little hole in Pitchers' forehead erupted in a burst of bone and blood and brain. The impact threw him against the door, then his lifeless body dropped into a squat and rolled onto the wet cement. An ugly spatter of thick red ooze ran down the door and marked an obscene trail to where the crumpled body lay.

The shooter unscrewed the silencer and slipped it neatly into the inside pocket of his leather jacket, then tucked the pistol in his jeans and pulled the jacket down to cover it. He turned his collar up against the weather and stepped off quietly into the darkened street.

Michael Leary had been strangely troubled all day. Working with a client like Peter Lade had been difficult from the outset, and now, as they approached the end of the second week of his trial, difficult had become irksome. The man seemed determined to be no help whatsoever in the carriage of his defence, and took a kind of sick pleasure in watching his lawyers fight his war without ammunition.

Sullivan recognised from day one that their client regarded it as a spectator sport. Apart from a two-minute introduction on the first day of the trial, Sullivan had studiously avoided any contact with him and had never once asked Michael to seek their client's instructions on a single point. He had known from the start just where to take this trial and how, and he seemed determined to win the case despite their client. He had mentioned several times that they would have the right of last address, and that meant he had assumed that Lade would not give evidence at the trial.

The trial had gone as well as could be expected. Davey had been a disaster for the Crown and the forensic evidence was falling neatly into place, with Eugene Sullivan using each new scientific witness to bring out a further anomaly in the story the Crown was putting forward. At this stage the jury seemed to be on side. They had clearly disliked Davey and now as each successive witness made a new concession, they listened carefully and nodded, confirming by degrees their earlier conclusion that Davey's story could not be believed.

What they did not know, as all the lawyers did, was that Graham Worrell had Dr Arrowsmith tucked firmly up his sleeve and was holding him in reserve until the final stages of the Crown case to maximise the impact of his evidence. When Arrowsmith revealed the autopsy results and told the jury about the stomach contents, he would reaffirm the accuracy of the confession.

There was no logical explanation for Davey's knowing in advance about the stomach contents unless he had been told about the oranges by the woman's murderer, as he had claimed. The jury had been made to think he was lying and, when they heard about the stomach contents, they would feel as though the defence had duped them.

Graham Worrell knew that, and that was why he was keeping his trump card until the end. Eugene Sullivan knew it too, and although he hoped for something to come out in evidence that might offer an explanation or an alternative theory, so far it had not happened and as the Crown case drew to its conclusion, the Arrowsmith evidence loomed as their Achilles' heel. Sullivan and Michael had discussed that at length and resigned themselves to the prospect of being struck a mortal blow before the Crown case closed.

Michael had given up a lot to fight the case against Peter Lade and now, it seemed, it was likely that it all would come to nothing. That was a part of what had troubled him all day. But it was more than that.

He had been deeply disturbed by the call last night from Gerry Manetti, who told him there had been yet another death in the Manetti family. Mervyn Henry Harris had died on Tuesday night in a motor vehicle accident in New South Wales. Police had recovered his body on Wednesday morning from a hire car which apparently failed to take a bend and plunged into a river just north of Newcastle. There were no witnesses to the accident but Harris had some heavy bruising to his forehead and it was thought he must have passed out and hit his head on the dashboard before his car went off the bridge.

Neither Gerry nor his wife seemed greatly saddened by the loss — as Gerry explained, Merv was not the sort of man you got close to. He simply wanted Michael's advice as to what should be done to wind up Merv's estate. Michael gave the advice, and that was it. But the news had left him deeply troubled.

Harris had meant nothing to him. He had never liked the man and the last time he'd spoken to him, Harris had flatly refused him any assistance whatsoever, despite the fact that he almost certainly could have done so. He was a surly, ill-mannered brute and Michael did not have a single reason to grieve his passing. But the news of Harris had left him thinking about a lot of ancient history. He'd had a restless night, sleeping fitfully, haunted by hideous dreams. When morning finally came, it was almost a relief to be awake.

He wondered whether it was simply fatigue that made him so depressed but as the day wore on his father was more and more in his thoughts. He remembered how totally he had believed in Brian as a boy, and how, as he and Dan were growing up, the integrity of their father had been the cornerstone of their lives. Somewhere along the line everything had become so terribly confused.

It was a busy day in court and afterwards Michael had conferred with Sullivan in the Supreme Court library, so that as they parted company outside the court in George Street, the chimes of the City Hall clock were counting down to six o'clock. It was getting dark a little earlier now and as he made his way down Adelaide Street, his mind revisited his melancholy with new clarity and insight.

The reason for his despondency was now clear. Mervyn Harris was the only person Michael knew who might have told the world the truth about the Mickey's Poolhouse case. He was the only one who could have confirmed that Brian Leary did not waste his life on an illusion and that his faith and perseverance had been warranted. He was the only man alive who might have publicly affirmed the integrity of Michael Leary's father. And now that man was dead.

As Michael walked past the City Hall towards the carpark he realised that it was this conclusion that had so eluded him. If Michael Leary ever could have done something to redress the wrongs perpetrated on his father, the opportunity had died with Mervyn Henry Harris.

Michael reached his car, unlocked the doors and climbed in. The engine kicked over and the Volvo glided towards the exit.

'Thanks boss,' grunted the carpark cashier as Michael passed a twenty through the partially opened window.

Two knuckles rapped against the glass behind him and Michael spun his head. An unfamiliar face peered at him through the passenger side window, and Michael looked back blankly.

'Change sir,' said the cashier.

While Michael struggled to accept the notes and coins being handed to him, he heard the car door opening behind him. When he turned back to the unfamiliar face it was inside the passenger compartment, and Michael saw it belonged to a lanky, unprepossessing man in his late forties.

'G'day Michael,' said the man. 'My name's Phil Vincent. I wonder if I could have a word with you.'

As he said this, Vincent flipped his wallet open, revealing a police badge.

Michael's heart lurched. 'What about?' he answered as calmly as he could.

The driver of the car behind them signalled his impatience with a blast of his horn.

Vincent swung his feet into the car and pulled the door closed. 'Pull out, and we'll talk.'

There was no mistaking the tone. Vincent was issuing a direction and he expected Michael to comply. As they drove out onto the city streets, Michael's mind raced, trying to organise his thoughts so he could have some control over what was happening.

'Just drive as though you're going home,' Vincent said. 'I'll tell you when to stop.'

'Look, what's this all about?' Michael blurted nervously.

'Your mate Peter Lade for one,' drawled the passenger, then added, 'and a bloke by the name of Merv Harris.'

'I heard he died in a car accident on Tuesday.'

'Just drive,' his passenger said.

They drove on in silence onto the South East freeway ramp towards the southern suburbs. Michael's heart pumped painfully as he thought about the warning Batch had given him and he tried to work out what he ought to do.

His passenger was silent and expressionless, intently following the road as it unfolded, and Michael tried to guess what his next move would be. Was this another threat or would they try to take it further now? But to what end? The trial was almost over. If they were trying to stop him acting in the matter, surely they had left their run a little late. It made no sense at all.

'Look, what the hell do you want anyway?' he demanded.

'To show you something,' said Vincent laconically. 'And you can't really look at it while you're driving, can you?'

As they drove along the freeway Michael tried to assess the situation rationally. The police could have no interest in him at this stage, it was ludicrous to think this man meant to harm him in some way. But then Batch had warned him and he had ignored the threat. And jumping uninvited into someone's car at night was hardly standard police investigative procedure. Every nerve in Michael's body was tense.

They came off the freeway by the second exit ramp and as they did so Vincent said, 'Take the next right and pull in by those trees.'

He pointed to the tract of parkland known as Thompson's Estate. Michael knew the area well and knew that a local Rugby team had started training there each Thursday evening. They would be out there now.

He pulled in by a line of trees that overlooked the oval, and as Michael saw the players on the field below, his heartbeat steadied slightly. As the Volvo drew into the cover of the trees the darkness swallowed it but twenty yards ahead of them and down a gentle, grassy slope the little oval was bathed in reassuring light. Michael stopped the car but kept the engine running and the selector shift in 'drive'.

'Okay, we've stopped,' he said. 'What's this all about?'

'Turn the engine off and kill the lights,' Vincent ordered.

Michael's right foot rested on the broad brake pedal. He eased it slowly to the right. In an instant his foot could jam down hard on the accelerator and they would burst into the bright light at the bottom of the slope.

'Not until I know what this is all about.'

Vincent slowly raised both hands, as if to demonstrate they were empty. 'Merv told me Batch threatened you.'

'You people don't scare me, you know!' Michael said, wishing the words sounded more convincing.

Vincent shook his head. 'You've got it arse about, mate,' he said. He was silent for four or five long seconds, then continued. 'I knew Merv Harris for over thirty years. He was probably the best copper I ever met. The best mate.' The man looked almost emotional. 'He rang me from Sydney last week. Told me he'd gone down there digging on this Probert case. Told me all about what you'd told him and how he give you the bum's rush. Seems he didn't like the smell of what you had to say so he did some digging of his own in Sydney. He found your old mate Bob.'

Michael slipped the gear selector into 'park' and turned the engine off.

'Do you mean Probert's flatmate Bob?'

'Yeah. He found the missing diary too.'

'What!'

'Or part of it,' continued Vincent, reaching into the inside pocket of his coat and bringing out a sheaf of papers. 'He sent me these.'

Michael flicked the cabin light on as Vincent handed him the little bundle of photocopied pages and in the dim light he devoured the contents of Shirley Probert's diary. He could see immediately that they seemed a record of some kind of blackmail plot. His brain worked feverishly to make sense of it, and where it fitted in, and what conclusions it might lead to.

'Wilson?' Michael questioned.

'Wilson is Tom Wilson from the Commissioner's office,' he said solemnly. 'G C is Inspector George Curran, now retired.'

The words hit Michael like a sledgehammer blow. The significance of what he had just read and been told left him speechless. The two men sat in the darkness looking at each other, pondering the inescapable conclusion they now shared.

'Pollard ... Who's Pollard?' Michael eventually said, looking back down at the document. 'What's this "Pollard statement" she refers to?'

Phil Vincent shrugged. 'Don't know,' he said. 'But that's where it gets really bloody scary. Merv figured Pollard must have been an alias for Probert so he asked me to run both names through the police computer. Neither one turned nothing up. A moll her age had to have some form so we figured she must have changed her name by deed poll. Merv thought she probably was born Pollard. We checked it out and found that Shirley

Probert changed her name by deed poll filed in the Adelaide Supreme Court back in 1973. Her real name was Gaye Mary Welham.'

'Gaye Welham!' Michael knew that name. The Fortitude Valley prostitute Gaye Welham had made headlines in the late sixties when she shocked the Queensland public with her claim that senior members of the Queensland Police Force were operating a highly organised protection racket for the brothels and the prostitutes of Brisbane and surrounding areas.

The controversy had threatened to prompt a Royal Commission which many pundits of the day predicted would unseat the government and it had continued to rage for many months, even after Gaye Welham had recanted and shortly afterwards disappeared from public view. Michael Leary was barely out of school when all that happened, but there were very few Queenslanders who did not know the name Gaye Welham.

'Looks to me like she came back with blackmail on her mind,' said Vincent, his sallow face jaundiced in the yellow light. 'And this time the boys fixed her up for good.'

The proposition that such senior policemen had conspired to end this woman's life was so extreme that Michael's fear came flooding back. He looked warily at Vincent's pale face. 'Why are you telling me all this?'

Vincent sat like a waxen figure. When he spoke his voice was quiet and controlled but stiffened by an underlying strength of purpose. 'Merv Harris didn't drive himself into that bloody river. They done it for him. It's time to pull these blokes up.'

It was a simple statement but a stirring one. Michael saw determination in this stranger's eyes, and courage, as well as a kind of honesty that, in a curious way, reminded him of Mervyn Harris.

He had gone to Merv for help because he had felt that no matter how much he had been diverted or corrupted and regardless of what he thought of Peter Lade, or lawyers, or the justice system, or anything else for that matter, Merv was, at heart, an honest man. For all his failings Merv was a man of personal integrity, who had lived his life according to his own code of conduct. He and Brian Leary were enemies but they had that much in common.

Phil Vincent took Michael through the documents, explaining what he could of each and suggesting how they might be used. He was convinced that Peter Lade had simply been identified as a convenient vehicle to offload the Probert murder case and if he were convicted the file would be closed. Which would make it harder to unearth the truth about those who put Merv Harris in the river. But Vincent, and others in the Force he said, were determined that the truth would be unearthed.

They were together for the best part of an hour before Michael offloaded his passenger in the carpark behind the Stones Corner Hotel. Vincent nodded and strode away towards a taxi rank without another word and as Michael watched him leave he thought how hard it must have been for him to do what he had done that night.

And he thought about how people like George Curran must have tapped into the personal integrity of essentially honest men like Phil Vincent and Merv Harris and so many others to forge the bonds of loyalty that formed the basis of his evil empire.

Perhaps that same integrity and loyalty would be the very things to topple it.

34

'Bullshit!'

Eugene Sullivan and Michael had been sitting in the living room for hours, trying to evaluate this latest information, but the old man kept returning to the same conclusion.

'It doesn't make sense,' Sullivan repeated. 'Gaye Welham's allegations were discredited nearly twenty years ago. Personally, I don't doubt that her allegations were entirely true but the fact is she publicly withdrew them. She was totally discredited. The police had nothing to fear from her after that. She had no real ability to blackmail them and even if she had tried, why would they do anything more than charge her with extortion?'

Sullivan was right. Everything Gaye Welham had to say had been said *ad nauseam* nearly twenty years ago. She had ultimately admitted it was all untrue. She would have had no chance of recycling it today, and even if she did it would hardly make the Sunday papers in a quiet week.

Sullivan and Michael talked about the issue until well after ten o'clock that night, examining it, dissecting it, approaching it from a hundred different angles but always arriving at the same conclusion. Some vital part of the jigsaw was missing.

As Michael drove home he asked himself a thousand vexing questions. What was Gaye Welham doing back in Queensland? Did she return with the intention of blackmailing some of the most powerful men in the state? And if so, what did she know that could have frightened them enough to kill her? It was absurd that anyone would take such drastic action to guard a secret that had been publicly exposed so long ago. And yet, if Shirley Probert's diary were to be believed, she'd said something to George Curran that made him very angry. Was he angry enough to have her killed? Curran must have known her real identity but he had dealt with her effectively before. Why take such drastic action now?

He must have known her real identity. The proposition lodged in Michael's brain and would not move. He tried to think of other things but he kept coming back to the notion that, in addition to Curran, at least one of the investigating police must have known who Shirley Probert really was.

And yet there had been no mention of her double identity anywhere. Not in the police reports. Not in the court hearings. Nowhere ... Why had the media not picked up on it? Why had no one realised that the dead body in the Golden Gate had once been the state's most controversial identity? No photographs of the victim had been published in the press except for a police shot of a corpse lying face down beside the coffee table and its carefully arranged magazines. It seemed the police had not distributed any other photographs. But someone must have known her.

After another restless night Michael woke the next morning feeling as if he hadn't slept a wink. His eyes were stinging and his head and neck ached. He looked wearily at the ceiling, then eased his eyelids closed.

Someone must have known her. The ravings of an ugly, squinting oddity filtered back: *I saw the photographs, and*

I told them that I knew that girl. She wasn't who they said she was. I told them I knew that girl a long time ago.

At ten o'clock that morning Michael was waiting in the legal visits area at the Brisbane Prison to see Stanley Rays, armed with the photograph of Shirley and Rita he'd had copied from the one Les Burrows lent him. He thought about Rays' words at their last meeting in the context of what he now knew — *She wasn't who they said she was.* At the time it had seemed an irrational comment by an irrational man. Now it perhaps had some significance.

Rays' hair had been shorn off completely and he had gained several kilos. But the nervous tic still contorted his face from time to time and his eyes were still vacant.

If Rays remembered Michael he disguised it well, and as the lawyer reminded him of their last meeting and explained his current role, he merely squinted, twitched and shook his head repeatedly.

Michael persevered: he thought Shirley Probert might have been known by another name; he could recall Mr Rays mentioning that police had asked him about a girl; Mr Rays had said she was not the person police said she was. Did Mr Rays recall that conversation?

Rays shook his head.

Michael was tired and frustrated. He held the photograph in front of Rays. 'Do you know this woman?' he asked brusquely.

To his surprise the convict nodded, then grunted the first word that he had spoken. 'Yeah.'

Michael held his breath. 'By what name do you know her?' he asked cautiously.

'Gaye.'

Michael's stomach churned. 'Where do you know her from?'

'She lived in King's Cross, years ago.'

Michael tried to assess where this new lead might take him.

'That's Romy with her,' volunteered Rays.

'What?'

The convict looked startled by the question. He squinted nervously and shrugged one shoulder.

'What did you say?' asked Michael, as casually as his mounting tension would allow.

'R-Romy,' stuttered Rays. 'That's Romy in the photograph with Gaye.'

'Romy?'

Rays nodded. 'She's a lot older there than when she lived down in the Cross but that's Romy all right.'

Romy — there was something about the name that tugged at Michael's memory. 'Romy who?'

'Just Romy.'

Michael inspected the photograph again. He could feel his heartbeat quickening as he struggled to unlock the mystery in his brain. He thought about the terror in Rita's face that night down in the Valley. Somewhere in his subconscious a distant bell was ringing but he had yet to work out why. His informant was hardly a reliable source, but the man certainly knew Gaye Welham, and Michael was convinced now that he also knew her terrified companion.

'Her real name was Sheila, I think,' said Rays. 'Yeah. Sheila Pollard.'

It took Michael the best part of the rest of that day to track down Johnny Forrest but after what Rays had told him he was convinced the exercise would be worthwhile. If anyone could join the dots up, Forrest could.

When they had met at the Shamrock, it was clear Forrest knew more about Shirley Probert than he was willing to disclose, but it had not been Shirley Probert he was thinking of when he spoke about people getting killed. If John Forrest did know Shirley Probert then he knew her real identity, and he knew that Gaye Welham had been playing a deadly game that threatened to get her good friend Sheila Pollard killed.

Michael tracked Forrest down at the office of *The Australasian Realtor* which purported to be a publication advertising real estate. It was on the second floor of a mostly vacant office block at Springwood. The interior had a temporary look as if the occupants did not discount the possibility of a need to relocate the business at short notice. Forrest welcomed him warmly, but with a hint of caution. They bought coffee at the downstairs snack bar and settled at a bench behind the pinball machines.

Michael wasted no time filling Forrest in on all he knew, including his conclusion that Forrest had known all along who Shirley Probert was and exactly what it was that she was up to and that somehow Rita, Romy, Sheila — whatever name he knew her by — was a part of it and furthermore that Forrest knew exactly what that part had been.

The fat man listened poker-faced, his eyes behind the horn-rimmed spectacles not once deviating from Michael's, his face devoid of expression, and his massive frame propped tentatively against the stool as if ready for flight. Michael reminded Forrest of his reaction when shown the photograph of Probert several weeks ago, a reaction that had gained significance when Michael learned of Probert's true identity.

When Michael handed Forrest the photocopies of the diary, he studied them, seemingly without surprise, and passed them back without a word. He picked up his coffee cup and took a noisy gulp.

'That Gaye always was as mad as a bloody meat-axe,' he said. 'Not crazy, but definitely a couple of sandwiches short of a picnic.'

He shook his head and sighed. 'I near shit myself when you showed me that photo at the Shamrock.'

'Why?'

Forrest hesitated for a long time, staring into space. His mind was ticking over almost audibly. The long delay before he finally launched into his story was positively painful.

'When the coppers got the irrits with her back in '69 Gaye went into real deep snooker for a lot of years. No one knew where she was. Then she showed up down the Cross a few years later and that's when she got to be great mates with Romy Pollard. That's Rita.'

'Sheila Pollard?'

'I guess so. Some of them sheilas change their name more often than their knickers. I dunno her real name. She called herself Romy back in them days. But she's been up here in the Valley for the best part of the last ten years working under the name Rita.'

Forrest's beady eyes stared in front of him, as if they saw a distant memory.

'What happened to Gaye Welham?' Michael prompted.

'Ten or eleven years ago she disappeared again and the word was she'd gone to South Australia. Then about three years ago she rung me from down south and told me she wanted me to help her put a scam together.'

This was what Michael had come for and he eased the question out. 'What was that scam?'

The fat man's puce complexion reddened even more. He spat the answer out. 'Fucking suicide, matey, that's what it was!' The intensity that burnt deep within those beady eyes was mesmerising. 'I told her to forget it,

Michael, just like I told you to forget it. Mate, sure as there's shit in a cat, anyone that touched that scam was going to wind up dead. And when I seen that photo of the two of them together, I knew straight away that the silly bitch had gone ahead with it.'

35

Graham Worrell walked into the empty courtroom shortly before ten o'clock on the morning of that Friday, the third of April 1987, smiling broadly. He'd had a pretty bloody good day yesterday, and he knew it. For two weeks he'd sat back quietly as that old fool Sullivan tried to systematically dismantle the prosecution case, posing irrelevant questions and raising preposterous hypotheses. But yesterday the post mortem evidence of Dr Frederick Arrowsmith had brought the three-ring circus to a grinding halt. As he led the evidence from Arrowsmith about the stomach contents you could almost hear the penny dropping, and several of the jurors gave an audible gasp as it finally did.

It was a magic moment. The only disappointment was the absence of that upstart Leary. He wasn't in court all day, perhaps because he could not bear to face what he knew was coming. But from that point on it was all over bar the shouting. Sullivan had asked Arrowsmith a few inconsequential questions, which merely served to underscore the fact that the defence had no effective answer to the evidence. When the judge excused the witness right on half-past-four, Worrell knew right then and there the case was won.

He would have closed the Crown case first up this morning had he not received a call just after nine from Eugene Sullivan asking him to recall Darryl Batch.

Worrell chuckled at how depressed the old boy had sounded. Bound to be nursing a monumental hangover as well as the realisation the defence was a dead duck.

The courtroom gradually filled with bailiffs, shorthand writers, police and public, and at ten o'clock the warders brought the prisoner in and lodged him in the dock. The jurors filed in and resumed their places, then old man Sullivan arrived with his henchman, Michael Leary, bringing up the rear. Worrell lounged back in his seat and savoured the ignominy of the humiliating defeat that awaited them. Sullivan looked so pale and drawn, so completely crestfallen, that Worrell found it hard to suppress another chuckle.

When Maxi Walker took the bench Worrell announced that Mr Sullivan had asked that the witness Batch be recalled to the stand, and he magnanimously added that the Crown was more than willing to accede to any request the defence team might have to ensure that the accused had every chance of presenting the best defence available to him. His Honour winced at this self-serving contribution and crustily directed the prosecutor to get on with it.

Worrell called Detective Sergeant Batch.

Darryl Batch strode through the courtroom like a heavyweight champion swaggering to the ring. As he passed the bar table he glanced disdainfully at the defendant's camp and then with head held high he passed the jurors' ringside seats and climbed into the box. He looked so invincible that Michael instinctively looked away. But then the image of a little man in a double-breasted suit, and the pain and anger that had surged in him all night long came flooding back and he looked back coldly and defiantly. Batch locked his gaze on him and kept it there. It was a look intended to intimidate and dominate but Michael comfortably returned it.

As Eugene Sullivan rose to his feet his face was ghostly white and his brow was knitted in the deepest frown. With a trembling hand he withdrew a single page of notes scribbled in the hand of Sergeant Phillip Vincent.

'Witness, at the time of Shirley Probert's murder you were stationed at the Homicide Squad office in Brisbane, were you not?'

Batch looked at Sullivan defiantly. The defence was about to mount a challenge but he would meet it, walking forward all the way.

'That's right.'

'Her body was discovered by uniformed police shortly after nine on the morning of the fourteenth of February 1986. What time did you start work that day?'

Batch was silent for a second, trying to anticipate the direction of the questioning. 'I was on days off actually. I was called in to work that morning when the Coast police notified our office there had been a homicide down there.'

'You were on days off. I see,' said Sullivan, leafing slowly through his brief as if he was just aimlessly inquiring. 'But you live in Brisbane, don't you?'

'Yes.'

'According to the investigation running sheets the Brisbane Homicide Squad was notified at 9.30 that morning.'

Whatever it was that Sullivan was getting at, he was not aimlessly inquiring. Such questions were more than padding. Batch breathed a little heavier. 'That'd be right,' he said.

'You know Constable Roy Garfield, don't you?'

'Yes.'

'He was the Scenes of Crimes officer down there on the Coast at that time, wasn't he?'

'Still is.'

'According to Constable Garfield's notes, you arrived on the scene at 9.37 am. Is that right?'

'That'd be right,' Batch grunted.

Sullivan was still leafing through his brief. 'Seven minutes after the Homicide Squad was notified?' he said, then paused and looked up at the witness. 'You didn't come all the way from Brisbane in seven minutes, did you?'

Batch hesitated, only briefly, but in the silence of that brief delay the jurors saw the point. The car trip from Brisbane to the Gold Coast took near enough to an hour. How had Batch got to the scene so quickly?

'No, I told you. I was on days off.' Batch seemed a little tense. 'I was actually staying at the Gold Coast at the time.'

'Oh, I see,' said Sullivan, then he paused as if to soak the answer in. 'So you were actually on the Gold Coast on the night Shirley Probert was murdered?'

The jury's eyes flicked back to the witness.

'That's right,' Batch said. 'Along with a couple of hundred thousand other people.'

Among the jurors there were raised eyebrows that asked why the answer was apparently so defensive.

It was precisely the response Sullivan expected, and he underplayed it perfectly. 'Yes,' he replied gravely, and turned a page as if to move on to another point. 'Mr Batch, the Homicide Squad running sheets show that at 9.33 am you rang in to say that you would go directly to the scene and secure it pending the arrival of your colleagues from the Homicide Squad.'

'That's right.'

Sullivan paused again and looked up at the witness quizzically. 'Well,' he said, as if struggling with a complicated proposition. 'You rang them. They didn't ring you. I take it from that, that by 9.33 you already knew a body had been discovered.' Sullivan let the jury soak that up. Then quietly, politely, he asked another obvious question. 'Who told you that, Mr Batch?'

Batch blinked. 'I'm not sure actually,' he hedged. 'I think someone from the CIB at Broadbeach rang me directly.'

'Who?'

'I can't remember, Mr Sullivan.'

'It's not noted in the investigation log. Presumably it wasn't anyone connected with the investigation.'

'I don't remember who it was.'

'Where did they ring you?'

'Wherever I was staying at the time.'

'Where was that?'

'I don't remember.'

'Why would they ring you up on holidays to tell you that?'

'Just thought I'd be interested, I suppose.'

Sullivan raised his eyebrows, and let that unsatisfactory answer sit quietly with the jury for a moment. Then he moved on robustly. 'Well, you *were* interested. In fact, you were so interested you went directly to the scene, and secured it pending the arrival of the Homicide Squad people, didn't you?'

'Yes.'

'Yes, and that involved clearing all police personnel from the premises and directing the uniformed officers to restrict access to all persons pending the arrival of the Homicide Squad detectives.'

'That's right.'

Another pause, then Sullivan made his next point. 'But you yourself remained in the unit, didn't you?'

Batch blinked again. 'I did, but I was careful not to disturb the scene in any way.'

Sullivan stared dispassionately at the witness. 'Is that so, Mr Batch?'

'Yes it is.'

Their eyes were locked together in the silence of the courtroom, the old man leaning forward on the lectern, the witness staring defiantly back at him. That silence made the jury wonder what the old man knew and what the witness might be hiding. They stayed like that for several seconds until finally the witness blinked and cleared his throat.

As if woken thereby from a trance, Sullivan stood upright and, looking down at his brief, continued authoritatively. 'At the time of her murder Shirley Probert was operating from those premises as a working prostitute, wasn't she, Mr Batch?'

'I believe so, yes.'

'And one of the necessary tools of trade of a prostitute working from her own premises is her diary, in which she records and schedules her appointments. Isn't that so, Mr Batch?'

'I wouldn't know, Mr Sullivan.'

Sullivan fell silent once again and then continued in a hushed and confidential tone. 'Really, Mr Batch?' he said quietly, his disbelief clear. 'Wouldn't you know that?'

'No.'

There was another pause before the barrister resumed. 'Shirley Probert had a diary in her apartment, didn't she?'

'Not to my knowledge, no.'

Sullivan's voice became sterner. 'I suggest that when you cleared that apartment shortly after half-past-nine that morning, Shirley Probert's diary was still on the premises.'

'No.'

'But by the time the Homicide forensic people came on the scene the diary had been removed.'

'No. The scene was fully secured. Nothing was taken out of that unit.'

Sullivan looked up to the bench. 'Could the witness be shown exhibit six please, Your Honour?'

The bailiff scurried to the associate who rifled through the pile of exhibits on the table in front of him, selected the one requested and handed it to the bailiff who handed it to the witness.

'There are nineteen photographs in that bundle,' announced Sullivan. 'They were all taken by technical officer Parker of the Homicide Squad at your direction. Is that so?'

'Yes,' said Batch, shuffling through the bundle.

'Photographs lettered H and I both show the entrance to the main bedroom.'

'Yes. There was a scuff mark on the bedroom door which we originally suspected might have some significance but inquiries in that regard proved negative.'

'In the background of both of those photographs can be seen a bedside table positioned on the far side of the bed.'

'Yeah, that's right.'

'And in each of those photographs the only items on that bedside table are a lamp and what appears to be a glossy magazine.'

'That's all there was on the bedside table.'

'Is it?'

The question was larded with disbelief and it seized the attention of the jury.

'Yes,' Batch answered.

'Are you sure of that, Mr Batch?'

'Yes.'

'When you first arrived at the scene Constable Garfield was in the kitchen area dusting for fingerprints, wasn't he?'

'I think that's probably right, yeah. I asked him to suspend that and leave it to our Homicide people.'

'That's right. But did you know that prior to your arrival Mr Garfield had already taken photographs of the scene?'

Batch squared his shoulders. 'No.'

'No, you didn't even bother to get a statement from Constable Garfield, did you?'

'We had our own forensic people examine the scene,' replied the witness in a voice that for the first time was uncertain.

'Yes, and as a result you never got to know that Garfield had photographed the scene just as it was immediately prior to your arrival. Have a look at these photographs, would you please?'

The bailiff took the bundle from Sullivan's outstretched hand and delivered it to the witness.

'These are the shots taken by Mr Garfield prior to your arrival,' continued Sullivan. 'There are thirty-four of them in that bundle, but in particular, I want you to look at photographs numbered twenty-four to twenty-seven inclusive. Each of those four photographs depicts the main bedroom, is that so?'

'Yes.'

'But there's something different in those photographs from what's depicted in exhibit six, isn't there Mr Batch?'

Batch blinked and tugged at the collar of his shirt. 'Yes.'

'Yes. In these photographs one can clearly see, particularly in photographs twenty-six and twenty-seven, what appears to be a small, blue, hard-covered book sitting on the bedside table, partially obscured by the magazine on top. Do you agree with that, Mr Batch?'

Batch blinked again and puffed a nervous little breath out through his nostrils. 'That could be right.'

Sullivan was building up a head of steam. 'Photograph twenty-seven provides a reasonably close view and shows that that blue book has an inscription in the corner, one quite decipherable to the naked eye. If you would like the assistance of a magnifying glass I'm sure that can be arranged, but I suggest to you that the inscription appears to read "Collins". Do you need a magnifying glass, Mr Batch?'

Batch stared at the photograph. 'No, that's right,' he grunted. 'I accept that. That could be right.'

'In fact, overall, the book has the look of a standard Collins business diary, doesn't it, Mr Batch?'

'It could be. I don't know.'

Sullivan paused again to maximise the impact of the question. 'What happened to that diary, Mr Batch?'

The policeman shifted in his seat. 'Well, you're saying that book's a diary, Mr Sullivan. I don't know that it is.'

'Well, never mind "diary" then,' returned Sullivan. 'Let's call it a book. What happened to that book? Where is it, Mr Batch? Do you have it?'

'No. No, I haven't got it.'

'Well, where is it?'

'Mr Sullivan, if you knew the number of books and magazines we took out of that unit — I wouldn't have a clue what happened to most of it. We have very limited facilities for holding exhibits. Half the time things that aren't needed are just thrown away.'

'But this book disappeared between the time the police first arrived and when the official photographs were taken.'

Batch shaped to say something but seemed to gag the words. He snuffled nervously and stretched his chin up from his collar.

Sullivan persisted. 'It was during this time that you were alone and unobserved by anyone in that unit.'

'There were plenty of police in the unit that morning. Anyone could have moved that diary.'

'But you secured the scene. You sent everyone out of the unit.'

'Someone might have taken it before I got there.'

'But why would they? Why would anyone take it away before the Homicide investigators got there?'

'I don't know.'

'What do you think was in that diary that would make someone want to hide it from the Homicide investigators?'

'I wouldn't have a clue.'

'Wouldn't you?'

'No.'

'Really, Mr Batch?'

'Really, Mr Sullivan.'

With a look of complete disdain, Sullivan straightened to his full height. 'Well, let's see if we can work it out together, shall we? I want you to cast your mind back a long way, back to 1969.'

It was an invitation into dark and murky waters and Graham Worrell sensed the danger. He jumped to his feet. 'I object to this, Your Honour. I really can't imagine what the relevance could be.'

As Worrell spoke Batch turned his eyes to Michael who met his gaze unflinchingly. They both knew what was happening, and Batch's eyes burnt with an intense determination. There was both menace and desperation in those eyes, the two so finely balanced that either might explode at any moment. While the lawyers argued the objection Batch stared stonily at Michael, silently instructing him that he had overstepped the mark, that he was dealing with a force that would destroy him in the end, just as it had dealt with better men than he in days gone by and that, whatever he might think, this fight was far from over.

He reminded Michael of a shark caught in the nets, thrashing wildly in a desperate final show of strength. This one had eaten up so many decent men that Michael could feel nothing but revulsion.

'Proceed,' said Mr Justice Walker, overruling the objection.

Sullivan resumed slowly, his voice as strong and insistent as the rhythm of a funeral drum.

'In 1969 you were a Constable First Class attached to the Fortitude Valley Criminal Investigation Branch.'

'That's right.'

'In June that year you arrested and charged a man by the name of John Edward Arnold with the murder of eleven people killed in the Mickey's Poolhouse bombing.'

The words fell into the deep silence of a transfixed courtroom. Barrister and witness faced each other in that silence while every eye looked on, every spectator intrigued by this new and startling tangent.

'That's right.'

'Yes. And you and five other policemen claimed that Arnold had confessed the crime to you in an interview room at the Fortitude Valley Police Station.'

Batch was snarling, poised like a hunted beast. 'That's right.'

'Yes. And that group of policemen included several well-known names.' Sullivan counted out the players on his fingers. 'The infamous Mr Barry Dent, an ex-New South Wales detective now serving a lengthy term of imprisonment in New South Wales on federal drug importation charges, Police Inspector Thomas Wilson, currently attached to the Office of the Police Commissioner, the late Assistant Commissioner Gerard Walsh, and the current Minister for Natural Resources Mr Frank Delaney. They were all there, weren't they?'

'Yes.'

'Yes. Some very powerful men.'

'Very senior, well-respected men.'

'Men who would have a great deal to fear from a perjury allegation.'

'I don't know anything about that.'

'John Arnold vehemently denied his guilt throughout his trial and thereafter continuously until his death in 1977. Isn't that so?'

'Yes.'

'He consistently maintained that at the time the bombing occurred he was on a beach at Surfers Paradise, over fifty miles away.'

'That's what he claimed.'

'Yes, on a beach with a girl he had met for the first time that night. A girl called Romy.'

The blood drained from Batch's face at the mention of the name. 'Yes. That's right.'

'Just before the Arnold trial in November 1969 a Sydney woman by the name of Sheila Pollard, also known as Romy Pollard, sent a signed statement to the *Courier-Mail* reporter Mr Gordon Yates, now deceased, claiming she was on that beach that night with John Edward Arnold, didn't she?'

'How would I know?'

'Because Yates sent the statement on to you police, I suggest'

'I can't remember. It was a long time ago.'

'I suggest to you that he did, Mr Batch, and that on the very next day Barry Dent and two other New South

Wales detectives went to Pollard's flat in Coogee Beach and ransacked the premises looking for her. They threatened and assaulted her then-boyfriend — a gentleman by the name of Mr Trevor Johns who is now a motor dealer at Parramatta — and they made it clear to him that they were looking for Miss Pollard.'

The form of the question was objectionable, and Graham Worrell knew he should probably intervene. But suddenly this witness had a dangerous feel about him and Worrell's healthy sense of self-preservation told him it was wiser to stay out of it.

'No,' said Batch unconvincingly. 'Not that I know of.'

'What you do know, Mr Batch, is this,' said Sullivan, his voice resounding through the courtroom. 'The Pollard statement, a statement that might have cleared John Edward Arnold of the Mickey's Poolhouse murders, a statement that corroborated Arnold's claims that you and other police, including a current high-ranking police inspector and a Minister of the Crown, had perjured yourselves, grossly and repeatedly, at the Arnold trial, that all-important statement was totally and utterly buried by you police and has never seen the light of day in sixteen years!'

Batch lashed out defiantly. 'No, I don't know that, Mr Sullivan. I've never heard of this Pollard statement.'

'Yes you have, Mr Batch,' snapped Sullivan. He paused. 'Yes you have,' he said again, sternly. 'You spoke to the deceased woman Shirley Probert about it at length on the telephone when she rang police headquarters on the fourth of February last year.'

Batch looked stunned. His mind was in chaos, feverishly scrambling for an escape hatch. How could Sullivan possibly know about his conversation with that slut Probert? Had one of the others rolled over and dogged on him? That weak prick Tom Wilson maybe.

Or Frank Delaney. Maybe BCI had bugged their phones. Or maybe Probert taped the call. Maybe the defence had tapes. His mind was whirring in a hundred different directions.

Sullivan punched each word out with the full strength of his powerful voice. 'Witness, I put it to you that when she was murdered Shirley Probert was trying to blackmail you police. She had got hold of the Pollard statement and she telephoned police headquarters several times in February 1986 threatening that unless she was paid $500,000 in cash she would expose your perjury at the Arnold trial and your subsequent cover-up of the vital exculpatory evidence!'

Batch's jaw moved but no sound came out. He was a spent force groping desperately for survival.

Sullivan continued with the onslaught. 'Evidence that might have proved John Arnold innocent!'

'I, er, I ...' Batch began, then fell silent, as the courtroom looked on incredulously, grappling with the full significance of what had just been said.

'A man who went to his grave wrongly condemned for the murder of eleven people!'

Batch said absolutely nothing and the silence stretched into a long ordeal, before the barrister continued more sedately, 'Mr Batch, you were in the military before you joined the police force, weren't you?'

'Yes.'

'Both in basic training in the Army, and as a police recruit, you were trained in hand-to-hand combat.'

'Yes.'

'As part of that training you were instructed in the application of the choker hold sometimes called the Gurkha Headlock.'

Sullivan had already cross-examined Dr Netting, so everyone in the courtroom knew that Shirley Probert had been murdered with such a hold. The point of the question escaped no one.

'Well?' insisted Sullivan. 'Weren't you?'

'Yes.' Batch's voice was no more than a feeble whisper.

'At the time of the Probert murder you were the owner of a Ford Falcon sedan registered number PEJ–401.'

'Yes.'

'On the night of Shirley Probert's murder did you drive that car to Surfers Paradise?'

'I, er ...' Batch blinked again, his eyes glazed with a kind of shell-shocked horror. 'I might have. I can't remember.'

'Shortly before 11 pm that night did you park that car in the vicinity of the Golden Gate Apartment building?'

'I, er ...' Had someone seen him? Was he followed? Perhaps they had taken photographs of his car. His mind careered irrationally from one proposition to another.

'Well?'

'Look, you seem to be accusing me of something here.'

'Never mind about that. I want an answer to my question.'

'I, er ...' His voice trailed away and he shifted in his seat. His skin was pale and moist with sweat and the jowls under the pugnacious chin quivered.

'Well, witness, what's your answer?'

Batch shook his head. 'No,' he grunted. 'I want to talk to a lawyer before I answer any more questions.'

The jury gasped and Mr Justice Walker sat back in his chair, his mouth agape.

Sullivan said nothing while the shock seeped through the courtroom. Then he spoke again, his voice clinical and incisive. 'Mr Batch, are you saying that you don't wish to answer my question on the ground that your answer might incriminate you?'

'I want to see a lawyer.'

Howard Walker leaned forward on the bench. 'Witness,' he said firmly, 'you must answer counsel's questions unless you are seeking privilege against self-incrimination. Is that what you are doing?'

'Yes, Your Honour.'

Maxi Walker's mouth dropped open and Sullivan resumed. 'Mr Batch, isn't it true that immediately prior to her death Shirley Probert was endeavouring to blackmail you and other very senior policemen?'

'I-I decline to answer that question.'

'She closely chronicled that scheme in her diary and it was for that reason you went to her apartment the morning after her murder and after her body was discovered and belatedly removed that Collins diary from the scene so that the investigating officers would not discover it.'

'I won't answer that.'

'Did you go to Shirley Probert's apartment at the Golden Gate on the night she was murdered?'

'No comment.'

'Mr Batch, were you present when Shirley Ann Probert died?'

'No comment.'

'You were, weren't you? That's how you knew she was eating oranges before she died. And that's why you were able to pass that information on to Reginald Davey before the post mortem report!'

The witness opened his mouth then closed it. Finally he answered, 'No comment.'

'Did you kill her, Mr Batch?' Again a painful gasp washed through the courtroom.

'Did you?'

The big man's pallid face was soaked in sweat and his mouth formed words that would not come.

Sullivan leaned forward on the lectern, his face contorted by the bitter taste of what he knew to be the truth. He gripped the rostrum desperately as his body shook with outrage.

'Did you apply that deadly choker hold and squeeze that woman's neck until her life just drained away? Did you do that, Mr Batch?'

The silence was excruciating and when the answer finally came, it crept out limply, in a hoarse whisper. 'No comment.'

From where he sat beside him at the table Michael could hear the rasp of Eugene Sullivan's rhythmic breath. The old man stared contemptuously at the witness, his chest and shoulders heaving with the strain of his exertions. His face was drawn, distorted by a lifetime's disillusionment, and ennobled by the ecstasy of this sweet, sweet moment. He could see John Arnold standing in the dock, and young Manetti, and that proud, courageous little man, his good friend Brian Leary.

He turned to Mr Justice Walker, his old eyes filled with moisture. 'In that case, Your Honour,' he said, a slight tremor in the mellow voice, 'I have no further questions.'

36

No one was more stunned by Batch's evidence than Howard Walker. He had prosecuted in the Mickey's Poolhouse trial and had always fervently believed in the certainty of Arnold's guilt. In sixteen years he had never had a single doubt so Batch's evidence left him absolutely shattered. After Batch stood down the judge had called both counsel into his chambers to propose that he disqualify himself as judge and declare a mistrial. The suggestion greatly appealed to Worrell who now wanted no part of the trial, but Sullivan knew that his client Peter Lade would never be more likely to be acquitted than he was now, on the evidence as it stood, before this jury, and so he urged the judge not to abort the trial.

Maxi Walker considered his position overnight, and ultimately agreed that the trial should proceed to its conclusion, adding that he had already directed that a copy of the transcript of Batch's testimony be forwarded to the Director of Prosecutions for immediate investigation.

Peter Lade gave no evidence at his trial and Graham Worrell gave the shortest closing address of his career. Worrell owed his considerable success in the public service to his innate ability to know which way the wind was blowing, and he now knew that this case was a very hot potato. He structured his address to demonstrate his own detachment and impartiality, and scrupulously reminded the jury of their duty to acquit if they were not satisfied of Lade's guilt beyond a reasonable doubt.

Eugene Sullivan's address was likewise brief. He spoke softly, wearily. He made no detailed reference to the evidence, no stirring speeches. He conceded that the jury might have absolute abhorrence for the accused man, and no concern at all for his well-being. But this trial was not about Peter Lade. It was about whoever murdered Shirley Probert, and if the man in the dock was not the murderer, then the murderer was still at large. He finished with a simple point, expressed sedately.

'The truth is that Peter Lade did not murder Shirley Probert. It is a disturbing, unpleasant, frightening truth, but it is the truth. And whilst there may be no merit whatsoever in my client, there is great merit in the truth, ladies and gentlemen, great merit indeed. Remember, it was a man of truth, a man of great wisdom, who said, "Blessed are they who hunger and thirst for justice". I urge you, ladies and gentlemen of the jury, I beseech you, hunger and thirst for justice in this case. Seek it out. Find it. And when you do, don't turn your back on it because it's too ugly, or too frightening, or too unpleasant. Face it, and expose it.'

The jury sat attentively, nodding solemnly from time to time, their faces painted with the grim recognition of the conclusion they were being asked to draw. Howard Walker reinforced it in his summing-up, which was longer than both counsel's addresses put together, and in which he made direct and pointed reference to the 'highly unsatisfactory' evidence of the witness Batch, and the 'gross inconsistencies' raised by the forensic evidence. The judge left absolutely no doubt whatsoever as to his view of the case, and when he finally sent the jury to deliberate at 12.45 on Monday the sixth of April 1987, he told them that the bailiff had arranged lunch for them, and he would therefore not take a verdict before 2.15, as though he confidently expected them to reach a decision quickly and easily.

As Michael Leary walked out through the front doors of the Supreme Court building, the fresh air rushed into his head and lungs and stirred him heartily. He felt like a thirsty man reaching an oasis, and as he looked at the old man ambling beside him he could see some colour in that tired face for the first time in several days. All around them journalists and cameramen were scurrying, taking photographs and video film of them as they moved slowly but constantly towards the footpath, dragging the frenzied little entourage along with them.

At first they ignored the journalists' questions as they continued their quiet way across the courtyard, but the noisy barrage persisted and intensified until the old man finally held up a hand like a passing monarch acknowledging his subjects and said dismissively, 'Please, ladies and gentlemen, the jury's verdict is still pending in this matter.'

The members of the press looked slightly puzzled but the sound of Sullivan's voice was like a royal decree that silenced them immediately, and they simply walked beside the lawyers for a little way, before they finally dispersed.

The Lade trial had become a media sensation from the time of Batch's cross-examination. The news had spread like wildfire that same day, and when the court rose to adjourn, a legion of cameras and reporters was already camped outside the courthouse. Since then it had intensified, with news breaking the next day that a woman by the name of Rita Pollard had approached the federal police in Cairns and had been placed in the Protected Witness Scheme, and speculation that a Commission of Inquiry may be formed.

Unhindered, Michael Leary and Eugene Sullivan walked towards the Adelaide Street traffic lights. Sullivan smiled wryly and arched his eyebrows. 'Old Maxi didn't miss them, did he?'

Michael nodded his complete agreement and added, 'There'll be an Inquiry into this I reckon.'

'Ah well,' said Sullivan philosophically, 'that's for the politicians to work out. We have to deal with things one client at a time.'

They walked on in silence to the intersection where they stopped and waited for the lights to change. The old man turned to Michael and said diffidently, 'I'm going to have a steak sandwich at the Plaza. I haven't done that in years. Will you join me?'

Michael smiled and shook his head. 'I'd like to but I can't. I'm meeting my wife downtown, and then we're both going in to see Neil Doyle about the new partnership arrangement.'

'Ah,' said Sullivan, his lined face softening in a smile. 'So BM Leary & Doyle will finally have another Leary in it.'

'As of Monday.'

The lights changed and they walked together to the other corner, where the barrister peeled off towards the Hotel Plaza and Michael continued on alone, heading down towards the City Square. He looked across to where the original old Inns of Court had once stood, a squat, unimpressive red-brick building that was now long gone. He remembered crossing Adelaide Street as a little boy straight from the kindergarten at the City Hall, hand-in-hand with his father and his brother Dan, across the tramlines, over to that little red-brick building. The city had a warm, familiar feel to it.

Colleen was waiting in Littleboys Cafe. As he slid onto the bench beside her he wrapped an arm around her waist and pulled her close. He kissed her and held her tightly for a moment. He had never felt more peaceful and fulfilled than he did at that moment. Every facet of his life was in perspective, every sadness reconciled, and every goal seemed attainable.

Colleen smiled that soft, sweet smile of hers.

'Good day?' she whispered gently.

'Good day.'

EPILOGUE

George Curran put the phone down and opened up his teledex looking for the next number. He had had a bad day so far, and he knew there was worse to come. He was surrounded by so many idiots and weak bastards that he was going to have to personally ring around a bit and put some lead back in their pencils.

That bloody Frank Delaney always did have a heart the size of a flea's dick and when the news first broke he had gone to pieces badly. He had looked a major liability until George got to him and put a bit of backbone in him, and he was going to have to do the same with the others. None of them had anything to fear except each other, and the only way that anyone could touch them was if they did not have the loyalty to stick to one another as they had done all their lives.

Rita Pollard was just a junkie moll who had the credibility of a two-bob watch, and even if they did have Shirley Probert's diary, it wasn't worth a pinch of parrot's piss without old Shirley and she wasn't coming back again. All they had was hearsay evidence, and it wouldn't make the grade in any court of law. So unless the coppers started rolling over, shit-potting each other, they were safe as houses.

The official line was to keep a lid on it completely; there was an investigation pending and it would therefore be improper to comment on the matter. The press were looking for a headline and any comment would just keep it on the boil.

The unofficial line was that Peter Lade was as round as a hoop for the Probert murder and the case had just been badly bungled by the Crown Prosecutor. Darryl Batch had been suffering from some major stress and was just not functioning properly at the time. He was given absolutely no advice by the prosecutor and the result was that he went a little funny and completely rooted up his evidence. He was one of them Vietnam blokes and had always been a few bob short. So the whole thing was a balls-up, but the truth was that Lade really was the murderer, and everyone would realise that as soon as the investigation was complete. It was just another case of a couple of clever lawyers doing down a dopey copper and hoodwinking the jury.

The press were dying to beat the whole thing up but George was confident that so long as he could tighten things up at this stage and keep a lid on everything and everyone, the story would run cold pretty quickly. On the Tuesday the *Courier-Mail* had published a copy of the Yates letter, which they had got from Crown Prosecutions but it didn't prove a thing. All it said was:

Dear Miss Pollard

I have received your statutory declaration, and I must say that I can appreciate your grave concerns that the wrong man has been charged. However, as a journalist there is little that I can do to assist at this stage, so I have sent your statement on to Inspector George Curran who is handling the matter. He will no doubt be in touch with you in due course.

That letter took them nowhere. It proved nothing. Without a copy of the statutory declaration it wasn't worth a pinch of shit.

No one could print the diary entries without risking defamation, so they wouldn't see the light of day. George had put a lot of work in on his contacts in the Opposition to convince them it would be totally improper to allow the contents of the diary to be aired in parliament. After all, they were unsubstantiated and the proper course was to allow the current investigation to proceed without obstruction. Luckily, there had been no mention yet of Frank Delaney or anyone within the government, so the Opposition boys seemed quite receptive. They knew there was no future in throwing gratuitous shit at coppers, because what goes around eventually comes around.

George Curran thought of all the gutless bastards surrounding him and wondered where to start. His mind drifted back a thousand years to when he first met Mervyn Harris. The kid was built like a Mallee bull and twice as tough. Right from the jump young Merv had understood what loyalty was all about and how to stick tight by your mates. He was the best copper George ever knew. But he never quite got smart. He never did ...

George Curran picked up the phone and dialled again.

AUTHOR'S NOTE

This novel is a work of pure fiction. It draws on my experiences over three decades practising as a criminal lawyer. As such I am sure it has an authentic feel to it, and features of it will seem familiar to many people. Some may be tempted to draw parallels with actual situations, events, and people. But it would be wrong and perhaps unfair to think that *Cop This!* deals with actual events, or that any of the characters represents any real person, living or dead. They do not. The story and the characters are completely fictional.

There is one exception to that. I couldn't help but weave Dan Casey into a story about passionate criminal lawyers, because, to me, he above all others epitomised that group. Casey was a real person, and should be remembered as one of this country's finest advocates.

In acknowledging those who have contributed to the book, I must first remember all those tough old cops who scared the life out of me as a young lawyer, and made me want to win. And also, of course, those dedicated professional advocates who showed me how to win.

Susie Rourke's early encouragement and assistance were invaluable, as were the tireless efforts of my wonderful agent, Trish Lake. I have been fortunate enough to receive guidance and help from so many people that I shall simply thank them all collectively, with special mention going to Helen Bowers, whose painstaking attention to detail drove me to distraction, but forced me to produce the story I wanted to tell.

CHRIS NYST

Christopher Nyst was born in Blackall, western Queensland, in 1953. Raised in Brisbane, he obtained a Law Degree from the University of Queensland before commencing practice as a solicitor in Brisbane, and later on the Gold Coast. As a lawyer he has been involved in some of Australia's most sensational cases. He is recognised as one of Queensland's finest criminal law advocates, and has been a regular speaker and guest lecturer on criminal law and advocacy. As a writer, he has made prolific contribution to a range of legal publications. *Cop This!* is his first novel.

Chris lives with he wife and four children on the Gold Coast, where he is a partner in one of the region's largest law firms.